The Tide King

The Tide King

Jen Michalski

Black Lawrence Press

Black Lawrence Press
www.blacklawrence.com

Executive Editor: Diane Goettel
Cover design: Pam Golafshar
Book design: Amy Freels

Black Lawrence Press
326 Bigham Street
Pittsburgh, PA 15211

Published 2013 by Black Lawrence Books, an imprint of Dzanc Books
Printed in the United States

Prologue—1976

Andrei thought they were strange as far as Americans went. He'd picked them up in his cab outside the Kaliningrad airport to drive them over the border to Reszel, Poland. They resembled the basic unit of family, one man and woman in their early twenties and an eight- or nine-year-old girl. But that was all. The woman seemed too young to be a mother, and the man seemed too old, somehow, to be a young man. The woman, an unattractive-looking rat with bulbous eyes, long nose, no chin, the color of jaundice, spent several minutes at the beginning of the trip explaining to the man, dark-haired, large and muscular, the top of his head pressed against the greasy roof of the cab, how to use traveler's cheques.

"You sign them like checks," she explained. "But they're really money—checks that have been already paid for."

Andrei turned his attention back to the road. The days and nights were separated by subtle gradation. Congested, industrial skies the color of bone and smoke bled into charcoal and faded into smoke and bone once again. One found different ways of staying awake, of keeping the lines between them sharp, understandable. Sometimes Andrei put horseradish in his coffee. Other times, he speculated about his passengers. The man, woman, and child baffled him. They had no baggage, except for a camper's backpack. They appeared too soft, too clumsy, to be fleeing the mob. Perhaps they were drug mules. But to go to Reszel, a town with a few tourist attractions, more of a "this-to-that" place, seemed crazy. Only the young girl, perhaps adopted, spoke Polish, a bit of Russian, both with a strange dialect.

He studied their expressions from the rearview mirror. Tourists liked for him to talk, point out the sights, few that there were, the whole nine yards. But then, they were not tourists. He lit a cigarette and fumbled with the radio dial until a station with a strong signal wove into the stale tobacco of the cab. A woman's voice sang out before being swallowed by a wave of guitar chords. Drums machine-gunned into the space between the chorus and verse.

"Who is Katarzyna Sobczyk?" The little girl stood in the well of the back seat, repeating the name the disc jockey had spoken moments before. She hugged the front seat from behind, her chin propped up on the shoulder rest.

"How you say," Andrei answered, waving his hand away from his forehead. "*Pop singer.* Big star in Poland with her band, uh, Czerwono-Czarni. Like, uh, *Fleetwood Mac?*"

The little girl shook her head, her eyebrows close together in puzzlement.

"You from Reszel?" he asked.

"Why? Do you know your way around? You get to the old Bishop's Castle, I can show you where to go."

"No—I take you in from main road. Then you tell me, okay?"

"It's easy to find," she answered, staring at her little fingers. "There is not much in Reszel worth remembering."

He'd seen someone like her in the circus, once, he decided. Like a midget but not. An adult in a child's body.

"Ela." The man, singular in syllable and intention, spoke, and the little woman-girl slumped into the space between her two companions in the back seat.

"Pretty girl," Andrei said to the man, who studied him for a moment. "Visiting family?"

"Just visiting," the man answered. The lights of Reszel grew like low-hanging stars, etching a canopy of night that replaced the blackness and straws of light from the cab's headlights.

"The castle," the little girl said, pointing to an illuminated turret topped with orange tiles. Tears appeared in her eyes, big childish drops that her eyelids reflexively sought to stop. "Oh, Matka..."

Andrei looked to the woman next to Ela for her response, but she did not answer, did not comfort her.

"Who are these people?" Andrei addressed Ela in Polish. She shook her head, motioned for him to stop the cab. The young woman pulled out a wallet fat with zloty, paid the total on the meter, gave him a generous tip.

"Will you be safe?" he asked Ela again as the man opened the right-side door and slid out, the absence of his weight buoying the cab.

"What does he ask you?" The woman, looking at Andrei with fear, irritation, in her gold eyes, asked the little girl, nudging her toward the open door, where the man fumbled outside with the backpack.

"He asks us who we are," Ela said as she hopped into the darkness. "Should I tell him we are gods who live in hell?"

"We are tourists," the woman laughed, fake, and nodded toward Andrei. "Thank you—goodnight."

"Bezpieczniej podróży," Andrei answered. He fingered the pile of zloty she had given him, crisp, and held them to the light, saw that they were real. He turned off the meter, flung the gearshift into reverse. And that is how he forgot about them.

1942

It was almost time to go. His mother, Safine Polensky, would see him out the door but not to the train station. She would not watch him leave on the train, his face framed in the window, his garrison cap covering his newly shorn head. She would see him to the door, where he could go to work, to school, to the store, and in the corresponding memory of her mind, he would return.

She opened the lock of the rose-carved jewelry box on the kitchen table with a butter knife, the key orphaned in Poland somewhere. He wondered whether she would produce a pocket watch, a folding knife, his father's or his uncle's, that he could fondle while trying to sleep on the hard earth, dirt full of blood and insides, exposed black tree roots cradling his head like witch fingers.

He opened his hand, waiting. She pulled out an envelope, old and brown, and the dark, furry object he regarded. A mouse carcass. A hard moldy bread.

"Burnette saxifrage." She put the crumbly mound in his palm. "Most powerful herb. I save it until now."

He glanced at the leaves and roots spread over his palm, dried like a fossilized bird. His lips tightened. His whole life to that point a stew of herbs—chalky and bitter and syrupy in his teas, his soups, rubbed onto his knees and elbows after school. Safine had brought them from the homeland, Reszel, Poland—stories of baba yagas and herbs and the magic of her youth. He may have believed once, been scared, as a child. He put it back in the envelope, more fragile than the herb.

"You take this." She grabbed his palm, her knuckles blue and bulbous. "Eternal life. You take it when you are about to die. You will live. This is the only one. You understand?"

He nodded, pushing it into the far pocket of his duffel bag, where he was certain to forget about it. Herbs had not saved his father from pains. They had not spared his mother's hands, curled and broken, her lungs, factory black. How would they save his head from being half blown off, his guts from being hung like spaghetti on someone's bayonet? He hugged her. She smelled like garlic and dust. Then he, Stanley Polensky, walked to the Baltimore station, got on the train, and went to war.

1943

They carried what they could carry. Most men carried two pairs of socks in their helmets, K-rations in their pockets, their letters and cigarettes in their vests. That queer little private, Stanley Polensky, also carried a book, and it was not the Bible.

"Polensky, throw that thing away." With the nose of his carbine, Calvin Johnson, also a private, poked him in the small of his back, where a children's book, *Tom Swift and His Planet Stone*, was tucked in his pants, under his shirt. "No wonder you can't get any."

"At least I can read." Polensky flipped him the bird over his shoulder. They were in a line, two men across, stretching for miles from Cerami on their way to Troina. Stanley Polensky was a boy who, back in Ohio, Johnson would have given the full order to. He would have nailed him with a football where he sat in the bleachers, reading a book. He would have spitballed him from the back of class or given him a wedgie in the locker room after track. Polensky had cried in his bunk at night for their first week at Fort Benning, wrote long letters to his mother the way others wrote to their girls.

Now, Johnson stared at his slight, curved back all day, the sun hotter than fire. On narrow trails in the hills, they pulled themselves up with ropes and cleats through passes that only they and their mules—the dumbest, smelliest articles of military equipment ever used to transport supplies—could navigate, driving back enemy strongholds at Niscemi, Ponte Olivo Airport, Mazzarino, Barrafranca, Villarosa, Enna, Alimena, Bompietro, Petralia, Gangi, Sperlinga, Nicosia, Mistretta, Cerami, and Gagliano. It would seem so easy if not so many men died, if Johnson was not walking on an ankle he'd jammed on a hill that had swollen to the size of a softball. And yet their toughest fighting was still to come, at Troina, with Germans shooting at them from the mountains in every direction.

But not today. Today there was sky and food and the Germans to the east of them.

"You want these?" Polensky tossed the hard candies from his K rations over to Johnson. Every day, they had scrambled eggs and ham, biscuits, coffee, and four cigarettes for breakfast; cheese, biscuits, hard candy, and cigarettes for lunch; and a ham and veal loaf, biscuits, hard candies, and cigarettes for dinner.

"I thought a nancy boy like you liked a little candy now and then." Johnson stuffed them in his mouth, pushing them into his cheeks like a squirrel.

"I haven't brushed my teeth in months." Stanley shook his head. "I'm afraid I'm going to lose them all."

"Well, I'll tell you what." Johnson lit his cigarette. "If I come across a toothbrush in my travels, I'll save it for you."

"I think you'll have better luck finding a Spanish galleon." Stanley lit his own cigarette.

"What do you know about Spanish galleons?"

"What do you want to know?"

"I don't know." Johnson closed his eyes. He had not done well in school. When he did not get a football scholarship to Ohio State, he thought he'd become a police officer, like his father. Knowing the war would help his chances, he'd enlisted the first opportunity he got. "What is it, like money or something?"

"No." Stanley drawled, smiling. "It's a ship."

"Warship?"

"And commerce, too. They sailed mostly in the 16th to 18th centuries."

"Is that what you learned in that Tom Swift book?" Johnson opened his eyes, studied Stanley lying on his back, knees swinging open and closed, smoke pluming upward between them.

"Wouldn't you like to know?" Stanley stared at the sky. His eyes broke up smiling when he looked at you, happy or sad. They squished a little, the outsides wrinkling, along with his forehead, his cheeks dimpling. Polensky was the youngest of six. Johnson had always wanted siblings. His mother had him. Another had died in the womb.

He imagined Stanley as a little brother and grimaced. But you took what you got, not what you wanted.

❀❀❀

They set the pup tent over an abandoned trench that they could roll into if any funny business found its way to the camp. They laid boot to head. Stanley was a kicker. It was easier if Johnson fell asleep first.

"Read me something from your book." Johnson laid his arms across his stomach. When they'd first started the whole bloody business, in Africa, he'd seen a soldier trying to hold in his intestines after getting shot, a slippery pink worm pulsing out between his fingers.

"Read it yourself."

"I'm tired. What's it about?"

"Well, every book Tom invents something new. So this time, it's the metalanthium lamp."

"Metalanthium lamp? What the hell is that?"

"It's a device that emits these rays that can heal the sick and bring people back from the dead."

"Sounds interesting. How does it work?"

"I'm not telling you anymore. You want to find out, you have to read it yourself."

"I don't have time to read." Johnson rolled over, away from Stanley's feet. "In case you didn't notice, there's a war on. Why are you carrying a children's book, anyway?"

"My mother bought it for me when I was a boy."

"Couldn't you have brought something more useful?"

But Stanley had fallen asleep, his snoring choked with hot, dusty mountain air. The sound reminded Johnson of the clogged carburetor on a motorcycle he'd fixed up one summer in Ohio. At night, his own mind churned. The war had been hard to swallow. He did not know what he had expected, but he had not expected this. The exhaustion. The hollow fear—fear so intense it burned a hole through you and left you hollow. The walking. They walked along ridges and through valleys for miles and miles, up and up on roads that lead to little towns full of rock and cement houses in which lived Italians with gaunt, piercing eyes who begged for candy or sugar and cigarettes and mostly had nothing because the Germans had taken everything.

The Italian women were attractive. Sometimes he would look at them as they took his chocolate rations, their long olive necks the soft fruits of their lips, and he wanted to lay with one on the ground. Not anything sexual, although he always thought of that. He wanted to lay on the ground with one to feel her heart through her chest with his fingers, the pulse of a vein on her neck, the soft skin on the underside of her arm, to remember what it felt like, the warmth of living skin, the soft quiet of humanity in measured breaths. The skin on the dead looked like rubber, and he did not understand the difference, the living, the dead. So many had died, men in little piles, only boys, really, their limbs thrown about like tire irons, hoses, their mouths open where something had taken flight. If they could all only go on living, with quiet pulses in their necks, wrists, little bird chirps. If no one had to die, except the very old.

Sometimes it got so bad, the need to touch, he wanted to hold Stanley. He thought of waking him up and asking for the book, to take his mind off things. But he was too tired to even open his mouth. He thought of Spanish galleons instead. For some reason he imagined that they were gold like coins and flew across the ocean. But for one to take you home, you would have to die.

Johnson guessed that was fair.

1944

They were on a warship stationed in the Isle of Wight. The bunk-room was still, the usual snores, jacking off replaced by the quiet of men's eyes blinking in the dark. Before they slipped into the sheets, they had made amends with their girlfriends, their parents, with God. When they finally stepped off the landing craft the next morning onto Omaha Beach, the First Division's fate would be clear, but they would not take any chances tonight. Stanley opened the envelope lying on his chest and felt the dry fibers of the herb in the lines of his palm, which were licked with sweat. His mother had sent him care packages at Fort Benning, North Africa, and Italy—knitted socks and dollar bills wrapped in cheese cloth, a few words written carefully on lined notepaper. But she never mentioned the herb. Perhaps it was bad luck to discuss it. He had forgotten about it completely until he sewed a torn pocket on his backpack that afternoon and discovered it pushed deep within. A bit of luck, he figured. That night, he laid it on the pillow next to him. His eyes blinked; the dark sleep, dreamless, weighed them closed.

"Wake up, Polensky." A hand, heavy, dry, covered his face. "Drop your cock and grab your socks."

Johnson, from Ohio. They had entered combat in North Africa, each killed their first men in the desert. They were uneasy, unlikely, friends. Johnson was tan and shiny, a farm boy who had lettered in high school before, as he explained to Stanley, a gimpy ankle kept him from getting a scholarship to college. Stanley swore he smelled like corn, although he probably smelled like Stanley and all the others—cigarettes and rotted teeth and stink.

Stanley turned in his bunk, feeling the film of sweat break from his body and release onto the sheets. His hand trailed on the pillow, feeling for the herb, but it was empty. He shot up, nearly hitting his head on the bunk above. A man stole something that wasn't hammered down, everyone knows. Veins pulsed in Stanley's neck, his biceps. But a flower? He might kill a GI before he killed a Kraut.

"Lose something?" Johnson, bent over, emerged with the saxifrage. "Your mother's corsage?"

"What time is it?" Stanley ignored him.

"Four-thirty." Johnson straightened. The doctor measured him six foot five during their physicals. Stanley had topped out eight inches shorter. "First wave 0630 to Normandy. Better shower, get that shit off your ass."

❀❀❀

One hundred thirty thousand men. Two years ago, Stanley could not have guessed so many to have existed in their divisions, much less his hometown, or the world. One hundred thirty thousand men dragged over the English Channel to Omaha Beach in battleships, landing craft, to fight like gladiators, mongrels. There were so many ships, Stanley wondered whether they could just cross the channel by stepping from one to another.

They climbed down the rope ladders of the battleship and into the landing craft, a steel bread box, that would shuttle them to the beach. The chop was terrible. Each wave sent that morning's oatmeal into the roof of each man's mouth, and they swallowed it again. Their helmets clicked together like teeth.

But the waves were too powerful; the landing crafts could not get in close enough to the shore to let the men out. They would have to swim. One end of the craft, its gate resting just under the water; the men stood and began to wade out waist-high. The first were sighted immediately by the 352nd Infantry German Division waiting ashore. From their concrete bunkers among the dunes and perches among the cliffs, the Germans scattered those first hundred men like pins. Shells exploded water into the boat, and the remaining men inched back, pressing against the sides as bullets rattled off the floor, walls, men.

"Picking us off like fucking lemmings," Johnson said from where he and Stanley sat in the back. He stood up and began to climb the wall of the boat. "Come on Polensky, you waiting to die?"

Stanley scrambled up the wall after Johnson, the weight of his packs and rifles pulling at him like children. The water stunned him for a second, and he was confused, thinking he was at Porter's Beach as a child, the chilled water of the Chesapeake Bay grabbing through the wool of his bathing suit and squeezing his nuts, his sister Kathryn bobbing beside him.

But it was Johnson beside him, the lasso of his arm pulling Stanley away from undertow of the boat. Stanley's fatigues stuck to him like skin. He wondered whether his rifle would work wet, if the grenades attached to his belt would go off after he threw them. He crouched in the water so only his eyes, helmet, bobbed above.

They waded to the shore, the water throwing up around them as the German shells exploded underneath, bullets flicking around them like whitecaps. No matter how fast he moved, Stanley fell behind Johnson's long stride, Johnson becoming his human shield, which filled Stanley with relief and disgust. Thirty feet in, to the right of Stanley, a man's upper body rose as if being yanked from the water by an invisible hand before sinking into the sea. The men thinned out closer to shore; if by miracle one were to make it to the beach, he was fired upon from several directions, his body a dancing pile in the surf.

The water squished in his socks and his underwear, and the straps of his backpack cut against his shoulder. He thought of stupid things while in danger, like his bedding being wet that night when he unfurled it to sleep, his cigarettes gone to mush. He touched his helmet, wondering if the herb he'd stuffed there that morning was secure. Suddenly Johnson lifted his rifle, set, and ran, firing at the shore. Stanley followed, although he thought it was a waste. He wasn't even looking at the beach. He was crouched so low that the current shoveled water into his open mouth and now here was Johnson, moving his big legs out of the water like pistons, lead flying from his rifle, a human tank forgetting it was closer to jellyfish than steel.

But Stanley followed. He moved his legs and spread out to the right of Johnson. He felt the burning in his hamstrings, the blood straining his heart, the veins in ears ready to spout like whistles. The shelling and fire screamed in his ears until it became quiet. The beach grew on each end; he could see the bunkers of the Germans beyond the dunes. Pinholes of light flicked from them; the water spit bullets around him in response. He aimed his rifle toward the holes and fired, the kick pulled him forward. He feared his skeleton, his muscles, might fall out of his body behind him. He clamped his mouth shut and felt the shells and pebbles of the surf scrape against his knees.

He had made it. He looked left for Johnson. Good fuck, the farm boy made it, too.

On the beach, they found a man who was not quite dead. They wanted to find a man who was dead, but they could not be picky. The man who was not quite dead was moaning and breathing thick, gurgly, lying on his stomach. Almost dead. He and Johnson rolled the body on its side and propped their rifles on its left arm. Above them, 50 yards up the beach, lay the Longues-sur-Mer battery, or the German bunkers, huge square cement structures that housed mortars and men. Artillery fire flashed from these holes and scattered the sand around them. Stanley reached for the dying man's helmet to put between the rifles, a barrier so they could peer up to shoot. A pack of cigarettes fell to the beach from it, which Johnson picked up and pocketed. Why Stanley hadn't put his own cigarettes in his helmet to keep dry, instead of the herb, he didn't know. There was no time to mull it over. They were alive, but only by luck and perhaps not for long. Around them, disembodied heads, arms, and backpacks floated in the air before gravity pulled them back to earth. Stanley coughed and shivered, peering up and sighting his rifle on one of the bunkers.

"I'll shoot and you toss the grenade," he said to Johnson over the fire. He may have screamed it, he may have thought it. Either way, no sound seemed to come from his mouth but Johnson understood, reaching toward his belt. The body flung backward at them like a flying log, taking fire. They braced against it. If the man had not been dead, he was now.

Johnson hurled the grenade. His long arm seemed to reach out and leave the grenade at the entrance to the bunker, like a gift. They ducked, felt the vibration rumble through the sand. The smoke from the grenade curled into the grey of the sky and the grey of the sky ate the smoke. It was impossible to see where anything began or ended.

Stanley felt a pull at his trousers. A tear in the side of his pants exposed flesh, blood. A bullet had grazed him, tearing a zig-zag down his leg. The Germans hidden in the cliffs around the bunkers were shooting at them. Johnson rolled to his left, stood up, and barreled for safety to a formation of rocks fifteen feet ahead. He waved Stanley on.

One of theirs, Green, was waiting there. Blood ran down his face, cleaning it of black soot on one side. Green jerked his head toward a rip in the fortified wire around the German embankments. The sand was slippery from the blood. Stanley spread his arms like a plane and continued running, his rifle flapping against his chest.

Beyond the barbed wire they waited, the men wearing the other helmets. They seemed surprised that Stanley, Johnson, and Green were there. Months of waiting at Omaha for the Allies to strike, and now they stood, unsure, like boys at a dance. Green pulled out his pistol and shot the first man he came to in the face. The man dropped, his body hitting the earth before his blood. Stanley shoved his bayonet low into a man's stomach, avoiding the ribs. Johnson held his rifle waist high and waved, spraying all those around him with bullets.

They did this for a long time. They killed men with helmets not like theirs. They stabbed them and they shot them and they lobbed grenades at them and they twisted their necks and they did this until the other men retreated. Then they smoked some of the cigarettes they'd taken earlier. Stanley knotted his handkerchiefs, wet and pink tinged from the bloodied channel water, and tied them around his leg. He watched the cloth drink up the blood until it was full, and then Johnson gave him his handkerchiefs while Green looked for the medic.

Some other men came over and smoked their own cigarettes. Everyone was dirty and smelled and shivered. Some cried. Some prayed, their mouths wide and moving. Some went through the pockets of the Germans and put watches, cigarettes, soft-edged pictures of girls into their boots and helmets. Stanley smoked his cigarette and wished he could tell his mother he was alive. Johnson stretched out his long legs as another man squatted, fanning a fire. Stanley laid his wet, torn cigarettes on the sand to dry. Most men were quiet, although some talked. Stanley wished they would shut up. It had been two years, two continents of this shit. The only way he could get through it was with silence, the air thin and yet full of salt, the beach full of dead men and yet life still lingering. His thoughts empty, body heavy.

"Come on." Johnson stood up. "We can't leave them like that."

That work, they did silently. They stacked the bodies of their men in rows like one would stack cordwood for the ships to take them to sea. Then they emptied their own backpacks, their bowels, and waited again for their orders.

They spent the summer moving inland toward Germany. *The war will be over soon,* Stanley wrote his mother. His twentieth letter. *The Germans are running like cowards.* He played poker with Johnson and Ennis, throwing pennies and cigarettes and girlie pictures into a German helmet they used as a pot. *I hope you are well and do*

not worry about me. He spent one week at Netley Hospital for his leg wound. *Nothing much has happened to us in Europe, except we are getting fatter.* He lost twenty pounds since leaving the States. *Hopefully by the time you get this, I will be on the train home.* In September, they entered the Hürtgen forest.

"I would die for a ham," Johnson let his cigarette dangle as he settled in the brush. It was a game they played sometimes, what they would die for, since they might die for much less.

"I would die for a turkey sandwich," Stanley answered. Spruce and balsam trees cloaked their eyes, yielding little forest beyond a few feet. The tree limbs, low, grabbed, and the men walked with a semi-permanent stoop.

"I would die for a woman's hips. I would put myself between them and sleep like the dead." Johnson grinned, his teeth white against the green cave. Water dripped constantly. The men could never find the source of it. Sometimes it confused Stanley, and when he slept for brief periods and woke, he thought he was at his parent's house, down the hall from the leaky faucet.

"Stay here." Johnson's arm would grab for Stanley's ankle as Stanley began to push forward through the brush.

"The sink is fucking leaking," Stanley waved him off, before Johnson yanked and Stanley fell down into the bed of pine needles that covered the forest floor.

"I would die to get out of this forest," Stanley said as they ate the last of their bread and coffee. The supply lines inland were farther away, their rations fewer.

"I would die for dry socks." The mud and fog lay on them like a film. In the dark undergrowth, the men rubbed against the trees and each other like ingredients in a stew. Where were the Germans?

Surely not as stupid as the Americans, Stanley thought, burrowing
through the forest, their tanks and artillery and Air Force stalled
by the dense formations of trees and rough terrain. The Allies were
all alone.

❀❀❀

Stanley peed in the snow. The cold air crept into his open pants
and ran down his legs. Before he could even finish the German shelling of the tree canopy began again, and Stanley crouched and hugged
the spruce in front of him without even pulling up his zipper. Around
him, splinters from the trees rained down like daggers, along with
hot metal. Ennis had looked like a wooden porcupine when they
pulled him back behind their lines a few days before. The shrapnel in
Ennis' chest had been bad, and he and Johnson, trapped in front of a
patch of machine guns, pressed themselves to the snow and needles
and mud for hours, Ennis between them, moaning for his mother.

Three days earlier, the First Division had discovered the Germans,
hidden and waiting for the Allies to amble past the river, when their
eyes were tired of the undulation of snow and trees, when their bodies were cold because, in anticipation of quick victory, the Allied
brass had not thought to ship winter clothes to the front. For weeks,
as the Northern chill swept in, Stanley and Johnson and the others
had measured their boots against dead men's, their inseams, their
chest sizes, looking to replace their wet, worn clothes with ones
slightly drier, slightly cleaner. Stanley wore two shirts other than
his own, each caked and itchy with medals of blood.

Stanley crawled on his hands in the red and brown snow back
to the slit trench he had dug with Johnson earlier that afternoon.
They had covered the opening with tree limbs and hoped it would

protect them from the shrapnel and wood. Inside, they were asshole buddies, sitting back to back, or asshole to asshole, chest high in the hole, branches and snow over them as they watched for movement beyond their line.

"You all right?" Johnson asked as Stanley shivered against him. After nightfall, it became frost. The dead men stuck to the earth.

"I think I'm going to have the runs something awful."

"Well, go have them the hell out there."

"You just want me shot at."

"Just go behind that tree over there. I'll cover you."

"Fuck you."

"I'm *joking*. Just be quiet." Johnson's hands felt frozen to his carbine. He would give his left hand, purple and granite under his glove, for a cigarette. He felt the pressure of Polenksy's back leave his, a creeping cold between his soldier blades, as Polensky turned around in the trench and squatted, helmet under his ass.

"You know, we should have a code word, a personal one, in case one of us leaves the hole." Johnson tried to talk over Stanley's sounds. A cigarette would go a long way to blunt the smell. But smoke could be seen at night. Rot, shit, and death smelled day and night, as assessable as air.

"What's wrong with the company's password?"

"Nothing. I just thought it would be good if we had our own. So I always know it's a Kraut in the burned-out house I'm about to fire into and not you."

"Jesus Lord Christ," Stanley grunted from his side of the trench.

"That's not a good one, Polensky. Too many guys already know it."

"Screw you. Christ…I ain't going to wear this again, that's for sure."

"Just clean it out with some snow. You may not need to protect that empty head of yours, but where are you going to store your socks and corsage?"

"Up your ass."

"Well, I know for sure that hasn't seen any action." Johnson aimed his rifle toward a flutter by the trees on his right. Geese? Squirrels? "How about metalanthium lamp?"

"That's your word?"

"Pretty good, huh?"

Suddenly, movement rocketed upward from the same trees. Mine? Mortar? Geese, definitely geese. The feathers and pulp floated to earth, shot by two others in the company. In response, the Kraut line lit up like flashbulbs. Polensky fell into position next to Johnson, his helmet, an overturned latrine, unstrapped on his chin. Around them, the snow spit bullets, feathers from feather pillows. For a second, Johnson closed his eyes, thought he would let himself get hit. To feel the cool, light fabric of a pillow, a flat one, a hard one, a moldy one, it didn't matter. His head whipped to the right, and he thought he'd gotten his wish. But it was only Stanley, punching him with an open palm.

"Wake up, dummy," he shouted at him above the soft explosions. "What the fuck are you doing?"

"Nothing," Johnson grunted, but he realized he was smiling. He liked this Stanley. He fired off a round. "Shithead."

"Go fuck yourself," Stanley answered, firing off his own. Johnson could see he was smiling, too.

The brass said the Hürtgen Forest was 50 square miles. It seemed to stretch to 100, then 200, then 300, as late October became early

November and late November became early December. Stanley did
not understand how they could not see the Germans and yet the
Germans could see them.

"They know these forests. They're stuffed in bunkers while we
walk right by them," Johnson said, coughing. Johnson had developed a cough-snore-shiver in his sleep. Perhaps Stanley could boil
the herb for tea, soothe Johnson's deathly rattle. *I still have the root,*
Stanley wrote to his mother. *Although I suspect I will have no reason
to use it. You never even told me how. Should I put it under my lip,
in a wound, perhaps?* His right foot smelled. There was no time to
unlace the boot and find out whether his toes had rotted. *We are
warm and fat and happy. Save me some Chinina.*

"Duck blood soup," Johnson laughed later, when Stanley
described Christmas dinner at home. "You eat everything, don't
you, Pole? Makes me want to come to your house to dinner after
the war."

"Right now, I would eat anything," Stanley shivered. He shivered
when he was awake and he shivered when he was dreaming. His
breath was staccatoed with shivers. He shivered when he peed and
he shivered when he shat and he shivered when he shivered. Stanley
would eat his shivers, if he could, but they would probably give him
diarrhea, he thought, like everything else.

They were still in the Hürtgen Forest, pissed as hell about it.
Stanley and Johnson had taken turns moving out ahead, little by
little, looking for mines and trying to clear brush for a path out.
The visibility was ten feet, at best, and the soldier, with his back to
Stanley, appeared from the foliage like a mirage. It had to be one of

their men, so close by. Stanley tapped him on the shoulder just as he realized the man looked wrong, the uniform, the helmet. As the man turned, Stanley pulled out his revolver and plugged him in the right cheek. The man fell, the wound cratering inward in his face like a black hole before bubbling up, blood oozing on the smooth, unshaven skin.

He was a boy. Stanley wondered if he was lost. His eyelids flickered, and Stanley wondered whether he should touch them, hold his hand. He kicked away the boy's rifle. The boy's fingers opened like petals. Stanley touched the boy's forehead with his left hand, his right cocked on his pistol, near his hip.

"Mutter," the boy said, a whisper wet with blood. When he reached up toward Stanley, Stanley shot him. The arm fell back toward the body. Stanley shivered. He shivered in his heart and his throat and the tears from his eyes warmed his face until it grew cold and sticky and he shivered again. He thought to eat his mother's herb, to protect himself. It could not hurt. When one no longer believed in anything, he considered, all things could possess equal power.

"You all right?" Johnson appeared from the brush, as Stanley groped in his helmet, feeling for the crumbled flowers. He put a hand on Stanley's shoulder. His grip was gentle, as if handling crystal, unlike his usual vice of fingers that dug right into Stanley's collarbone.

"Yeah." Stanley put his helmet back on quickly without retrieving it and rolled the boy over, face down, in the snow.

They walked in a diamond formation: Stanley walked in the back, Johnson in the front, one man, red-haired, was to their left, another, blond-haired, to their right. Stanley didn't know their names. It seemed a waste to learn them. Wood and shrapnel fell from the sky, mixed with snow, hitting the ground in hisses. The trees burned standing still. Stanley listened to the fire eating the wood, the snap of twigs and branches as they broke free of the parent trunks and fell down to the forest. Smoke poured from the nooks and crannies of the burning bark, and men were forced to crawl. On the ground, the red-haired man, in front, would tap the top of his helmet and point in the direction of movement, and they all would crouch and fill that direction with fire, grenades. But then the blond man on the right threw a grenade that hit a tree and bounced back toward them, and they dove leftward and rolled down a small hill.

"I would die for a stick of gum." Johnson entangled himself from Stanley. The smoke cleared, briefly, and the hard marble of sun blinked through the treetops.

"This might be your lucky day." Stanley nodded. Before them, a formation of rock appeared in the trees with a low opening, two by eight feet. A bunker. The red-haired man stood off to the side of it. He tossed in a grenade as they turned, covered their ears. Then they waited for the smoke to clear before joining him at the hole.

Stanley was the shortest, so he got on his knees and crawled in. He imagined a speckling of dead pale boys, boys with smooth faces and darting eyes, but it was empty with black. He tapped the inner mouth of the cave to make sure it was still secure. Then he pointed his thumb up, and the others joined him.

"Now this is living," red hair said in the darkness. He lit a cigarette and stretched. "We stay here until the war ends, okay?"

"At least for a nap," Stanley agreed, pulling his blanket out of his backpack. "We'll take turns on watch."

They slept on ground that wasn't wet and in corners that weren't windy. They slept with their helmets off, their boots unlaced, oblivious to the shelling outside. When they woke, their stomachs were relaxed, growling. They wondered how to get back behind the line for rations, wondered where they were.

"I say we stay in the hole," the red-haired man said.

"Yeah, and when one of our own boys throws another grenade in here, then what?" the blond said, tightening his laces. They were broken and did not go all the way up the boot.

"That's why we take turns on watch." The red-haired man shook his head.

"And when our whole company leaves us behind?" Johnson loaded his rifle. "We'll starve to death in the woods."

"Moving thirty feet a day?" red-haired man sneered. "Not fucking likely we get left behind."

"My orders were to take the forest," Johnson craned his head out of the hole. "I don't know about yours."

Their mood was sour. They decided to follow the ravine that led from the bunker.

"All aboard the Kraut trail," Johnson laughed. "Think they'll shell us here?"

"I say we're mighty close to something." Stanley lit a cigarette. "Think we're near the West Wall?"

"By God, we should be so lucky," the blond man said. "Then we can shoot the hell out of them and go home."

Stanley could not picture home. His mother's face appeared vaguely, the smell of her, the sound of her. The hardware store where he worked on Eastern Avenue. His school, Baltimore Polytechnic. He could not be sure whether any of those things had happened or whether they were a dream. Whether he had always been at war and would always be. They walked along the ravine for hours. Sometimes they would come across a body of a German, always picked clean. One body was missing its fillings, the mouth open and exposing bloody stumps of gumline.

"We need to find some Krauts so we can take their braut," the blond man said.

"I'd even eat the fucking Krauts," the red-haired man said. "Maybe we should go back and find our men."

"Maybe you're right," Stanley said. "Even if we find the Germans, they'll probably outnumber us."

"Our men are probably ahead of us," Johnson said, his head nodding forward. "That's why we're seeing so many dead. I told you we got left behind."

"Not likely," the red-haired man said. "I'm going back. The whole month, I ain't seen nobody get ahead of me. If there's somebody ahead of us, it's a different division. Which I'm more than happy for. Let them take some shots."

"I'm with him." The blond turned in the slit trench.

"Come on, safety in numbers." Red gripped his rifle. "Let's go back."

"What say you?" Johnson looked at Stanley. Johnson was the leader, but Stanley wanted to find their squadron, food.

"Let's go back." Stanley didn't look at Johnson.

"The Pole has decided," Johnson said, spitting in the trench, kicking at the snow-dirt with his shoe. "Let's go."

They turned around and followed the slit trench back to the bunker. Then they climbed up the slope they had fallen down earlier.

"Let's sweep out and move forward," Stanley said. Stanley moved in front, Johnson in the back. The shelling shook and shredded the tree canopy above them, branches falling like swooping vultures, pelting their shoulders and arms, leaving welts. The raining wood and shells filled the air with the sound of sanding metal, and Stanley could not hear anyone, only see their jaws moving, their eyes flicking back and forth as they scanned the area for mines, for Germans, for secure ground in front of them. Stanley wished they had stayed in the bunker. He glimpsed a man running through the trees, white and red cross armband. A medic. They knew how to get back to the line. All they needed to do was follow him. Stanley motioned to the men and ran toward the figure.

He had not gotten far when the ground swelled behind him like a wave, sweeping him off his feet. A shell. His body hit the dirt at angles—elbow, knees, ankles—before rolling. When he stopped, he felt for his legs, moved them, and stood up, crouched over.

"Johnson?" he called back. The area from where he had been thrown was peppered with wood and metal. Blackened bark. Gray and red snow. Johnson's helmet.

He followed the trail to Johnson, what was left of him. Blood spread from the left side of Johnson's groin, his left leg scattered around him, bone broken and carved like scrimshaw and strewn with strips of muscle and skin. Johnson shivered, coughed, and looked lazily up at Stanley, drunk with shock. Stanley called for the medic. The blond man staggered up and then off, shouting for help. Stanley tore a strip of cloth from Johnson's backpack and made a tourniquet. Johnson's big long face caved in from his cheeks to his chin. His eyes fluttered.

"Johnson." Stanley shook him. But Johnson was going. Stanley took off his helmet and scooped the herb out of the lining. He opened Johnson's mouth and pushed it in.

But Johnson didn't chew. Stanley opened Johnson's mouth and pulled a third of it between Johnson's gums and teeth. He picked off another piece and put in the red, beating hole that was once Johnson's hip, leg. Then he moved Johnson's jaw with his own hands, pushing Johnson's tongue aside, grinding the herb with Johnson's teeth. Johnson's mouth was dry as cotton, and the herb coated the soft pink insides. Stanley stuck his finger in Johnson's mouth and pushed the flakes, the unchewed pieces, into Johnson's throat. Johnson gagged, sitting up and coughing, hands at his neck. The green-brown flakes flew out, covering Stanley's face and shirt. Stanley wrapped his arms under Johnson's chest and jerked upward. Stanley jerked and Johnson coughed and the herb chunk flew into the snow.

"Medic." The man dropped his kit beside Stanley. Stanley moved back and caught sight of the spat-out herb. It glowed in the detritus, unearthly. Stanley's heart jumped. He reached for the glowing orange saxifrage. The medic turned, shook his head, frowned.

Johnson was dead. The medic tagged him, took one of his dog tags, and scrambled back in the forest. It seemed wrong to leave Johnson like this, any of them like this. Maybe Stanley wouldn't fight anymore, stay here with Johnson, work the herb into his wounds, down his throat. He could stick his knife into Johnson's chest and massage it into his heart.

The trees shook around him. Men shouted in the distance, the trill of bullets, explosions. Small fires baked in pockets of black trees. When another shell landed to the left of Stanley, he could feel the warmth of it on his leg. He did what he later imagined any other person would do. He ran.

1806

They traveled in the highlands west of Reszel, Poland, Ela Zdunk and her mother, Barbara, like they always did, looking for rare species of flowers and roots. They walked miles in the mossy, swampy darkness, digging around the bases of beeches, spruces, and sycamores, bending under brushes, getting scraped by thorns and stickers and bitten by bugs. For as long as Ela could remember, the villagers visited their one-room shack outside of Reszel, the bone house, as it was called, to buy tinctures for their ailments. They had probably visited her mother for longer than the nine years she had been alive, for her grandmother had served the villagers in this capacity as well.

Witches, they were sometimes called. But as long as the tinctures worked, no one became upset. They overlooked, or allowed, out of supposed generosity, Barbara Zdunk and her daughter to live in a hut of mud and river rocks and animal bones on a little patch of hill near the edge of the woods, where the ground was barren and cracked and the coyotes howled and nobody bothered but the gypsies, and only then for a little while. From their spot on the unprotected hill, Ela and her mother could see the thick ring of poplars and willows that surrounded the city below, the dense maze of terracotta-tiled roofs protected within it. When the customers were particularly foul or rude, Ela stood on the hill and squashed their houses between her thumb and forefinger.

They traveled so far west in the highlands that they passed through the forest and came upon a clearing, burned to black chalk by a lightning strike, and nothing grew in this grave save for a plant with three to four long stems, little white bouquets of flowers topping them. Burnette saxifrage. Ela remembered her mother talking about such flowers. They were part of the old folklore, when the goddesses purportedly roamed the earth. Her own mother did not pay much attention to the stories except to pass them along to the older, more superstitious villagers in order to sell them her tinctures.

"There were once three scythe-wielding goddess sisters," she told Ela as they picked the flowers. "Who brought death. One of the sisters, Marzana, hurt her leg and lagged behind them as they moved through the towns, lusting for blood. But no matter how much she begged for them to wait, they went on without her. So she sought revenge. She limped through the villages the sisters had not yet visited and told the townsfolk to eat and drink saxifrage to protect themselves from her sisters of death. They did, and they survived."

"Is that why these flowers survived the white heat?" Ela asked, rubbing her hand in the coarse soot. How anything had survived, had grown here after the lightning strike, she did not understand. In the past, she'd seen trees halved, rock blackened by the swords from the sky. "Marzana gave them the blessing?"

"It's not likely, the lightning, my sweet. The saxifrage is hardy, like weeds. It needs not much love to prosper." But in truth, Barbara did not know why they grew in the dead soil or why they did not succumb to the lightning. She caressed her cheek with the petals from one of the flowers and felt a tickle, a surge down to her feet, as if the herb had captured the electricity from the strike. But when she brushed her cheek again, the sensation did not return.

"Matka, do you believe such a thing?" Ela smelled the flowers, running her thumb and forefinger down their long stems.

"Believe what?"

"In magic."

"Of course not—but the roots and leaves we find have healing properties, some by themselves and some mixed with others. And maybe we'll be able to help Antoniusz. Would you like that, Ela?"

"I would." Ela skipped around in a circle. "Maybe when Antoniusz is healed, you will love him?"

"Come." Her mother Barbara gathered the herb in the apron of her skirt, and beckoned. "Time is not to waste."

❀❀❀

There were two men who loved Ela's mother, Bolek and Antoniusz. Bolek was sixteen, a farmer's son, one of many spit in Reszel, Poland, hard like rock and yet soft with youth, a sheep's head of blond hair that would probably thin as had his father's, eyes like river water, the brain of a squirrel. For years, he had visited Barbara, to get tinctures for his father's gout, his mother's headaches. Barbara had watched the sweetness of his boyhood, when he had fawned over Ela and confided that he wished men could have babies, shrivel into the erect swagger of manhood. And yet he could still charm them, bringing grapes and cheeses he had filched from the village, his angled jaw and easy smile reminding Ela of a jackal. When Bolek came, Ela's mother sent her outside to play far from the bone house. The first few times she heard her mother screaming, she ran home and tried to pull away Bolek, who lay on top of her mother on the straw bed, by his knobby toes.

I am feeling pain in a good way, Ela's mother explained, shooing her away. *Because Bolek is helping me with my back.*

Antoniusz was the other man who visited. Although Ela's mother talked with Antoniusz for hours, she did not let him help with her back. A friend of Ela's father, Jan, who had died in one of Poland's many uprisings, Antoniusz still led the underground resistance. Although Ela did not understand most of it, Antoniusz and her mother often talked about the continual partitioning of Poland among the Russian, Prussian, and Austrian empires as the gentry of Poland, who favored political alliances over a strong state, sold out to the highest bidders. The resistance, mostly peasants who were tired of both sides and who yearned for freedom most of all, had survived in pockets under Antoniusz's leadership, who had too many connections in the village gentry to be killed.

But the same gentry weren't afraid to send a message to lesser men and women, especially witches, fox dung like Barbara Zdunk, and drove her off her land shortly after Jan's death. In their new home at the top of the hill, Ela's mother had collected branches, thick as wrists, and the bones of boars and bears to build the skeleton of a shelter and packed it with mud from the forest. At one end, she tunneled out a chimney, which she lined with river rocks and the bones of bats and rabbits and birds. She collected wisps of straw that had traveled outside her neighbor's barns and made a mattress for her and Ela, then a baby, to sleep.

Although he had survived the uprising through the fortune of his connections, the indifference of fate had thrown Antoniusz from his horse years later. His leg had been broken in so many places that he walked with a limp and could no longer work in the fields, forced to whittle pipes and other objects, relying on his sister's care. Barbara was convinced she could strengthen the bone, soften the scars of muscle that were his calves. After they dried the leaves and roots of the burnette saxifrage they had collected, Ela's mother seeped them in potato vodka. She added other ingredients—a Chaga mushroom tonic she had used to rid the villagers of consumption, dandelion root for liver sickness, some extracts of amber—and seeped them as well, some for a few days, others for a few weeks. Some jars grew dark and cloudy while their secrets brewed, and others stayed clear. She also set aside a second batch of ingredients Ela recognized as those her mother sold in her "love" potions to the younger women of the village.

"Are you making Antoniusz my father?" Ela asked as her mother set some unused burnette saxifrage on the window ledge to continue drying.

"Antoniusz can never replace your father, in your heart or mine." Barbara bent toward her, brushed a lock of hair from her forehead. "But perhaps we, or I, can grow our hearts larger so that there is room for Antoniusz also. Would you like that?"

"But who will help with your back, Matka?"

Her mother laughed, her head arched backward, and Ela put her hand on the creamy trunk of her mother's neck, felt the vibration of enjoyment in her throat without understanding.

"Don't be mad, little one." Barbara grabbed both of her hands and kissed them. "My back is better. Who knows? I may not need Bolek after all."

"I don't believe it was Bolek who helped your back, anyway." Ela sat back on the straw, and Barbara rubbed her feet. They were little, smaller than Barbara's hands, smudged with dirt.

"You don't?" Barbara kissed a big toe. "Why not?"

"Because Bolek's too stupid. Yesterday, he even left with his shirt on backwards."

"Well, he was in a hurry." Her mother smiled. "There is still a war to fight, and he may not come back. Let's pray for his victory and safety."

"Don't worry, Matka—I will protect you while Bolek is gone!" Ela took Barbara's face in her little hands, probing her eyes until Barbara looked away. Ela's eyes were the same color as Jan's, and his memory lived in them, green lichenous orbs that made Barbara shiver. Ela's hair fell heavily, like a shawl over her back, almost to her bottom, rich chestnut like a horse's mane. The memories of him flared in Barbara's gut, like sour goat's milk, his broad back, his flat hands and soft voice, the way he held her in bed, and some days burned more than others. She knew there would never be an herb for this.

"You will get married someday, to a brave soldier." Barbara pulled away and began to straighten the bed. "And where will I be then?"

"I'll marry a king, Matka, and you can live in our castle!" Ela bounced.

"You don't really believe you will marry a king, Ela, do you?" Her mother bit her lip. "We are peasants. You and I are considered worse than that. It is enough that we are allowed to live. Do not let the fire of your pride burn a target on your back."

"But if Poland becomes free like Antoniusz says it will, I can marry anyone I want." Ela shook her head. "Is that not right, Matka?"

"Yes, you're a smart girl." Barbara stood up. "You will be as wise as your father some day. Come, help me pick some horseradish for dinner—Antoniusz will come soon."

❀❀❀

"It is a fool's errand," Antoniusz agreed. "For Bolek, surely, but Dąbrowski especially. Does he think Napoleon won't double-cross him again?"

"Maybe he thinks a defeated or weak Prussia is the best hope for everyone," Ela's mother answered.

They talked of such things as Ela played with her lalka, the names of men floating around her like bright butterflies that eluded her attempts at capture. The lalka had real hair, the toymaker in Reszel who sold it to Ela's mother claimed, dark like Ela's, and its arms and legs moved as well. Ela liked it so much Barbara had bought another, a blonde with blue eyes, for her birthday the following month, and hidden it under the bed.

Ela smelled Antoniusz's pipe, the musk of cloves and tobacco, and felt happy. When he was around, she could hear her father's voice in the rustle of the forest, see his thick shoulders in his shadowed form. Antoniusz's mangled leg, thin and weak, was tucked under the stool, while his healthy, firm one lay in front of him. A low fire heated a cauldron of horseradish soup in the corner of the room.

"If Prussia goes down, Napoleon will install a French government, not a Polish one," he argued, leaning over and coughing, his face almost in her mother's lap. It was much too crowded for three in the bone house, barely livable for two.

"The Polish Legion is his mongrel." Antoniusz cleared his throat and sat up. "We're lucky if we get a few scraps of rotten meat out of the deal."

"For people who do not get much meat, it is a king's ransom." Her mother crouched before the pot. The steam reddened her cheeks, and when she turned back to Antoniusz, he smiled, blushed.

"Since you are so worried about him, maybe I will try to talk Bolek into joining the underground resistance instead of Napoleon's army under Dąbrowski." Antoniusz rubbed the thigh of his good leg. "He will be safer with us, and fighting for our cause, not someone else's."

"Thank you, Antoniusz." Barbara ladled soup into bowls and put them on the table she had dragged from the trash of the sweetshop in town. "The Wysickis are my customers, and I shall feel terrible if their son dies for nothing."

"So many die for nothing," he shrugged. "Ones who fight for something, ones who don't. Everyone dies. Does it matter what they die for?"

"It matters to me," she said. Ela's mother had told her Antoniusz had lost both his wife and child many years ago, in childbirth. "I know we have been through so much, but we must live for something, and also die by it, too."

"I want you to be very careful in town when you run your errands," Antoniusz said between slurps of soup.

"But…why?"

"Dąbrowski's army will begin attacking Prussian interests and sympathizers. Shops, homes, properties, castles—nothing will be spared. Of course, you are probably safe because of your distance, but with your excursions to the city…perhaps it is safe for you to stay out here. I…I can bring your tinctures to town."

"Antoniusz, no." She put her hand over his, and the long strands of hair he had combed over his bald spot began to stick up. His skin, porridged, reddened. "That's very nice of you, but…everyone knew Jan. And even if they don't respect me, think I'm some dirty witch, surely they'll respect Jan's legacy."

"As you wish." He stood up, hunched over, and straightened his jacket. "You were always firm with your thoughts."

"Matka has a stone head," Ela, who had been silent to this point, blurted, and Antoniusz laughed.

"She'll be wiser than Jan in half the time." He rubbed Ela's head. It fit, almost entirely, in his palm, like a river stone.

"That would be a blessed thing." Barbara nodded, and let Antoniusz kiss her on the cheek before leaving.

"Antoniusz, I hate it when you go." Ela grabbed onto his good leg, her eyes wet. "Why do you have to go?"

He looked at Barbara, who gathered Ela close to her.

"We aren't the only people he cares for," her mother answered. "He has a sister who loves and depends on him very much. And many men follow his lead to free Poland. We cannot weight him anymore than we do."

"I'll be back soon, love." He knelt, a little laboriously, down to Ela. "I am carving a horse for your lalka. Its legs will move! And perhaps I can borrow a little of your hair for its mane. When it grows a little longer, I will be back with my shears."

Ela nodded and smiled, but her eyes, still wet, tipped her thoughts. Barbara held her close as Antoniusz walked down the hill, leaning on his cane, a man too wise and beaten for his years.

❁❁❁

The tinctures smelled sharp, moldy, and at times lightly fragrant. When Barbara was ready to test them, she had Ela catch some field mice. She took a knife and made cuts of different lengths and deepness on their bellies and their limbs, their bodies squirming under her fingers, and stopped the bleeding with the vodka. Then she applied the mixtures to their wounds, murky dressings that bubbled and clotted in the blood. She put the mice in glass jars Antoniusz had brought her from the village, trying not to watch their tortured forms scramble against their glass prisons, the bloody paw prints streaked on the glass.

During the next few weeks, they would study their progress while continually applying the tincture dressing. But when Barbara returned from washing the laundry a few days later, several mice were quiet, and she assumed that they were dead. She pulled out the first mouse, the one with the shallowest cut; the cut had disappeared. She rubbed the mouse's hair, feeling its skin, smooth and intact, on its stomach. She wondered whether Ela had switched the mice to play a trick on her. She took out the second mouse. She had made a deeper cut in its stomach, and when she turned it over, she could not find that wound, either. Then she pulled the third mouse out, the one in which she had made the deepest cut, almost severing its right hind paw. But both hind paws of this mouse were fine.

"Ela!" Barbara stood at the entrance of the bone house, letting the mice fall out of her hands. They scrambled away, little currents firing through the grass. "Ela! What have you done to the mice?"

It didn't matter what animals they used—mice, birds, frogs. Barbara, with the sweep of her knife, would leave animals clinging to life, cuts so deep that organs, bright and smooth like unborn children, peeked from underneath layers of tissues. Tendons trailed behind legs, bone gleamed white. After a few drops of the tincture and rest, they healed, in days or weeks depending on which mixture was applied. The only constant between the potions was the lightening-struck saxifrage, and the more saxifrage, the more potent the potion. Barbara cut off the paw of a wild rabbit completely, in desperation, in disbelief, and threw the rabbit in a pot. All night, she listened to the scraping of three legs against the sides of the pot, waiting for the sound to subside.

Barbara shook Ela awake when the first slither of light bloomed from the chimney. They carefully removed the lid of the pot. The blood-smeared rabbit did not move, but Barbara could see its quick breaths pushing its fur in and out. She turned the rabbit over. Where there once was a bloody stump was now a skinned-over dwarf paw, pink with nubby nails. Barbara tied a brightly colored thread tightly around the base of its tail and set it free. When Ela ran up to the bone house a week later, she swung the same rabbit by its upper paws, and two hind paws, each mirroring length and width, dangled before her.

Barbara and Ela ran errands in Reszel, dropping off tinctures, leaving an invitation with Antoniusz's sister for Antoniusz to come for dinner. When they returned from the village, Ela's mother killed one of the rabbits that they had not treated, slicing its throat and draining its blood into a jar for later. She tied its carcass to a sturdy stick and roasted it on a spit behind the bone house with wedges of potato and rosemary. Inside, Antoniusz's tincture, brown-clouded and sour, waited in a glass vial. The rest of the untreated saxifrage flowers were spread on a rock by the door, waiting to be seeped eventually in Barbara's love potion, the rest ground in powder for use later. But when the time came for him to arrive, she and Ela stood on the hill and could not spot him walking through the fields. Plumes of dark smoke rose from the village, furling up to the clouds like an umbilical cord.

"Matka, the city is on fire!" Ela grabbed at Barbara's hip.

"It'll be all right." Barbara stroked Ela's hair. "It's probably just a stable or something."

The smoke curled and funneled and was still whispering through the darkness when Barbara put Ela to bed. It would not spread, Barbara told her, but whatever it had been had been significant. Ela knew. The air was brushed with burning wood, the sear of heat, and her eyes watered. She closed them, her dried eyelids tickled by the straw, and listened for Antoniusz's step on the path.

She was nearly asleep when she heard the rustling of brush, stones skittering underfoot. She opened her eyes and stood, joining her mother at the door, following the shadow's progress across the fields.

"Barbara!" The voice was Bolek's, and a minute later, his soot-smeared face began to form in the bone house. "Quick, get me under cover!"

"Are you all right?" Barbara felt his body in her hands. Ela could feel the heat of his clothing. Threads of fabric on his shoulders and elbows sizzled.

"You need to hide me." He pushed past them into the shack. Barbara took one last look in the dark for Antoniusz before beckoning Ela to follow her inside. The smell of flesh, cooked, burnt, slapped the back of Ela's throat as it overwhelmed the shack, and she gagged. Bolek's overshirt lay on the floor, and some of his flesh did also, curled, the color of lamb fat.

"Bolek!" Barbara turned for her treatments. "What is all this about?"

"The fire." He sunk to the floor, rubbing his hands on his knees. "We burned it. We burned everything."

"Everything?" She sank to her knees on the floor beside him. As she stripped him of the remaining swaths of fabric, they could see the extent of his injuries—the oily red muscles of his back, exposed and twitching, his left hand a charred stump. She coughed on the smoke and drew the collar of her dress over her nose and mouth. "Oh my god, look at you!"

"We only meant to burn a few stores, places owned by the Prussia lovers." He wet his remaining thumb with his tongue and smoothed it over a welt on his arm. "But it got out of hand. Oh, Lord, what have we done?"

"Your parents, Bolek—what about your parents?"

But Bolek only shook his head. He began to cry. Barbara linked her arms lightly around his shoulders, drew him to her breast.

"I wanted to be a hero—I didn't want everyone to die."

"Oh, Bolek, you're but a child." Barbara wove her fingers into his thick, sooty curls. "A child."

"The Prussians will come—they will find all of us and kill us," he said. "They are already moving through the fields, killing everyone, even children."

"No, they'll do no such thing," she answered. "Just be calm, please. Be calm."

"Barbara, I have been unfair to you, so unfair." He grabbed her hands. "In that I have never asked you to marry. Please don't let me die. Your potions—please do something!"

"You're not going to die." She squeezed his hands.

"Do not make such promises if they're not the truth." His teeth chattered as he fought back more tears, his face red, the cords in his neck tense. The salt of him and something rawer, primal, grabbed at them. "You must know that if I survive, I should like a life together with you and Ela. I am strong—I can provide. We'll go far away and I'll take care of you, I should... you would like that, wouldn't you?"

"Shh." She put her finger before his lips. "There will be time to talk later."

Ela hurried to the river to collect water for Bolek's wounds as her mother instructed. On her return she could feel it, a footstep hum deep in the earth. Something was close. She hurried, stubbing her foot on a rock, her lungs burning from the black that wove the air like a fine lace. If she did not hurry, Bolek would die, and if they did not leave, the soldiers would catch them. She thought of Antoniusz, willed him to come and help.

In the darkness of the hut, she could make out her mother sitting on the straw, preparing the tincture.

"Matka, I'm scared." She buried her head in her mother's side as Bolek moaned from the floor. "Bolek is talking funny."

"He is seriously injured, my love." She bent and dipped a rag in the bucket, touched his back with it.

"Oh, my dear Barbara, I will be hero to you yet," he giggled, delirious. "Grab me my gun and I shall protect you. Where is my gun?"

"Stop." She pushed his hands toward his lap. "I'm going to clean your wounds and apply a tincture, and everything will be okay. Do you hear me, Bolek?"

"What is this?" Bolek picked up the spindly root with the fan-shaped flowers from the rock and smelled it. They were uncured, waiting to be soaked with dandelion and Chaga mushroom.

"Something that will save your life," she answered. The ground underneath her feet vibrated with the gallop of horses. Bolek grabbed for the bucket, took a large drink, and threw up. The bucket slipped out of his hands, spilling the tincture to the floor.

The soldiers were so close. Ela's mother stood and grabbed the remaining saxifrage from the windowsill. "Ela, come here."

But she did not move. Her mother lurched toward her and pried open her little mouth, smudged with dirt and sweat. She pushed the herb into it.

"Chew, my love." She pushed Ela's lower jaw up so that it met her upper jaw. "Hurry."

"Where is mine?" Bolek moaned. He leaned unsteadily toward them. "You cannot give her all of it."

"Shh, there is more," Barbara answered, placing the herb in his hand. Suddenly, his eyes grew wide as if God himself had returned. But when she looked, it was not their maker but men in tricorn hats, waistcoats, stockings, one crouched in the doorway, two just outside. She could see down the barrels of the muskets they leveled at them.

"Traitors, filthy traitors." A man, hairs of copper curling from under his hat, spat at them. "Did you think you'd get away with this, arsonists?"

"It was not me—I, a townsperson, am innocent." Bolek stood up shakily. But he set his jaw, clenched his fist, his eyes unwavering from the man's. "It was witchcraft—I saw it with my own eyes."

"Witchcraft?" The man laughed, his mouth so wide Ela could see the spaces, far as countries, between the few yellowed teeth in his gums. He set his musket on the ground as he rubbed his blackened cheek with his palm. "You are the speaking the truth, lad? There're no witches in Prussia. We're not governed by spooks."

"What do you call all this?" Bolek waved his arms around the bone house. "This woman has been selling her witchcraft around the village for years. We all buy it because we're scared of her. You killed her husband years ago, and this is her revenge. And we're paying the price for it."

"Imbecile," one of the musketeers bellowed from outside, but the man waved him off.

"So why are you here, then, boy, conspiring with this witch?"

"Because I want to be a hero, like everyone else." He nodded toward Barbara. "I came here to capture her. Even though she could turn me into a frog or set me on fire just like the town, I knew I needed to separate her from her magic and bring her back for justice."

"Liar!" Barbara exploded. She looked at the musketeer pleadingly. "Pray tell, sir, who is the one covered with soot, burned? Not me. My tinctures have no such power. My own mother made the same tinctures for your mothers and fathers. You probably even know of her, Agnes Zdunk."

"Exactly. Her mother gave tinctures to the villagers." Bolek pointed his finger at Ela's mother as he swayed back and forth. He would die soon, Ela knew, and yet he would still attempt and betray them to save himself. But she was too scared to do anything. "Are they not dead now?"

"Of old age, you fool," Barbara answered.

"Enough." The musketeer picked up his musket. He pointed it at Bolek. "You—outside."

He did not look at Barbara as he passed. The musketeers gathered her remaining vials, glass jars, saxifrage flowers.

"Burn it all outside." The lead musketeer directed. "If she's really a witch, I don't want her instruments available to her."

"I'm not a witch." Barbara shook her head over and over again. "I am a woman of medicine. I have been treating that boy's parents for years. He came here tonight and asked me to hide him. He said the whole town was burned, and it was his doing. My daughter and I have no stake in any of this—we don't even live in Reszel."

"You are a widow—you may not be a witch, but you have a desire to avenge your husband, do you not?"

"I do not—I just want to be left alone!"

"Well, the matter should be easy enough to solve." He leveled his musket at Ela. "Are you a witch or aren't you?"

"No, I'm not a witch. Please, stop! Stop it!" Barbara reached for her, but the soldier grabbed her arms and twisted them behind her back. "Good lord! She's a child—a child! Don't you have children?"

The soldier kept his musket aimed at Ela as he spoke to Barbara. "Again. Are you a witch?"

"No . . . no," she said. He cocked the trigger. "Yes. Yes! Take me, leave the child. Please!"

"You're a liar, and if you're a witch, so be this child."

The house exploded with the smoke and sound of the musket, sucking time and air inward, never to be released. The shot hit Ela in the chest and she lay with her lalka in the dirt, hard and milky like a broken vase. She heard her mother scream and struggle against the soldier as he dragged her from the bone house. Soon she was outside her body, following. Outside, she hovered over them, over the shadow of Bolek, his heavy breaths filling him up and then shrinking him as her mother struggled to get at him.

"Bolek, she's dead! Ela is dead!" She clawed the air between them until it was thin and ragged, but he stood unflinching, breathing heavily. "You have taken everything from me! And why—because you are a coward?"

He bobbed his head, laughing like a loon, but his body slumped. She could not believe he was going to get away with it. The lead musketeer emerged from the bone house and threw her mother's remaining tinctures on the ground. He started a small fire and rolled the glass and alcohol and herbs into it.

"Young peasant." he said to Bolek. "You will be well rewarded by the Prussians for your bravery in bringing this Satanic menace to our attention."

Bolek lifted his head, and Ela could see his smile, self-satisfied, through her tears. But it was only for a second before the soldier pulled his sword from his side and, in one stroke, lopped Bolek's head off.

"Stupid peasant." He kicked Bolek's head, no longer smiling, across the field. "Enjoy your reward."

The soldiers laughed. The fire burned blue and green and then orange as everything spat and cracked and turned to black.

"We'll take this one back." The copper-haired soldier nodded at Barbara. "If she is a witch, surely it can be proven. And until then, let her bewitch us with her fruits."

And with that, he dropped his pants and moved toward her mother.

1945

He woke up in blackness. It choked him like a coffin. The trees of the Hürtgen forest and the large bowl of gray sky above them were gone. He tried to sit up, but darkness pressed on him like heavy taffy, ensnarling his limbs. No birds sang in the black trees he could not see. He vaguely remembered winter, the Germans, the cold.

His hip ached. He dug his hands through the black weight to his thigh. He felt a stump where his left leg had once met his hip, the skin smooth and round like a baby's head, a mossy substance covering the tip like afterbirth. A memory of men, of Stanley Polensky and others, swam before him. But they were not here, nor were the others in his unit. In his mind, he could see them around him in the forest still, lumps in faded fatigues, helmets upturned like opened walnuts.

He thought of his parents in Ohio. He imagined them sitting in the living room, listening to *The Abbott and Costello Show* on the radio, interrupted by a knock at the door. It would be the only knock, as their nearest neighbors were a half-mile north, they were expecting, the knock they'd hoped never to get. His mother's hands would clench her knitting, her fingers moving over the seams, counting them absently as the officer at the door took off his hat and his father turned toward her, his face like a quarry. He thought of his room, the clothes he would never wear again, the line of sun crawling over his bedroom wall and dresser in the red dawn that he would never see. He imagined the wife he would never touch, whose shoulder he would squeeze in the car on the way to somewhere, anywhere, as long as she was beside him. Would he ever kiss anyone again? Would anyone ever love him, beside his parents?

He thought of the field behind his parents' house and the beet and carrot seeds he would never again press into the yielding earth with his mother during the spring, his hands still chapped from the raw March. He would not hear the sound of husks swishing in the wind in the late summer, the smell of warmed dirt and motor oil and the sound of crickets and the glow of the moon from his window.

He thought about the war. He wondered where the war had gone, if everybody had died. If he was dead. If this, this suffocating purgatory, was all he had for all his prayers.

He had fallen asleep. When he woke up, his left leg itched. He still could not see and could barely move. His hands swam to his phantom thigh and grazed something firm, fleshy. Now, his stump ended at his knee, smooth and round like a baby's head. A sticky glue clung to the end. He felt sweat in his armpits, in his crotch. It was warmer, smellier in this darkness. He could see slits of light above him, like cracks around a basement door. He had dreamed, or hallucinated, that he was a full amputee.

Where were the men? It was so quiet, a few birds, rustling leaves, a voice, laughter, far away. He pushed against the weight above and around him, remembering the shells raining from the canopy of trees and the bullets whizzing like mosquitoes.

Whatever the medic had done, it worked great. Johnson ran his hand over his exposed knee. No gangrene. A completely healed-over stump. That man deserved a medal. If he'd only been good enough to save the whole leg, but this was better than nothing. Johnson wondered how he lost it in the first place. All he knew was that he was pissed as hell at Polensky. Leading them back to the forest like that, when they could have followed the ditch. Nearly gotten him killed.

It was not Polensky's fault. If Johnson were, in fact, dead, if this were hell, or the afterlife, he could not be mad at Polensky. He could have followed the ditch if he wanted. He would tell Stanley, if he could, that it was okay. That he was sorry for being such a jerk, for teasing him all the time. When he thought about it, although he played poker and talked rough stuff with Green and the others, Polensky was the only one he'd ever told anything to. About his childhood nightmares of faceless men who kidnapped his parents and led him into the field to beat him. About how he lost his virginity to an older woman, Eva Darson, a divorcee who didn't go to their church but who always smiled, a mouth of slightly crooked teeth, and asked him about his parents when he was at the drugstore. That she had asked him to come over to help move her couch but they had moved their lips, their bodies against each other, against things instead. That he thought of marrying her once, that he liked how she ran her index finger along things, sizing them up, speaking her mind in a way that most women had not been taught, or allowed.

"I am half Spanish." She'd bounce the bottom of her coffee-colored hair with the palm of her hair. It fell in bangle-sized curls around her neck. "If we do not speak, we do not breathe."

He did not spend time with her because she was half Spanish. He supposed he felt sorry for her. She always prepared extravagant dinners for him—pork loins and sirloins—although he was too young and probably too self-absorbed to consider how she managed them on her meager resources. Once she gave him a bottle of cologne, called Garcon, that he hid, like a girlie magazine, on the top of his closet shelf, lest his mother smell something on him other than the Skin Bracer aftershave she bought him for Christmas and his birthday, like an obligation. Eva always had cigarettes, which she liberally encouraged him to smoke. He supposed now that she had done these things to extract some sort of promise from him that, even if he didn't love her, he would always be available to her. That he would always worship and admire her with the dewy eyes of youth, that she, in various stages of emotional starvation, could at least quench her thirst with a tall, cool drink.

She did not love him, he knew. She did not love anyone, as far as he could tell. Her drunk of a ex-husband who couldn't provide for her in the way she was accustomed, the men she'd dated who could barely spring for dinner and a movie, always skipping those acts and wanting to add a third, which usually took place in her bedroom. The girls at the telephone company where she worked, who gossiped and were boring and never heard of the Louvre. Eva required a sophistication and kindness and curiosity from every-one that she assumed she had herself, if only because she always reminded him she was all of these things.

"I can't help it; I'm a sophisticated woman," she had apologized after he asked her, with his money, to buy his mother a nice blouse at Pennelmen's Department store. "I would never step foot in Pen-nelmen's. The cheapest fabrics you ever saw. And no imagination, no style. I mean, maybe that's okay for an old woman...you should let me get her something at Barrett's."

"I don't think my mother would wear anything from Barrett's," he answered, looking in his wallet. And even if she looked good in the frilly chenille, the billowy scarves, and other French-looking outfits, he couldn't afford it.

"Well, I will not set a foot in Pennelmen's, I'll tell you that. My reputation couldn't stand it." She lit a cigarette and crossed her arms, ending the conversation. She had compromised enough in her life, she'd always told him—and look where it had gotten her!

It was not the sex, not only the sex—the sole benefit he imagined most boys to derive from such a relationship—that he continued to see her. She was a good-looking woman, for thirty, and had a quick wit and could flatter one with a single raise of her eyebrow. But why he thought he had loved her, he didn't know. He supposed he felt sorry for her. It was the hole of the persecution in which she was buried, by men, women, by society, she had impressed upon him to believe, all while she stood there holding the shovel.

"People from Ohio, they just don't know anything." She floated her eyes to the ceiling, taking a cigarette herself. "They certainly don't know how to live."

Well, he had certainly lived, and he had seen some things. He had lived, she would be happy to know. If he saw her again.

He dug at the darkness, twisting his body in increments so small, it was a miracle there was oxygen to breathe. But he could not squirm without becoming tired. He felt himself doze off. When he awoke again, his left leg burned. His hands went to his phantom calf and grazed something firm, fleshy. His stump had grown again. He wriggled the toes on his left foot, all five, and the steely, curly hairs he remembered on them burned as the nerves beneath them fired their own internal gun battle. He breathed and choked on the acrid stink of flesh. Jesus. He had dreamed, or hallucinated, he was a below-knee amputee.

Where were the others? He wiggled, kicking his legs, his arms in little motions. He was buried in rocks, maybe. Had there been an explosion? And why was he not broken into so many sticks, marionette limbs?

His voice. It sounded so far away, like those other voices. Murmurs of men close by but far away. Was he hearing things? He inhaled, wondered whether his lungs were punctured. Once he inflated the branches of lung in his chest, a few deep breaths, he shouted over and over again in the rocks. Why would he wake up after such catastrophe, only to die in rubble? He had to be found. His parents had to know. Stanley Polensky had to know. He shouted but what sounded like a wounded gurgle came out. He gurgled until he was too tired to make a sound.

When he awoke again, he was so hungry. The rocks were softer; he wondered whether it had rained. He could see ribbons of blue sky above him, and he kicked and pushed and managed to move the rock above him slightly to the side. Something fell on his face, a bat, a mouse, he was not sure, and he closed his mouth and pressed his eyes shut but it did not move. He rocked his body back and forth, widening the space around him. The rocks oozed wet and stink on him and the squiggly feeling of maggots. The ribbons of blue sky widened, and occasionally a fly swarmed in, crawling on his face. He shook his head back and forth, back and forth, and the thing on his face fell to the side. Curiously, he touched it with his tongue. It tasted salty, sour. Rubbery. Fleshy.

"Oh Jesus, we got an animal down there or something," Johnson heard someone say.

"Well, let's not sit around and let Sarge find out," another answered. "Come on, let's scare it out of there."

Suddenly the pile of rocks above Johnson was rolled away, one by one. The air grew fresher, the sky brighter, and Johnson could see that the rocks wore fatigue wool, canvas jackets, socks. He was buried in a pile of corpses. As soon as his arms were freed, he began to push against the bodies around him. The sourness in his stomach rocked against his cheeks.

"Oh, Jesus. Oh shit." The men, fresh-scrubbed privates by the look of them, wiped their hands on their thighs. They squinted their eyes, grabbed him by the shoulders. They shook him. "Are you all right?"

At a clearing station of the Graves Registration Service, T/O 10-298, north of the Hürtgen Forest in Aachen, Germany, Johnson waited for a private to find him some clean clothes. He could not be picky. He was lucky that he had not been buried already, that his personal effects were not shipped to Depot Q-290 in Folembray, France, where they would be sorted and sent to the Army Effects Bureau at the Quartermaster Depot in Kansas City, Missouri, as one sergeant had painstakingly and eye-glazenly explained to him. He was given wool pants that were too short, a shirt that scratched at his chest. Still he'd had a shower, the first in presumably months, since D-Day at least. He'd used a whole bar of soap on his balls and ass.

"The form pinned to your body said you died of shock from an amputated leg." The platoon leader looked over his makeshift desk at Johnson's full set of appendages. "Now how do you suppose those EMT tags got messed up?"

"I don't know, sir." Johnson rubbed the leg in question. "I don't remember much of anything."

He suddenly remembered the corsage. For some reason, Johnson thought maybe Stanley Polensky had been trying to stuff it into his mouth. He shook his head, licked the inside of his cheeks. He had imagined so many things—his leg all sizes of amputation, the changing of the seasons. He knew for certain he'd been left behind—whether by the Allies or Germans he wasn't sure—left for dead.

"Now you don't suppose you were faking it, were you?" The sergeant frowned, drumming his fingers on the desk.

"Fake an amputation, sir?" Johnson sat up. He'd heard about the deserters but had never thought he'd be assumed one of them. No one had mentioned that the right pant leg of his old fatigues was missing, that the torn cuff, up near his groin, had been tinged with blood. Why he had not kept the pants for proof he did not know. Shock, he supposed.

"Let's say for a minute the medic pinned the wrong tag on you, made a mistake." The sergeant leaned back in his seat. There were lines on his face angled in every direction—at the corners of his mouth, across his forehead, vertically in the sunken parts of his cheeks—but Johnson didn't believe him to be any more than twenty-five. "And maybe you played dead for awhile on the ground. Tired of people shooting at you, maybe. Couldn't take it anymore."

"No, sir." He didn't tell him about the hallucinations. "I must have passed out somehow—the shelling, maybe. I remember a big explosion. And then I remember waking up in the ground."

The sergeant sat with his index fingers in a triangle, touching his lips. Johnson was not sure what he debated—whether John-

son would make a stink about being left for dead in a pile of bodies, or whether the Army should prosecute him for full desertion.
Whether he should be examined for fugue, or brain damage, before
being sent back to the line. Whether he was so much human collateral to be worth the trouble.

"Sir, I wouldn't lie to you," he offered. "I enlisted, and I'm prepared to stay through the end."

The sergeant sighed. "What's your outfit?"

"First Division Infantry, sir."

"I'm sending you to the hospital," the sergeant said finally, light-
ing a cigarette. With this decision, his energy increased. His eyes
burned like coals. "Those boys need every warm body they can get
right now, but you've been sitting here like you don't know your ass
from a hole in the ground, and, honestly, I don't think you're faking it. I mean, you haven't eaten for a couple of weeks, you've been
transported in a truck with the other bodies... it just don't make
sense. I'm not sure how I'm going to report this, but I would prefer
you don't talk to anyone until we get it straightened out. We'll be in
touch with your family, to redact our mistake." The sergeant stood
up, and Johnson followed.

He did not talk to anyone at the base about the mix-up, how so
many human bodies were lumped into piles without sheets or bags
to cover them and all the other things that Graves Registration was
not supposed to do, but what he most wanted to talk about was what
had happened to him, exactly—how he had been dead, maybe, or
almost dead, and something had happened so that he was alive.
Something had happened in the darkness that was not supposed to
have happened. His religion could not explain what had happened
and his parents could not explain what had happened and the Army

sure as hell could not explain what had happened. It came down to Polensky, he reasoned, the last person who he saw in the forest. Stanley and thing he stuffed in Johnson's mouth.

Maybe Polensky was a witchdoctor; maybe he had gotten a formula from one of his Tom Swift books. Johnson would get back to the front and grab Polensky by the neck and he'd better start talking or he'd break it. Or maybe he would thank him for saving his life. Right now, he just wanted to not throw up, to break down in tears like a little girl, like Stanley. He bummed a cigarette from a soldier outside the mess tent and stretched in the grass, hoping the sun would bleach out the burn of memories that were seared in his limbs. He watched another truck arrive, full of bodies. He pushed himself up on his own two legs and felt his muscles expand and contract as he walked over, the air swimming down his throat. The sun warmed the top of his ears, the back of his neck. He saw the arms and legs, trunks of others piled one atop one another, and those men were dead. The sun warmed their bodies but when the night came, they would cool again, and nothing would make them move their mouths, laugh, open their eyes. They would not tunnel their way out of the pile. They were not so lucky. Why was he?

When he made it to the truck he was crying, tears like he hadn't cried since he was six and his father put down their bird dog, Shotzie.

"Hang in there, buddy." A boy-soldier, the barest of fuzz on his chin, a sprinkle of freckles across the bridge of his nose, knocked him on the shoulder. "The first few are weird, but then they're just bodies. Nothing to get upset about."

"How long you been here?" Johnson asked, wiping his eyes. He felt the muscles in his arm simmer, his fist clench. How could he disrespect those men, men Johnson had played poker with, catch with, shared cigarettes? He imagined the small explosion of pain in his fist when it would meet the bone of the boy's jaw.

"A few months. It's gets old—you'll see." The boy grinned, and before Johnson could react, he held the legs of a dead man in his arm, boots dry caked with mud and blood, the boy straining to square the man's head and shoulders against his chest. The boy jerked the man's shoulders upward as the face, placid white and set like wax, lobbed to the side. "You ready?"

The boy moved backward, and Johnson moved forward. And they took the men to a shed and collected their things from them, pocket watches and crucifixes and girlie pictures and foiled-wrapped chocolate. The bodies had only one dog tag—the other had been taken by the medic when he declared them dead in the field of combat. Johnson and the boy went through a box of tags brought in by the medics and matched them up to the bodies, making them men again briefly, before they were zipped into bags to be interred at the temporary military cemeteries all over Europe. When the boy wasn't looking, Johnson slipped one of the tags from the box up his sleeve and held it against his wrist, underneath his cuff. Before dinner he squatted behind the mess tent and retrieved the tag: CALVIN E. JOHNSON. He slipped it on the chain on his neck, reuniting it with its partner. He rubbed them together against his thumb and forefinger, feeling his name and number and branch of service agitate the skin. But he felt not like man nor body. He pulled at the chain against his neck until it snapped, watching it slither with the tags through his fingers. Wherever they fell on the ground, in a jumbled dance, was where he left them.

❀❀❀

The War Department wished to inform them, Johnson's parents, that the death of Private E-2 Calvin Ernest Johnson had been a mistake. While a telegram went out to Bowling Green, Ohio, to correct the Army's error, Johnson was loaded on a litter in a military ambulance, driven to a train station near Hampstead, England, and then, assuring them he could find his way just fine, he boarded the special hospital car of his own volition. The red tag that he had removed from his chest and attached to his wrist was correct this time as far as Johnson could tell. He was alive and headed for Camp Upton, Long Island, New York. It was mid-April, 1945.

The soldiers at Camp Upton Convalescent Hospital were not severely injured—broken bones, second- and third-degree burns, a pysch consult for "psychoneurotic disorders." One tried to avoid the latter. Nobody wanted to go home branded as someone who couldn't cope, when so many others had. At least, if they hadn't, they weren't saying.

The days were long. He read detective paperbacks to a corporal who'd been burned at Cisterna. The man lay on his stomach sixteen hours a day before he was turned over to have his dressings changed. He bowled with a private who'd taken shrapnel in his eye at Salerno. He swam laps alone in the pool in the evening, the lights of the pool giving it an unearthly sheen, feeling his right leg, then his left, slice through the chlorinated water. He opened his eyes underneath because when he closed them for extended periods he saw men disemboweled, crushed, burnt like the turkey his mother had left too long in the oven a few Thanksgivings ago. He lay in bed, smoking cigarettes, watching the big hand, then the little hand, make its rotation on the ward clock. The cinderblock walls shone smooth with painted seafoam; sometimes after falling asleep from exhaustion, then waking up with the sweats, his hands clenching the bed sheets, he stood up and pressed his cheek against the cool wall. He wrote letters to his parents, commenting mostly on the food, some of the other soldiers on the ward, a pretty nurse or two.

But he felt like a mistake; a healthy, shiftless mistake sleeping in a clean, firm bed. A mistake that drank hot coffee and ate scrambled eggs and not cold canned rations. The others didn't ask him about his wounds, or lack thereof. They looked at him with a knowing glance; in private, perhaps, they speculated: shell shock, suicide attempt. The more generous, maybe, pegged him with infection, influenza.

"We're rubbing down your rough edges before we send you back," the nurse from the counseling service explained as she took his blood pressure, listened to his heart. The staff doctors administered the same psychiatric tests they administered to him before the war. He passed. They gave him sodium pentothal and put him under hypnosis, but the same dream, image, whatever it was, waited for him, like a movie that ran on a continuous reel. Polensky was in front of him. It was cold as it had ever been and almost impossible to fathom how cold. Snow gusts swirled through the trees, along with an occasional storm of hot splinters, pine needles, shrapnel from the Germans shelling them. Suddenly, the air was sucked away before returning and knocking him off his feet, slamming him onto his back. His ears rung. The sky vibrated above him. He tried to sit up, numb, but could not. He felt his body, his chest and stomach, then he moved his fingers down to his legs. First his right, and then his left. His blood ran cold as he realized there was fabric, wet and sticky, but no leg. He tried to sit up again. Polensky leaned over him. He could see the faded blue of Stanley's eyes, the whites around them as they widened. Stanley fumbled in his helmet. Johnson tried to tell him what a fool he was—*do you want to get shelled in the head, you idiot?*—but he put it back on. He then stuffed something dry and fibrous in Johnson's mouth, taking his hands and moving Johnson's jaws up and down to simulate chewing. It hit the back of Johnson's throat, choking him. Someone new then appeared in front of him, a medic. He pinned something on Johnson's collar.

The Army psychologist looked at him. He had the same tired lines of the sergeant back at the Graves Registration Service. There was little he probably had not heard, and their directives were similar at all levels—to send men back to the front. For the psych unit, that is, those soldiers whose war existed in their minds, it had taken the form of calling them cowards, soft. But Johnson was not soft— he had landed in Algeria as part of Operation Torch, Operation Husky in Sicily, Normandy, Germany. He had been in almost two years of continuous combat.

"I dreamed that I got shelled in the Hürtgen, that I lost my leg," Johnson explained. "I remember being in so much pain. And then I wake up, months later, in a pile of soldiers. And they tell me I was tagged as death by amputation. Does that make any sense to you, doc, seeing as I have two perfectly good legs here?"

"It's possible that that, while you were moving in and out of consciousness, that you heard other conversations on the battlefield." The doctor rustled through his papers. The walls of the room also were foam green, as was much of the hospital, a soothing color, some said. It made Johnson think of fatigues, light happy ones—

baby fatigues. They had all gone in as babies, he thought, and they left with lines on their faces, eyes that could only see the past, and yet not make any sense of it, to the detriment of the future.

"So..." Johnson pressed.

"Well," the doctor coughed. "Say someone else was hurt nearby. Someone else lost their leg. The other soldiers are shouting that Scotty Private has gotten his leg blown off, needs a medic. And the medic that is treating you, that will attend to Scotty Private shortly, accidently writes 'leg amputation' on your EMT tag."

Johnson nodded, looking at his hands. Every day he looked at his leg, trying to find something different about it. A stray hair, a scar. He tried to remember the moles on his leg before, whether they had changed positions.

"Does that make sense to you, Calvin?" The doctor tapped his pencil on his papers.

He supposed it had to be true. How else to explain he was alive? There were no such things as witch doctors, metalanthium lamps. He watched the doctor scribble a few notes in his chart.

"Let's say you were in a coma." The doctor said. "And that you have recovered. Do you have any questions?"

Johnson shook his head. He was prepared to go back and, if he was to come back here, actually have a real injury. But then Germany surrendered to the Allied Forces the last week of April. Instead of being shipped back to the First Infantry Division, he was sent home on furlough to await reassignment to the Pacific.

1807

She dreamed of dirt. It was the longest dream, all of dirt, the feeling of worms around her, the footfalls of birds above her, sticking their beaks in the ground and wrenching the worms from her. She hoped, in her hysteria, that the birds would wrench her from the ground. Her heart leaked cold all over her chest, and then it stopped, clenching like a fist and turning into itself. It began to pulse warm, and she could feel her toes and her fingers. When a worm crawled near her eye and was plucked from the dirt by a bird, she could see light through the hole it left behind. Her eyes moved to where she thought her hands would be, and she spread her fingers, feeling the cool, muddy earth around them. She moved them back and forth, a little at first, and then in wider arcs as the ground around them collapsed and the ground around her legs as well and suddenly she was able to sit up. She opened her eyes, expecting Matka to be beside her on the straw bed, her lalka under her armpit. But she was on the ground outside the bone house.

She wondered whether Matka had gone to town. There was so much she did not remember between going to sleep and waking up. She wondered whether she had a fever, whether Matka had buried her to quell her temperature. Perhaps she had needed more ingredients for a tincture and would be gone only a little while. Ela vaguely remembered soldiers, rabbits, Bolek. Her mouth was dry, coated with a chalky, flaky substance. She drew it out with her finger but could not quite identify it. She stood up in the hole and was surprised to find not one lalka beside her but two. The second had blonde hair and blue eyes. She shook them carefully free of dirt and then found her way through the woods to wash herself.

By the creek, she laid her dress on an exposed rock, splashing water on it and rubbing. She dipped her naked body in the water, cool and clear and lifting the dirt off her, little cloudy rings spreading into the creek like the haze of her dreams. One stain, a reddish whorl on her chest, did not wash away. It was round and scarred, just over her heart. She knew it was not something she'd had before, and she wondered whether her heart had been stolen. She pressed her fingers in her ears and held her breath. Her heart beat in her veins, as always. She traced the depression in her skin.

"Matka?" She called into the trees. Branches stood erect. They seemed to ignore her. Even the birds were quiet. She strained to hear leaves under feet, her mother's hum, the splash of water against the sides of the well bucket. "Matka?"

But she was all alone. She wrung out the dress to dry and sat on the bank, letting the sun warm her skin.

At the front of the bone house, a skeleton of bones, clean, white in a rust-dirt blanket, lay near the hill's edge. She approached it slowly, feeling her throat close, her heart hum dully against her chest. Inside the skeleton's hand was a flower, white with a root, curled over from the bend of the fingers. A flower. She put it in the pocket of her dress and then lay her hand near the hand of the skeleton, relieved to find it too big to be her matka's.

But she was not relieved long. She looked around her and saw that the road of the hill to their hut, normally well traveled and flattened into the earth, was overgrown with weeds and grass. She crouched and listened very hard to the ground like her matka had shown her. Silence. A silence that comes with time, forgetting, settled heavy over her like a humidity. It pressed at her chest, her eyes, and she did not know what to do.

The bone house had become porous. From holes in the arc of the ceiling, swords of light crossed through the center of the room, as if exposing the tumult that had occurred. Her mother's tinctures and herbs were missing. The mattress was stained with old blood, rust colored and faded. Their few pieces of furniture—stools and a table—were broken and splintered. A damp, earthen smell of absence lingered. How long had she been in the dirt? She was no bigger than she remembered—it could not have been for long. She shut her eyes and groped for her mother—her scent, her voice, the intangible weight of her presence. But something had closed in the world, a door, a window, and she could no longer feel even the dimmest breeze of her. She dropped on the mattress, away from the blood, shut her eyes tightly against her tears, hoped things would be different when she woke up. She would have to be a big girl and wait.

She dreamed of fires, an herb flower, chalky in her mouth, her mother. And she also dreamed of Antoniusz.

He would know where her matka was. Perhaps she was with him. Although she'd never been to Antoniusz's house, she walked toward the town to find him. At the first house she came to, on the outskirts of Reszel, a woman hung blankets in the green valley. The grass was lush and alive and so unlike the charred hill of her house.

"Antoniusz? Do you know where he lives?" Ela asked her, and the woman looked at her with soft, wet eyes. She patted the ground near her damp bundles.

"Looking for your father?" She pulled at Ela's clothes and pinched her cheek. "No meat on you, that's for sure. So many families torn apart after the fire." She clucked her tongue. "It's a shame."

The woman went in the cottage, stone with a thatched roof, and brought out some goat's milk and bread. A man, her husband, followed.

"She's looking for her father, she says—Antoniusz." The woman ruffled Ela's hair as she tore the bread with her teeth.

"Antoniusz?" The man scrunched his dry, brown face at her. "Antoniusz has no children. He lives with his sister."

"Where?" Ela stood up, wiping the milk from her face.

"Up aways, a good afternoon's walk." The man pointed up the road. "Too far to walk on little legs. I'm going to town later. I'll give you a ride in the wagon."

When he was ready, Ela climbed on the bench of the hay-filled wagon beside him. The town grew before them, the red roofs and stone walls, in various stages of construction, and they were different from the ones she remembered from the older, finished stone ones.

"Why is the town different?" she asked.

"From where you come, little one?" The man asked. He rapped the reigns softly against the behind of his horse. "Did you hear of the fire?"

She remembered the dream and shook her head.

"Do you have parents?"

"I want to see Antoniusz."

"Antoniusz hasn't been well since they burned the witch." The man shook the reins and frowned.

She choked; her chest trembled. Witch was what some of the villagers, the mean ones, the ones who spread gossip or thought her mother overcharged for her tinctures, called Matka. Did he speak of her mother? She felt everything inside of her crumble like old stone, and the rubble filled her lungs and she cried out, gasping for air, her eyes singed with tears. She pressed herself against her knees, felt the dusty stone drain from her like sand. The farmer put his hand, big and calloused, on her back as she emptied the contents of her stomach over the side of the wagon.

"There, there, now. Why don't you lie in back on the hay?" He stopped the horse. "Back there, it is not as rough a ride for little stomachs."

"I'm fine." She shook her head, lacing her arms around her stomach, empty and twitching. "Please, take me to Antoniusz."

"What is your business with him?"

"It is my own," she answered. "Why … why did she burn? The witch?"

"Why, it is known to everyone, I thought." He chewed on the inside of his cheek for a minute. "And perhaps those who do not know have ears too young and tender to hear."

"I am old enough to know, and if you do not tell me, I will find someone else, like Antoniusz."

"Well, better me than Antoniusz tells you." He bent toward her. "Did you not lose someone in the fire, child? Your parents, your brothers and sisters, perhaps? Then you have the witch, Barbara Zdunk, to blame, just as we all do. Some say she avenged Pilowski, our master, for killing her husband and daughter. But why, why burn the whole town? Why kill so many innocents, all for personal gain? And Pilowski is a good man—he pays us better for our crops than some of the others. He could have punished us all. But he burned the right one. And let it be a lesson to the rest of them and their silly uprisings—Antoniusz included."

"There is no such thing as witches." Ela felt her cheeks burn, her fists clench. She would make a tincture, she vowed, and kill him. "You are a stupid old man."

"Who taught you your manners?" He lifted his hand and made to slap her. "Surely you are an orphan. No one in our village would allow such a mouth."

"I would not want to be the child of any fool in this village," she answered and hopped down from the wagon. A stone hut leaned at the top of the road, just outside the town, and a man, folded and beaten like a weathered sack, sat outside on a carved wooden bench, whittling a piece of wood.

"Antoniusz!" she shouted, and when he saw her, he stood up slowly, his mangled leg even more shrunken than she remembered it.

"Young thing." He hobbled toward her, drawing a dirty wool cloak across her shoulders. "What business do you have with me?"

"It's me, Antoniusz! It's me, Ela!" She ran her hands on his good leg, feeling its warmness, inhaling the faint traces of pipe that lingered on his clothes. "Do you not know me?"

"What kind of laugh do you play on an old man?" He pulled from her grasp, and nodded toward the wagon, where the farmer sat watching. "Idzi, whose child is this?"

"I haven't the faintest." Idzi shrugged, drawing up his reigns. "A dirty orphan that I will call the magistrate on if she keeps talking her mouth."

"Antoniusz!" She grabbed his good leg and did not let go. "Please, you have to believe me! Where is Matka?"

She felt his hands underneath her armpits, herself lifted up. She met his eyes, brown broken spires that drew in her features before rejecting them, the way an ocean rejects a shell. His brow wrinkled, his eyes wet before he blinked and put her back down.

"By God, if you don't look like her." Antoniusz reached and touched her hair, her shoulders. He looked past her. "Idzi, I will take care of this. I am sorry that I have detained you."

The farmer shrugged and went on his way to Reszel.

"Would you like some milk, little girl? A little honey?"

"I want Matka." She buried her face in his stomach. "Please tell me where she is."

"Come." He moved toward the cottage. Inside, she ate some bread and apple slices, hoping she would not throw them up as well. She studied the carved figurines that lined the walls of the cottage, little men and women and birds. He watched her eyes, the folds of his face leaking sorrow despite the firm lines of his brow. After a time, he reached into a box by the table, emerging with a wooden horse. He placed it in front of her.

"Is this the horse you made for my lalka?" She ran her fingers over the wood, so smooth and oiled, and moved the legs. When she moved one of the back legs upward, like she remembered him telling her, its stomach opened, revealing a hiding place. Antoniusz rubbed his fingers against his forehead until Ela was sure the skin would begin to tear.

"I do not know who you are," Antoniusz said finally. "She has been dead for the year, almost. And her mother as well. Clearly you have heard the stories from someone, and you pretend to be her. Even down to the dress. Unless, of course, you are but a ghost, torturing me until the end of my days."

"I'm not a ghost," she answered. She looked at her hands, so small, even as her mind, her understanding, her memories, her sorrow, had grown. "I am Ela. I have been her forever."

"I buried the girl myself after the fire. I shall prove you are an imposter." He stood with surprising vigor, purpose. They got on his horse and rode to the bone house. The sun stabbed through the woods and Antoniusz knelt by the dirt behind it. The hole had healed over, a scab of earth with irregular borders, but still flat. Antoniusz bent and attacked it with his hands, digging and scattering dirt to all sides, his bottom lip low and dripping with sweat as he sank lower and lower into the earth. She went to the river to get him some water, and when she touched his back he ignored her, his shirt wet and sticking to his muscles, stringy like an old goat's. She went inside the house and lay down on the straw bed, sleeping without dreams. When she woke, the sun lay low in the trees. Outside Antoniusz still knelt by the dirt. The hole was the size of her, a depth of several feet, and she looked at his hands, dry and cracked and covered with dirt and blood, and they both looked at the empty hole, Ela clutching her lalkas.

"She spoke the truth." Antoniusz shook his head, and something in him looked so torn that her eyes hurt to look at him. He took a lalka from her and smoothed its hair, still dull with dirt. "And we did not heed it. I am so sorry, my child."

"What do you mean?" She clutched her dolls tighter.

"She was tried as a witch, my dear, for burning the village."

"But it was Bolek! I heard him tell my matka himself. I remember!"

"Of course, it was impossible to prove her innocence…but she implored me, while she was imprisoned, to get an herb, a tincture, from the house that she thought would protect her from the stake. She said to gather and hide you as well, that you had eaten the herb and would have survived. But when I came, you were dead. That I did see. So I buried you. But here you are, and I cannot believe it."

He put his hands, smeared with dirt and blood, to his face and wept. Ela put her hand on his heaving back.

"Child, I have failed you. You and your matka both." He leaned over, letting his arms fall into the grave. "And I am not fit to live on this earth."

"But what about me?" She pulled at his shirt, feeling the strain of his weight, whatever he carried, against it. He leaned forward, as if to crawl all in the way in, before pushing himself out of the grave and sitting on his hauches.

"You are a little girl." He turned and gathered her in his arms. "You are a little girl who needs a father."

Ela lived with Antoniusz and his sister. They did not speak of the tinctures. Antoniusz insisted she not try to make them.

"Antoniusz, why do I grow no bigger?" Every few months she measured herself against a mark she'd made on the wall, just as her mother had made notches in an old oak by the bone house. But her line, made with a stub of coal, grew fatter, not taller.

"It is a mystery." He stood with his hands on his hips, his brow furrowed. He did not look her in the eye.

"Why do you lie?" She put the lump back into the pocket of her smock. Although not height, time had given her bravery, suspicion, an adult's ability to reason.

"I do not lie, child." He put a hand, large and calloused and spotted, on her shoulder. He was becoming an old man, that was clear. "Your mother was a powerful woman, in her way, with her herbs. She may have done more than save your life."

"But what?" She wanted to be as big as the other girls in town, the ones whose limbs became long and graceful like the necks of swans, whose lips filled like the flesh on cantaloupe slices.

At night, she studied the herb she had taken from the skeleton's hand, remembering a potion, a lightning strike. Perhaps in time, the clouds in these events would clear, revealing the whole sky. She hid it in the stomach of her wooden horse so that Antoniusz would not take it and erase the last bits of her memory. She already was forbidden to travel home to the bone house, to the woods where the herb might still grow. At night, she lay awake and prayed to her mother to give her the strength to go home and find the truth that eluded her. She also prayed, squeezing the coal for luck, to grow, to grow so much her feet pressed against the wall of the room in which they slept, or at least long enough to reach the end of the bed. But each month, each year, the line of coal opposite the bed grew darker, fatter, never higher.

Antoniusz knew about the herb Ela kept in the wooden horse, but he pretended not to. Barbara would have wanted him to take the herb to be with Ela forever, but he could not bring himself to consider it, not when he had failed her. And yet, it would have been the only fitting punishment, to live forever with the knowledge he had let her die. There would have been a way to get her the herb from the bone house to the castle prison, where they had kept her before the burning, wait for her to arise from the ashes like a phoenix, if he had only believed her.

Like a veil over everyday life, the scene from that night replayed itself, the soldiers chaining Barbara, drunk with starvation and sleeplessness, to the stake, piling the faggots to mid-calf. The crowd leered and decreed vengeance for their loved ones, so many lost in flames almost a year before. He had been ashamed for feeling faint. Even after so many men had calloused his eyes to death, the sight of Barbara was a knife through the ropes holding his knees to his body and he fell to the dirt, feeling the sparks from the faggots catch his cheeks like the devil's tears. He closed his eyes when her screams began, crawling toward the sound, feeling the fire wash him in greater waves, hotter, in his face, and he felt convinced that he would climb into the faggots and burn with her.

But hands grabbed him, not of God, but of men; they held him back and someone covered his ears and when he opened them, Barbara, mouth open like the brightest angel in heaven, full of song, was screaming.

They tied him to the bed at his sister's house for seven days. He moved against the ropes and chafed his body but he could not escape, the ropes, her face, the scream. He peed and shat himself and cursed and cried. After four days, he drank a little broth, a little tea. By the seventh day, they removed the ropes but he could not move, could not walk. The fire burned lazily around the edge of his eyes, the smell of hair and flesh. Barbara's face blurred in corners but disappeared when he tried to look directly. His sister wrapped him in clean clothes and he drank the broth, a little milk, a little stewed carrots. He began to crawl. His sister found him some balsa wood, a piece as big as his head, and left it on the table. He stared at it for days until the balsa wood became other things—a soldier, a ship, a catapult. He crawled to the table, running his hands over the wood and Barbara's face, still in the cottage, receded a bit more. His sister gave him a knife, and he buried it in the balsa wood, ripping half away, and then little pieces, shavings like faggots.

He owed Ela this truth, his complicity in her mother's death, and he decided to wait until she grew older to tell her. But she did not grow in body, ever, even as his sister died of consumption one winter and his leg became weaker, the strength of only a twig. But he did not speak of the herb, nor did she.

He waited still. They grew potatoes and bought a cow. They lived many more years alone, and Ela cooked and mended Antoniusz's clothes and cut his hair, white and oily and thinning. When she suggested making a tincture to calm the fires in his leg, to build his strength, he left home and did not return for three days, white and blotched and stinking of vodka when she found him in a tavern in Reszel. She did not mention the tinctures again. But he began to whittle less and less, and sometimes he merely ran his fingers over the figurines he had already carved, as if conceding that his best work had already been done.

When Antoniusz was ready to go, he took no chances. He took the horse, now old and as broken as he, and rode it north to the Baltic Sea, where Ela could not find him, press the herb upon him, make him live forever with a kindling leg and an ashen heart. At the docks, he sliced the horse across the neck and tied himself to its leg. Then, with his wavering strength he rolled it off the docks. They plunged together into the sea, and after a splash, a bubbling, he died, too.

She waited many years for Antoniusz to come back, even when it was impossible for him to be alive because the earth would have asked for his old bones, and she no longer had a father, either. But Ela was still a little girl, even as her mind had begun to weave all manner of thoughts, complex and layered, rich, and desires, deep in her chest and loins, and she did not get older. One day, she packed the wooden horse with the herb and a few other trinkets and went back to the bone house. It had not changed, except for a slight weathering by the seasons, and she had not, either. It was one small comfort.

1945

Stanley's mother had been dead for two months when he finally got the telegram. They had passed through the Harz Mountains, happy green lumps against the spring sky, into Czechoslovakia, when he requested to go home on furlough. But then the war ended, and Stanley went home for good. When he docked at Locust Point in Baltimore, he smelled the factory smoke belching out over the harbor and thought of the stories of Dachau and Auschwitz. He imagined the Domino Sugar plant, or the American Can Company, a three-story warehouse on Boston Street where his mother Safine had worked as a child, packed full of hair, charred flesh. A room full of watches, jewelry. A room full of skulls. It was the smell, though, that remained with him, deep in his nostrils, of human rot. He had smoked cigarette after cigarette by the boat rail until he couldn't smell anything.

The buildings in Fells Point had bowed with age but were not broken, not like the piles of bricks and dust that demarcated most of Europe. At 919 South Ann Street, his mother's pansies, pink and yellow, still perched in their windowsill pots, unaware of history's realignment, and the marble steps out front still gleamed like bone.

"She go in her sleep. Is likely her heart." Linus, his father, blotted his eyes with his handkerchief. His cheeks, still damp, had settled down his face above the corners of his lips, where his beard began. He was frailer than when Stanley had left, although that was to be expected. Still, Linus's white hair, his yellow and blue eyes, the dried spit on the corner of his lip unnerved him. Her death had rotted him worse than any pint of whiskey.

"How was the funeral?" he asked. In the kitchen, he made coffee and placed the mug with the unbroken handle into Linus's hands, whose fingers, crippled with gumball knuckles, half closed around it. He lifted the mug and pushed it into his beard where, eventually, it found his lips.

"Beautiful service—Henry and Thomas and Cass pallbearers."

All of Stanley's brothers and sisters had moved out while Stanley had been overseas. Henry, Thomas, and Cass worked at the steel mill in the county, over on the Patapsco River. Their jobs and their ages had kept them out of the war. In letters, his mother had updated Stanley about Julia's wedding, Kathryn going into the convent, Thomas' baby, but none of them had written to him personally.

"You ask Thomas for work, he could prolly get you job." Linus leaned back in the wooden chair. It grunted under his weight as he packed his pipe. His suspenders, he grabbed close together in the front. As each place on his waistband frayed, thinned, Linus had moved the clips little by little to newer spots, until they too became frayed. Now the suspenders were dangerously close to touching.

"I'm not asking Thomas for a job." Stanley lit a cigarette. The brothers had gotten rich, according to his mother, working double shifts at the mill, making the steel for warships and planes. They seemed to forget that it was his own hide, freezing in the trenches, that had paid them to do so.

"What Thomas done to you?" Linus lit his pipe, sucking at it with little-girl breaths until it glowed.

"Nothing, that's exactly what Thomas has ever done for me." Stanley sat across from Linus and reached into his duffel bag for his comb. He felt what was left of the charred herb in the front pocket. He thought of Johnson. He had thought of him on the ship home—the man underneath his bunk had not snored like him. He thought of Johnson in the woods, lying there every day, farther behind. Further dead. He slid the herb into the front pocket of his pants, feeling the pulse of blood in his fingers. He hoped he would see his brother Thomas after all. He needed an excuse to fight.

He went up to his parents' room. It was as he remembered, the Bible on the end table, the white blankets tucked tight on the mattress, the crucifix above the bed. The afternoon light cut a line across the bed. He opened the closet, pulled out a dress and brought it to his nose. The smell of garlic made him cry. He ran his hands across the other dresses on the hangers, wondered why Linus had not gotten rid of them. Perhaps Linus would give them to his daughters. Perhaps they would use the fabrics, thin and dated, to make Linus shirts.

Stanley shrugged off his boots and lay on the bed, closed his eyes. Below. Linus coughed and tapped his pipe. It was quiet, and Stanley fell asleep. He dreamed about Johnson. He was alive, coming toward him with a mouthful of herb. His eyes were bleeding. Snow was everywhere. Black spikes of trees shot from the ground. Johnson was shouting something, holding his rifle at his waist. Before he reached Stanley, he turned into a Kraut. Stanley pulled his revolver out and shot him. The Kraut stopped and looked at him in surprise. *I'm sorry*, Stanley said. He dropped the gun in the snow, put up his hands. The Kraut sat down on the earth and lay back, his face to the sky, arms behind him like a sunbather. *Mudder.* The Kraut, the boy, Johnson, wept.

Stanley woke up. He walked into the bathroom. It was bare and clean like his mother's room, and the simplicity, the sanctity of it, comforted him. He filled the sink with water, scrubbing his face, his hair, his teeth with soap. He plunged his face in the basin and caught the line of it in the mirror as he stood back up. He touched his cheeks, his ears. They seemed different, although they were the same size, shape, as he had always remembered them. But something was different. Had he come back a man? He had cried, cried like a baby those first few weeks at boot camp in Fort Benning, wondering why he ever enlisted. There were better ways to see the world, to be Tom Swift, to feed his curiosity of foreign lands. But now, the fear in him was dead, along with everything else. He simply didn't care about anything anymore. Stanley Polenksy had left this house, left for the war, but he had not come back. And he could wait for him no longer. He walked down to the bar to get some whiskey.

He got a job shucking oysters south of Baltimore, at Locust Point, in 1946; at least that's what the calendar in the foreman's office said. Time did not feel as if it had restarted since he'd been back. It was low-paying, women's work, but he would not go to Sparrows Point and work at Bethlehem Steel with his brothers. He stayed at home with Linus. In the evenings, he drank on Lancaster Street, where no women came, except the fat horse of a bartender whose armpits mooned with sweat while she dried draft glasses. Nobody talked to him. He didn't shave every day. Sometimes the person in the mirror behind the bar looked like someone else, and he liked that. But sometimes he'd see Johnson, the German boy, in the faces of the other grimacing, sweating men around him, and he'd buy a pint of whiskey and take it home so he could drink in the dark of his room. Sometimes he'd put the radio on. The rye settled over him like a velvet cloth, along with the voice of Bing Crosby, blotting out most of the dead men, mostly Johnson. Johnson's frowning face, choking on the herb. Stanley kept the rest of the crumbly mess in his pocket but didn't know why.

One night, he went to a bar over on Thames, in the grittier section of Fells Point. He would have never gone to such a place before the war, but he'd been tossed out of his usual bar, on Lancaster, the night before, because he pissed on a man in the bathroom. A mistake, he'd tried to explain. Sometimes he went places in his head, back to Germany, to Italy, and he'd smell the shell fire, the blood, tinny and sour, the diarrhea and beans. He'd see the shadows of men in trees, feel the zip of bullets by his ears. He went to these places but his body stayed in Baltimore and he didn't always know what it was doing in the meantime. He had pissed on the man—he must have been at the next urinal—and then he had to fight him.

The man was older, a shriveled wharf rat, pickled and brined from the docks. His fingernails were yellow and curled, like his teeth. He lunged at Stanley, unsteady and smelling of piss. Stanley punched him once in the gut and folded him over. Then he let the men in the bar grab him by the cuff, push him to the ground outside, and kick his ribs until he curled into a ball. *A mistake*, he said as they went back inside. *Don't come back*, they responded.

The bar on Thames Street was crowded. It smelled like underarms, like beer and rot. It smelled familiar. He bought a whiskey and made his way to the back. Two men were playing poker at a table. Russians, Stanley thought. Their eyes were sharp, dark like dogs; their spirits were clear, like vodka.

"You play?" One, with a face flat like a board, a nose broken down into a hook, looked up at him. In the army, when Stanley wasn't firing his rifle, sleeping, or jerking off, he was playing poker.

"A little." He waved his hand in the air. The Russian smiled.

"Take his place." He nodded at a heavy form, passed out at on one end of the table, before pushing it onto the floor. The Russian kicked it for good measure, and Stanley heard it grunt. He felt for his Colt in the back of his pants. He picked it up in an alley shop off Greenmount after the war. He had hated guns when he had one, all those years in Europe, and then after the war, he hated not having one.

"Vadim." The flat-faced man nodded. He wore a sleeveless undershirt that looked like it had been dipped in cooking oil. On his arm was a tattoo of an owl with raised wings, a top hat, and bowtie. He nodded toward the other man, who was wearing a vest but no shirt. "Nicolai."

"Stanley." He sat down at the table and bent over to tie his shoe. He could see the gun, straight and clean, in Vadim's waistband. A TT Tokarev.

"You boys in the war?" Stanley picked up his cards. They were worn to felt, greasy on the edges.

"Why you need to know?" Nicolai smudged his cigar into an ashtray, brought his glass to his lips.

"I'm a vet myself." Stanley shrugged. It occurred to him the money he planned on winning could be put to good use. He could take the train to Ohio, find Johnson's parents, and let them know how Johnson died, not honorably for his country as they probably thought, but because of his own foolishness, his vote to go back along the ditch. On the other hand, it seemed a stupid thing to do, to snatch whatever veil of delusion lay like gauze over their eyes just to heave an anvil off his own chest. But maybe it would be of some comfort to them that their son had not died alone, in pain, that Stanley knelt before him and mourned his ascent into the afterlife.

"We are all brothers here." Vadim cupped Stanley's shoulder with an open palm, stirring the soup of his murky plans. Stanley rubbed his eyes, cleared his throat. "We all on same side. To victory, eh? Here, I give you a shot."

Vadim brought an unmarked bottle from under his seat and poured it into Stanley's glass. They raised them, and Stanley watched the fluid rise to the rim before ebbing. He opened his mouth and the liquid went hot, icy, down his throat.

"Spasiba." Stanley nodded. "Thank you." He looked at his cards. It occurred to him suddenly that the Russians would not let him win, and that if he somehow did, perhaps they would kill him.

The war had made him many things—alcoholic, apoplectic, apathetic—but if they were going to try to plug him in the alley later, he was going to win the dingy, greasy shirts off their backs first. He tossed aside two cards as Vadim dealt him three more. Nicolai raised a modest sum, and Stanley saw him. Vadim folded.

"Two pair." Nicolai laid down two fours and two eights

"Three pair." Stanley tossed three sevens over top. "Are we gonna start betting real money, or what?"

He wondered how the Russians got so quickly to the States after the war, if they were in the Red Army. Their faces were pebbled with scars and sunburn. Nicolai's nose was fleshy, an older man's. Vadim's palms were roped with burns and creases. Stanley sipped at his vodka, spitting every other sip back into the glass. The light, dim above him, hummed against his ears, along with the voices in the bar. The air was so wet and hot that he could eat it. He hoped he would not go places in his head when he needed to stay here, think about the game, think about how he was going to get out of the bar, winnings or not.

"I've seen things," he slurred as his winnings grew. His fear grew, too. He had not expected to win so easily. "I've seen some shit."

"You know what this is?" Vadim pointed at the owl on his arm. "Is tattoo I get in prison."

"He kill three men." Nicolai lit another cigar. "Is tattoo you get if you murderer."

Stanley tried to remember his Latin. He repeated his multiplication tables. But the room still carouseled slowly. And the Russians did not seem to get any drunker. He did not want to be pushed off his seat by Vadim, on top of the stinking carcass already there. He lit a cigarette and picked up his cards.

"You like prop-ert-y, Mr. Soldier?" Vadim ran his ringed fingers through his greasy hair and touched his cards. Stanley squinted, trying to see if the smudges on Vadim's cards were new or old. The boys in First Division used to mark the cards in any way they could—tobacco spit, dirt, blood. Stanley had played with cheaters, even won. But those boys had never tried to kill him later.

"What kind of property?" Stanley breathed through his nose. The sour, onion smell of the men cleared his head a little. Nicolai burped. Flecks of something dotted his lips.

"Is farmhouse on other side of bay." Vadim patted his pants pocket, emerged with a yellowed title. "A man I take from instead of money in card game last week. But I stupid. I should have just make him get me money, you say?"

"The Chesapeake Bay?" Stanley fondled the paper. He did not have anywhere to be. He imagined working his body to exhaustion on some farm somewhere, falling into bed every night, not thinking. No boss to tell him not to come to work still dank with whiskey.

"Yeah yeah." Vadim nodded. "Es worth something, if you like farming. We left Russia so we not have to farm, you know? So I win all my money back from you, then I sell stinkin' farm and open leather shop."

"Why didn't you sell the farm first, before you gamble all your money away?" Stanley pondered aloud, stroking the blond stubble that never quite thickened into a beard.

"Why not you shut up?" Vadim leaned over. His eyes were ravines of red meeting the dark brown iris. Their focus wavered slightly. Stanley smiled, and dragged his cigarette.

"All right." Stanley fingered the title disinterestedly before cutting the cards. "I guess it's legit; throw it in."

Vadim shuffled the cards, grinning like an ogre. Nicolai began to giggle, holding his belly. Stanley reached to pick up the title again, half expecting see Cracker Jack written at the bottom, but stopped. He picked up his cards and bet modestly, even though he was a four of clubs shy of a straight flush. He wondered if he should blow the game, if the Ruskies were letting him win, setting him up with the money just so they'd have a chance to kill him later. The Ruskies in the Red Army were the lowest bastards he'd ever seen; the villages the Army went through after the Reds were decimated, full of disemboweled men, raped and carved women, children with slugs between their eyes.

But it was possible that they were just really drunk and stupid. If that were the case, they were trumping his drunk and paranoid. Vadim chewed on the end of his cigar and pushed some more bills into the pot. Stanley sat for a long time, trying to throw them off. He rubbed his forehead and sighed before he added his own money.

He studied the crowd, looking for an opening to beat it the hell out of there. Vadim dealt Stanley a four of clubs. He wondered whether to excuse himself, go to the bathroom, give them a chance to substitute his cards or theirs. But something in him had stirred when he saw that title. He saw a chance to be alone, to sort out whatever the hell had happened to him, to right his ship. He would quit drinking. He would be a good son. He'd be a good American.

"Well, look who wins the big pot," Vadim laughed when Stanley laid down his flush, and he knew the fix was in. Vadim had lost too much money, too much face, to be such a gracious loser.

"It's been a pleasure playing cards with you fine gentlemen of the Red Army." Stanley held out his hand to Vadim, then Nicolai, as he scanned the bar with his eyes. "Give a big salute to Stalin for me."

Just then a seaman staggered forth from the bathroom. Stanley stood up just before he reached their table, stuffing title and money in his pants pocket. Nicolai stood up just as the seaman walked between him and Stanley, and Nicolai pushed at him. Stanley began to squeeze his way to the front. Bodies multiplied between him and the door, perhaps because of his drunkenness. He pulled his Colt from his back pocket and tucked it in his right shirt sleeve, above his hand. Nicolai pushed the seaman onto the floor and began to pursue, but Stanley was halfway through the bar. A hand grabbed him as he pushed his way ahead.

"Ten cents?" A man the color of liver asked him. His yellowed eyes floated on a fifth of liquor, if not more, by Stanley's estimate. "Lend a guy ten cents?"

Nicolai was only one man from him now. Stanley hooked liver man's barstool with his boot and pulled it hard, sending him tumbling to the floor behind him. He could smell the cool, salt air from the open door, glimpse the cobblestone and the night harbor before Vadim filled it from the outside.

"Some of us, we take back door," he grinned as Nicolai cuffed Stanley's shoulder from behind. "What, you think we come to this country yesterday?"

"Come on, Mr. Soldier." Stanley felt Nicolai's gun in his back. He had survived Europe only to get killed by a bunch of greasy dumb Ruskies.

"I won fair and square," Stanley said, although he supposed the argument was more for his benefit, for God, than for theirs. They walked along the cobblestone streets, thick with the smell of fish and salt, Vadim in front, Nicolai behind, like a drunken marching band, until they found a narrow alley well off Thames Street, where the bums slept. Where Stanley would be sleeping forever, soon enough. They hadn't gotten his gun, but Stanley didn't see how he could shoot them both. At the very least, he needed to shoot Nicolai first, whose gun was nosed so far in Stanley's back, he could feel it in his stomach. Vadim wheezed in front of him. He lurched left and right, and Stanley was hopeful for a moment that Vadim would pass out, making Nicolai pause, perhaps, loosen his grip. Stanley let his Colt slip from his forearm into his hand.

"Not here," Nicolai said, when Vadim stopped. "People live here." Stanley looked at the open, second-story windows from the backs of brick rowhouses overlooking the alley. He couldn't imagine who lived down here. But a woman sat in one, smoking a cigarette. Her blonde ringlets bounced as she leaned over the sill. *Help me*, Stanley mouthed.

"I'm tired. Shoot him now." Vadim turned and coughed, emptying his chest of yellow phlegm before spitting it on the ground. A shot whizzed by Stanley's head, and it was enough of an opening. He turned and shoved his gun into the gut of Nicolai, who had crouched behind Stanley, intending to use him as a shield from the errant gunman, and fired twice.

Stanley heard another shot, from Vadim's direction, and then warmness in his left shoulder. He turned, on his knee, and fired three shots into the middle of Vadim's shadow, which staggered back. Another bullet split the air from the window. It hit Vadim in the neck, and he slumped over.

"Up here." The girl in the window motioned to him. Stanley patted Nicolai's pockets, pulling out some loose bills, before he went over Vadim. They had done it in the Army for years, stealing from dead soldiers. Only it wasn't a crime then. Not that there was very much—a few tens, loose bullets, a button—on the Russians. Vadim and Nicolai were probably small peanuts, not part of any group. No group that would be hunting Stanley in the days and nights ahead, he hoped.

But there was still the police. Stanley looked up at the window. The woman had retreated, but the light was still on. A stone wall, five feet high, separated the yard of the rowhouse from the alley. He scaled it and tried the back door. It opened, and he went inside.

He stood in the kitchen. It was dark and sparse and clean. A teapot sat on a stove burner, an ashtray on the counter. Stanley moved through the living room, where a sailor snored on the couch, his back to Stanley. Ladies' things, lipsticks and pantyhose, rouge brushes, laid scattered, along with cheap perfume vials, and Stanley wondered whether he was in some sort of brothel.

"In the back," a woman's voice called down, and Stanley went up the stairs and opened the back bedroom door. She sat on the bed, a child with a grown-up's face, drawn with lipstick and eyeliner. Or maybe she was a child with a baby's legs. Stanley focused, squinting his eyes. She was a midget in hemmed lingerie, sewn to accommodate the squat trunk of her body. Her legs, plump and formless, swayed from where they hung off the bed. Her toenails were little red squares the size of confetti.

"What're you looking at?" She lit a cigarette that, compared to her, stretched like a javelin, and set it in the ashtray.

"Nothing." Stanley cupped his hand over his shoulder. It began to burn worse than anything he'd known. He could feel the blood running over his fingers and down his hand.

"Christ—you're bleeding all over my bedroom." She hopped from the bed and waddled over. She stood to his waist, and Stanley had to crouch so that she could examine the wound. "Looks like a flesh wound."

"It wasn't your bullet."

"Pfh—I know it wasn't my bullet." She went to the closet and pulled out a bed sheet. "You see that shot I put into ugly's neck?"

"Your first shot missed pretty bad." Stanley let her peel the shirt off. He was in too much pain to do anything. The wood floor pressed into his kneecaps, and the whiskey still pressed on him like a boot heel on his neck.

"I couldn't get a clear aim on the guy, and I didn't want to shoot you, neither." She left the room and returned with a bowl of water and some soap. She dipped one end of the bed sheet in the water and wiped the blood from his shoulder. She soaped it a little and wet it and then dried it. She ripped a large swath from the other end of the bed sheet with her teeth and tied it tightly around Stanley's shoulder while he grimaced, stared at the crucifix above the bed. A Catholic prostitute.

"Where'd you learn to handle a gun?" He had seen the ladies, sometimes children, in the villages with rifles, discarded lugers, but their handling developed from necessity, and it showed. They were just as likely to hit a tree or even themselves as they were a soldier.

"This ain't exactly Sunday school, this side of town," she answered. "If this don't stop bleeding, you're gonna have to walk up to Church Hospital on your own. I don't want to get in no trouble."

"I should be going, anyways." He stood up, and the room crashed against him in waves.

"You're not going anywhere." she pushed him by the legs toward the bed. "Just sit down."

"What about the cops?"

"You think the cops don't have better things to do than to come here?" She laughed, and it was a pretty laugh. Stanley closed his eyes and imagined it coming from some other woman, a real one, before he felt terrible for thinking it. "Don't you worry about the cops. I'll probably have to call four or five times to get them to take away your friends from the alley, anyway."

"They're not my friends."

"I didn't mean it like that," she said.

"I'm sorry." He leaned over on the bed, feeling sick. "I gotta get up for work tomorrow. I shouldn't even be here."

"That's what they all say." She walked toward the door and threw the sheet out in the hallway before locking the door. "By the way, you owe me for that sheet."

"Of course." He nodded, feeling in his pockets for his winnings.

"Relax for now, all right?" She fumbled at a desk, a small desk, the type one would find in grade school, before turning around with something clear in a shot glass. "Have some vodka."

"No thanks," he shook his head. "I couldn't drink any more if you paid me. If you had a few aspirin…"

"I'll go up to the drug store when it's morning," she answered, climbing on the bed beside him. He felt his body stiffen. He had never been so close to a woman before, certainly not a midget. The combination, both alluring and off-putting, made him long for some known comfort, something that had eluded him since he enlisted.

"Why are you crying?" She touched his knee. "Does it hurt real bad?"

He began to shake, tears escaping in fistfuls. He missed Johnson. He missed his buddy and he shouldn't be afraid to say it. He missed other things he didn't have, whatever it was he was supposed to have after graduating from high school, returning instead from a honeymoon of death and rot and stink. Marriage? Children? The pictures in the paper of the men in their military dress marrying their high school sweethearts angered him. Why weren't they as paralyzed as Stanley, not quite home, not quite anywhere else?

Perhaps he was being a baby. Johnson wouldn't have acted this way. It should have been Johnson who survived; that much he knew and wished.

"I'm sorry." He turned his head. The room was cool, pink-gray, as the rising sun slowly filled it. Stanley could see the little desk and a vanity with the legs sawed in half. The only thing that was its true height was the bed. For customers, he imagined. "You've been real nice, and I don't even know your name."

"Cynthia Meekins. But you can call me Cindy. What about you, baby doll?"

"Stanley. Fish that piece of paper out of my pocket, will you?" His face pressed back against the mattress in a pool of his own sweat. If he wound up dying, which at some points he dismissed but other points, when he faded in and out of consciousness, when the walls began melting and the roses on the wallpaper began swirling into boars and coyotes, was convinced, he wanted to give her the deed to the farm proper. If it was really a farm.

"Let's see." He felt her little hands moving in his pockets, fleshy spiders, but even so, he felt his erection press against the bed. "Looks like you got seventy-five dollars, a dried-up corsage, and, oh, here's something"

"Don't throw that away." He lifted up his head as high as he could. "The flower, I mean." Although he did not know why he kept it, the stupid herb that didn't do anything, didn't save anyone. If his mother believed in it so much, why didn't she take it herself, make sure she was alive for him when he returned from Europe? But, with it in his hands, fragile and crumbly, he relaxed, breathed easier.

"Looks like some kind of property deed." He heard Cindy unfold the paper. "To someplace in Fruitland. Where the heck is that?"

"It's on the other side of the bay, the Eastern shore. You ever been?"

"Honey, I ain't been more than twenty blocks outta this neighborhood in any direction."

"Well, listen, if I die, I want you to have it. The money too, of course. But this way, I'm giving everything to you proper, and you don't have to worry about whether you feel like you're taking it from a dead guy."

"You're a strange one," Cindy laughed. He felt her hand in his hair. "You're not going to die. And you don't seem like a criminal to me."

"I'm not," Stanley said. "I just got a little drunk, got a little lucky at poker, got a little luckier that you were staring out the window."

"Well, I'm just a nice girl, too, aren't I?" He heard her voice, slightly wistful. "Don't think I haven't tried to get respectable employment. But lotsa places, they don't hire people like me—they say we'll scare the customers. Or we're too short to work the registers or the machinery. They all tell me to run off to the circus. I ain't no freak, Stanley. I just want to work respectable like everybody else. A lot of guys, they like the kinky stuff. They like little girls, right? But they ain't going to actually screw or marry no little girl, get run outta town by a lynch mob."

Stanley drifted away. He wasn't sure if it was the wound or his usual drifting. He dreamed of circuses, of Cindy riding a Shetland pony, hanging on by the neck, her little legs bouncing off the shoulders. Both wore their hair in ringlets. Johnson was there, too. He sat in his own cage, looking glum. Above him, a sign read THE BOY WHO NEVER GROWS UP.

"Stanley." Cindy was shaking him. "Stanley? You okay?"

"Just sleeping," he said.

She petted his head. "You want me to run to the store, get you some aspirin now?"

"Stay. I need someone to wake me up if I start to go again." He turned on his side, feeling a little stronger. His shoulder burned like fire, and he wondered whether a cold shower would help.

"Just stay down for a little bit, Stanley." Cindy hopped off the bed. "You like eggs? We got a few eggs left, some Tabasco. I'll split an omelet with you, okay?"

"Just hurry back," Stanley called after her. Although he supposed it wouldn't matter once he was dead, he wanted someone to see him die. So many men had died in the fields, in the dark, in the middle of fighting, without anyone to say goodbye to. Even Johnson, left there to rot. Had the cleanup crews brought his body back to America, or had they buried it in the Hürtgen?

Cindy came back before long with a hot plate of eggs and splash of coffee. She put the plate between them as Stanley eased himself up on his elbow. He could see better now, with the sun up. She had a pretty, baby doll face: an upturned nose, lips in a permanent slight pucker, a round chin and chubby cheeks. She had breasts like a real woman, but there's where the similarities ended. He wondered whether she wore children's clothing. He wondered how the men could fuck her, how she could take a larger man. He could not imagine fucking her himself, even kissing her, and yet her voice drizzled over him like honey. She was how he imagined a woman would treat him, a woman he wanted to marry. And yet, she was a child.

Stanley sat up gently in bed, wondering if, after breakfast, his cue to leave would be short in coming. He tested the weight of each foot on the floor before pushing off the bed. The room vibrated faintly, still, like a spun quarter laying down to rest, and he made it to the window, sticking his head out, just before the eggs and last night's whiskey plumed out of his mouth and in the small concrete yard below. Beyond the fence, he could not see Vadim and Nicolai. She must have only had a head shot on each. Maybe the wrong sex had been enlisted to fight.

"Stanley, what's wrong?"

"Come with me," he heard himself say. It wasn't a proposition, he didn't think, but he wasn't ready to let her pass by his life. She was the first solid thing he'd seen, touched, since sailing back to Baltimore. Not an anchor, more like a buoy, something steady in the undulating sea. "I got this farmhouse, see…"

"I got a room here, a job," she answered. "You're sweet, baby, but I don't even know you."

"Well, here, take this." He handed her half the bills. "For your trouble. But I'm going to this farm. To start over. If you want to come, come over to the ferry docks. I'm leaving as soon as I can."

"Do I look like a farmer girl to you, hon?"

"You don't look like a sharpshooter, either," he said. She opened the closet and rummaged through the few shirts, dresses.

"Here." She held out a large, purple satin women's shirt. "Here— this looks like it might fit you. One of the girls, Rhonda, left it behind. Let's see that wound."

She peeled the bed sheet off. The bullet had carved an alley across the top half of his bicep. It wept blood, but Cindy was able to wrap a smaller bandage of bed sheet around it before helping Stanley into the shirt.

"Thanks a million." He leaned down and kissed her cheek. "I'm sorry we have to part ways like this."

"Just stay out of trouble, huh?" She answered as he opened the bedroom door. "If you bother me at three in the morning in the alley again, it'll be your head I'll be aiming for."

"Well, if I have to be shot at one more time, I'd want it to be you." He smiled before frowning. It was probably the stupidest thing he ever said. He wondered if he'd ever learn how to talk to a woman. But she laughed and beamed at him, a little too long, and he thought he'd better leave before the space between them filled with branches that pulled at their arms and legs and organs and got them tangled up in each other, like Siamese twins.

"Stanley, wait—" Cindy grabbed at his leg. "Can you get that suitcase down from the top shelf?"

They slid into a bench under the deck of the ferry with Cindy's suitcase. Stanley had not even stopped home to say goodbye to Linus. It was like he had never been home anyway, a listless ghost that dissipated when Linus opened a window. Cindy dabbed the dirt off Stanley's face with a spit-moistened tissue. He was tired still, so tired he might die. But he was so afraid Cindy might be a figment of his own imagination, his angel taking him to heaven, that he slapped himself awake in his wounded shoulder. Blood dotted his purple satin shirt, and the fabric strained against his back. The plank rose from the dock, and slowly, Baltimore shrank until it became a miniature city, too small even for Cindy. He felt like they were running away to the circus, although to many aboard, they probably looked like they were already in it.

1946

The man who came back from the dead, they called him at church. The man with nine lives, they called him at the drug store. At the gas station, they called him lucky. Calvin smiled, laughed, let his back get slapped by his father, his cheek pinched by the wrinkled ladies who smelled like rose water, let himself get roped into football games when the kids at the playground called after him, begged for a game of catch.

"Can you believe it?" His father laughed to his friends. "It's like God gave us our life back."

His mother touched Johnson's shoulder, lightly. She had been touching him more since he returned. He wondered whether she thought he was real, whether she'd go to grab his arm and her fingers would sink into it like sand.

"Leave it to the government to make a clerical error." His father rocked on his heels like a proud father. "Worst month of our life because some paper jockey got the wrong man."

They called him heroic, brave, honorable. He always knew the men who said these things to him had not served. The men who served said nothing. He'd see them at the movie theater, sitting next to their girls, their wives. They stared in their popcorn sacks as if they'd lost a tooth in it. At the dance hall, their hands would hold their girls close, but their eyes would be far away. He held girls close as well, mindful of their gravity. Without them, he would certainly float away.

When they dropped the bomb on Hiroshima, Nagasaki, Johnson's father came through the door of the house, late edition of the newspaper in his hand.

"You know what this means, boy?" He slapped Johnson on the back. "We won, we won it all!"

He wondered about the other men in his platoon, Polensky, Abraham, mostly Polensky. Did he go back to Baltimore, or was he an occupier? He'd have to write the platoon. He waited in the line, filled out forms, talked with a few of the other soldiers returning, had no equipment to return. He listened to occupational counselors, who stressed on him the decorum of the GI, one's presentation at the employment office, job interviews. The need to take advantage of civilian goodwill toward vets, turn it into a good-paying job. Find a girl, pick up a hobby. Return to a normal he had yet to know.

"Maybe I should go to school." He put down his fork one night at dinner.

"What would you study?" His mother scraped her plate by the sink, shaking her head. She dried her hands and returned the table, straightening her dress, a simple cut that she had sewn from some old satin curtains. Materials were still in short supply; she made him two ties from the same curtains, embroidering a duck on one and a deer on the other. Animals he didn't think he'd ever have the heart to shoot again. He'd worn the ties to church in her presence but carried his old tie from high school in his truck in case of an interview for the postal service, for a job administering civil service exams, an electrician's apprentice.

"Architecture," he answered, dabbing his lips so she couldn't see his face.

"Architecture," his father laughed. His nose was thick, his eyes wide and steady on either side, like Johnson. Slow and deliberating. Dumb to some. Like his son, he had been a pupil of the physical field in high school, not the academic one. He'd served in the first World War and still had the shrapnel in his shoulder to prove it.

"Yes, architecture." He stood and put his dish in the sink.

He'd been captivated by the architecture the corporal at Camp Upton, who'd been drafted out of Princeton, had described to him. He talked about buildings, the arch of stone and metal girders. Vertical space. The only way to move—up. Johnson imagined rebuilding churches, houses, storefronts, in London, Salerno, Berlin. He imagined making structures that could withstand all manner of bombing and blitzing. A city of clean lines that paid homage to the past but looked forward to the future. And even if his ability matched more of card houses than cathedrals, he knew he did not ever want to draw a gun again. He wouldn't have to tell his father, he figured, for a semester, at the very least.

Johnson enrolled at Bowling Green State for one class. His mother spent the evening starching and ironing his one white shirt while he sat at the kitchen table, writing his name in the clean, unmolested notebooks. CALVIN JOHNSON. Before the war, he had assumed he would take over the farm. But the war had made him bigger and everything else in his life a little smaller. He hoped his greed for the big world was not bigger than his ability. He had held a rifle. He had shot men and thrown grenades and looked into the unmoving faces of his battalion mates in the sand of Normandy and the snow of Germany and he had been left for dead. He could surely become an architect.

But he still sat in the family pickup in the parking lot, watching the young men with pressed slacks and quick steps enter the arts building. Their faces were smooth, their smiles as light as their consciences. The girls were lithe and graceful, and he could not imagine going to the drug store to socialize, drink egg creams. Not when his hands felt too awkward and his tongue too big and his left leg not quite his. They probably thought he was a chump, a stupid farm boy who couldn't get a college deferment to keep out of the war. And he wanted to knock all their blocks off. Why had he thought this a good idea? He drew his books toward him, so important to him the night before, now seeming like cheap imitations.

Maybe he just wouldn't go. He could drive across town, to where Eva Darson lived. She had written him during the war; he'd responded once or twice. But Europe had opened his eyes, the women, the cities, the culture, and he thought he was better than her. No, it wasn't that. It was just that he was young, and there was a lot to see before having to settle on the known. But maybe he was no better, deserved no more, than Eva Darson. She would be wearing the slip that he liked and would put lots of lime in his gin to conceal the fact she could only afford the cheap stuff, and they'd sit on her couch that had been clawed to shit by her cat and make out a little, maybe more. She would be grateful. Maybe it was all they deserved.

He imagined the slightly smug smile that stretched his father's lips rubbery, the touch of relief in his mother's, the wrinkle in her forehead unfurling, as he returned that night, no longer a student. He got out of the truck and walked to the humanities building.

The classroom for Introduction to British Literature smelled like chalk; the fluorescent lights scrutinized every pimple and discoloration on the student's faces. He spotted a seat in the back and kept his head down, aware of his size, his age, and awkwardness. He felt the desk scrape his knees as he watched the professor, a man in his sixties with neat silver hair clipped close to his skull. His brown wool suit jacket stretched across his waist; he looked like he'd made it through the rationing okay. He thought of the pot roast his mother had made with the few scraps of chuck she'd gotten from the market. Where she had gotten that extra dollar, he didn't know. But cooked with carrots, potatoes, and barley from their own farm, it was a godsend, a rich fur that nestled in his stomach like a bunny rabbit in a hutch.

"Welcome, ladies and gentleman, to Introduction to British Literature." The man wrote on the blackboard in light, quick strokes. "I'm Professor Shillings. This is an introductory requirement for bachelor degree programs at Bowling State. If you feel you are in the wrong class, please leave now and do not interrupt us by your departure later."

She was in the third row, to Calvin's right. Her long, dark hair was exotic to him, at least in Ohio, where bloodlines ran brown and blonde. She wore a light blue sweater that hugged her shoulders and elbows lovingly. He watched her milky arm rise, her hand flick through her hair.

He opened his notebook and began to take notes, afraid to look at her again. His fear, his embarrassment was slowly replaced by anger. He had dug out foxholes until his fingers bled and he'd huddled aside fucking Stanley Polensky in them. He'd shat, had diarrhea in the same holes while Stanley laughed until it was his turn to shit, too. He knew more about Stanley's bowel movements than his father's. And he was supposed to take this know-it-all professor in English class seriously.

"I'm going to ask a question, and I need a volunteer." Professor Shillings raised his head, his forehead wormy, and scanned the class. His gaze settled on Cal. "How about you, young man?"

"Tell me the question first." Cal gripped his pencil in his fist. "And then I'll let you know whether I'll volunteer."

"Hmm." Professor Shillings frowned, then smiled. Boys snickered, letting their crossed legs unfurl. The girl with the dark hair looked back at him, and he froze. "Things don't work quite this way here in my class, Mr. ...."

"Johnson. You wanted a volunteer. I didn't volunteer."

"Very well, Mr. Johnson. I choose you to answer my question. What do you think all literature, through the centuries, has in common?"

"I don't know." He felt the veins in his neck inflate, an area in the back of his head boil.

"Is that your answer, Mr. Johnson?" Professor Shilling raised his fist to his mouth, coughed. He leaned over his podium and examined his fingernails.

"Well, I suppose I wouldn't have to take the class if I knew." His pencil snapped, one half of it rolling to the floor. He trapped it under his foot, his church shoes. They weren't as smart as the shiny, soft leather loafers that tapped, slid on the floor around him.

"Mr. Johnson, if that is your attitude, I suspect you won't do very well in my class. And that you may as well save yourself the embarrassment of dropping out later by leaving now."

"My attitude is that if you're going to try and make me look like a fool, I'm not going to let you. I'm no fool, and I'm here to learn."

He sat up in his chair. "I'm here to learn what all literature, through the centuries, has in common, *sir*."

"Veteran?" Shilling raised his eyebrows slightly, and then nodded. "How about someone else? You in the second row."

Johnson stole glances at Professor Shilling when he thought he wasn't looking. He copied Professor Shilling's words into his notebook and he avoided his sweeping gaze when he asked questions. After class, he let everyone file out before he walked to the front of the classroom.

"Sir, I apologize for my behavior this evening." Johnson stared at his hands, grasping his books. "I don't want special treatment. I served, and I want my education so I can get a job. I follow orders well, so if you tell us what we need to know, I'll work real hard to get it right."

"I appreciate your candor, Mr. Johnson." Shillings snapped the locks of his briefcase shut. Cal could see the top of Professor Shilling's balding head, oily crown. He stepped back. "But this isn't the Army. You may have taken orders there, but in university you cultivate independent, critical thinking. And our opinions, your thoughts, are much more important, much more interesting to me than rote—er, following orders."

"Well, I haven't done too much thinking about literature, Professor Shilling, but I'll give it my best shot. I promise."

"Well, that's all I ask, Mr. Johnson." Professor Shilling smiled slightly and turned. "Now, if you'll excuse me."

Shilling put on his hat and nodded before walking out the door. Johnson looked around the classroom for a moment before following, not wanting to leave. The walls of these buildings harbored great secrets, he surmised. Why men fought wars. What they did once they were over.

"I hear he's a bit of a rat."

The girl from the third row stood a few feet away in the empty hallway, her books pressed against her chest. Her eyes, wide and brown, smiled at him.

"He seems all right." Johnson kicked at the linoleum. "A little stuffy, maybe."

"I'm Kate." Her hand, small and delicate, raised, her fingers slightly outstretched.

"Calvin Johnson." He took it. He could not remember the last time he'd held something so delicate. Maybe the hatchlings on the farm. Soft furred, chirpy hearts. He removed his hand quickly, not understanding the danger he felt. She was not holding a grenade, a revolver. They walked side by side by the classrooms, opening and expelling their students. Their chatter swirled between them; his neck felt hot.

"Are you a freshman?" She seemed unperturbed by the commotion.

"Yeah, kind of. I mean, I'm not from high school. The Army."

She nodded as well. A pause stretched into awkwardness. "Well, I'm sure my father is waiting. I just felt bad . . . Shilling giving you a hard time like that." They stood at the entrance. Johnson spotted a man near the parking lot, hands in his wool trousers, his sports jacket open casually. He sized up Johnson with a disinterested nod as Johnson quickly closed his jacket over his tie with the duck. "I'll see you around, Calvin."

"Sure." He nodded, and he watched her legs move away from him, her hand in her hair, the way it splayed over her back. As they moved together toward the car, a green Ford, new off the lot, it seemed, she turned her head toward him and waved.

"How was class?" His mother sat on the edge of the glider while he scraped the last of the glazed apple off his plate.

"Good. Pie's perfect." He leaned over and kissed her. "Everything's perfect."

They looked at the moon, the same moon he'd seen in Africa, Normandy, Germany. The moon that betrayed them, their movements. The moon that hid the sun. That night, it was just the moon, maybe a little more.

❀❀❀

From the *Anglo-Saxon Chronicle*, he read about the great kings of England, Henry and Richard and Edward. He read slowly at the kitchen table, sometimes aloud to his mother when she wasn't listening to the radio. In the living room she sat on the couch nodding, her mending resting between her hands, a baby of brown and blue threads, mostly his father's shirts and sometimes his uniforms from the force. Sometimes she lay her head back, eyes closed, and he could not tell whether she was listening, and sometimes he'd change his voice to differentiate between the characters and his mother laughed, a half sigh and half giggle.

He read *Beowulf* and understood the horror and beauty of the battles in a way he had not in high school. He could not wait to read *The Iliad* and *The Odyssey* again. And maybe his mother would listen and they would have something else since the war that they could share.

"Worried about class, Calvin?" his mother asked one morning, serving him waffles. He had spent most of the night in the bathroom, bathed in a cold sweat, his heart humming in his ears. It had been something practically undetectable, unthreatening to civilian life—an unusual sound outside, a foot snapping a twig. Or so he had thought. After he'd checked the barn and the surrounding ground, he sat on the porch smoking a cigarette. In the corner of his eye, he'd see a shadow move, but when he turned to focus, it was no longer there. It reminded him of nights on foxhole duty, trying to detect a shadow, an outline, in blackness, back in the months before the snows. Was it one of their men, a Kraut? Should he risk shooting into the night, giving away their position? He smoked another cigarette on the porch, and the shadows were everywhere—in the corn, by the barn, behind the truck. There were hundreds of men swarming like silent wasps, a swirl of lost souls, but when he ran out into the middle of the yard, daring them to take a first shot, no one fired. He ground out his cigarette and went back inside to the bathroom. His balance felt off; he thought he might vomit. His father almost stepped on him at five-fifteen, when he stumbled in for his shower.

"I've got a paper to write," he answered, cutting the waffles along the squares. He tried to keep the syrup contained within the spaces, but the knife was dull and his precision clumsy and many of them bled onto the plate. "About war in early English Literature."

"You were never much of a writer," his mother said, joining him at the table, patting his hand. She put her hand on his shoulder as if in apology for the truth. She'd never diminished him or his accomplishments in his life (*if you'd concentrated more on sacks, you would have been starting at Ohio State* was a scrap of wisdom his father liked to hurl at him on the weekends, when they listened to the games on the radio), and he was hurt that she'd start now. But perhaps she thought it was cruel to be kind, lest he muddle too far along and drop out, become bitter.

"I'll figure it out," he answered. His plan was a bit disingenuous. Each class he had sat a seat closer to Kate, and although she said hello to him and smiled, he didn't know how to approach her under any premise, except perhaps to appeal to her greater intelligence, which she displayed modestly when Dr. Schillings called on her. Once or twice, Johnson had raised his hand, in response to questions so easy some didn't even bother, but he wanted Dr. Shillings to know his intentions, to acknowledge his earnestness and motivation. Still, he was carrying a C minus and needed a good term paper grade to ensure his passing the class.

"Have you written your term paper yet?" Johnson asked Kate when she lingered in the hall one night after class, tying a shoelace, retying. It could not have been for him, he was sure, but he was more than happy to take advantage of her delay.

"Oh," she sprang up quickly. He felt the breeze her body generated on his neck, and he felt his cheeks coloring. He coughed, fist to his face. "Hi, Calvin."

"Hi. Did you, uh, finish your term paper?"

"I'm sorry." She blushed also. "I'm almost finished. How about you?"

"I haven't." He scratched the back of his head. "I mean, I've got some ideas… but I'm not much of a writer. I was wondering if you wanted to read what I had…I could buy you an egg cream or a hamburger or something."

"Well." Kate smiled. He could draw the line of her face in one stroke, so smooth and gradual the curve from chin to cheek to eye. "I suppose my parents won't mind a study date."

"Oh, I don't want to make anybody mad." His shoulders tightened, feet jumpy. He scanned the entrance ahead of them.

"No, no." She shook her head. "It's perfectly fine. Why don't you meet me tomorrow at seven?"

"Okay, great," he answered. As relief filled him, it drained quicker out his chest. He'd written not a word of his term paper.

At home, he sat at the table, crumpled pages surrounding him. *In Beowulf nature is violent and death is uncontrollable. Beowulf is a warrior, like I was. Once you enter a world where nothing makes sense, it is hard to leave it.* He smoked a cigarette on the back steps. *Many people think Beowulf and everyone had what was coming to them because they were pagans, but a hell of a lot of Christians lost their lives for God and Uncle Sam in Europe and the Pacific.* He heated the leftover coffee in a pot on the stove. *I think Kate is a woman I will fall in love with.*

He awoke because his mother was frying eggs. Sleeping on the hard table had stiffened his neck. He sat up and pulled his work to his chest. His balled-up notes were gone, and he wondered whether his mother had uncurled them carefully and read them in an attempt to gauge his academic prowess, whether she'd seen the one about Kate.

"You'd better wash your face." She touched his back, betraying no thoughts. She had not asked him about the war. He wished she would. "The eggs are almost done and you need to milk Tawny."

He dragged himself up to the bathroom and plugged the sink to shave. He had pinched a nerve in his arm by falling asleep on it, and the razor in his right hand moved crazily across his face, catching its edge and cutting his skin. He dropped the razor in the water and put a finger on his cheek where a cut had bubbled with blood, shaving the rest of his face with his left hand. He stuck a wad of toilet paper the size of a quarter on the wound and hoped he wouldn't still be wearing it that night like some high school kid.

❀❀❀

He wore his high school tie and the short-sleeved button-down he'd worn at graduation years ago, even though his time in the Army had filled his muscles out and the seams cut his biceps when he bent his arms. He'd spent a half hour after dinner sweeping the dirt off the floor mats of the truck, taping the rip in the seat, and wiping the dashboard and windows until they gleamed. He sprayed a little bit of his mother's White Shoulders in the cab until he thought maybe Kate would think he had another girl, and then he drove through town with all the windows open, airing it out.

As he waited for Kate outside the steps of the school—she took a second summer class—Introduction to Calculus—he glanced at himself in the rearview mirror. The first thing he noticed was that the cut on his face was gone. Not even the faintest of red lines remained on his lower cheek. He opened the driver's door so that the interior light would come on. His skin was free of blemish. Perhaps he had not cut himself as badly as he thought. Perhaps he needed more sleep. From the corner of his eye, he saw Kate's form on the stairs, and without thinking about it any further, he hopped from the truck and hurried up the walk.

❀❀❀

"Well." Kate leaned over, a strand of her hair brushing the top of his hand. "Shall I take a look at that paper of yours?"

At the end of a long, double-horseshoe counter at the drug store, Johnson watched her eyes move back and forth over what he had compiled, hastily, that morning after breakfast. He followed the line of her shoulder next to his down to her side and hip, afraid and transfixed by her proximity. Her perfume layered the air along with the grease of twelve-cent hamburgers and percolating coffee, the steady beat of the jukebox. She was not like Eva, and for that he was thankful. She had a confidence that did not announce itself from her lips; it emanated in the way she sat, the way she moved and turned his typewritten sheets with her fingers, slowly, with interest.

"I like this line, Calvin—*Like Henry in Henry V, once you enter a world where nothing makes sense it is hard to leave it.* But I think you need to follow it up with an example, maybe from your own experience." She tapped her pencil against her cheek. He liked that she was able to compliment his work but also criticize it, unlike the girls in high school, who repeated his opinions like parrots, who smiled at him bashfully and sat with their hands in their laps, shoulders turned inward.

She did not look away when he caught her looking at him, her dark eyes soft smudges of charcoal. She blinked in a manner less seductive and more puzzled. "So what's Europe like? How come you never talk about it?"

"I don't know. I guess no one has ever asked," he answered, stirring his coffee, even though he took it black. Everyone was afraid to ask, as if he would have a nervous breakdown in front of them. "Well, the churches in Italy are beautiful. Even the ones that were destroyed. And the mountains in Africa. Even the snow in Germany, as cold as it was. Of course, Paris. Sometime it's strange sleeping in a bed, night after night, when for months at a time, you slept outside on the ground and, in a strange way, you owned the world. Or the world owned you."

"I like that." She rested her chin on her hands. "My brother Stephen and I used to play soldiers when we were younger. We both fantasized about it a lot, going to war, the noble sacrifice, seeing the world. Of course, it had a very Homer-esque quality to it."

"You wouldn't want to go to war, believe me."

"Why?" She cocked an eyebrow toward him, tilting her head slightly and smiling. "You don't think girls are tough enough? You're not one of those boys, are you?"

"It's not that." He shook his head, his cheeks flushed. She could have told him then that women had two heads, and he would have agreed with her. "I mean, plenty of women served honorably as nurses and stuff. It's just...when it's happening to you, the horror of it becomes unreal. You get used to...terrible things. And then when you come home, safe from it, you can't believe you ever thought anything you saw or did was okay. I don't think anybody should have to live like that." He closed his eyes, struggling to explain the emptiness that filled him with such weight. He may have lived, but he'd left something behind. His heart, his sense of wonder. His future. He wondered if he needed to go back to the Hürtgen forest to get it.

"Calvin?"

"I'm sorry." He opened his eyes. "Sometimes it's still hard to talk about. There's a lot...I haven't told anyone"

"Will you tell me?" She touched the straw of her egg cream to her lips, and it was more of a command than a question. She was like Eva, more than he'd thought. She was fearless. But was she persecuted? She drank from the glass, opaque with milk and sweetness, her eyes trained on him like a bird dog.

"Maybe another night...I promise. So what about the paper?" He changed the subject, although he was unable to concentrate. A vein pulsed on his head. He knew, at that point, that he would not finish school, do anything. His world was inside him, what had happened to him in the war, what would happen to him. It consumed him.

"Well, I think you should concentrate on the violence aspect of Beowulf, maybe, instead of Henry." She dabbed the wet ring from her glass on the Formica countertop with her napkin. "Both Grendel and Beowulf were violent, but one was heralded a hero and one was feared. But a lot of pain and suffering, as you mention here, was caused by both, and will continue, because someone is always avenging someone."

"Sounds like you've got a great idea for your paper," Johnson smiled.

"I already finished my paper. On King Cnut." She turned her head, taking in the soda fountain around them.

"Who was he?"

"The king of Denmark, England, and Norway, during the 9th century. He was pagan but converted to Christianity and was a great statesman. In fact, his subjects believed he could do anything, even turn back the tides. So one day at Westminster he kneeled before the Thames and ordered the tides to turn away."

"Did they?"

"I guess you'll have to read it and find out." She finished the last of her float and blotted her lips. "You'd better get home to get this written, huh?"

"Can I ask you a question?"

"I'm a horrible typist, so please don't ask me to type it for you."

"No, no—it's just...you're not like any other girls I know. I know that sounds like a line, but it's the truth. Do you want to go out with me? On a real date?"

"Oh...I think I should be getting home." She grabbed for her purse, a sudden, stilted motion, and it fell to the floor, her compact and lipstick clattering and rolling away from them, along with his hopes.

He crouched, his fingers straining for her things. On that first date that would never happen, he would have told her the things she wanted to know. He would have told her that, since the war, the world moved by him on a screen, like those AFO reels civilians watched at home of troop movements, of minor setbacks, or high-stakes advances, of the inevitable sacrifice otherwise known as casualty. The theater was dark and he was alone and there was nothing to do but watch the story of the war over and over, his death and rebirth, until the doors of the lobby had opened, and Kate stood, a dark silhouette, beckoning him into the light of the lobby.

"I'm sorry I was so forward." He stood by the passenger side of the truck, hands in his pockets, as she clutched her purse. "I really do appreciate your help with the assignment. I'll uh, see you in class, then."

"Goodnight, Calvin." She moved toward him. "I'm sorry I… it's just that… the thing is… well, I think you're the most interesting boy I've ever met."

Before he could react, she placed her lips on his. He could feel things in his heart, moving around slippery in his mouth, marbles of love and desire and marriage, marbles that had never risen above his pants with Eva, along with other lumps that he swallowed as she rested her head on his shoulder and they breathed the small space of air between them until there was no air left. Love was hunger, was suffocation. But also soft quiet, the rise of her chest on his, the weight of her head on his shoulder. Her head came up and they kissed again, Johnson holding her face in his hands so she could not slip away.

❀ ❀ ❀

Spears of fall began to poke at the bubble of summer—a few unseasonably cool mornings in August while Calvin planted the broccoli, cauliflower, and radishes in the field; a sweater draped on his mother's shoulders as she knitted on the glider; his father's gun parts gleaming on the table as he cleaned and assembled them for goose season. In class, he sat in his usual seat behind and to the left of Kate and wrote short-answer essays on *The Odyssey* on his final exam. When he finished, he stayed at his seat, watching the slow wave of Kate's hair cascade down her back as she looked to the ceiling, turned her pencil on her cheek and then moved it feverishly across the bluebook. When she closed it and stood, he did too, and followed her up to Professor Shillings, who held up his palm to Johnson as he turned to follow Kate.

"I'll be reading with great interest." Professor Shillings raised an eyebrow as he took Johnson's bluebook. "Maybe we'll see you for the fall semester, Mr. Johnson?"

"I haven't registered yet," he answered. "I liked your class, sir. Thanks for the opportunity to take it."

Kate waited for him in the hall.

"How about an egg cream?" He smiled at her. He looked forward to talking about their schedules for the fall, kissing in his truck in the parking lot behind the bowling alley. She had grounded him. He didn't feel essential to himself, even alive in a normal sense, but he felt tethered to Kate, her gravity keeping his moon rotating, surviving its long trip around the galaxy.

"When were you going to tell me that you were going to New York?" They sat in the truck behind the bowling alley. He lit a cigarette and stared at the tip of the neon bowling pin that cleared the roof and poked at the sky.

"I'm sorry, Calvin. I wanted to from the beginning, that night at the drug store, even. But I wanted to spend time with you. I've always wanted to go to New York University. I just stayed close to home during the war so my parents wouldn't worry. I think they were hoping I'd be engaged or married by now to someone at Bowling Green and ready to pop out a baby."

"What if I asked you not to go?" He turned and put his hands on her shoulders, his eyes locked on hers, and he tried to burn his feelings into her irises, her corneas, so even if she left, she'd see him, a shadow that stretched over her.

"I'd say you were asking a lot of me."

"But I thought there was something between us..." he groped for words. She had erased his entire vocabulary, and new words had yet to form. "A connection. The way we talk...you're scared of what you're feeling."

"Maybe. I don't know." She dropped her head, searching for her own. "But I know I want to go to New York and I want to study art history and work in a museum and I've always wanted these things and you just can't sweep into my life, Calvin, and expect me to change everything."

"I'm not asking you to change anything. I want to be a part of your life, Kate. I'll come to New York. I'll find a job, anything."

"Calvin, you need to find your own place." She smoothed the collar on his shirt. "I don't want you to follow me. You started going to school before you knew me. You wanted to be an architect, remember? And rebuild all those beautiful churches? I don't want to be the person who makes you stop that."

"If I rebuild anything, it's going to be with my hands. I'm too dumb to be an architect." He turned from her. "I'm sorry, Kate. You're a smart girl, and I hope you'll do something with your studies and not just wind up getting married to some rich guy."

"Calvin, you're going to do great things with your life." Kate smiled. "And I'm going to see you do them. It's just that, right now, I need to go to school."

"I understand, Kate. You don't have to apologize."

"You will write me, won't you? I should love to get letters from you. And I will write you back, I promise."

"Sure, okay." He shrugged. He would go to New York. He would find her and woo her. He did not know what else to do.

"Oh, wait." Her hands went to her neck, and when they came together in front of her, they held a medal of Saint Christopher on the chain. "I want you to have this."

He took the medal and turned it over.

"Si en San Cristóbal confías, de accidente no morirás," he read the inscription. "What does that mean?"

"It means if you trust St. Christopher, you won't die in an accident," she answered. "I want you to be safe in your travels. For when we cross paths again."

"You really think we're going to cross paths again?"

"Of course," she smiled. "I'm just going to school. We're not banished from each other forever, two wandering souls. You have to give it back then."

"Why?"

"It was my brother Stephen's," she explained. "He died."

"When?"

"About a year before you came home. Of leukemia. For months,

I dreamed that I would die so I could go visit him. I talked to him in those dreams, and I believed for a long time that those conversations were real."

"What made you stop dreaming?" Calvin pulled a cigarette out of the Pall Malls on the dashboard and pushed the cellophane pack toward her.

"Well, it wasn't real...that kind of stuff," she shrugged as he lit her cigarette, then his own. "I mean, when people are dead, they're dead."

"You don't believe in miracles, or ghosts, or eternal life?"

"I don't even believe in God, necessarily," she answered, exhaling. "Although that is strictly between you and me. My parents thought that sending me to boarding school would teach me how to knit a doily and drink tea and think thoughts becoming to a lady. And they would never have agreed to let me study in New York if they thought I didn't think those things."

"So why are they paying for you to study in New York?"

"Because I told them I'd join the circus," she laughed. "I guess I've always been a little fragile since Stephen passed away, and I know they want to keep me happy, lest I break down and be hospitalized and become some spinster. Plus, I kind of hinted to them I'd absolutely settle down when I was finished. That I just wanted to be cultured, a good wife. Ohio is terribly isolated, you know, and I could find a good family to marry into in New York rather than stay here and risk being some backwards rube."

"Well, you're a pretty girl; I'm sure you won't have any trouble."

"Oh, geez, you probably think I've flipped my wig." Kate touched his arm. "I never tell anyone things like this, honestly. I just knew...you'd understand. I've always known. That first night in class, you felt so out of place, and I've felt that way so much in my life. Not that I show it…but I completely understood how, to you, everything here after the war feels kind of phony."

"Do you really? Do you really understand anything about the war, about what happened to me?" He turned to face her. He let the chain slide from his hand onto the seat between them before scooping it up. "Now, I'm sorry, Kate—I didn't mean it like that. Sometimes I'm a little touchy about what happened…in Germany."

"Take me home, okay?" She stared through the windshield as the streets put distance between what they were before, what they were to become.

"Kate, please write." At her house, he grabbed her arm before she climbed from the truck. "I want you to understand me. And I want to understand you."

She picked up the chain between them and studied it before affixing it to Calvin's neck.

"I'll see you in a few months. I promise. Write me back." She kissed him and leapt out, heading toward the light of the porch before he could respond.

He did not know if he could wait those few months. He needed something, something that would tie things up, make him feel complete again. He wrote Stanley Polensky a letter at his Baltimore address, and when he did not hear from him he wrote to Green, from their unit. Green thought that Polensky had gone to Montana with some of the others to get jobs at the National Park Service. He remembered the Pole talking about it during the war. He had loved the big ponderosa pines out in the Hürtgen, the smell and look of them, even as Johnson could never imagine them again without thinking of diarrhea, of blood, of bone-hurting cold. But Polensky saw the good in everything, and now that Kate had taken what was left of his heart, Johnson needed a little bit of that goodness. He also needed to tell Stanley a few things—first, that he was his friend and brother. That he would die for him. And that only he would understand the strange tale of the Hürtgen forest. Maybe he, man of medallions and lamps, would know what it all meant, if anyone could.

1894

Seasons opened and closed their eyes, batting leaves from trees, crumbling the stones of the bone house, lining the skin of the villagers. Children once her age had their own children, and their own grandchildren, and sometimes their own great-grandchildren. But she did not grow any bigger; her head got no closer to the ceiling of the bone hut, and she needn't not stoop to enter.

She picked burnette saxifrage, white, fan-shaped, from the far end of the woods, where she had gone with her mother long ago. They grew in regular grass and not in a circle blackened by the lightning. They did not look as radiant as the one she had hidden in the bone house, that had survived the fire and the ages, nestled in the skeleton hand of Bolek. But she dried them and boiled water and tried to make the tinctures she had made with her mother. She caught rabbits and mice and cut their bellies, their limbs. She buried them in the grave behind the bone house when they bled to death, variations of the tincture lathered over their wounds. She cut herself, jagged lines as wide as her arm, her thigh, and watched the blood drain for a minute before the edges of her skin began to draw together, the blood disappearing. When she awoke, the signs of her mutilation had dispersed like the morning fog, her skin shiny and taut in the sun.

"Do you think I should try a little more Chaga mushroom?" She asked her lalka, the raven-haired one her mother had given her, as she boiled potatoes to make vodka. It was named Barbara. "A little less amber?"

Barbara never spoke; her face, depending on the light through the roof or Ela's emotional weather, revealed a wry smile, a cooing sympathy. Sometimes at night it seemed to leer at her; others, she seemed remote, her eyes, her smile, reserved for someone or something else. Those days, Barbara wound up across the room, her legs flailing in the air, her face on the stone floor her own mother had made years before, pressing the largest and flattest rocks she'd found into the earth.

"What do you think of the little girl down the hill?" She tossed a potato, eyed and hard, in the air while looking out the entrance of the bone house. Several years ago, a family built a small stone-and-wood cottage down the hill and tried to farm rye. Most of the lots had been parceled and halved and quartered over the years, and those peasants who were not so lucky tried with little luck on the rocky, nutrient-less land in the widening perimeter of miles outside Reszel. The father had left several months before, and the expressions on the mother and daughter's faces had gradually changed, like the slow but irrevocable wear on a rock formation, from hopeful pride and excitement to confusion to the beginning dampness of despair, before the deluge. The broken, the hopeful, were the most desperate. The loneliest. The little girl became aware of Ela. Ela caught her staring up at the bone house from the valley below. "Do you think she likes us?"

Barbara smiled affirmatively from the bed, where she lay next to the blonde-haired lalka. This one had no name, no story. It merely smiled and backed up Barbara.

"I will wait a little longer." Ela came back to the boiling pot and dropped the potato in it. "We must let her come to us."

"You're not a witch." A month later, the little girl stood by the opening of the bone house. "My matka says, when they burned the witch, they burned her daughter, too."

"I am not a witch," Ela agreed. She had seen the girl's mother often in the village, while buying cabbage and oxen bone, things the villagers gave to her for free, along with milk and honey and lamb's meat, if she promised to stay away, not to bewitch them.

"I think you are lying." The girl half-skipped around the bone house, her curiosity buoying her bravery. She had played a little closer to the bone house each day, throwing rocks up the hill and drawing pictures in the loose hillside with sticks, returning home when her mother called her back. "She said a witch lived in the bone house, that I shouldn't come here. Are you a Baba Yaga?"

Ela smiled. The girl, four or five, was too young to be scared of her, to understand the things she represented, by her continued vitality, to the older villagers—death, brittle bones, tepid health. But these things were natural and did not have their source in Ela. They were a conclusion to a story, an end to a beginning, a night to morning. Things Ela could only dream of.

"I have a lalka." Ela cut to the fat of the girl's heart. "Would you like to see her?"

"Are you sure you're not a Baba Yaga?" The girl stared at the doll resting in Ela's arms. Ela imagined the girl had been told stories about Baba Yagas, witches who turned themselves into young, beautiful princesses and lured men to their huts. They lured children, too, and ate them, packing the bones in the mud and stone of their houses. She had heard such stories herself from her own mother. But the promise of a doll, to love and hold even for a few minutes, to a girl who wrapped cloth and hay around sticks and pretended to nurse them, would be too tempting, Ela figured. She had all the time in the world to find out.

"I'd better not." The girl moved her right foot backward toward the hill, then her left. Then her right again.

"What's your name?" Ela asked. She brought the doll to her cheek. "I'm Ela."

The girl retreated farther, feeling for the incline of the hill with her feet.

"Come back tomorrow." Ela smiled still. "Maybe I will find you your own lalka."

❊❊❊

She left the lalka, the second one, blonde and almost as new as when her mother had bought it, by the clothesline of the girl's little stone cottage. From the hill, she watched the girl's mother come out and beat a quilt that hung from a rope tied between the cottage and a tree. It was hard not to see, a heap of white and gold, like a fallen angel, at the base of the hill. She could make out legs and arms and fingers. And the little girl who peered out the window at it could see them, too.

If the girl's matka glanced to her right, she would see it. But like most of the villagers, who traded with her for tinctures, always giving her, out of fear, more for them that she'd asked, she knew the girl's mother would ignore her, pretend she did not exist, and if all else failed, bargain to keep Ela from cursing or bedeviling her.

Ela never saw her look, but when she finished beating the quilt, she walked over to the hill, picked up the doll, and threw it back toward the bone house as hard as she could. The girl's eyes followed its trajectory before they disappeared into the darkness of the cottage.

The moon sat high, the sky purple, full of hot breath. Ela rested at the top of the hill, feeling the faint breeze pull the strands of hair from her wet forehead. With surprise, she watched the little girl steal from the cottage and scramble up the hill, her eyes greedy and shiny, full of doll cheeks and hearts.

"You came." Ela's shoulders went up; she smiled. "Come."

The girl's eyes went toward the bone house, and her mouth opened, hungry for the doll, but Ela took her hand. Together, they entered the edge of the forest.

"Do you hear the wood owl at night?" Ela asked, and the girl nodded, afraid to breathe. "I will show you where he lives."

They wound through the dark trunks and thick undergrowth. The girl became less scared. The crickets talked to the frogs, who talked to the owl. They were as busy as the village on trading day, when the girl and her mother took their cattails and milk and other meager crops and tried to get for them a few cups of flour, a bowl of oxen tail.

"See, you are not as alone at night as you think," Ela smiled. "There is always someone awake."

"Where is your matka?" The girl asked, and Ela did not answer. She bowed her head so low the girl held out her hand, afraid she would trip on a stone or a root. What was at first affected, a ploy to fool the little girl, became real as grief poured from a spot above her and filled the bend in her neck, her eyes. She was talking to an actual person, albeit a girl, who did not think she was going to kill her. She realized she missed simple things, the sound of a voice in response, even a word, yes, no. A nod. The pressure, a light itch, from the fingers.

In fact, the girl seemed to pity her. She squeezed Ela's hand reassuringly. "I bet you could live with me and my matka. My name is Safine."

"That's okay, Safine; no one wants me to live with them." Ela shook her head, wiping her eyes. "My mother died. I have been alone for a long, long time. I am so lonely for company, but the villagers think I am a witch. They do not understand why I grow no bigger."

"I am big for my age, my matka says. Maybe you are small for yours?"

"No." Ela patted her shoulder. "I will tell you sometime. Tonight, let me enjoy the fact that I finally have company."

❀❀❀

Every night, Safine stole away and saw Ela. Sometimes, they walked in the woods; other times, they lay on the grass in the moonlight, talking softly. Safine told her that she and her mother hoped to go to America soon to be reunited with their Ojciec, who had sailed months before to get work in a city called Baltimore. *To work in the factories*, Safine explained vaguely. *To make us rich*, she said surely. They were not able to harvest a big enough crop of rye on their land in Reszel; there was no other choice.

One night, they even went inside the bone house. To a stranger, Ela supposed, it was small and dark and smelled sourly of herbs and vodka, but her quilts were soft and warm, full of colorful swaths she had gotten from the women in the village who by turns pitied and feared her. Ela watched Safine's eyes sweep the house, looking for the angel-haired, nameless lalka, bite her tongue not to ask about it.

But Ela sensed her disappointment, and the next night, when Safine went to the hill, Ela waited, a doll in each arm. She held out the blonde doll, but Safine did not take it right away.

"Where did you get such beautiful lalkas?" She asked. Her eyes said it all; it seemed too good to be true, something Matka had always warned her against. Only a Baba Yaya, Safine's cloaked eyes reasoned, could produce such beautiful dolls.

"My matka gave me them." Ela's arm dropped back to her body, the blonde lalka's hair swinging toward the ground. "I have been waiting so long for a friend to play dolls with."

Ela pulled the wooden horse from under the bed and opened the secret compartment, revealing the herb. Despite its crumbled brown leaves, she felt a charge move down her fingers and into the air as she fondled it. She did not know why Safine would be the one; perhaps time and loneliness had left her impatient, careless. There would not be another opportunity. She breathed deeply and looked at her.

"If you want the lalka, it's yours," Ela explained. With one hand she held up the lalka, and the other the burnette saxifrage. "But you must eat this herb. It will make you stay young and beautiful. Your hands will not curl like your matka's; your face will not line, and your lips scowl. You will experience a long, prosperous life."

"Tomorrow night, may I take it?" Safine answered, shifting her weight from foot to foot. "I do not feel so well tonight."

"Do not fear this." Ela put her hands on Safine's shoulders and sought out her eyes. "I would never harm you."

"I know." Safine nodded, and bent over so Ela would not see the quiver of her lip. "But I must get home tonight because I feel very tired. I shall take it tomorrow, when I feel better. I promise."

"Please, trust me." Ela smiled. She drew the lalka and herb behind her back, out of sight. "It's all right."

❀❀❀

"Why do you not grow any bigger?" Safine looked up at Ela the next night, sitting in the tree next to their cottage. She swung her bare feet in the air, not meeting her eyes. Safine hit the bark of the tree with her hand. "How does the herb work? You must tell me, or I cannot be your friend."

"Come back to my house and I will tell you." Ela jumped down from the tree, a little smile staining her lips. Safine looked back at her own house for a moment before following.

"Before my matka died, the soldiers had come to our house for her lover, who did a bad thing." Ela sat on the bed, holding the lalka and the herb. "A bad thing he blamed on my mother. But my mother made medicines, and some of her medicines were made from this flower. I ate this flower before the soldiers came. Antoniusz, my stepfather, says the soldiers shot me, and he buried me himself. I didn't remember anything for a long time after that. But I woke up in the ground. Little by little, I dug myself out. When I got out, so much time had passed, my mother was already dead. And many springs have passed since. But I am still a little girl."

"But why?"

"It was struck by lightning, this flower—I have tried other flowers of burnette saxifrage, and cannot replicate the medicines. It must be the soul of the lightning captured inside. It healed all the rabbits and frogs we maimed. And it healed me. I am very old, and I cannot die."

"But why?" Safine shook her head.

"The herb—do you understand?"

Safine looked at the flower as Ela held it out to her.

"If you eat it, you'll never die." Ela nodded to her as Safine shook her head. "Won't it be fun? We could play dolls and live in my cottage and the villagers will give us things because they are scared of us and want us to stay away. We can have beautiful clothes and honey and butter and dolls and even meat."

"Can my matka take it, too?" Safine asked. "I would miss her."

"Take it." Ela pressed the herb up to Safine's lips. "Take it for me."

Safine scrunched her face, the way a child might resist medicine. She opened her mouth the width of a finger and then widened it.

"Safine!" The scream came from the entrance of the bone house. A moment later, it was joined to Matka's body, still in her nightclothes, followed by a man from the village, brandishing a torch. She picked Safine up and pushed at Ela. "Get away! Get! Get, you witch!"

Ela stuffed the herb into Safine's palm, and her fingers closed over it tightly. Safine's matka mumbled prayers, curses, as she ran down the hill, Safine tucked against her.

"We mean no harm to you." The man backed out of the bone house, torch in front of him. "The mother wants her baby back, that's all. They're leaving for America tomorrow. Please leave them safe through the night. Here."

He dropped some goat meat wrapped in cheesecloth at the entrance of the bone house. Ela followed him outside, in time to see Safine and her matka disappear into their cottage. She wondered if it was too late to get the herb back. The next day, she watched the man load Safine and her mother and their belongings into a wagon and head toward the village. She searched the cottage, empty and swept clean, for the herb. She searched the grounds around the cottage, the soot of the fireplace. But the herb was gone, along with Safine, forever. She went back to the bone house.

"We were not patient enough." She threw the blonde lalka against the wall. She took Barbara by the arms and shook her, hoping that the dainty smile, the mocking eyes, would fall off her face. "Why did you not speak your mind, warn me? Why do you want me to be alone, to live old and haggard in the heart and mind, but young in body? Stop laughing at me. I am tired that you laugh at me."

She threw Barbara next to the other lalka and built a fire outside. When it crackled orange, coughing black puffs of smoke, she tore off their arms, then legs, and fed them to the flames. Their smiles remained, weak but preserving, martyrs to the end.

"You shall seal your own fate." She twisted off the heads and threw the bodies and heads into the fire. Their cloth unfolded and burned. "You are not even human."

Was she? She watched their smiles disappear into the soot and was relieved that she was finally free of them. But she felt sick. They were gone, and she remained. She was really alone, with no one but herself to blame.

1947

When they had moved into the farmhouse, it looked less like a house and more like a collection of boards that been blown together upwards. Window shards jutted from panes like incisors, a wilderness of weeds and stones grew from the baseboards, and the nearest neighbor looked to be a quarter mile away south. But, Stanley found, it was less than a mile from the dump, and when he felt better, when Cindy had washed his wound in warm soap and water and dressed it for five days straight, he dragged home a table, a sofa they'd later discover to be infested with spiders, and various slats of wood that he hammered into crevices, converted into shelves, and used to repair the porch steps. His skin healed over the wound, wormy and shiny, and he could not lift his arm all the way above his head.

Until they could afford to fix the upstairs window, they slept in the living room on a pile of quilts they had gotten from the Salvation Army. During the day, Cindy worked with her sewing kit on the front porch, trying to give her silky, gaudy clothes a drab, humbler life of knee-length dresses and shawls and blouses. They drank watered coffee grounds for weeks on end and tossed Stanley's combat boots at the things that scrambled in dark corners.

Stanley picked up work at a neighboring farm for harvest, corn, working twice as hard with his good shoulder and arm. He bought a truck that didn't run and rebuilt the engine by reading a manual, and Cindy cleared out a small square of land behind the back of the farmhouse, where she planted carrots and kale, green beans, tomatoes, and potatoes.

But the piety of their present life could not bury the bones of the old. Stanley bought a fifth of cheap whiskey and hid it under the porch. It was his only ammunition against his dreams. Every night, when he settled from the pain in his shoulder, shrugged off the ache of the fields, and floated into the ether dark of his mind, Johnson would be waiting, demanding to know why Stanley hadn't saved him. In each dream Johnson met a different death—explosions, shrapnel, rifle wound, gangrene, influenza—his body bloody, dismembered, burned, and pale. Johnson's mouth did not move in the dreams, but his questions grow more insistent, his brown eyes sharpening, locking onto Stanley with such force and tenacity that he woke up shivering.

"Why don't we go out tonight, baby?" Cindy washed the tomatoes in the kitchen and put them in a pot to boil and can for the winter. She stood on the stool Stanley had made her, her legs pale drumsticks underneath her skirt, and when he moved behind her, the curve of her hips and buttocks pushed against his stomach. "It's so quiet out here, I can barely stand it."

It didn't matter to Cindy how the men looked at her—with scorn, with bemusement, with pity, or with longing—so long as they looked at her. She drank from the syrupy attention gotten as the result of her beauty and her deformity just as greedily as Stanley from the bottle. Stanley—and her inability to drive the truck—was all that stood between her and her admirers and detractors.

"I don't know." At the sink, he wrapped his arms around her, feeling his erection swell against her leg. "We can't really afford it."

"Honey, I swear I might go crazy if we don't go into town—just to window shop?" She turned her head and puckered her lips the way he liked. "And maybe you can do a little window shopping later."

The trump card, if there ever was one. Perhaps they were not truly compatible, but they were man and woman, the most natural compliment, and for Stanley, that was enough. But maybe it wasn't enough for Cindy, who'd been with men before him, men of all shapes and sizes. In all those years lying on his bed as a teenager, reading books, he hadn't read much about women. He didn't know if Cindy, riding on top of him like a child on a miniature pony, liked his cock, whether her orgasms, big productions of shuddering and hyperventilating and pounding his chest with her lemon-sized fists, were real, but he loved everything about her because she was a woman, silky, milky, her breath on his shoulder light in sleep, the feel of her lips on his brow when he woke up shivering, Johnson dead again.

Johnson. He could go to Ohio and see about Johnson's family. They could go to Ohio, if Cindy wanted to come. And if she didn't want to, then perhaps it was for the best. Their relationship, and its failure, it would not be the first or last mistake either of them would make.

Cindy became pregnant. Stanley had not been not sure if she could get pregnant, if it was possible, given her condition, her compressed woman-ness that he assumed extended to all of the inside of her, but then slowly the front of her began to stretch, smooth and round, and she began to throw up in the morning, loud, gut-spilling retches from the upstairs bathroom that woke Stanley down in the living room, Stanley who had surrendered to slumber only precious hours before, his dreams finally too tired to haunt him.

They had not talked about children, but he figured it was assumed, the product of the time-tested man-woman equation. He felt safer, that with impending motherhood, the attention of men would be replaced by the attention of child. And maybe Johnson would go away, too, seeing that Stanley was firmly planted in civilian soil, and a new generation, shiny-eyed myopics to war and atrocity, was on its way.

"What do you want to name it, baby?" She called from the living room as he stood on the porch smoking a cigarette and drinking coffee water. The morning settled cold like dust on his shoulders and hands, and he brought his mug, steaming, closer to his face. Winter was coming, and neither of them had a good coat. Cindy's was now too small, and Stanley's wool overcoat from the Army was lost back in Baltimore. And now there would be baby coats and baby food and baby things on top of everything else.

"We could name him after your father, if it's a boy." She stood beside him on the porch, her head nestled into his waist. He wondered if the baby would be a midget. He did not feel sorry for himself if this was true, but he would feel sorry for the baby. He wondered whether Cindy would be okay having a baby. He'd already wondered, so many times when they were having sex, where exactly things were located in her body, whether he was stabbing vital organs, tearing tissue to shreds, poking holes in things. But Cindy had never complained, and she complained no more even now that she was pregnant.

"Now why in the hell would we want to do that?" He kissed the top of her head. "I'd rather have a girl, anyway, pretty like you. Now go inside; you're going to catch your death."

The season had ended at the farm, and now a twenty-dollar-a-week pension from the Army was all that stood between them and their first winter. Some of the men who worked on the farm shot deer and lived off the meat, and Stanley had considered this, except he did not have enough money saved for a rifle. Not when Cindy had to go to the doctor and she needed new clothes and new shoes, too, because her feet had swollen.

"You're so good at cars, Stanley." Cindy pushed the bowl of beans to him across the table. They had eaten beans, which Stanley had gotten from the church's charity pantry on his trip to town, three times that week. "Why don't you get a job at a garage? You're so smart and did so well in school. Maybe we could move closer to town and you could work in an office and do something. Make friends. Have people over, go dancing."

"I don't know." He moved the beans around in his mouth but didn't taste them. The baby was not nearly born yet, and she was already building their postpartum social life. "I like being out here in the middle of nowhere. I'll get a job—don't worry. Something has to shake out. Someone's always got a job for a vet."

"You and fifty thousand other vets, right? You could go to school on the GI Bill and learn a trade or something."

"Let's wait until the baby's born—we've got too much on our plate right now."

"If we've got so much on our plate, how come I've got so much energy?" She swept the kitchen floor and sang. He wondered how a woman, dwarfed by her own broomstick, could have a locomotive in her big enough to power those vocal chords. She sang songs from her childhood and songs she remembered from the radio. When she got tired of those songs, she made up songs of her own. The songs comforted him, like his mother. Although his mother had not sung—it was her noise, the clanging pots and thumping rugs and splashing laundry water and chopping vegetables, that cloaked him in the soft dew of youth. He dropped his head on his hands as Cindy's voice washed over him like a cat bathing her kittens.

But he still had not found work, and he could not cancel Cindy's appointment he'd made at the doctor's because she'd know he had taken their last few dollars and spent it on more whiskey. Outside the house, so cold a bird could drop from the sky in an ice cube, he lifted her up in his arms and settled her in the front seat of the truck. He figured he'd beg, grovel at a few places while Cindy was at her appointment and maybe even have a job by the time she was finished. He walked her to the front door of the doctor's office, kissed her hair, which smelled faintly of roses and oil, and walked to the post office to apply for the civil service exam. Then, he drove to the outskirts of town to see whether the shirt factory was hiring. Fabrics were no longer being rationed, since the war ended, and rumors floated at the post office that the factory was going to triple its production from the previous two years'.

Cindy was waiting outside at the curb when he returned, her arms linked underneath her little scallop of belly.

"What's the news?" He swung her up into his arms and kissed her cheek before depositing her into the truck. "Why didn't you stay inside, where it's warm?"

"I'm never going back to that peckerhead," she answered, her little features stewed into a frown. "What a lotta nerve he has!"

"What'd he say, baby?"

"He asked me if I knew what kind of risks I was taking, having a baby—that I had no business putting my health and the baby's health at risk like this."

"What does he know? Women only a little bigger than you have babies just like women two times your size."

"I'm just so tired of it, Stanley." She rubbed her stomach absently. He could see the straps of her Mary Janes, the ones he'd bought just last month at the five and dime, stretching, her flesh red and sore and poking out. "Some people act like I shouldn't do anything, shouldn't say anything, shouldn't even be alive. Of course, the men weren't complaining when I was their little fantasy doll, right?"

"Don't worry about them. I love you. And we're going to have the most beautiful baby in the world."

"I'm hungry, Stanley. Do you think we could stop by the diner near the police station?"

"I would, if we had any money."

"What about them few dollars we had left over?" When he didn't answer, she hit him on his bad shoulder. The pain razored up and down his shoulder and elbow before bottoming out.

"Christ, Cindy—why you gotta do that?" His fingers went white on the steering wheel.

"Because you are the most unreliable SOB I have ever met! Can't you do anything right? I have to save your ass from being killed, nag you into getting a job, you spend all our money on booze... Jesus Christ, Stanley. You're supposed to take care of me."

"Well, I guess there's nothing I can say about that." He always knew when to fold them. Cindy stared at the diner, as if willing it to rectify their situation.

"You go to the diner anyway, Stanley," she said finally. "I got an idea."

He wondered if he would spend the evening washing dishes in the diner kitchen but instead outside the door she pulled the wool hunter's cap off his head and dropped it open side up. She plopped on the steps of the diner and began to sing.

"Jesus, Cindy—get the hell up." He grabbed her arm. She shrugged him off. "We don't need no charity."

"We do when you act like a peckerhead and drink away all our money," she said while smiling, and continued to sing.

"Christ, I'm not going to take that. You weren't getting shot at overseas. Hell, you weren't even shot by your boyfriend, but you sure plugged me good."

"Yeah, and if I had a gun I'd plug you again right now." She stared at him, and her eyes plunged into his chest, extracting the warmth of love and companionship that she had slowly filled it with in the last year. Or perhaps he was mistaken, and his chest was merely a balloon, fooled by the pressure of mere air.

He went back to the truck and sat in the cab, staring at her like a puppy locked inside. He vowed to make things right, to get a job like any self-respecting man. But he did not know if it would be enough. He watched as a tall, soft man in a suit and cowboy hat approach Cindy, reach for his wallet. The man bent his head back as he laughed. He wiped his forehead with a handkerchief, impervious to the falling thermometer, and bent over and shook Cindy's hand. Stanley strained to see the bill that the man left in his hunting cap. Then he watched Cindy pick up the cap and the money and follow the man inside.

He waited for her to come get him. He kicked at the baseboards of the truck, squirmed in the seat to get warm. He thought about driving away, about not letting a damn woman push him around. He was disappointed he was not that type of man. When she came out, an hour later, she was rosy and warm, carrying a brown paper bag. The man tipped his hat to her and waved to Stanley in the truck before heading up the street.

"Well, I see you still know how to sucker the men out of their money," he spat when she opened the cab.

"Shut your stupid ass up, Stanley, and help me in the cab."

"I don't see why I should," he answered, but he did anyway, secretly happy that she was back, that she didn't walk down the street with the heavyset cowboy man and out of his life forever.

"You wouldn't believe it, Stanley." Cindy's rubbed her little hands together in the truck as he started the engine. The smell of pot roast filled the car, and he swallowed once, twice. Down the street, the headlights of a sedan traveled through the purple dusk past the doctor's office and over his fingers, dotted with goosebumps. Cindy had made gloves for Stanley from her old wool coat but he stupidly had left them home. "I was singing there on the sidewalk thinking that you were right, that it was a terrible idea, and a man come by and heard me singing. He said I should be on the radio and bought me dinner and gave me his card! He wants me to come down to the radio station and sing a song! You woulda known if you hadn't been such a stubborn ass and stayed outside with me."

"You could have invited me in."

"I ain't your mother, Stanley. You could have come and at least protected my honor."

"You shouldn't have been begging in the first place. We got beans at home."

"Well, I hope you enjoy them while I eat this leftover pot roast, mashed potatoes, and blueberry pie," she answered. "Now shut up and listen to me. He said he was having tryouts for a radio program like the Grand Ole Opry." Cindy hit his arm. "Ain't that something, Stanley!"

"Would they pay you?"

"Well, the singers would get ten dollars a week for being on the radio show."

"We could you get you a new coat." He guided the truck onto the highway. "And some things for the baby. But is it okay, with you being pregnant and all?"

"I don't know," she shrugged. "Why not? I sing all the time. Isn't this great, baby? We'll finally have some money."

"Yeah," he agreed, tightening and loosening his hands on the steering wheel. "So when you going to do it?"

"Well, he said to come to the station on Saturday. By then, I'll have a bunch of songs practiced and ready."

"Well, even if it don't turn out to nothing, I'm proud of you, baby. Maybe you'll make a little money to last through the thaw and I can go back to the farm."

"Hell, maybe this'll be something bigger and we won't be talking about being farmers no more. Earl Wooten—he's the guy who owns the station—said he's hoping to send some of the singers out to his brother Wendell in Nashville for recording contracts."

"You don't want to be a farmer's wife?"

"I never, ever wanted to be a farmer's wife," she answered, and took his hand. "I thought it might have been obvious to you by now. Now, hurry up and get home or your food's going to get cold."

"My food?"

"I asked Earl if he would buy a plate for my poor, proud husband who'd rather freeze to death in the truck than take charity."

"Well, you know what's wrong with that, right?'

"What? I shouldn't have gotten you any food?"

"No, you shouldn't have called me your husband until I had a chance to make it official." He pulled the truck to the side of the road and turned to her. "Cynthia Meekins, will you marry me?"

"Well...of course, silly." She smiled, as if he had brought her some crudely composed painting from elementary school. "You could have asked months ago, or when I got pregnant, even."

"I was waiting until I could afford a ring."

"I don't need a ring, Stanley—I just need your word. Besides, we don't need to worry about weddings right now. Maybe I'll be able to buy myself the biggest ole' ring you ever did see if I sing my cards right with Wendell."

He nodded, but the whole thought left a bitter taste in his mouth, one he could not rid himself of even after a plate of pot roast, mashed potatoes, green beans, and blueberry pie.

Earl Wooten was a resourceful and unlucky man. At least, that was how he explained his current ownership of WXFB radio in Salisbury to Stanley and Cindy. In his office, Cindy sat in her best dress. They stopped by the department store on the way to WXFB so Cindy could get a free spritz of perfume from the fragrance counter. "Oh, my, aren't you a pretty little girl!" The saleswoman, beaked and boned, leaned over Cindy until Stanley cleared his throat.

"My fiancée would like to try that Shalimar." He nodded to the bottle.

"Of course." She reddened. "I'm *so* sorry. Geez."

"That's okay—thanks so much, ma'am," Cindy beamed, as she always did—her public persona was finely calibrated to handle any variety of humiliation. But not Stanley's, and Cindy tugged him away from the counter before he considered knocking the other perfumes—the White Sands and Christian Diors that lined the glass counter—onto the floor with a flick of his elbow.

Earl's secretary led them to a wood-paneled, smoke-clouded office with a square glass window to the broadcasting booth. Framed records on the walls hinted at respectability, although they were not names that Stanley had ever heard of. He stood, hands in his pockets as Earl grabbed and kissed Cindy's hand, offered her a faux leather seat with a duck-taped arm.

"You ever gambled, son?" Earl, looking at Stanley, positioned his girth, packed tightly into his six-and-a-half-foot frame, on the edge of his desk with unusual delicacy. He crossed his leg, and Stanley noted his thin ankles, long fingers. "Let's just say I lost a bet and won a radio station. My brother, he's even got worse luck. He lost a bet and won a recording studio! Course, the studio ain't here—it's out in Nashville. Nashville, you're sayin'—why not New York or Chicago or Los Angeles where all the big boys are? Well, let me tell you something—Nashville is hot. Country music is going places, and your little lady here, well, she ain't no bigger than a pushpin, but she got a big voice."

"So how are you gonna make her a star?"

"Record? Well, let's not get ahead of the game, here." Earl lit a cigarette. "We're going to let the little lady sing a song live on the air, and if our listeners like it, we'll have her come back in as part of the barn dance ensemble. We got all kinds of radio shows, you see—Jimmy Ray Housin and Betty Dandy. And now we're gettin' together one of them weekly radio barn dances like they got at WLS-AM in Chicago."

"Sounds fair, Stanley." Cindy nodded, her eyes seeking his approval. "Kind of like the free spritz of perfume—you like it, you might buy it."

"You know your business, little lady." Earl grinned, his face squeezed into folds from his cheeks to his forehead, his eyes little black pins under his eyebrows. "I can tell who's doing the thinking in the household. So, are you ready? Stevie over there in the booth's got a guitar, he plays almost anything out there."

"Does he know 'Keep on the Sunny Side'?"

"Of course he does, little lady." Earl guided her through the door. "Stanley, why don't you have a seat? We can listen from here."

Earl came back and offered Stanley a smoke.

"Is it too much trouble to take two?" Stanley asked. "We've been a little tight for money, especially now Cindy's pregnant."

"Yep, yep—congratulations, son. It's marvelous what medicine can do these days for, uh, people who…" Earl stared at his lighter. "Well, when I seen her outside the diner, I thought she was the cutest little kid. And I thought, here we've got another little Shirley Temple or Peggy Lee. I was counting my money already! But imagine my surprise when she turned out to be that pint-sized little thing."

"Yeah, she's pretty gifted singer, I'd say." Stanley pressed on the balls of his feet.

"It's such a shame. I mean, she could be a star if she were…you know…"

"No, I don't." Stanley lit his cigarette and leaned forward, ready to jump over the desk. "Maybe you should say what you're really thinking?"

"Well." Earl exhaled and touched the back of his head with his palm. "I told my brother all about Cindy, how I thought...well, she's got a great voice for radio. But she's no...I mean, what picture you got by your foxhole during the war, Stanley? Betty Grable."

"You're saying nobody's going to be interested in Cindy because she's a midget?"

"*I* don't think that's true. Like I said, she's a little button. But there's also...well, she's pregnant." Earl stubbed out his cigarette. "My brother, he runs that side of the business. I'm just on the radio side. It's my responsibility to listen, not to see."

"Then why the hell is she here, then?" Stanley felt his jaws, his legs tighten.

"Well, I don't go back on my promises. I asked her to come in and sing, and people is gonna hear her, right? I think they're almost ready." Earl stood up, patting his forehead with his handkerchief, and motioned him to the window. Cindy stood on the radio jockey's chair, her lips close to the microphone.

❀❀❀

Stanley did not know how it happened, exactly. When Earl came by one winter morning with plane tickets to Nashville to record a demo at his brother's studio, Cindy had been recording for the "Happy Hayride" show for almost three months as 'Lil Cindy Sunshine. She was the talk of the tri-state area, although, thanks to Earl's carefully timed studio sessions, no one in Maryland-Delaware-Virginia had ever laid eyes on her.

"You're not going to Nashville to do anything." He stood in their renovated bedroom, with window panes and a real bed frame and mattress courtesy of Cindy's earnings from Happy Hayride. "You're almost four months pregnant."

"Since I'm the only one earning any money in this house, I think that decision should be mine, don't you?" She lay on her side, head propped on her elbow, looking at sheet music of the songs Wendell wanted her to record in Nashville.

"They'll probably use your voice and put some other girl's picture up—Earl already told me he can't do anything with you because you're a pregnant midget."

"He didn't tell you that." She stared at him with narrowed eyes. "You take that back."

"I may be unemployed, but I'm not a liar." He moved toward the bed. "I'm sorry baby. You don't need him, anyway. I love you just the way you are."

"Don't touch me." She squirmed out of his grasp and hopped off the bed, padding toward the bathroom and shutting the door. "You've always been jealous of my dreams."

"Baby, I'm sorry." He knocked. "I'm not jealous of your dreams. I just think we should have the same dreams." But weren't his, chasing down the parents of a dead comrade in Ohio, just as selfish, as foolish?

He sat outside the bathroom door.

"We can make this work, Cindy. The two of us. I'll get a job and you'll never have to work again, I promise you. You'll be royalty, Cindy. My royalty."

He sat outside for a long time, listening to her motions inside, a slight cry, the toilet flushing, water running. He dozed off until the door opened suddenly and he fell inward, looking up at her from the tiled floor. She held a wadded, soaked facecloth dabbed with pink.

"Stanley, I lost the baby." Her stubby legs stepped over his head and down the hall. "I need to talk to Earl."

1947

When he hit McDonald Pass outside of Helena, Montana, where the two-lane blacktop curved and disappeared into mountains of pine and fir trees, Johnson had been on the road three days, his tires were sizzling, and he prayed to God for the first time since the war. He'd gone west past Helena, looking for some cabin that a man in a bar back in Kansas had told him about, a hunting cabin that wasn't locked, where he could spend the night. But the details, scribbled in pencil on a napkin in the man's drunken, unsteady hand, made less sense the farther west Johnson went, and he looked for a place to turn around in the winding mountain road that resembled the man's arched, urgent script. He prayed that his tires, leaving black horizontal smears of rubber across the road as he braked, would not blow out and send the truck tumbling into the Rocky Mountains. The chassis shuddered as he fought against the steering wheel, sending silt to the edges of the road.

He slowed the truck to a crawl and coasted to a spot where he could see a good mile in front and in back of him. To his right, the Rocky Mountains climbed, obscuring his view of the North, and to the south, the road dropped away into the deep blue Montana sky. He inched the truck back and forth across the width of the road, noting where his rear tires grabbed the edges of the narrow shoulder before it descended. He pulled at the steering wheel, traces of last night's whiskey from some whistle stop in North Dakota beading on his neck and forehead and the palms of his hand.

He spotted a late-model truck heading east in his rearview mirror and pushed on the gas pedal, backing the truck westward before grabbing the clutch to move into first and forward. But he idled, in the transition, perhaps a second too long, his thoughts bottoming into the dark well of uncertainty, what he was doing in Montana, if he would find Stanley, where he had gone off the path, a side route where roads disappeared into mountains without the promise of emerging, and he felt the right rear tire spin because there was nothing under it. He pressed the pedal harder and leaned forward in the seat as rocks and dust swirled behind him and the right wheel sank into a soup of stones and silt. As he and truck tilted backward, moving toward the sky, Johnson pushed open the driver's door with his left arm. He dropped from the truck and rolled to his left, the ground unforgiving to his shoulder and face. From the corner of his right eye, he saw the front of the truck, wheels in the air like a bucking bronco, the engine whining for a moment in the rush of motion, the futile spin of suspended tires, before sound and truck were sucked into the below. A second passed, two, and the sound took up where it had left off, like a radio coming back into reception, as metal twisted and glass shattered and tires exploded, a vehicular accordion moving through the chords of its swan song.

He heard the other truck, now only hundreds of feet away, its brakes slowing the tires, its engine shifting downward in gears, and he became aware of his body, of the raw abrasion that clung to it like a dew, and he bent his elbows and knees and neck without moving from the ground, where gravity had locked his stomach and chest and back until the enormity of what had happened could be processed by his head. He laughed, feeling a tooth loose in his bottom jaw, a stiff, unbendable left index finger, and he saw boots, scuffed bald on the toes, the steel of the toe almost peeking through, little caulks on the soles, by his head.

"You all right, buddy? Jesus."

He forced his eye upward, toward the young man, blond, cleft chin bristled with stubble, with deep-set eyes looking at him from a height that may have been heaven.

"I think I need a ride into town," Johnson answered, closed his own.

❀❀❀

"I think I heard of a Stanley at the Fire Service," the man, Lane Gustafson, answered. "You looking for a forestry job?"

"Yeah—Stanley's my friend. We served together." Johnson sat on the passenger side of Lane's truck, patting his face with a handkerchief. A dotted pattern of blood emerged on the yellowed fabric as he moved it over his cheeks and forehead. He was sure his index finger was broken. The middle joint had swelled to a plum, almost as purple. He could not bend it; it was as immobile as a knife in a full jar of peanut butter.

"You want to go to the hospital, have that looked at?" Lane nodded at it as he steered them along mountain roads at speeds that made Johnson a little queasy.

"Naw. I'll get a little ice somewhere. Back in the war, we called this a boo-boo," Johnson answered.

Lane laughed, and Johnson took note of the throbs reporting

from the various centers of his body: his lower back, his left forearm and elbow, his neck, his left thigh. The memory of his stumps entered his consciousness as randomly as a lightning flash on a clear day, and his first instinct was always to bury it in a stiff drink. Johnson turned and watched the buildings roll by on main street—the Martha Hotel, F.W. Woolrich, the Harvey Hotel. Mountains towered over the far end, a protective giant that closed the valley of firs and pines and bright peaked houses in its arms. Lane guided the truck off the main strip and eastward out of town.

"I know a bar," Lane seemed to read his thoughts. "Let's get the shake off you, man."

Johnson settled his shaking hands into his lap, where Lane could no longer see them. He seemed to skirt harm more than most people. Perhaps that was an understatement, or perhaps the strangeness of it kept him constantly vigilant, afraid that the truth of this statement would catch up with him and pronounce itself boldly; that he was actually a freak, a demon, a ghost. That something really had happened over in Germany.

The handkerchief he pressed against his face stopped absorbing blood. When he flipped open the sun visor and glanced into small rectangular mirror, covered with a paste of smoke and dust, to his surprise, he noticed that his cuts were pink and closed, on their way, he supposed, in another moment, to disappearing completely. He curled his hands into fists and realized his index finger bent along with the other fingers, its plum-sized joint now just a peach pit. He covered his left hand with his right and hoped Lane would not notice, but he was too busy trying to find reception on his radio, the thick tuner bar moving lazily across the numbers.

"Can you pull over for a minute, buddy?" Johnson turned in the seat, unrolling the window, letting the wind dry the sudden sweat on his face and neck. Before the truck's tires had stopped rolling, he jumped from the seat and crouched on the rocks and dirt by the shoulder, vomiting up God knows what from whenever he'd eaten last, acidic brown plumes tinged with red that singed the dirt and leaves and sent up an ominous smoke signal in the wake of their destruction. His clothes were drenched in sweat. He was in the middle of crisis in the middle of nowhere. He looked at his hand, wriggling the jammed finger, bending the joint. It moved as free as a stick through the air. He felt his skin, the sides of his face, as if they would supply him with answers. He felt his heart clicking in his chest—he could not be a vampire or a zombie or countless other versions of the undead he'd seen at the movies.

"I need you to take me to Stanley now," Johnson said when he climbed back in the truck.

"Calm down, buddy." Lane laughed at him before pulling off the road. He picked up his cigarettes from the dashboard, waving them up and down, back and forth, as if to tantalize him. "I don't even know where this Stanley is. We'll need to ask around a bit, and we may as well do that at the places that men usually go, right? Now, have a cigarette and calm down. Where are you from?"

"Ohio," Johnson answered, pulling one from the pack, slapping his jacket pockets for a match. "I think my lighter was in the truck."

"That's a shame about your truck." Lane held out his Zippo. "Maybe later we can get down there, have a look, get your stuff out. You gotta be careful on these roads."

"I'm just happy she got me here. This is where I needed to be."

"You run into some trouble back there in Ohio?"

"No." Johnson shook his head. He stared through the windshield before him, trying not to look at his finger, trying not to think. His brain pressed against his skull, and he put his fingers in his ears for fear it would seep out. "Just need to find Stanley real soon. What about you?"

"I'm taking it easy. They're starting building on the new dam soon. I'm going get a job there—the money's great. You oughta come and get a job with me at the dam, Johnson."

"I really want to try and find my friend at the fire service. It's kind of important."

"Well, not before we get you a drink, my friend. You almost met with the angels back there." They watched as lightning, silent, cracked over the mountains. "Besides, it might rain. Keep ourselves under cover until it passes, you know."

"Couldn't hurt." His feelings were fire in his pores, sweat on his skin, knots in his stomach. "I am feeling a little thirsty."

"Can get mighty hot in Helena, my friend." The Pint, a little roadside bar, came into view. "You'll have your work cut out for you at the Park Service."

"Why do you say that?"

"The land is dry grass in some of those gulches up there in the mountains, and it's damn hot in the summer—hundred degrees in the middle of the day. Lightning strikes, and the fire races right through them." Lane laughed, a raspy cough punctuating it. "You'll be praying for a job at the dams, then."

Johnson followed Lane into the green-paneled one-story building. Lane was taller than Johnson, lankier, with a relaxed gait about the hips, shoulders back. A man who never felt in trouble, Johnson figured. A man who was not apologetic about having a whiskey at eleven in the morning. Lane rolled the box of cigarettes into the

sleeve of his undershirt and swung the door open wide. In the darkness, Johnson could make out the outlines of men at the bar, and
when his eyes adjusted the lines of them deepened like carved rock,
the only soft things about them were the worn white undershirts or
plaid and the knees of their canvas pants.

"Well, if it ain't the good-time boys." One of the men said. He
held a shot glass in his fingers and the whiskey disappeared down
his throat with efficiency and ease.

"Coming from one to another." Lane slid onto the vacant seat
next to the man and patted the stool on the other side. "Sit down,
Johnson. What's your poison?"

"Whiskey," Johnson answered and nodded at the man. Over the
top of the bar, behind the counter, two timberjacks were mounted
in an X. Faded photos of lumberjacks, logging competitions, and
woods dotted the walls. A musty billiards table rested under the
dim halcyon of a hanging lamp, and some woman with a child-like
voice sang a slow and pretty country song on the jukebox.

"A midget." Lane nudged Johnson and pointed his head over to
the jukebox. "Can you believe it? Little Cindy, she calls herself."

Johnson ceded she sounded familiar. He'd probably heard her
on the radio on the miles from Ohio to Montana. He listened to the
radio or he sang out loud, out of tune, to crowd out the other songs
that cried like mythical sirens from just beyond his ears: the war,
his parents, Stanley, and Kate. He did not know whether second
chances existed, and if they did, whether he was deserving of one,
but he was alive, by chance or by design, and he did not want to
dwell on the choices he had made to this point. He was afraid that
he would choose to relive the past, to rearrange facts that had no
bearing on the present situation, a ghost walking across the foyer,

its ancillary object long disintegrated.

"This here is Johnson," Lane said to the leathered man to his right. "His truck rolled off MacDonald Pass this morning."

"No shit." The man laughed, moving empty shot glasses on the bar like a magician trying to hide a ball. "Your wife in it?"

Johnson took his own whiskey and set the rim of the glass to his lips. He drank before speaking. "You know Stanley Polensky at the Park service? I come to see him."

"Never seen him here. Probably a boy scout. All the rangers are, mostly. The only boys who'd touch a drop are the smokejumpers, and hell, I'd be drinking too if you were going push me outta plane into a forest fire." The man coughed, wet and phlegmy, wiping his bulbous nose and stubbled jowl with the back of his hand. "What, you looking into forestry work?"

"Maybe."

"This here is collateral central for the fires, ain't that right, Lane?"

"They have been known to round up the drunks here, give them a Pulaski axe, and tell 'em to cut fire lines." When Johnson's face didn't register, Lane waved his hand. "You know, dig ditches in front of the fire—contain 'em."

"I ought to go find Stanley right away, see about a job." Johnson stood up as Lane's hand pressed on his shoulder.

"I'll drive you over there, Johnson. It's only over in Nine Mile. Let's have a few drinks. Let's celebrate your good fortune. Who knows, maybe you'll want to take the summer off, like me, wait out the dam jobs. All right?"

"All right—just one more," Johnson agreed as Lane signaled for the bartender.

❀❀❀

The bar's occupants had multiplied steadily over the hours, and not because Johnson began to see two of everything. The sharp clack of billiard balls, laughter, smoke, bodies, and heat crowded into Johnson's back and in his brain, a sweet confecture, and he had not thought of Kate for a few hours, making him happy and disappointed at the same time.

He thought about his truck, a pulverized animal in a gulch of the Rocky Mountains. He tried to remember whether there was anything he needed in it—personal papers, a clean shirt, everything and nothing. He thought about his finger. If he could only find Stanley, straighten this out. Perhaps he'd find him today, tonight, and it would all be over. He stood up and went outside. The heat hit him like a train as it wafted up in waves from the road. The sky, so far away, seemed like blue glass, reflecting the heat back to the earth, cooking the drunken stew in his blood and his stomach. He leaned against the wall and closed his eyes. He wanted to go home, back to where everything made sense. He was not sure where that was.

When he opened his eyes, he saw the smoke, a small plume from the mountains, like a giant smoking a pipe. He heard the heavy clank of suspensions, the churn of engines as the trucks came down the road, trucks that bore the green and white shield of the Forest Service. Equipment rattled around in their beds, and instead of passing by the bar they slowed and pulled into the crowded parking lot.

"Get in." One of the rangers, a thin, wiry man who emerged from the first truck nodded at him. "We need all the warm bodies we can get."

He found Lane cradling his head on the bar and hooked him under the armpits, dragging him out onto the dusty gravel before climbing in a truck full of men with bulging eyes, lopsided grins. He looked around for Stanley, even though he would not be among these men, the flotsam and jetsam of Helena. The smell of burning wood and brush had reached the road, and the smoky plume had become a monstrous cloud. He felt the shift of gears in the truck, its wheels begin to roll, and they were on their way, drunks to a forest fire.

From the truck, they climbed into a boat that took them down the Missouri river. There were no roads; pine-studded cliffs rose hundreds of feet on either side of the river, as if the hand of God himself parted them. In pockets of lower elevation bobbed little docks for boats that ferried picnickers and sportsmen and rangers into a territory that had seen little taming since the days of Lewis and Clark. From the boat the cliffs grew, straight, long molars that had erupted from the ground.

They could feel the heat before they even got to the base of the gulch, where the fire burned. They could hear it along the road that wound around the base of the gulch. It snapped branches, sending random pops through the air, along with the crackle of drying, burning leaves. Johnson could feel the heat and the smoke line the bottom of his lungs, a velvet aftertaste of soot and carbon. They disbanded the trucks in single file and a man, tall and pocked-faced with a prominent nose and high forehead, stood before them. Johnson studied the quick efficiency with which the man moved, as if every second on earth were calibrated with the same urgency. The man studied them quickly as he assigned them their tools: Pulaski, two-person saw, shovel, water can. He assigned Johnson the Pulaski, a wooden shaft with an axe on one end of the head and a pick on the other. Johnson felt he must have appreciated his broad shoulders and back, certain that he could chop down small trees standing in the fire's path and break open the earth, parting the dirt into a chasm, a fire line, that the fire could not jump across, thirsty for more fuel.

"All right," the man, Mantee, spoke, and his voice was sharp, like metal, clipped. Johnson wondered whether he had been a corporal or a sergeant. "We've already dropped thirteen smokejumpers in to flank the fire and keep it on the south side of the gulch. You're to meet up and support them, building a fireline and clearing shrubbery. I'm your foreman; you listen to everything I say. At no time during a fire are you ever safe, so always keep yourself between the river and fire. You might need to escape to the river if the fire gets out of control."

The twelve men seemed to slouch collectively as he set them at rest, the saws and axes suddenly more burden than they could care to handle. The memory of ice-cold beer in frosted glasses back at the bar grabbed at their hearts like a first girlfriend. The heat swooned heavy over them, buckling their knees and soaking their brows, and they had not even broken camp yet.

"Okay, let's move." Mantee picked up an oversized water can with one hand, clutched a compass in the other. "Last report from the radio tower had the front of the fire about two miles from the river."

Johnson found himself next to last in line. Lane had made sure to get behind Johnson, giving him a wink and grin.

"What the hell happened to your hand, Johnson?" Lane pointed to his left hand, his smile wiped into a frown. Johnson expected to find it suddenly missing, mushroomed to the size of a sausage or covered in blood, oozing gangrene. The way it should have been.

Relief washed through him, warm like piss. But he held his finger up to the sky and found that nothing was wrong—the peach pit from earlier that morning had shrunk to its more regular shape of oversized marble, the color and texture of skin uniform with the rest of his hand. He squeezed and wriggled, felt no pain.

But Gustafson had seen it too, the malformed member before its renaissance of health. And Johnson knew, for the first time, that he was not crazy.

He could not think about it now. They walked through a thick growth of Ponderosa pine and Douglas fir, a tinderbox of needles that lashed at their faces. Above them, a blue china sky became milky with grey plumes. Ahead, a clearing beckoned; beyond, one could see the slurry orange lollipop of fire that tumbled slowly down the south side of the gulch like a slinky. As they got closer, Johnson could see that it moved in waves, dancing a little bit forward, backward, before making short sprints across fuel-heavy areas. Still, it kept under the tree crowns, away from the branches and leaves. They would start the fire line in the clearing, he heard Mantee say from the front of the line, men separated ten or twelve feet apart, digging trenches that would meet up at both ends. It was not much different than the war, he reckoned, except the enemy could grow exponentially and unexpectedly. And these men were not soldiers; they were drunks, slurry-smile good ol' boys and liars.

"Johnson," Lane said behind him, and Johnson glanced over his shoulder as Lane doubled over against a tree, the remains of his last three or four whiskeys watering the base. "Christ, the smoke's so thick."

"Come on." Johnson felt little earthquakes in his stomach as he straightened up Lane by the armpits. "Don't think about it."

Before them, the faint smoky shadow of the tree line seemed to go on forever, thicker and with a glimpse of an upward slope— perhaps the northern side of the gulch. They were on the far arc of the fire trench, working toward its middle. But already they could not see the men twelve feet in front of them; the smoke and the heat crackled as intimately as if they were in a closet. Johnson bent his knees low, trying to find the heavier, cooler air near the forest floor. Each time he swung the Pulaski behind his back and speared it into the ground, it was as if he was spearing himself and not the earth. Pain and nausea zig-zagged through him, and he could no longer see the trench he had begun. He thought he heard the voice of Mantee calling to the men.

"What is he saying?" He shouted to Lane, who rested on his knees behind him. He did not know whether it was fire or voices, the screaming white noise, but he knew his hands burned with such intensity he could see the flesh begin to redden. He nudged Lane, who fell to his side. A roar swept around them, like an eighteen-wheeler or a train bearing down on them, and Johnson turned to see if such a calamity was possible.

But it was the fire, the giant swell of burn that consumed the oxygen in ragged, hungry breaths through its insatiable mouth. The fire had moved upward into the crowns of trees maybe seventy-five yards away.

"Run!" He shouted to Lane, but he couldn't even hear himself, only knew that his mouth had formed the words, and to back them up, he grabbed Lane's arm and began to pull him through the growth and up the slope. They were a quiet breath machine, tongues leaving the caves of their mouths as they opened them wide to breathe the thin air, hot and filled with smoke. It burned at their lungs and stung their eyes; bright red and blue stars filled their vision and their legs seemed filled with cement.

The fire was twenty yards away, maybe less, and Johnson could feel the heat in waves at his back, his lungs gasping for the thinning air. He saw Lane drop beside him, his boots kicking stones and roots down the hill as he scrambled for footing on the ridge. They were thirty yards, maybe more, from the top of a ridge and would not make it. Johnson thought of his finger and had an idea. He pinned Lane to the slope with his body and tucked in his flailing limbs as the fire burned over them, a howl of flames and crackling wheatgrass and smoke and wave upon wave of searing air until it was quiet and they lay on the black slope, the ashes falling over them like snow.

"Jesus, are you okay?" Lane wriggled underneath Johnson, but Johnson could not answer. He rolled slightly to the side, feeling cold on his back and legs. He reached around and touched where his shirt, his belt, would be and felt oily, separated flesh, hard blades of rib. He looked down at his feet and saw the heels of his boots melted against ankles, his pants burned away or grafted into what remained of his skin. He opened his mouth to dislodge the sand-papery sack of his tongue from the roof of his mouth, and when he worked up enough precious saliva, he spoke.

"Are you all right?" he asked as Lane scooted away from him.

"Oh dammit, Johnson. Oh jeez. I'm okay." He patted an earlobe, singed, and brushed at some minor burns on his hands and legs. "Oh Christ, look at you."

"Give me some of your water." Johnson looked, reached for Lane's canteen, which had been buried under his stomach.

"Sure, buddy, sure." Lane made a face as he unscrewed the cap. His hands shook as he held out the canteen to him. "Where do you hurt?"

"I don't hurt anywhere," Johnson answered. He was euphoric, actually. "Just thirsty."

"Yeah, I imagine you wouldn't," Lane answered, and Johnson knew vaguely what he meant. He remembered when he was in the army and received treatment for a shrapnel burn, how one of the nurses had explained that sometimes burns can be so deep that the nerves are burned as well. Those patients, she added, usually died. "We need to get you out of here."

Johnson stood gingerly on the slope. He felt the bones of his heels touch the warm, soft carpet of soot that now covered the hill. The backs of his legs were a pastiche of exposed muscle and skin and strips of canvas, a white glow of bone at the heel. He touched the back of his head and felt only skull.

"Get help," Johnson said.

Lane moved up the slope, looking back at him, not with concern, but with sadness. Johnson would be dead when he returned, he thought, and Johnson figured he would be right. A vacuum of air and popping rocks, twigs surrounded him. No birds or wind. He thought he could hear the Missouri running downgulch of him, but it sounded so close at times he thought maybe it was the rushing in his ears. He felt asleep and awake at once, a dreamy happiness flooding his circuits along with the uninhibited endorphins and toxins. He strained to hear other men, a rescue party, cursed Lane for leaving him to die on purpose, even as he knew at some logical level that it would take hours for a team to get here, whether by boat down the gulch or helicopter. But he could not tell one minute, one hour from the rest. He stood on a hill, ashen and pocked with stumps, black stones, and he wondered whether he had time-traveled back to Germany, whether he was in Dresden.

Damned if he was going to stay here. He crawled slowly up the slope, trying to stay off his heels. He had gotten twenty feet before he realized he left the canteen behind. He kept moving upward, reasoning in some way that the river was closer, that there was more water in the river than in the canteen, and he could not waste any more time. He thought about Kate, in New York, and was saddened he would not be able to tell her of his demise, or even see Stanley, so close, somewhere in these woods.

At the top of the slope was a reef barrier, tall white saw rocks jutting out with little space between them. Johnson squeezed himself through a slit and saw the glint of the moonlit river below. If he could make it to the river, baptize himself in its cool embrace, he could fill his mouth and his reserve and he could make it. At the very least, he could quench the terrible thirst that scraped his throat and glued his eyelids together, that spasmed his stomach like a wrung-out dishcloth. He stood up, and in a minute of hysteria, thought he would run like hell, that he could feel no pain, and that it would be over fast.

He took a few large leaps before losing his balance on the impacted stones of the slope, and he rolled and bounced, airborne at times, down the hill and into the river with a rush. The water filled his back and legs with white-hot pain, and as he drank the dark water, it seemed to leave him as quickly as he drank it in. He vomited hot into the cold space around him. The basin of night was bare on the east side of the Missouri. A skeleton of trees scraped the cloudless sky. No owls or night creatures convened, as was their ritual, to discuss all matter of nocturnal importance. It could have been hell on earth, or it could have been actually hell. All he knew was everything was dead, and he was alone, too tired to get out of the water.

1938

She dreamed of violins, playful notes that leapt up and down the scale like mice. They became louder, louder still, and when she woke up, they were outside, a cacophony of horseshoes, bells, the crunch of wagon wheels. From the door of the bone house, she watched the gypsy caravan disassemble in the valley below, two squat rusted trailers on tall wagon wheels from which eight Romani emerged. Older women in scarves, the color of cinnamon and tough as jerky, strung a clothes line between two trees. A man, his beard dark like ink, squatted in front of smoking kindling. She was so mesmerized by the emerging makeshift village of the travelers, she did not see him loping up the hill on the right side until he stood in front of her, a barefooted boy, thin and dirty but clean with youth and curiosity.

He smiled at her and tapped his chest. "Ferki."

She smiled and tapped her chest. "Ela."

Ferki curled his fingers as if holding a spoon and ladled air to his mouth. He pointed toward the campfire, where some of the older women cut onions and forest mushrooms into a now-smoking pot. She followed him down to the campfire and sat to the side, waiting for the women to scowl and wave her away or look at her fearfully, giving her a generous serving of stew in the hopes she would leave them alone. Their eyes studied her in quick thrusts upward as they concentrated on peeling and cutting and feeding the fragrant broth that made her stomach claw against her sides in hunger. They asked Ferki questions in Romani about her. He shook his head and shrugged his shoulders, his mouth full of gaps from his baby teeth, half-filled with incisors that sprouted like glaciers anchoring his gums. No, he did not know whether she was a Pole or a Jew or Russian, whether she was an orphan or a witch. He only knew she was a girl, a girl he wanted to play with.

The women murmured among themselves. Finally, they looked at her and smiled, handing her an earthen bowl filled with stew.

"Te avel angla tute, kodo khabe tai kado pimo tai menge pe sastimaste," Ferki's grandmother, named Tsura, said. Her eyes, cloaked almonds, sat far in her face, as if she saw everything from a distance deep within her. *May this food be before you, and in your memory, and may it profit us in good health and in good spirit.*

❀❀❀

Ela had known gypsies before. They had come through once, many years ago when her matka was alive, trading herbs, tinctures, some fabrics which were now part of her bed quilt. In the years since, she'd seen their caravans from the hill of the bone house, small plodding dots heading northwesterly, toward the sea. But they had not come this close in a long time. She watched the women boil dandelion roots and elderberries and sage while the men loaded a smaller wagon with fabrics, jerkied meat, and jewelry to take to the village to hawk.

"Germans everywhere," Ferki explained to her in broken Polish when she asked him why they were heading east. "The Russians no better. Jekh dilo kerel but dile hai but dile keren dilimata."

One madman makes many madmen, and many madmen make madness. She had heard talk in the village when she went down to trade her tinctures—small things, mixtures for gout, for headaches, for fever—that she remembered her matka making. Talk about Germans invading, about people leaving. It was not anything to which she'd paid much attention. Poland had changed so many hands since she'd been alive, it was hard to keep track of the ruling parties, their petty laws and greed. She floated above them, a ghost, a menace, a shadow. She did not understand why they fought so long, so hard, even died for a land they would only have for a little while. The land always won in the end, slowly grinding their organs to rot, their bones to dust. And yet every generation thought they would conquer it for all eternity.

Except for her. Despite her best efforts, she remained to see the same mistakes over and over again.

"You come with us." Ferki kicked a ball made of old rags toward her. She moved it back and forth between her feet. He made a gun with his fingers and pretended to shoot her. "The Germans shoot Roma on side of road, in towns, in Serbia. Say we spread disease, are spies."

"I don't know," she answered in broken Romani. If she disappeared, the villagers would burn her house to the ground. The local priest would bless the earth. She would be a nomad. But they might kill the villagers, too. It was hard to know, these days, who would be called a witch and killed.

"The land is our home." Ferki spread his arms wide, as if to hug it. He smiled at her. He would be a beautiful man. She imagined the slight hook of his nose, his full, red lips, the fold and curls of his earlobes and the gentle slope of his hair over his head, the way its chestnut curls licked his ears and the back of his neck. She imagined clinging to his body, the itch of his chest hairs and groin as they rubbed against her, the pulse of his gorged member, but this would not happen. She may see him become a man, she may see him to the grave, but she would always be a girl, and the earth would not break her.

He walked toward her, his arms still wide, and then he drew them around her. Had Antoniusz been the last man, the last person, to hug her? Ferki smelled like curry and sweat and dirt. She ran her hands along the smooth cliffs of his neck, pressed her cheek against his before grabbing the cloth ball and kicking it as far as she could. She watched as he ran, light, wiry, after it, the soles of his dirty feet catching the sun. She could not be broken, but if she was not careful, he would melt her.

Ferki and Tsura followed her to the clearing where she had found the burnette saxifrage. She pointed at the sky and then the earth as Ferki explained to his grandmother, adding "cccrrracckkkk!" and waving his arms for theatrical flourish. Tsura touched the earth, no longer black, covered with a century of blown dirt and seeds, and began to dig. She motioned for them to help her, and they knelt in a circle, raking their fingers over the earth, the hole around them becoming bigger and bigger, layers of sediment and clay exposed until they happened upon a small area of white ash, several feet in, no more than a handful. Ferki's grandmother scooped it into her palm and dropped into a leather pouch tied to her waist.

Back at the bone house, Tsura gave Ela a knife, sharp with dull rubies on the handle. Ela held it against the creamy white of her inner forearm and pressed, the dark blood bubbling to the surface like lava. Tsura bottled the blood in a flask and pressed a cloth over the cut and then dressed it with a spiderweb that had been seeped in black wort.

"We wait." Tsura nodded at Ela's dressed arm. "To see this healing."

"We won't wait long," Ela answered.

In the bone house, Ela sat every morning and made a cut on her arm, from which Tsura could collect a sample. Then they ground and pestled the dried herbs and mixed them with the white ash. Ferki brought in the rats and frogs, which they cut and applied the paste to and waited. All the animals died.

"Sometimes the Gods' powers are one time." Tsura searched for words. "I chirikleski kul chi perel duvar pe yek. *The droppings of the flying bird never fall twice on the same spot.* Then they cannot be taken advantage of, and so they are also properly revered."

"My grandmother means, if everybody can live forever, what is the use of it?" Ferti added, lying back on Ela's bed.

"But if no one can, it is of no use, and if one person can, it is a curse," Ela answered. They looked at her in confusion, and she frowned. "Curse!" She said louder. She put her hands to her neck as if to choke herself and then pointed to the sky.

"No... you stay now. I want you stay. We will help you." He rested his hand on her shoulder and smiled, his hodgepodge of teeth filling his face. She imagined his face growing around his teeth, his eyes burrowing deep into his face, his eyebrows covering them. His muscles growing, stretching his skin, and then the reverse when his muscles sunk like Tsura's, hung from the bone. Skin slipped from her cheeks like curtains as if something inside her had been used, reused, finally abandoned.

"Everyone has gift that is only theirs," Tsura shook Ela's chin in her hands. "Some can be seen more than others, that is all."

The men came back one afternoon with their wagon and motioned for the women to help pack the trailers. From their tight faces dripped worry that seeped into the camp. Were the Germans already here? According to the talk the men had picked up in town, their territory had been expanding further and further east, and the Russians further west. For months there were rumors of the Nazis taking the Jews and the gypsies to camps, an invasion of Poland. It was already hard enough to trade in the towns, Ferki told her, given the natural, centuries-long distrust of the gypsies, but the German would put them into *Zigeunerlager*, or work camps, or they might kill them on the spot. The Russians would send them to Serbia. Ela watched from the door of the bone house as Ferki carried bales of blankets on his young back, the bead of sweat that formed on the top of his lip. She wanted to hold his head close to her chest and kiss his brow.

"I am worried for your safety," Ela said to Tsura as she helped to pestle some of the burnette saxifrage.

"Es okay. We survive a long time. But you will show us how to survive longer."

Tsura stood close, rubbing her hand. She put her finger in the bowl and held up a finger covered with grains. She poured the remains of the bowl into her pouch. With the ashes, it would be all they had to work with during their trip, wherever it was they were going. Heated words between the men, Ferki's father and another, floated into the doorway. Whatever they decided, there would be no time.

Ela looked around the bone house. It had always protected her, she thought as she grabbed Antoniusz's wooden horse and brought it to her chest. But perhaps she had been the one who protected it. She wrapped it into the multicolored quilt and tied the ends and then sat on the bed.

"Hurry," Tsura called from the door and hurried outside. Ela listened to Ferki call her name. She dug her feet into the earth and closed her eyes. If she left her mother's house, she could never get back to her. She was sure of it.

"Ela!" Ferki's voice was closer, just outside the house. She imagined the silk of her mother's hair as it tumbled down her back, the touch of Matka's hand on her shoulder, caressing it.

Then it nudged her *go, go.* When she moved to the door, Ferki was already there, waiting. He grabbed her by the arm and they ran toward the trailer.

They rode at night, traveling narrow cattle trails through the open fields, far from the little jumbles of villages scattered like campfires across the countryside, relying on the moon to reveal an intruder. They slept during the day deep in the forests, one eye open. They learned to tell the sound of a branch broken by a human foot from one made by a goat or mountain lion. There were uncooked potatoes to eat and cold pottage, a wheat stew. It took its toll on the younger Romani through temper, dark eyes, dry coughs, runny bowels. Tsura became sick. She lay in the back of the trailer under a pile of blankets with Ferki and Ela while Ferki's parents sat outside in the front, where they had affixed a wooden bench to corral and guide the horse. Ela fed Tsura the mint and sage and burnette saxifrage she had ground into a tea, but her tinctures left Tsura almost as quickly as they entered her, and if they made a complete crossing of Tsura's stomach, they exploded as hot, sour liquids from her as she shat out the trailer door, Ferki holding the rest of her inside by her arms.

"My spirit has been taken," she murmured, eyes closed, a sunken pillar in a pile of cloth, the reservoirs to her wisdom sealed forever. "Leave me behind."

"Never." Ferki dabbed her face with a cloth, damp from the bucket of water that needed to last them all. For how long, no one knew. The forest they were traveling through was unfamiliar; they had encountered no brooks or rivers. No one wanted to think about what might happen next, but they each had taken pains to urinate into something that was theirs alone, a cup, a flask, a bowl, and guarding the precious liquid against the bumps and twists that the wagon wheels found on the forest floor as if cradling a zygote in their womb.

"Do not waste the water on me." Tsura tried to sit up. "If I stay, you will go faster."

"If you leave, we all will die." He kissed her cheek. "As your soul goes, as do ours."

A meeting was held. The trailers would separate so they could travel faster, smaller, like coyotes and not dogs. Ela went with Ferki and Tsura and Ferki's parents. They rolled onward in separate directions, their wooden wheels splitting stones and cracking branches, but still maddeningly slow. The horses spooked easily, and they stopped many times as Ferki's father spoke softly to them, rubbing their necks. They could cover so much more ground on foot, Ela knew, but Ferki would not leave his grandmother, so she did not ask.

They took turns, Ferki's father and Ela sleeping, then Ferki and his mother. With an eye open, they listened for the sound of the Nazis in the distance. They were arrogant, it was known, shouting and laughing in German, never needing the element of surprise because of their brute force.

At least, Ela listened. Ferki's father slept like death, silent and unmoving until the trailer stopped and everyone changed their positions, nibbled at the hardened biscuits and potatoes full of eyes and roots that lay like small islands at the bottom of growing sacks. When it was their turn to sleep, Ela lay awake, the dream world and the real world before her, holding hands, courting. She missed her time with Ferki; she longed to press her face into his neck, to be comforted by his smells as Tsuri's began their own slow and inevitable leeching into the trailer, sweat and rot and bowels that festered in every corner. Sometimes he would tap on the roof of the trailer, softly, from where he sat on the bench to let her know he was there, that he was thinking of her. That he would not forget her.

The trailer ground to a halt, throwing Ela forward, out of her half sleep. She shook Ferki's father as he swatted at her with his hand.

"*Jal avree.* Go away." He frowned and furrowed his brow. "Another minute."

"We're stuck." Ela pulled at his ankle until he sat up. Outside, the horizon glowed orange, revealing the last few glimmers of the world. The trees huddled before them in dark shadows. They seemed to sway closer and then farther from them. Ferki's father stumbled out of the trailer, kicking his legs as he struggled not to fall in the mud.

"Come." Ferki took her hand and they felt their way in the darkness, gathering branches, pressing them to their chests until they began to drop them. If they did not work quickly, they would lose time, the cover of night, to put distance between the rumbling trucks, the searchlights that sometimes swept through the trees ahead and behind them. Ferki and his father threw the branches they collected and leaves into the mud by the wheels as Ferki's mother fed the horses the last few bits of straw. Ela walked the perimeter of the trailer, looking for berries and other edibles, medicinal plants for Tsura, when she saw Tsura staggering away from the back door of the trailer.

"Don't mind me." Tsura smiled at her. "I have to go the bathroom. And then I will fly like a bird to the clouds, tweet, tweet, tweet."

"May I be of help?" Ela looked toward the trailer, which rocked back and forth, the wheels trying to catch the dry material.

"No, no. The fresh night air." Tsura said over her shoulder as she teetered, holding her skirts. "Already I feel better. Like the snakes in my ears."

It was only natural she would become delirious from her continued loss of fluids. Ela took her own skirt full of berries and jasmine flowers back to the trailer and opened the wooden jewelry box that Tsura used to separate and store her herbs. Perhaps she could ground some more psyllium and mint together, making a fibrous concoction to better bind Tsura's stools. But when she opened the door on the right, one of the wooden slots, the one where Tsura kept her belladonna root, was empty. Ela left her berries in a pile and ran out of the trailer.

"Ferki!" she shouted as she ran in the direction that Tsura had taken into the woods. She had not gotten far when she saw her, slumped under an oak, face flushed, her chin pressed into her neck.

"Puri daj! *Grandmother!*" Ferki had overtaken Ela and lifted Tsura's head in his hands.

"She ate the belladonna," Ela explained, opening Tsura's eyes, moving her head back and forth. Her eyes did not track; they locked on Ela's shoulder. "Wake! Wake up! When did you take the belladonna?"

"I saw her going through them this morning." Ferki looked at her Ela, his eyes rimmed wet, his bottom lip loose, exposing his lower teeth. "The herbs. She said she was getting some mint to chew on."

"We need mustard and salt." Ela put her fingers in Tsuri's mouth. "To make her bring it up. If it's not too late."

"You have to save her." Ferki grabbed her arm and pressed his knife across the soft underside of her arm. He pulled it across and it sank, without resistance, into her skin. A sea of red spilled over the edges of the cut as Ferki pressed her arm to Tsuri's lips. "Drink, Puri daj. Drink."

In the distance, they heard an engine. It was not good if they were near a road. But if they were near a road, perhaps they were close to water, to help.

"Javen daj! *Come here!*" His mother called after them. "We get the trailer under cover."

Ela could feel Tsura's breath, light and quick on her arm, begin to slow. She pressed her arm closer to her, even knowing that her blood had never saved anyone. It smeared across Tsura's face, making her look like one of the clowns that sometimes came through with the circuses. Ela tried to wipe it with her the top of her hand.

"Javen daj! We must go," Ferki's mother called. "I do not say again! Akana mukav tut le Devlesa." *I now leave you to God.*

"Go." Ela looked at Ferki. "I will stay with her."

"Never."

"It is too late for her. *I* will be safe—you know that."

"Tsura." Ferki cupped her chin and pressed his ear against her mouth. When he pulled away, sucking in his breath, her lips had left a blood kiss where his ear met his cheek.

"Akana mukav tut le Devlesa!" Ferki's father appeared at the head of the woods. He beckoned to them.

"Javen daj's dead!" Ferki yelled.

"They are coming!" His father waved them toward the truck. The engine was louder. Clipped German bit at the air. His hand froze in mid-air as they heard Ferki's mother scream, voices they did not recognize mingled with it. His father began to wave them in the other direction. "Go! Go! Run!"

Ferki stared dumbly at his father as he hurried back toward the trailer. Ela grabbed his arm and pulled him the other way into the forest, his feet stumbling in the roots, kicking up leaves, his breath choked wet with tears, until something settled in him, the force of life, and he began to pull her, faster and faster until they were gone from where they were, no idea where they were going.

❁ ❁ ❁

During the day, they slept in the trees. Ferki tied one of each of their ankles to the branch on which they lay with the torn-off arms of his shirt so they would not plunge to the ground. They hugged the thick branches with their bodies, and as they fell asleep, their grips would loosen, awakening them. But they were safe. By day, they searched for a stream, a pond, a stagnant circle of water, to wash off the blood and grime. They had heard the dogs, some days as soft as whispers, other days just over a hill, down in a valley. It was possible that they knew Ela's scent, that they had found Tsura and smelled it on her. That they were gaining.

"You go on." Ela stopped walking. The woods spread around them like a maze. Every tree the same, a sliver of moon through a canopy of leaves to guide them. "I will be decoy, you get?"

"No." He grabbed her arm and jerked her along. Branches whipped at her face. "We go together."

"They smell me." She stopped again. "You are free."

"My heart is chained to you." He cupped her face in his hands. "I have no family but you. If I do not have you, I have nothing. And I may as well be dead."

They went on. They sucked the juice from berries and chewed leaves. Their stomachs, empty, knotted like vines as they moved past seemingly the same trees, the same ruts and indentations in the earth. At night, they again shimmied up the thickest trees, the oaks, and tied themselves to the branches. At night, they wondered whether they would die before they were found. They wondered, sometimes, if they wished the opposite.

"We will get married when this is over." Ferki still talked of the future. He nudged her when she could not walk further, massaged her stomach when she was doubled over with the cramps of hunger, saved berries in his pockets and pressed them into her mouth when her mouth was so dry she could no longer speak, when her throat cracked and she coughed, the violence of her convulsions vibrating through the forest for anyone to hear.

"It will be a great honor," she answered. "To be your wife." They did not speak of her curse, even as his clothes, aside from being torn and stained from the forest, had begun to tear at the seams of his calves, his shoulders, as he grew, and she did not. His voice, a soft melodic stream, at times fell into a cave, deep and sharp, before it fell into a stream.

"I wish we had the herbs." She picked at plants, unfamiliar, familiar, and ground them between her fingers, smelled them. "We could find a way to protect you."

"It is my job to protect you," he answered, drawing a strand of hair behind her ear.

"I pray to my mother—she will tell me what to do." She did not tell him she had prayed to her mother most nights, with no reply. But perhaps she was far, far away, and it would take a long time for her prayers to reach her.

"Your mother tells you to stay with me—we'll be okay." He bent over and rubbed his foot. He had torn it shimmying down a tree trunk a few nights before, the cut since muddied with dirt. She had rubbed the husks of the walnuts they ate to dress it, but they were not eating enough to heal, for the healing powers of the herbs to work with their bodies. Now, a thin veil of pus leeched from the cut. "When this is over, we will figure out something. We'll never be apart—you have my promise.

They came upon a Bartok, a wide, stout oak with low, thick branches the size of other tree's trunks.

"This is good sign." Ferki smiled at her in pink dawn light. The forest began to rouse with bird songs, the travel of squirrels and foxes. "We shall get good rest in God's arms."

She climbed up the tree, and he followed.

"The branches—too wide for tying." Ela frowned.

"We not need—we sleep at base of branch, next to trunk." He leaned against the trunk and motioned her to him. She backed herself into him, and he wrapped his arms around her. "I can feel something—people, water. They will not turn away children. We will be safe for a little bit, maybe."

"Kocham cie," she whispered to Ferki in Polish. *I love you.*

"Te iubesc," he answered in Romani. She turned her head, and his lips caught hers. She held them with hers, hoping she would fall asleep like this.

"Sleep." He pushed her head on his shoulder. "I join soon."

She dreamed of a barn, a few strands of dung-sticky hay to sleep on, a fingerful of cold water to whet her mouth. She did not dare dream of a bed, food, warmth. She dreamed of her matka in heaven, wondered how she would get to her, see her again. She did not fear death, even as her life force propelled her from it. If it caught up to her, somehow, she would welcome it like an old friend.

She dreamed of dogs, German shepherds, with hair sticking off their neck like spikes, their hackles striped down their back, teeth white against their black muzzles. They barked from below the tree, circling, and she was glad she was only dreaming.

Ferki shook her. The dogs did not disappear. They circled the base of the Bartok, changing positions with fluidness, like water slipping around river stones, a devil's dance, baring their teeth and calling to them in growls and barks. Four soldiers in uniform, Nazis, joined them, with harnesses and whips relaxed in their hands, gloved with leather. The smoke from their cigarettes swirled up into the trees as they laughed. She picked up bits of their German as she straightened herself on the branch.

"Look, it is Hansel and Gretel in the tree." One of them slapped his thigh. His eyes were brilliant blue, like the sky. She did not think a man so evil deserved such beautiful eyes, or his squared, dimpled chin.

"You are false gods," she spat at them in Polish. "You are beneath dirt."

"Oh, no, no—not Hansel and Gretel." Another ribbed him, ignoring her. "They are a rare species—Juden birds."

They all laughed harder, bending over, as the dogs circled the tree again and again, hairy sharks, their barks searing her spine.

"Kocham cie." Ela kissed Ferki's cheek and steadied herself to standing. "When I jump into dogs, you jump the other way and run."

"No." He grabbed her arm, tried to pull her back to him. She opened her mouth and bit him as hard as she could on the forearm. When he left go, his mouth opened wide in pain, she leapt from the tree and tackled two of the dogs, pulling at their necks and gouging their eyes as they sank their jaws into her legs as if they were mere twigs. Their teeth tore into her muscles, and even though she could not die, she could feel pain. It covered her in a cold sweat and burned her like fire.

"Oh, dear—the Juden bird cannot fly." One of the soldiers aimed his luger at her. Suddenly Ferki fell from the tree on top of him, wrestling for the gun. The dogs crowded over her, biting her cheeks. The blood ran over her lips, her eyes. One emerged with her nose in his teeth. She heard the scuffle of boots on the forest floor, and then a single shot. But she was too weak, the crush of hairy bodies on her, to see who had won. She imagined this was what dying felt like. She closed her eyes tight, as blood filled her throat and trickled into her lungs. She hoped the dogs would tear her to bits and eat her to nothing. She hoped, when she and Ferki would meet again, it would be in heaven. She hoped, as she closed her eyes, that she would finally see the earth for the last time.

1960

They were somewhere between Nevada and Kansas, stuffed in a station wagon with a bunch of pickers, Dwayne Zukes and Bobby Hill and Terry Mann, when Heidi was born. Two hundred miles, an inch on Dwayne's roadmap, a thousand in the prairie dark, snaked from the piston-powered engine of their wagon to the gig in Kansas City. If only the road, if only the road was all, but now, sometime after midnight, the snow began to fall like an act of malice, swirling and bleaching the night with salt. Stanley stopped the car and the pickers slid out of the backseat, checking some of the equipment that they had tied to the hood.

"The baby's coming now, honey, snow or not." Cindy lifted her legs and pressed them against the dashboard, so short there was barely a bend in her knee. Her naked toes grew blue as her face began to color and contort in rhythm with the mysterious will of God contracting and moving within her, the same mysterious will that planted seed in Cindy's 41-year-old womb.

Of course it was not his. He knew it because of the way Cindy sat on Dwayne's lap at the bars, snuggling against his head. How they'd disappear for hours in the pickers' hotel room to work on music, how, certain nights, Cindy would come in and straddle him, demand they have sex, as if to cover her bets. He did not know what to do except sit in the bar and nurse whiskey and accept that he had failed as a man but was pretty good at being a roadie, driving the car on the two-lane highways while everyone slept, dragging amps and putting together drum kits on stage.

And now he was going to be a father, at least in name. It had been hours since he'd spoken to Cindy, after she agreed to the gig in Kansas City at the last minute, on their way home from Reno, when they should have been headed straight for the nearest hospital. When he put his foot down, and she threatened to leave him there at the shack its owners had billed as a casino and club, the New Texas Lounge. By its looks, he wasn't sure what was so new about it.

He put out his cigarette and turned toward her. The new had already gotten old, the dates that their manager arranged haphazardly for them across the country, as if he were shooting rubber bands while spinning in a circle. The sleeping in the car, the show promoters skimming money off their ticket sales, the pickers—great guitar players but lousy men—the jeering, the leering drunks in the audiences who called Cindy names, sometimes threw bottles. It would have been enough for Stanley. But for every breakfast of coffee and toast, every lost shoe and blown tire, every boo, there was applause, encouragement, people who bought their single and fawned over Cindy. And that was enough for Cindy to stand the rest of it.

And now there was the child. He leaned over her and held out his hands as Cindy's face went red and purple and white and then went again like Christmas lights. He patted the claw of her fist that had begun to separate the vinyl fabric of the front seat from the stuffing. He tore off his jacket, an old shearling rancher's coat, and held it between her legs, ready to cloak the pink nub of hairy eraser,

Calvin or Heidi, that had appeared and bring its little plum-sized heart next to his, and Cindy's hair, long and blonde, caught her lips as she groaned and pushed once, twice, three times, and the slippery girl wormed out into the cocoon of Stanley's coat, Heidi.

Heidi. Her breath made a little cloud above her face, so honey dark in color, before Stanley pressed her against his chest, wrapped the cord around his index finger and nicked it free with his pocket knife. Cindy wiped herself with the quilt, the quilt they slept under, would have to sleep under whenever they slept next.

"Jesus H. Christ. Look at that." Dwayne, whose Indian skin glistened with the same syrup color as the baby's, shook the snow off his shoulders and climbed into the back seat. If he had any thoughts about his new fatherhood, they came second after his guitars, strapped to the hood. "Two miracles tonight—my Gibson's okay, and a baby."

"Can we make it to town?" Stanley felt sleepy, the warm bean on his chest beginning to stir and cry for food, shelter. His baby. He cupped the caramel head with his pink hand, felt the wet of her dark hair against his palm. Dwayne's baby. He handed her to Cindy and revved the engine.

"It's as white as a sheet out there. But I don't see what other choice we got." Dwayne said as Terry and Bobby piled in, bringing with them the snow and the cold.

"Close the doors. I gotta feed her." Cindy unbuttoned her blouse, the rawness of birth now hidden under the blanket. She brought the baby to her breast as if she were brushing her teeth.

They rode in silence, inches, white, creeping. The sound of snow crunching under tires, pickers breathing, baby suckling. The white erased them from everything in the world, everything from them.

They were quiet in its vortex, except for Heidi, who had screamed as if they all owed her something.

❀❀❀

Cindy was awake. She was awake when on stage, signing photos, and doing interviews at the radio stations. She was asleep in the car, in the hotel room, feeding Heidi, and whenever Stanley wanted to kiss her and maybe more.

She was awake now because of the call. She called Eddie every few days to check in, and after today's call, lipstick containers and fake pearls and hairbrushes rattled and rolled across the vanity until Stanley lifted his head from the pillow.

"What?" He was up with Heidi until just a few hours ago, hours that felt like minutes. "You'll wake the baby."

"Oh my dear Lord, Stanley, 'Forever in My Arms' is number 1 on the Billboard!" Cindy half-skipped, half-danced over to him. "On my mother's grave, baby. This is not a joke."

"That's great." He turned over, his face in the hotel room pillow, sour and lumpy like a kindergarten bean bag. Good things for Cindy seemed to mean trouble for him. They had not been home in five months, even with a newborn baby.

"You know what this means honey?" She stood by the bed, stroking his hair. "It means we're gonna be on the Opry! Wendell told me, once we hit the top 5, we were going to get a call. He was promised. Oh, Stanley, they do love me!"

"Even if they didn't, baby, I would still love you." He sat up in the bed, rubbing his temples. He had stopped drinking on the road but still felt like shit. Hours and hours of padding around the hotel room, the hallway, backstage, coaxing Heidi to sleep. Colic, the doctor back in Nashville had said. Babies need to be home. They need stability, regular feedings. Not the road.

Just one more gig. Cindy had said it again and again. So they don't forget us. I'll be a mother forever, but I'm only a star now. So Stanley padded back and forth in his socks while Heidi cried. I won't be a baby forever, she seemed to say. But Stanley would always be her father. Even if he wasn't. He cradled her head and sang to her, the little golden stranger with yellow-green eyes and caramel hair, and walked in circles until she was heavier than the forty pounds he'd dragged on his back through Europe, heavier than bodies he dragged into shallow ditches and unused foxholes. Heavier than Johnson in that space where his heart used to be. Then she would smile and coo, staring at Stanley with love, her eyes like little drops, little shards, of Dwayne's.

"I know you love me, baby." Cindy crawled on the bed. "But it's good to know other people do, too." Her hair, still in various stages of primping from last night's show, framed half of her face, the other side matted where it lay on the pillow. She looked like some sort of mythic creature, a temptress turned siren. She smiled at him and he touched her face, a face he did not recognize some nights, behind the stage lights and the lipstick and rouge. A little woman propped on a stool in the front of the pickers so the audience could see her, a little woman with a big voice. Perhaps, he had never known her. Perhaps, he was one rung of the ladder on which she was climbing her way to adulation, to acceptance. A hunger for approval, for love, that seemed insatiable. A love Stanley had thought, foolishly, he could provide solely. And her love for him? On stage, she was everyone's savior, dressing their wounds with her voice, her eyes.

"If one person loves you, that should be enough." He took her hands and squeezed them, smelled the woman of her. He pushed her back on the bed, released her hands. He felt himself push against his pants as he straddled her. "You don't need anybody after that."

"Baby, not now." She wriggled underneath him. "I have to call Wendell back. We've got a lot of free dates next week. There's got to be a barn dance or radio show we can do while we wait to hear from the Opry. I bet they'll give us a spot on the Louisiana Hayride after that show we did on KWKH."

He leaned over her, his strength quelling her struggle, as he loosed his drawers. Heidi began to cry in the crib, a little cry that cracked his spine upright, sending pressure to his head, a headache. He gathered her and brought her to Cindy, who took her to her breast.

"Think we got a little country star on our hands, baby?" She stroked Heidi's head. "Momma's baby. Maybe we can get mother-daughter act going, when the time's right."

"Isn't one selfish little country star enough?" He grabbed his shirt and his boots, his erection sinking. "I'm leaving."

"Where are you going to go, Stanley?" She laughed at him, laughed at him like he was nothing, the baby sucking at her breast. "Home and drink yourself to death?"

"I'm going to Ohio. There are things I have to do."

"Oh, that's right, your little dead soldier friend." She pulled Heidi from her breast and placed her in the bassinet. "I wonder who you really are in love with, Stanley. It would make much more sense, wouldn't it?"

"You have to burp her." Stanley dove toward the bassinet and cradled Heidi on his shoulder as she cried, then burped. "We know who you're really in love with, and it ain't me or this baby."

"Go to Ohio or wherever, you goddamn pansy." Cindy lit a cigarette and picked up the hotel phone. She reached into her purse and pulled out two one-hundred dollar bills and they fluttered toward him, birds with broken wings. "Just get out. I'm going to the Grand Ole Opry."

He went to the bus station to purchase his ticket for Bowling Green, Ohio. But as he waited on the bench, smoking cigarettes, he thought of Heidi's eyes, her sprout of hair, her little hands that had begun to memorize the contours of his face, hands that grasped frantically until she felt him, his shirt or his forefinger, his earlobe. Her weight pulsed in the muscle memory of his arms and chest. He felt tears in his eyes, her place in the foxhole in his heart right next to Johnson.

He went back to the hotel. Cindy looked up at him quizzically from the phone. She did not stop him as he packed Heidi's bassinet and her bag and put her in the stroller. At the station, he traded in his ticket to Bowling Green and bought two bus tickets to Maryland. As he watched the fields of wheat and corn and barns and water towers and bus exhaust accumulate between him and Cindy, he thought of what he would do to Heidi's room at home. A bunny painted on the wall, a crib. A doll. He could read her books, Tom Swift and the Hardy Boys and Nancy Drew. He could find the child who abandoned him when he left for war. He did not have much to give her, except for his undivided love and attention. He figured it was a good start.

1970

He awoke in the womb, water pushing into his lungs and eyes, dark and soundless. But he was a man and the womb a lake, its enormity both alienating and suffocating. He flapped his arms to drive himself up to the disk of pale light that rested on its ceiling, where the black gradually dissipated into layers of hazel and green. But he could not move, his foot prisoner to something in the cloudy blackness below. He groped around his ankle and felt a rock, its slimy ridges resisting his grip. There was no need to panic, no matter how hard his lungs screamed, the crescendo of synapses in his primitive brain that warned him of danger, of possible death. No, he had been awoken once, awoken again. Now he was alive again, and he'd chew his fucking foot off if he had to.

He hugged the sharp boulder and tried to loosen his foot, but he could not straighten it flat enough to wriggle it free from this narrow crevice. He wondered whether he even had a foot when he descended, a gelatinous mound of burned flesh, whether it had grown back and now was trapped in the place that had welcomed, anchored him, until he was ready to be born again. He strained, tried to push the rock from its location. His lungs burned, screaming for air, his eyes full of fireworks. He wondered if he'd pass out and wake up again, unable to dislodge himself, stuck in a Sisyphean nightmare.

He held onto the rock and twisted his leg as far to the right as he could, until he could feel the muscles and tendons straining, a pop, and then a warming, increasing pain as the space in his broken ankle filled with blood and produced a clot and fibroblasts to mend the space. He could feel the heat coming off his body, the accelerated steam engine of his healing. He yanked his foot, a broken hinge, out of the space before it had time to mend and floated up to the surface.

The sun burned his eyes, and he squinted as he paddled toward the shore. The lip of land greeted him with sharp teeth, the rocks tearing into his soft, milky blue skin, as he washed up against them, and blood seeped out of his hands and arms like a surprise. The pain came first, a bloated ache through his body, as he gasped for air, air, to fill every spider branch of his lungs, every tendon and muscle, for air to inflate his heart and arteries, to move the dark sludge of his blood. The smell came next, a sweet, bloody sour eggy steak. His smell. He closed his mouth as a spasm of air and gastric juices made its way from his stomach to his throat and pressed his face into the pebbled shoreline.

A rifle clicked overhead. He strained upward to the blur of body before him, the limp pale blonde hair, an ear. A woman. As his eyes adjusted to the light, the blur of her became older. Calm, flat lines weighed her lips and eyes; lines like tree branches grew from between her eyebrows and across her forehead. The weight of her cheeks set her mouth into a frown. She was not an angel, he figured, but she was his saint.

"Don't move." She leveled the barrel at his head. "Do you speak English?"

"Yes." He made to stand but his skin was soft, wrinkled, on his feet, like a little baby man, his legs puffy. He wondered whether his bones had molted. He flopped in the pebbled bed. He must have looked like a seal man, an alien, the living dead at best. But she did not frighten, did not flinch.

"Where'd you come from?" She steadied the rifle.

"Ohio." He held up his arms, the skin thin and sagging on the undersides. "Please. I'm not going to hurt you. If you could help me up—"

"Ohio? You're from Ohio?" She leaned toward him, studying his face, his seal skin. Her eyes narrowed then widened. Her jaw dropped. She stepped back. "Oh my goodness, you're a man."

❊❊❊

From where he lay on his stomach: soft cedar wood walls, a quilt on a hand-carved rocker. A cabin. She had carried him here on her back, feet forward, and he'd watched the river bob farther and farther away, a narrow path growing behind them as they moved steadily upward. From the bed, he watched as she heated water on a stove on the other side of the room.

"I'm awake now," he called. He didn't want to scare her. He counted two rifles, a hunting knife, in his limited sweep of her quarters. It was one room, maybe fifteen by twenty feet, a basic stove and ice box wedged into the corner opposite the bed on which he sat, the only bed. A table with a red gingham tablecloth was pushed against the wall at the other end. A glass vase with some fresh wildflowers seemed the only decorative touch. Two windows on the front side of the cabin supplied light. The front door opened onto a screened porch half the size of the cabin.

She turned and placed a cup of tea on the floor near where his right arm dangled. "You can sip at that if you want—there's some chamomile petals in it."

"Who are you?" He lifted his head and shoulders and steadied the cup to his lips. It was heavier than he expected, or perhaps he was weaker. His skin still rippled loose from his muscles, as if the glue of his body had evaporated.

"My name's Margaret, but people call me Maggie." She came to him and slid her hands under his armpits, turning him rightward and upward as his legs dangled off the mattress. An ice bag was tied with a kerchief to his broken right ankle, with a makeshift splint from a split log. She stood before him in men's dungarees, the sides unbuttoned to allow the spread of her hips, and a denim shirt with the sleeves rolled up. Her skin, clear and brown, glistened from the heat. A looker when she was young, and a looker still if she had cared about those kinds of things.

"I'm Johnson."

"Johnson, huh? I've been calling you a lucky son of a bitch ever since I found you washed up off the lake." She straightened the sheet around his shoulders as he sipped at the tepid liquid in the cup.

"There was a fire." He set the mug down between his legs, conserving his strength. "Down at the gulch. Burned like a monster."

"What fire?"

"The one in the big gulch—you know where that is?"

"I know it where it is—everybody in a hundred miles knows it." She walked across the cabin, turned to look at him. "But there hasn't been a fire there since '47."

❀❀❀

She patted his back as he vomited over and over into a tin bowl. He vomited so much he didn't think he could vomit any more of himself. When he was done, he sat shivering in the blanket as she heated up some broth and potatoes. But he still could not believe it, that he had been in the lake for 23 years. The situation in Germany was hard enough to accept. This hardly seemed possible.

"I apologize." He wished he hadn't awoken, only to be this sick. "I don't mean to take up your bed."

"It's all right." She said from the sink. "I don't sleep very well, anyway. This soup needs to cook a little longer. It's not much, but you can't take much right now."

"Tea's okay." He motioned to the mug with his head. "I bet I was quite a sight, huh?"

"That don't even begin to describe it." She sat on the rocker by the bed and began to chew on a piece of jerky. "I've been wondering all kinds of things while you've been sleeping, about you washing up here, about the fire, about your family. About whether I'm really talking to a human being or... something else."

"Something happened to me back during the war," he explained. "In Germany. And I haven't been right since. It's driving me crazy— it's like... I can't get injured. Apparently I can't die. Have you ever heard of such a damn thing? Who the hell would want such a thing?"

"The government." She leaned toward him, her blue eyes mere slits. "I knew it. They're probably making soldiers who never die, that can fight all their wars for them. The government is up to their elbows in all kinds of stuff we don't want them to know, like UFOs. And Vietnam."

"Vietnam?"

"The new war—there been others since Germany. A lot has happened, even I know."

"But you believe me?" He leaned forward, their noses almost touching. "You don't think I'm crazy, do you?"

"Well, I seen some weird things in my life." She sat back and looked into the distance. "I seen a flying saucer over the lake one night. And I seen a bear walk on its front paws instead of back ones, like it belonged in the circus. I ain't one to say something can't happen. Besides, I'm up here in the mountains. They coulda blown up half the world and I wouldn't know it. And I wouldn't care."

"But why did you take me in?"

"I don't know." She shook her head slowly, looking at the air in front of her. "I didn't know what you were, but you looked so sad, like some doe caught in a trap."

"You have any family?"

"My daddy died ten years ago. I live alone." She slumped in the rocker, her knees spread. "The other girls always made fun of me at school for living out in the woods, and the men...sometimes some smart aleck from the Forest Service ties one on and comes up here, thinking he's gonna get a little hanky panky with me. I'm pretty accurate from 100 yards, they find out pretty quick."

"So you're up here by yourself?"

"I know how to take care of myself in the woods," she answered, her eyes level and penetrating. "I grew up here, and I'm going to die here."

"I didn't mean to upset you. Not really having a home, I say it's nice to feel like you've got one."

"How on earth did you get to Montana from Ohio?" She pulled a foot up on the edge of the rocker.

"I was looking for somebody. Somebody who might know why I'm like this, what's happened to me." He let the sheet fall from his chest. The smell was stronger underneath. "Jesus, how can you stand my smell?"

"I got a big jar of vapor rub. Kills most smells. But I would be lying if I said I'd forget the smell of you." She ripped a chunk of jerky with her teeth. "And the varmints been coming up to the cabin something awful. Plunked me a few raccoons. Had to scare off a mountain goat yesterday."

"Well, once I get better, I won't be any more trouble." Would he get better? Outside the window, through the porch, he could see pines and fir, the cloudy bowl of early spring above them.

"Don't worry about it. I'm not scared, if that's what you're worried about. I could kill you ten different ways before you even got off the bed."

"I'm the one who should be scared." He smiled. "And I guess I am, a little. Especially of how I look."

"Well, you look a little more human than you did when you washed up."

"Could I trouble you for the mirror on the wall?"

She did not look at him as she handed over the rectangular slab. And after one look, he did not look at himself, either.

Now that he was conscious, he dreamed of the fire. It seemed like yesterday to him and not over twenty years ago. He woke up with the heat on his back, his hands gripping the sides of the mattress, just as the fire made to sweep over them. He wondered what had happened to Lane, if he survived. What had happened in the world while he was sleeping. Perhaps he was still dreaming. In bed at night, he knocked his head against the wall of the cabin, harder and harder until he thought his crown would break through to the other side.

"Jesus Jiminy, will you stop doing that?" Maggie mumbled from the rocking chair. "This is not a dream, Johnson. Next time you start banging your head, I'm going shoot a tranquilizer in you."

He wanted to go to town, as soon as he was able, and find Stanley. Maggie did not make trips to town often. Since he'd been at the cabin, Maggie had gone once, bringing canned beans and bread for herself and jars of baby food for him, but she never mentioned any news of the outside world. Perhaps she did not want to upset him. Sometimes she caught him staring in disbelief at the free calendar from the marina that hung by the stove. August 1970.

But she was gentle. Every night she dabbed his back and legs with a cold rag with which she had seeped chamomile flower, explaining it would fight off infection and dull any pain. His hands faded to white and then warmed with peachy ochre. Thin white hairs grew between his knuckles and then thickened.

"I don't really understand it." Maggie wrung the rag into a tin bowl between her bare feet. She brought it back up and dabbed his neck. "I have half a mind to call Dr. Porter down and have him take a look at you. Every day I wake up and you're alive, I can't believe it's hardly possible."

"Why don't you call him? Maybe he knows something." He liked when sometimes he felt her fingertips on the sides of his back, his neck. It had been a long time, Kate, since anyone had touched him with any intention. He longed to ask her for more, to touch every part of him, to prove to him he was alive, that she was alive, but felt he'd already taken too much. Already, when she fell asleep in the rocking chair, he pushed himself to a sitting position and practiced sleeping against the wall so that soon he could insist she take the bed, he the rocker.

"I don't know what Dr. Porter knows that I don't," she sighed. "My father grew up around the Flathead Indians. They used osha and gumweed for a lot of general healing. But I never heard of an herb that makes you heal like this. You sure the government ain't gone done something to you, Calvin?"

"I don't think so. Why would they leave me in a pile of bodies?"

"Maybe they treated all of you. Maybe you're the only one who woke up." She leaned back in the chair. "My daddy and me, we have a few folks we trust in the town, but I don't trust anyone else, really. Especially the government."

"But you trusted me. And I could be the government Martian spy you're all spooked about." He smiled. His skin was still rubbery, not entirely responsive to his muscles, and he imagined the loping, sloping jack-o'-lantern of his face, like a stroke victim's.

"Don't make me have to shoot you, Johnson," she answered, picking up the bowl, in which lukewarm water and sloughed skin lay, forming a paste. "I lay awake all night already wondering why I didn't leave well enough alone."

❀❀❀

Although she didn't drink, when Maggie went to the post for her usual supplies one week, she came home with a flask of whiskey.

"That got Mr. and Mrs. Rumsey a twitter," she laughed, watching him take a small sip while standing near the window. He'd practiced walking around the cabin, building the muscles in his legs, testing the weight of his ankle. He could make it from bed to stove and halfway back before feeling tired, before having to steady himself on the back of the rocking chair. "I told them I was having a little trouble sleeping and needed a nip before bed."

"How can I pay you back?"

"You don't worry, Johnson. You may be many things, but you ain't been much trouble. Maybe if you can help me with the corner of the ceiling over there before winter comes. It looks like it's ready to leak."

"I don't want to cut into your season." He knew she earned her living as a game guide, taking groups of recreational hunters hunting for deer and antelope in the fall, bison in the winter, sometimes black bear in the spring. She made him split with pain laughing as she told him stories of the men staying in the lodges across the lake who needed help shooting game, how she'd have to stand right next to them and fire exactly when they did, insisting the bullet that killed the deer or antelope was indeed theirs and not hers. They never argued with her, and they came back every season. And she lived well enough off the money and the game, making venison jerky and stew and fillets of antelope that she sold to some of the restaurants to supplement the gnarled, undersized potatoes and radishes she harvested from her rocky garden.

"It's maybe another month before the hunters will start coming." She put away the canned milk and anchovies and woman products she'd gotten from town. "I really should have been canning some of the carrots and potatoes."

"I could help you." Johnson sat up in the bed, pulling at the band of the boxer shorts Maggie had given him, her father's. He was thankful for the hand-me downs, but they did not leave much to the imagination. Although he supposed there was not much Maggie didn't know about him physically by now. He watched the muscles of her arms move as she boiled the water for coffee, the broadness of her shoulders and the soft back of her neck where her hair was swept up in a bun.

"You help me with the roof," she answered. "You save your strength until then."

"Tell me something about yourself, Maggie."

"I'm not that interesting of a person." She did not turn to face him. The skin at the base of her neck was flushed, whether from sun or embarrassment he didn't know.

"Tell me about your father. I feel mighty strange wearing another man's underwear. You can at least do me that favor."

"He was the most honorable man I've known." She came and sat on the rocker, her hands clasped between her legs. "He taught me everything I know about hunting, fishing, the woods, God. My momma, I didn't really know her that well—she died when I was so young. But my father wasn't scared of raising a little girl. I had dolls at Christmas and my birthday."

"You ever had a boyfriend, Maggie?"

"I've got more of daddy's stuff." She stood and moved to the foot of the bed, where a large cedar chest stood. An elaborate scene was carved on top, a clearing of river in the woods from which an elk drank. "I never could bring myself to get rid of it—figured I'd take it in a little and wear it myself. But I'll take it in for you. Not all the pieces, but some of them."

"That's very nice of you." He studied his feet. His hair and toenails had grown back, although his skin was still baby smooth. "Thank you."

"Well, anyone'd be so nice." She held up a green flannel shirt with blue checks. "This one would look good on you."

"Yeah, that one I'll wear when I go to town."

"You want me to take you to town, is that what you want?" She stood up, looming over him, and he flinched. He'd seen her chop wood through the window, drag a 20-lb sack of flour from her motorboat and up the hill to the cabin, carry him back and forth to the outhouse like a doll. "You tired of being cooped up with a crazy old girl in the woods?"

"No," he answered. He reached up and took her hands. "I just don't want you to get in any trouble, that's all."

"That's a crazy idea." She pulled her hands away, brushing a strand of blonde hair from her face, where it pressed against her lips. It looked fuller and softer, and he wondered whether she had washed and combed it recently. "Why someone helping somebody would get in trouble. That's the craziest idea I've ever heard."

She left the cabin, and Johnson watched her through the window walk aimlessly around the clearing in front of the cabin, clenching and unclenching her fists, kicking up the dirt. When she came back in, ten minutes or so later, he pretended he was asleep so she would not have to explain herself to him.

※※※

"See how these fit you." The next day, Maggie placed her father's old logger boots on the floor by his feet. They were broken like an old back, the unlaced mid-calf sides falling open on each side, a long tongue unfurling from the opening. The soles still held their caulks. He pulled them over his pink baby-seal feet, and he stood in them unlaced, feeling his toes graze the roof of them.

"They feel good," he answered, and Maggie made an irritated sigh, bending over him.

"You gotta put the socks on, lace them up tight." She pulled the boots off and he felt her hands, full of life and circulation, graze his feet. She stretched the socks snug and reshoed him, pulling on the laces until the leather fit around Johnson's foot like a second skin. She sat back on her haunches, her legs and hips spread firmly through her dungarees, her hands on the tops of her thighs, and her body began to shake. Tears ran fast down her big moon cheeks, her eyes bluebells after rain. He put his hands on her cheeks and felt the warm salt flow move over them. She grabbed his wrists but did not pull his hands away.

"I miss him so much," she said finally. Johnson pulled her up on the bed so they were sitting side by side, and he held her, the storm of her swelling against his chest, his arms, and after awhile he could not tell whether he was holding her or she was holding him because he was crying, too, for Kate and Stanley and his parents and for Maggie and her father.

"I know, Maggie." He stroked her back. "I know."

"With you here, it's almost like…he's not gone. Except he used to sleep in the rocker when I was younger. When he got older, I made him sleep in the bed, and I slept in the rocker, except in the summer sometimes I'd sleep on the hammock on the porch. After he died, I just talked to myself for hours, and nobody answered, of course. My daddy used to call me his little magpie, said I talked till my face was as blue as my eyes. He used to get so mad at me for staying here with him, saying I had to find a husband. But I never wanted to leave him. And he was right, wasn't he?"

"It's not too late, Maggie. You're still young." Johnson pulled

away to face her. She was not Kate, but she would make someone—
like Stanley—a fine wife.

"Huh—you see me getting all dolled up for a church dance or
something?" she snorted. "I'm thirty-eight years old. I don't even
own a dress. I don't need nobody."

"Maggie, you're a good-looking woman," he said, and she stood
up after he had stared too long at her.

"Why don't you try out the boots?" She stared at the floor, her
hair out of its ponytail and spilling into her face. She fetched a
handkerchief out of the breast pocket of her dungarees and wiped
her tears. "I've been so busy a'blubberin."

"You mean outside?" He looked at the door.

"Go on." She waved him away, still sitting in the rocker, clutching her handkerchief. "Get yourself walking. Hunting season isn't
going to wait for you."

"Of course." He nodded.

"Go on." She did not look up at him. He turned and walked out
onto the porch. It was the first time he'd stood on his own outside. A
hammock was tied at one end of the porch, and some fishing equipment, a kerosene lamp, and a wooden oar, broken, against the wall
on the other side. He opened the screen door. The slope was fairly
level here. Through the trees, he could see the glint of the water.
He could hear an engine motor a few miles off and wondered how
close they were to the road. He took small steps until he reached
the source of the water. The mountains flanked each side of the lake
for several hundred feet, overhanging the water in some parts, and
ponderosa pines and evergreens grew along the elevation. Savage
and beautiful and largely uninhabitable except by people like Maggie and her father.

He could leave now. He could make it down to the road, hitch a ride to the ranger's cabin, the forestry service, whichever came first. They would take him to the hospital, he figured, make sure his treatment had been proper, and he could find Stanley Polensky. He needed answers, now more than ever.

But he turned back. On the trail back, he picked some forget-me-nots, other wildflowers that grew close to the water. He walked, one foot very deliberately in front of the other, and leaned against trees when he tired. He thought of the wiry girl underneath the calloused hands and thickened middle, the small but respectable swell of her breasts, her water eyes, the way her face broke up into pieces when she laughed, loud and easy and that way she dressed his back. He entered the cabin, letting the screen door fall shut behind him so she would not be startled, and when he entered the main cabin, she stood at the stove, boiling potatoes and carrots and salted venison. He replaced the wilting flowers in the vase with his own and sat at the table as she brought over two plates.

"I feel good," he said as she fumbled with the silverware and napkins. She looked at the vase but did not reply. "I bet I could walk all the way to town this week."

"Well, that's good to know you're thinking of leaving. I'm needing you out of here soon, anyways." She retrieved two mugs and filled them with coffee. He picked up his fork and knife as she sat across from him.

"I think I could probably sleep in the rocker tonight." He looked at her. "You probably need to be getting your rest."

"It don't make no difference to me." She stabbed at the venison with her fork and began to saw it with her knife.

They cut and ate the venison and potatoes and drank the coffee and listened to the crickets, the nightbirds, the trout jumping out of the lake, the tick of the Bakelite alarm clock that rested next to the Bible on the bedside table. The evening came like a cloak over the cabin, and Maggie lit the kerosene lamp by the bed. He stripped down to his boxers, folding the clothes and putting them on top of the cedar chest, as Maggie sat on the rocker in her dungarees.

"Take the bed, Maggie." He stepped toward the rocker. "I'm strong enough to sleep sitting up. Lord knows I got through the war sleeping all kind of ways."

"I'm all right." She crossed her leg and her arms. He leaned over her and grabbed her under the armpits, bracing with his legs to pull her upward. But before he could lift, she kicked him in the shin with her boot. He crumpled to the floor, afraid for a moment that she'd broken his leg.

"Aw shit, Maggie." He hugged his leg, rocking back and forth. "Just take the goddamn bed."

"I'm fine here." She bent forward slightly, peering at him in dimness. "Are you all right?"

He lunged toward her from a sitting position and grabbed her arms, pulling as hard as he could until she was on the floor with him. From his knees, he grabbed the runners of the rocker and dragged it across the floor toward the door.

"What the hell are you doing!" She wrapped her arms around him and tried to dislodge his grip with her fingers. "Let go of my goddamn rocker!"

"You sleep in the bed or I'll turn it into kindling." He pulled at the runner and legs, trying to separate them. He stopped and looked at her. "I don't really want to do this. I just want you to relax. I want…to take care of you for once. Is that all right?"

"I don't need nobody doing anything for me." She stood up and retrieved the rocker, returning it to its spot by the bed.

"Are you afraid I'm going to leave, Maggie?" He sat on the bed. "Or are you afraid I'm going to stay?"

"I don't…I don't know what you're asking." She straightened the snaps of her dungarees, refolded her sleeves. "I already told you the season's starting soon."

He leaned back against the wall, feeling the stubble on the back of his calves and thighs. It had started growing a few days ago, the last thing that would return him to being Johnson. He closed his eyes, concentrating on the shallow breeze that limped over these late summer nights, kissing his bare shoulders, underneath his chin. The events of the day drained him, and he found himself inch toward the forgiving mattress. He felt additional weight strain the bed, and when he opened his eyes Maggie lay with her back to him, hugging the other edge. He lay on his side facing her and pressed against the wall so that they were not touching, and he watched her back rise and fall until he fell asleep.

Johnson thought about Helena. The longer he stayed in the cabin, and Maggie ventured to town for supplies or parts for the boat or even just to catch up on town gossip, the more he starved for sustenance beyond the scraps that she tossed to him as she deemed fit—while they sat on the porch at night sharpening her knives or early morning out in the secret fishing spot away from the other boaters, in the bed they sometimes shared, on the chilly nights, although not as lovers.

Helena was his business. And so was Stanley Polensky. He hinted to Maggie that she might need help carrying the groceries or the ammo from the store, but she laughed.

"I done it all these years, Calvin." She'd stand in the rocking boat as he unlooped the rope, watching the distance between the dock and the boat grow. "I'll be fine. Those rugs and quilts need a beatin'. I'll see you before dinner."

One night he begged for the hammock, which Maggie usually took at night, claiming his back was bothering him. Then, at dawn, he stole away to the dock, untied the boat, and drifted 50 yards off the shore before turning on the engine. Still, the motor whirred through the trees and echoed off the rock like a sledgehammer. But there was nothing he could do now. He headed down the shoreline, following the curve of the river until he reached the dock where he'd climbed on the boat that took him to the gulch fire. He tied Maggie's boat to a spot on the dock and nodded a good morning to a man putting his tackle box in his speedboat. The man, older, swallowed by overalls and a sleeveless undershirt, bent his brow into a stare. Another man, who leaned against the door of the boathouse fondling his pipe, looked at Johnson, then Maggie's boat. Before they could strike up conversation, Johnson walked casually down the road.

After about a mile or so, he reached downtown Helena, found the one-room library, and waited on the front steps until it opened. The librarian showed him how the old newspapers were stored, on microfiche now, little print on film rolls like movies, and he looked at the articles, reading about the Mann Gulch fire, the smokejumpers and ranger who perished, pictures of deer burned to death where they stood as the fire raced over them. He read quotes from the ranger about the fire becoming a blowup, a dangerous ignition of conditions which sends the fire up in the air and through the air at incredible speeds.

He read for hours, slowly, moving his finger over the lines, looking for clues about other missing, dead. But even though he had not expected to find his name, he did not find any mentions of any other missing firefighters. No quotes from Lane Gustafson or Mantee or a Stanley Polensky, and he did not know why this had surprised him. The only person who knew he was alive in Montana, perhaps in the world, was Maggie.

And she was going to be pissed at him. He hurried along the main street but stopped in front of a sporting goods store. The size of the cooler, a deep green Coleman, so shiny and new, caught his eye. Color everywhere, in the clothes of the women, the cars, orange and red and cobalt, big engines that sounded like airplanes. Strange, whiny guitar music from the windows as he passed. Men wore their hair long, curling over their ears, their sideburns touching their chins. They passed him on the street, looking at him from behind mirrored sunglasses and smiling. Were these boys, in their denim jackets with the fringe, their heeled boots, even born when he was buried in the ground? Were they even born when he was sunken in the water? They walked away languidly, as if poured down the sidewalk. It was as if he had stepped into the future. He supposed he had.

Back at the dock, the man with the pipe waited with the deputy sheriff. Johnson didn't have any identification, so he didn't feel compelled to tell them his name. Accordingly, they didn't feel compelled to give him lunch, coffee, or cigarettes in the holding cell while the owner of the marina went out to Maggie's cabin to bring her into town.

"Yeah, I know this man." She wore her best shirt, a simple white blouse and a pair of denim jeans. She did not look at him. "He's been helping me out at the cabin. I sent him down for a can of coffee. I got to get ready for the season."

"I'm sorry about that, Maggie." The sheriff cupped her shoulder. "I know you're busy up there this time of year. He just wasn't very accommodating in helping us get to the bottom of things."

"He don't talk much." She shot Johnson a glance. "I think he's a little soft in the head."

Neither of them spoke on the way home. Johnson concentrated on the bobbing and crashing of the boat against the water, the crystalline blue sky, the blinding noonday sun on the water.

"You mind telling me what the hell that was all about?" At the cabin, she banged a pot on the stove and heated water for coffee. "I thought you'd done run off for good. Maybe that's what you was planning?"

"I wanted to go to town. It's not like I haven't hinted about it a hundred times." He stood in the doorway of the porch.

"And what the hell do you need there, exactly?" She lit a cigarette and spooned the instant into two mugs. "Don't I bring you everything you want?"

"I never said you didn't. I just wanted to make sure there was a town. For all I know, I could be in heaven or something."

"You're a real kidder." She exhaled and poured the steaming water. "I ain't laughin'."

"I just wanted to read the newspaper. About the fire. I wanted to know if I'd been listed as missing. I got twenty years to catch up on. You should see the cars they're driving now, Maggie. The engines are so powerful. And the way people dress. The things you can buy."

"I could have told you that. Nobody ever said nothing about anybody missing in the fire." She thrust a cup toward his hand. "And I already asked around town about your Stanley Polenksy. No one's ever heard of him. And things might change, but people don't. That's all you need to know."

"But—"

"You know, why don't you just leave if you've got ants in your pants? The season is starting, and I'm going to be too busy to worry about you."

"I can't."

"Why not?"

"Because you're the only person who knows that I'm alive, who knows anything's wrong with me." He turned to her in the doorway. "Who believes me. I owe you for that much, and plenty more."

"You don't owe me anything, Calvin Johnson." She walked past him and sat on the porch steps, cigarette between her fingers, coffee mug snug between her palms.

"But you keep me here like some animal at the zoo." He touched her on the back. "I don't mind working off any debt, but I need to be able to come and go as I please. We're not married or anything, you know. And, to be honest with you, there's someone else."

"Don't you think I know that?" He could hear the break in her voice, feel the slight heave of her shoulders. "Don't you know you say her goddamn name every night? How do you think that makes me feel, after you ask me to share the goddamn bed?"

"I'm sorry, Maggie." He sat down next to her. "I didn't mean it that way. I like you so much, and I think you're a great woman, but I love someone else."

"It don't matter, anyway. I can't love no one no more, Johnson."

She stood up and walked into the cabin. "My daddy dying, it tore the seam in me. I ain't enough rope left to lend."

"Maggie, just tell me what you need from me, and I'll stay as long as it takes." He stood in the doorway and watched her slam her mug in the sink, the sickening sound of it vibrating and settling.

"You get the hell out of here." She moved to the cedar chest without looking at him. "I mean it, Johnson. I got some money. You take it, take the bus out of here, find your friend."

"What about the roof?"

"It's best that you go right away." She swung open the cedar chest and emerged with an envelope. She licked her finger, and counted out ten $20 bills. "I realized that when you were gone."

They rode in the boat down the Missouri. Johnson stared at her back, the width between her shoulder blades, imagined his head nestled between them. It was possible to wear her down, to massage open the heart, to be patient and let her tell him, in her own way, that she loved him. She already had. But why would he subject her to such cruelty, when all he saw in the shadows of his thoughts was Kate, just out of reach, around the corner, behind the door?

She stayed in the boat. He hugged her while they moved this way, that, against the tide. It felt more like they were hanging onto something other than each other. He thought about asking her whether he could visit, but as soon as he stood on firm ground, his weight on his own feet, she waved a little wave and the boat bounced away, seeming to glide over the choppy waters, not touching anything.

1964

In the forest, there were sounds. She did not know what they were at first, the clipped song above her, far away and close. Her fingers spread in a cold soup of mud. Water pelted her face. Rain, so much rain, making the dirt soft, gauzy. And birds. The song of birds. She stared at hands, small and pale with deep whorls on the fingertips, little hair. Smooth skin that glided gracefully upwards and connected to shoulders, her shoulders, a torn dress, an exposed nipple on a flat breast. She felt her feet in the mud and pressed, pushing herself up to stand. She was in a gully, a mud slide. A depression in the earth made by rain. So much rain, the only good thing about it was the way it cleansed the dirt from her legs and her hands and her hair.

Where was her matka? She remembered the bone house, a trailer chased by death. Mongrels. A woman with sunken eyes, blood-smeared lips. She moved her feet in the mud, a slippery floor of fish, and felt them graze something of permanence. She knelt and removed it from its grave. A long bone, longer than her own forearm. A glint of white, like diamonds, grew in the mud as the rain attacked it, had its way with it. More bones, slighter larger than her own. An arm bone and a leg bone, ribs.

A skull. She brought it to her own face. A slightly older child than she. Above its left eye the skull had caved in from the clumsy precision of force. She put her finger through it and felt the power and trajectory of it. It seemed to cave in her own skull, stir the memories that had settled like the paste of leaves and grit on her. The officer's bullet. Ferki and the trees. Ferki. Her heart was alive and it pounded pain through her, releasing memories like a gorged stream. Weakness washed over her. She squatted and wove her hands through the little white pieces that had comprised one of Ferki's hands, and already they were fragile, like winter branches. She put them in her mouth, to warm them, to taste them, but Ferki was long gone, with his grandmother Tsura and perhaps his parents and her own mother as well.

A grave washed away by rain, so much rain it seemed determined to reveal the dark secrets of the world. One by one, she found the pieces of Ferki, and she was angered that he had been dead so long, with no one to know, not even her, except the Nazi soldiers that put him there. And she was angered that the grace of God had shined on him, taken him away, and left her here in the mud. For what?

"Niech cię szlag trafi!" She shouted at the sky. *Drop dead.* "What did I ever do to you?"

She gathered the bones in the bottom of her dress, so thin and threatening rupture, an embryonic sack ready to birth a skeleton, and walked. She walked and the sun sunk and rose. She walked barefoot, her hair knotted and frizzy, layer upon layer of salty sweat drying to her face. She walked until she came to a farm, where a man spearing hay dropped his pitchfork and hurried to her.

"Child," he said in Polish. "Oh, child. Where have you come? And what is that you're carrying?"

"My husband," she answered, and because her arms were so tired, let him rain from her dress to the ground.

❁❁❁

Alojzy the farmer and his wife, Anatola, fed her stew. They grew potatoes and rye and their children, Benedykt and Daniela, went to school in town. Their house, with three small bedrooms, a sitting room, and a kitchen, was to Ela a palace. But they moved in and out of the kitchen, around the kitchen table, in the sitting room, with great difficulty, as if they lived in the bone house. It was easy to see what the problem was—so many things! A wooden box that glowed in the corner and from which voices and strange music vibrated, to which Daniela swayed in a way that would cause Ela's matka to slap her. Chairs that were dressed with fabric finer than any of her dresses. Tables and papers. Light that came from the ceiling and from statues on the tables. She pressed the switches on and off for minutes to watch the little suns appear and disappear. Pictures on the wall, not drawn, but of the family, captured on the paper. Photography, Alojyz explained, scratching his beet-shaped head, a frown above his whiskered chin. A spring of blond hair sprouted from the top of his head like a carrot tussle.

"Where is it that you come from?" Anatola was hardy, like an ox, and seemingly as strong. Her features lived in the puffed folds of her face, her eyes blue and hard like marbles.

"Reszel," Ela answered between bites of meat. In the corner, a cast-iron box held fire and kept the stew warm, along with coffee. Alojyz had put Ferki's bones in a sack so that their dog, Opi, would not bother them. They rested under her chair. From her chair, her bare foot grazed the top of the burlap to ensure that they remained.

"Oh, yes." Alojya left the kitchen and returned with a piece of paper, which he spread out on the table. "You see, Reszel is here."

She looked at the picture of a green blob with blue at the top. Words were written all over the green blob.

"What is this?" She leaned over her bowl and studied it. Perhaps it was a potion.

"A map." Alojya coughed, looking at Anatola. "I show you where you are, from like, bird's eye, from the sky, and where you are from."

"How do you know from the sky where you are?"

He ignored her, pointing his finger toward the middle of the map. "Bydgoszcz. We are here." He moved his finger up higher and more leftward, toward the blue. "Reszel here. Not very far, but far enough. How did you come about this way?"

"What is the blue?" She trailed her hand on the paper.

"The sea." He shook his head and folded up the map, disappearing from the kitchen. Momentarily, he returned with another piece of paper.

"You see?" There were lines that went up and down, making boxes. "This is the year. 1964. September 1st."

"Where are the Nazis?" She peered at him. "Will the Nazis come for me?"

"She is not old enough," Anatola shot a look at her husband. She rubbed a cup made of glass with a rag. "She must have had family tell her."

"The Nazis killed my husband—you understand?" She nodded her head toward the burlap sack. "They kill him and I hide. I . . . fall asleep. Then I come to you. This is the truth."

"Child, it is not possible." He pointed to the piece of paper again. "This here, you see? 1964."

She stood in the chair. "Well, how long have I been asleep, then?"

❀❀❀

They arrived from Reszel, from the Child Welfare Services. When they came to Alojya's, a middle-aged woman with outdated glasses that slid down her nose and a younger graduate from the University of Warsaw who was being groomed to take her place as supervisor, Ela learned of other strange things that had happened over the years, excluding the wars (they were a constant): carts that moved without horses but with the speed of them, telescopes that one wore in front of one's eyes to see better, clothes that looked like she did not know what. Especially Daniela's. Everything had shifted, the world a foreign place that did not have room for her. And yet, it refused to let her go, a tree from which an apple did not fall, soft and rotten and swaying in the breeze.

"My name is Ana." The older woman put her suitcase down on the kitchen table and held her hand toward the younger woman. "And this is Emile. We'd like to be your friends."

What Ela said was, "I'd like you to help me." What she thought was, *I want you to help me die.* Surely, it could be done—metal birds in the sky, soldiers with rifles that shot many bullets at once, wires strung across the sky on poles, and people's words sent across them—why could they not kill her, chop her up in little pieces and bury the parts far from each other, not like the mongrels, who even the Nazis had driven away, beat when they had began to pull her limbs from her body?

"Oh, dear." They looked at each other when Ela pulled Ferki's skull from the sack and placed it on the table.

"My husband." She said matter-of-factly, as if his presence gave her an advantage, authority. But she realized, more than anything, that she was entirely alone. She was alone and no one could help her, not even herself.

"Don't cry, little one." The older woman patted her shoulder as she cradled her head on the table, big boulders of tears tumbling from her eyes and dripping down her forearms. "We're here to help."

At the facility outside of Reszel, they weighed and measured her and took her vitals. They bought her corduroys and a turtleneck with an embroidered turtle on the collar, fitted her with Mary Janes. They bought her a lalka. It peed like she did, but only water, and its eyes closed when she laid it down. They asked her about her mother, how old she was. *Amnesia.* She asked them what herbs they had used to bewitch it so. *Schizophrenic.* They consulted the Diagnostic and Statistical Manual of Mental Disorders. *Delusional.* They gave her a bed in the orphanage and did psychological and IQ testing and set up interviews with potential foster parents. She refused to leave her bed, bit at the hands that came toward her, that tried to take Ferki's skull, which she cradled at night, eyes closed, rocking.

Flat affect. *Behavioral issues.* She was tutored in the modern dialect, but when not in class, she reverted to her old language or did not speak at all. She found she liked Chips Ahoy! and stuffed cats.

Couples came and examined the orphan girls lined up in a row in the play yard. Ela was always the plumpest, healthiest; her hair shone like liquid silk, and her skin was unbroken and taut and vital; yet her slit of mouth and her hard eyes repelled them, sent them looking for a lipstick in their purse or for their wallet in their suit jacket as they moved onto the next girl, emaciated but with a soft wetness in her eyes, a ragged boy's haircut they could soften and curl, tight shoes they could replace with a roomier pair, things they could fix.

Seasons changed; twice she ran away. Both times, they found her
in the forest grinding leaves and twigs together into fine powders,
any number of natural toxins she had collected there to constrict her
breathing, to stop her heart, to swell her lungs and throat, to paralyze
her. And she had lived through all of them, nights of terrible vomiting, diarrhea, headaches, delirium. Eventually, she woke up from
the fever dreams, as if they had never happened. At the facility, she
saved her pills under her tongue or coughed them back up, hoping to
save what she thought would be a lethal dose. In dreams, she pleaded
to her matka for the answers. So many years, many lifetimes, had
dimmed her memory of her mother's words, her scent. There was
no scent among the antiseptic surfaces, the steel tables and cement
walls of the orphanage. She peed in her new clothes and rubbed them
in the dirt outside the playground; they always came back from the
laundry, bright, soft, smelling like nothing. She did not understand
how they could erase her so thoroughly, and yet she was still there.

Every month, they took her vitals, identical to last month's numbers, the last six months—weight, centimeters, blood pressure, cho-
lesterol panel, as if the numbers had cloned themselves, had cloned
another Ela.

"Kallman's syndrome, Dr. Czyeski thinks," Emile explained to
the nurse as Ela sat on the metal table, waiting for her two Chips
Ahoy! in a napkin. "The children—they never age."

At the university hospital, they gave her a teddy bear and stuck
her in the arm with a needle. They fed her barium and injected
gadolinium contrast and radiographed her neck, her uterus, her
brain. And when they could find nothing, and could find nothing
else to do, they contacted the only person they knew who might
want her—Dr. Henry Palmer, a gerontologist in America.

It just so happened that his wife could not have children.

Emile went with her on the plane. She kept a vial of liquid Xanax for injection if Ela became agitated on the flight, a bag of graham crackers as another means of placation. She fingered both when the plane took off and Ela went into a litany about the devil bewitching the silver bird, that they were flying straight to hell, and decided on the graham crackers, pressing them into Ela's palm. Ela crunched them dryly with her teeth, little brown boulders tumbling out of the corners of her frowning lips, before falling asleep. They landed at JFK and were met by Dr. Palmer. He was tall and handsome in a suit, his dark curly hair brushing the collar of his white shirt. She thought she might find him attractive, think about him naked, if she did not think of Ferki still.

He wore a gaudy tie, orange and purple splotched sunset patterns, as if to reassure Ela he was harmless. He clutched a new lalka in his hands, dark haired with a green dress trimmed with lace. She had tired of these children's things, had even beheaded the one at the orphanage that peed and left the head in the fruit bowl. But this one looked like her mother, she decided. She accepted it as he held it out, smiling.

"Hello, Ela. I'm Doctor Palmer. I'm very happy to meet you." He crouched down to her level. She touched his face, very clean shaven, inhaled the spice of his aftershave.

"I am happy to meet you, too." She curtsied, like they taught her at the orphanage. You catch more flies with honey, she figured.

She read the street signs at the intersection as the cab went further and further from the airport. 34th Street. 67th. Finally, they stopped at 87th off 1st. Each side of the street was lined with thin brown brick buildings, three stories, blocky and uniform.

"Is this hospital?" She asked from the backseat of the cab.

"Oh no." Doctor Palmer laughed, placing his palm on her shoulder. "This is my home. Your home."

She wondered how they would live together in the bed if she was not entirely a woman. Perhaps it was okay in America to marry, to sleep with little girl women. Perhaps America was truly free, as she had been told.

The woman looked too clean, too refined, to be the maid. Her mane of strawberry hair curled away from her face unnaturally, stiffly. She wore makeup and her sleeveless brown dress was open immodestly to her breastbone. She bent toward Ela, the round cantaloupes of her breasts filling the opening, grabbing her arms.

"Is this our little angel?" Her nose almost touched Ela's. "Oh, Henry, she's a darling. Our little girl forever."

"Ela, this is my wife, Carol Palmer." The doctor put his hand on Ela's shoulder. "But you could also call her Mrs. Palmer, or Carol, or mother, or just mom."

Her room was painted in shades of pink and lemon yellow. A bed with a ruffle canopy. A stuffed giraffe. A small desk painted white. A dollhouse called "Victorian" that was only a little smaller than the bone house, with little lalkas and things to lie and sit on. Everything smelled of candy, or flowers. She put Ferki's skull on the white-painted bedside table that had bumble bees and butterflies stenciled on the side. But, the first night, she slept under the bed. Even there, she could find no dirt, nothing to press her cheek against, to remember home. The second and third nights, the Palmers searched the house frantically, opening cupboards, closets, fireplace grills, before finding her asleep among the potted geraniums in the gardener's greenhouse on the roof.

Twice a week, a woman came to work on Ela's English. She gave Ela a marble notebook and told her to record her thoughts in English, a diary.

I do not like color pink I would be better green.

The next week, the painters came with drop cloths and covered Ela's furniture, floor. Two days later her walls were emerald green, with matching bedspread and area rugs.

I like more Chips Ahoy! With her afternoon snack of carrots and apple slices, two Chips Ahoy! rested on a napkin.

Once a week, she went to the lab with Dr. Palmer. He held her hand as they walked through the rows of steel hoods and tables, past men in white coats with little coats tied across their faces. Animals that would have been happier in trees and holes and even on the plain earth grabbed at her from cages. They put Ela in small room, not a cage, and they hit her knee with a rubber hammer, listened to her heart with the silver medallion, shined light into her eyes and mouth and ears. They looked at her womb, took scrapings. They took blood from her arm with a sewing needle and tube. They gave her a lollipop. Then, she sat in a laying chair and talked to a doctor about anything she wanted to. She did not know what to say. She talked about the toilet paper in the bathroom, how it seemed too nice to put on your dupa.

I should like the animals be let go.

The animals remained, except if they died, in which case, they were replaced by new animals.

I should like animal of my own.

One day, Dr. Palmer brought home a kitten. Black with a white face and paws. Ela named her Psotka, *prankster.* She slept at the foot of the bed and batted Ela's feet.

"Why don't you write something about your mother and father in your diary?" Her speech therapist urged. That day, they worked on fruits: oranges, bananas, apples, lemons.

Mr. and Mrs. Palmer they take my blood.

The Palmers enrolled her in The Chapin School for Girls on 84th street, second grade. The other girls complained she smelled of onions.

"I don't know what they are talking about." Carol Palmer knelt by the clawfoot bathtub, sleeves of her cashmere sweater rolled to her elbows, scrubbing Ela's back with lavender soap. Ela stared at her reflection in the water, her face dark, shape-shifting. "You smell as good as any one I have ever smelled."

Every Thursday, she went past the cages of the animals and the doctors poked at her and took things from her, her blood and urine and spit. They did something to them that turned them into numbers that Dr. Palmer went over at his desk.

It is something more than Chips Ahoy! I need.

"It's a vitamin," Dr. Palmer explained at breakfast, over his newspaper. Mrs. Palmer smiled and nodded. The lady in the black and white dress, black and white every day, brought her breakfast—oatmeal, half a grapefruit, a slice of toast with jam. And a red and white cylinder, like shiny plastic candy. "It won't harm you."

The vitamin made her sleepy. She took a nap in gym class in the pile of jump ropes. When she awoke, the girls had tied one each to her legs and arms. One to her neck.

"We could get her a private tutor." Carol Palmer spoke into the hallway phone, her tennis racket slung over her shoulder. Psotka batted at the yellow balls on her socks. "I just don't know what to do, Henry. Sure, her English is not perfect, but she doesn't smell, and she looks like an ordinary little girl. I know...I know she's not. Listen, I'm late for my lesson. Melanie is coming for speech at four."

It is not vitamin I need.

"Honey, I want to talk to you about something." Carol Palmer sat at the edge of her bed, where she played with Psotka. She held out a napkin with two cookies and a glass of milk. "One of the other mothers at school mentioned you told her daughter you were a witch. Did you tell her that?"

"No, she call me a witch." Ela took one of the cookies, pinched her stomach. "I was picking leaves for tinctures, and she ask me what I do."

"What do you mean, tinctures?"

"I take leaves from the greenhouse at school to make medicines. My mother and I, we make medicines for healing."

"Oh, that's right." Carol clasped her palms together. "Are you trying to make the medicine that made you this way?"

"I don't know if I make that medicine here. I make that medicine at home."

"Honey." Carol Palmer touched her ankle. Her nails were painted blood. Very *fashionable* (her new vocabulary word) for women here. "This is your home."

"I mean in Poland." Ela put the cookie back. "My Poland home."

"What medicines are you making here?"

I would like to grow bigger.

A green and yellow capsule appeared next to the red and white one at breakfast. It made her body tingle. On the weekends, instead of watching Saturday morning cartoons she went with Dr. Palmer to the Institute. She drank funny-tasting milkshakes and went to sleep and when she woke up, the whole weekend had been taken from her by the milkshake. Her body hurt. She did not go to school on Monday.

"Don't worry, Ela." Dr. Palmer lit a cigarette in the study. "All children have growing pains. And we are hoping you have growing pains, too. With this medicine, we think that you will be able to keep up with your classmates in size."

Third, fourth, and fifth grades, she was still the size of a second grader.

❀❀❀

"It is a small operation." Dr. Palmer sat at his desk. She was to call him father, but the vocabulary word that seemed to suit him better was *visitor*. Carol Palmer sat across from Ela, holding her hand. She was not quite a mother, but she made Ela liver and onion sandwiches like she liked and let her watch *The Monkees* on the television, the color one, in the master bedroom. Ela liked the boy with the knitted hat. He reminded her most of Ferki.

"You don't have to, if you don't want." Carol Palmer squeezed her hand. "He is your father, but you can say no to him."

"I have already done this," Ela explained. "I already tell you what happens."

"Well, we'd like to see for ourselves, take samples of the tissue as it…regenerates. But mostly, we'd like to see for ourselves."

Friday afternoon, a car came to the school and drove her directly to the Institute, no afternoon snack. She went to sleep on a big white bed with tubes in her arms and mouth. Such a big to-do, she thought, to chop off her pinky. When she woke up, a bandage the size of an oven mitt covered her left hand. At home, she waved the stub in the air and giggled as Carol Palmer put her hand over her mouth.

"And now, they say, the magic happens!" she laughed.

There were more operations after it grew back, but they were inside of her. She woke up with scars on her stomach, over her heart, and then she underwent x-rays and the scars disappeared and they drew new scars to see whether what they had taken had grown back.

Every time I grow back but I do not feel whole.

Eighth, ninth, tenth grades, she did not grow. The girls called her midget, snickered behind her back, locked her in the bathroom stalls. Her mother had taught her never to use the tinctures for harm, so she had no other choice but to fight back on her own.

She tripped girls in the hallway, hid their clothes while they showered after gym. She squirted mustard and ketchup packets she had gotten from the cafeteria onto their seats.

"Ela, you're not in the third grade anymore." Carol Palmer lit a cigarette at the Manhattan deli where she sometimes took Ela for liverwurst. "You need to behave in a manner becoming of a lady."

"They do not act that way."

"Your teachers…have found no evidence of other girls teasing you." Carol crushed the cigarette in the kidney-shaped ashtray between them. "Look, I know it's hard when you don't feel like yourself…"

"I am old woman. I am not a girl." Ela chewed on her soda straw. "I have no interest in Calculus or British poetry. I go back to Poland now. I do not want to be here anymore."

"Oh, honey." Carol shook her head. "How could you mean that? You have everything here."

I want to go home.

Psotka was sick. She was only eight, but she did not eat. Ela felt her ribs, fed her lavender seeped in milk. She thought of the animals who looked at her in the labs, who pleaded to be free. She thought she saw the same stare from Psotka, the same droop of head, the same sigh.

From chemistry class, she knew how to make the tincture: vinegar and baking soda. After school in her bedroom, she ran a tube from a covered pitcher into a plastic sandwich bag and waited for the gas to fill the bag. She fit the bag over Psotka's head, petting her coat with the other.

"Wieczne odpoczywanie racz Jej dac Panie," she whispered. *Eternal rest grant unto her, O Lord.*

"Ela." Carol Palmer dropped the glass of milk, napkins, and cookies in the doorway. "What are you doing to Psotka?"

From behind the locked study door, they talked about her in murmurs, voices rising and falling in frustration. Ela went up to the roof and lay between the mums. She had wanted to bury Psotka in the park, Carl Schurz, a few blocks from their house. But it seemed that her opinion, spoken or written, did not carry much weight anymore. The handyman took Psotka away in a trash bag. She wondered if it ever had.

1972

The farmhouse had aged, its white clapboards needing a fresh coat of paint, the front steps sagging from the weight of time and weather. Branches of the oak tree he had climbed as a boy poked at the upstairs windows, as if looking for a fight. There was a newer car in the driveway, a brown Buick, but Johnson knew his parents still owned the house because of the tulips his mother cultivated every spring in the little garden that surrounded the porch like a moat. It was Sunday morning, and he waited for them to go to church. He held his breath as they emerged, gray haired and frailer, his father's jowls touching the collar of his shirt, the flesh on his mother's upper arms sagging, as if gravity were trying to pull them into their graves.

Tears ran rivulets into his cheeks. He had prepared himself for this, for his return to Ohio, but despite the warnings from his head, his heart had fed on the warm honeysuckle of memory, which contrary to everything else, did not age, except for himself. He wondered briefly whether he was a memory caught in the folds of time, or perhaps a ghost. Maybe he was not real, nor Maggie, nor anything that had happened once he had left Ohio. But the barrier between the world before him, where time had moved along, and his, did not seem to have a beginning or an end, as thin as air but as impenetrable as a boulder.

What had his parents thought when he had not written them or called upon arriving in Montana? Did they call the police, urge them to contact the station in Helena? Had his father driven out to Helena himself, visiting restaurants, hotels, and bars, describing his tall, muscular son with the slightly crooked nose, his hazel eyes and dimples, a boy who looked like any other boy but who was theirs and was missing; had there been a report filed? Had they given up, or had they not even tried, fearing he had become one of the lost men, who had returned from the war but had not stopped fighting, the drip of alcohol into the bloodstream the only anesthetic for spiritual casualty.

He watched the Buick back out of the driveway before scrambling for the rear of the house. Outside the door, a broken planter stood, one that had once held sunflowers. It seemed strange that his parents, so meticulous that they replaced or repainted all outdoor ornaments every season, had left it to disintegrate, slabs of faded terra cotta that had fallen outward like petals and mixed with dirt and stone to form its own curious layer of earth. He lifted the circular bottom plate and found the back door key in a wormy crater underneath. He wondered if they had left the key there, if they had not the heart to close the door on him.

The smell of coffee and his mother's perfume still lingered in the kitchen. He pressed his palm on the stone countertop, feeling sick from the scent. The sickness was in his heart, not his stomach, a cloud with hammers that drummed over his chest and made the back of his neck sweat. He inhaled the traces of gardenia and honeysuckle, hoping he'd pass out and wake up, his paper on Beowulf on the table, a half-filled coffee mug, his life still before him. But he would have to go back further than that, before the war, when he was still a boy, still normal.

But he was home now. Maybe he was still normal. Perhaps it had all been a strange dream. But the kitchen was different—new cabinets and appliances—an oven in the wall, a refrigerator with two long vertical doors, one of which had a lever sticking out of it. He pulled the lever, and then pushed it back, jumping when cold, square boulders tumbled out. He squatted and picked them up, feeling them melt on his palm. Ice cubes. Had he broken the refrigerator? He pushed the lever again. More ice tumbled out. A refrigerator that dispensed ice cubes. It was like everything that had changed when he was gone, so inconsequential, so significantly massive.

Still, he was home now. Perhaps it would all end. He needed to know for sure. He scooped up the new ice and put it in a paper towel with the old ice, numbing the pinky finger of his left hand. Then, with his right hand, he reached for the butcher block, pulling out his mother's butcher's knife. In the back yard, he found a mostly level stump, a tree that possibly had been diseased, too close to the Johnson home, and therefore removed. He knelt and folded the fingers of his left hand into a tight fist, except for his pinky, which he extended as far from the others as possible. Then he lined up the butcher's knife with his pinky and drew back, closing his eyes.

His scream hurt him more than the pain; high, then low-pitched, like an animal crouched in the shadows of its life as death closed from the corners and softly kissed light to darkness. He staggered around the yard, holding his hand in the flimsy paper towel, wetting Maggie's father's flannel shirt with warm, sticky blood. When the white-hot sensation that traveled from his fingers to his teeth became recognizable as pain, rather than an altered state of existence, he stumbled back to the house and to get paper towels from the kitchen. He was never much of a planner. He sat on the steps outside the back door and unthreaded the shoelace from one of the logging boots and looped it around what remained of his pinky, pulling tight. He pulled until the remaining skin, just below where his mid-joint had been, began to close inward toward the bone. But the blood was everywhere, the step, his shirt and hands, splashed on the tops of his boots, one loose and laceless.

The pinky. It remained on the stump in a pool of blood. He scooped it into a bloody towel and stuffed it into his pocket. Then he took off the flannel shirt and mopped up the stump and the steps before wrapping the rest of the paper towels into the shirt and heading inside. He sat at the table, shaking. What had he done? The familiar contours of the wooden seat, the squeaking of the legs, leaned against his heart, and he could not stop the tears from tumbling down his cheeks. Here, he had sat eating dinner every day of his life—pot roast and chicken pot pie and beef stew and mashed potatoes. Here, he sat in December 1941 and announced to his parents he was enlisting in the Army. They had been returning from church, in the older, green Buick, and the first thing they noticed was crying. People crying in the streets downtown, huddled under their mufflers and woolen caps, wandering through space like empty wrappers. They huddled in small groups, their faces broken, before dispersing again into pairs of twos and threes.

"Turn on the radio, Harv." Johnson's mother touched his father's shoulder in the front seat.

The voice of the disc jockey filled the car. *Japanese warplanes have attacked Pearl Harbor...more than two thousand Americans killed.*

He was young, and there wasn't much to think about, in terms of consequences. He was young and didn't know what lay ahead, which was the beauty of being young—so many risks taken before one has the sense to realize the dangers. He was young and going to fight.

"Of course," his father merely had said after Johnson stated his intentions at dessert, after his mother served the tapioca. He pushed back in his chair and patting his stomach, bulbous like an onion over his slacks. "It's the honorable thing to do. The American thing to do."

"Harv." His mother dropped her spoon. Her face, broad and unassuming, had knit itself into lines of worry as she had prepared dinner. It had permitted the minimal movement required for her to consume food, but now the tension in it had snapped completely. Her eyes bulged from her face, her mouth hung open, her bottom lip was wet and flecked with tapioca. "He could get killed. He could get hurt. We might never see him again."

"Mom, I'll be all right," Johnson said. "Don't cry, now."

"Well, the thing is, Helen, they gonna draft him eventually, anyway." His father lit a cigarette and pushed the pack across the table to Johnson. "Here, you're a man now, Calvin."

"Thanks, Dad." He pulled a cigarette from the pack of Lucky Strikes and fumbled with the matches so his father would not know he'd been smoking since he was a junior, behind the football field and the barn and the drugstore.

"When I was in the war, our replacements were terrible." Calvin's father talked, cigarette bobbing in the corner of his mouth. "Could barely aim a weapon. And they got killed as soon as they stepped off the convoys. If Calvin enlists early, he'll get better training. He'll have a better chance now than later."

"A better chance to live?" His mother pushed back her chair and stood up. She leaned over and snapped the cigarette in Calvin's mouth. "That's what we're talking about? Improving my son's chances of living?"

She hurried from the dining room, the back door slamming behind her. Calvin put the broken cigarette in his father's ashtray and didn't ask for another.

"She'll be all right." His father exhaled. He looked thoughtfully into the distance. Or perhaps he had indigestion. "This is a new ball game, with the Japs attacking. And we'll all need to make sacrifices. You're doing the right thing, fighting the right fight. I'm proud of you, son."

His father had not been terribly proud of him up to that point. He did not get a scholarship to Ohio State. He did not get the grades for anywhere else. He knew his father wanted him to join him at the police force, but the precinct at Bowling Green suffered from a severe lack of adventure to a boy who'd not been anywhere except for Yosemite the summer he was fourteen.

But his mother, he had not wanted her pride, only her love. She sat outside in the small gazebo he and his father had built the summer before. It was cold and she did not have a coat. He sat opposite her on the round bench inside the gazebo as the air whipped through the sleeves of her dress, blew up her apron.

"You don't have to go." She looked at him, and what she was saying with her eyes was *I don't want you to go.*

"There's no other choice," he answered. "Our country needs me."

"I need you, Calvin. Your father." She wove her hands together. She always wove them together after finishing half of her desert, as if she was not allowed, did not deserve, any more than she had already taken.

"Mom, you can't say that. If Pastor Smith heard you…"

"I don't care about what the pastor hears or doesn't hear. You're our only child, Calvin. Now. There was one before you…but we lost him before he entered this world. I never told you because we didn't see the point in burdening you with it, but I'm not going to lose another."

"I don't see what other choice I have," he repeated. He rose and wrapped his arms around her. She felt stiff, empty, like a turkey carcass after Thanksgiving. "I'll be all right."

Now, at the table, he wondered if there had been another choice. Perhaps he could have gone to Canada, or to Mexico. Maybe none of this would have happened. He could have returned a few years after the war, gotten a job, gotten married. Had children. Made his mother happy. She had only wanted his love, and he couldn't even give that to her. He put his head on the table and cried, his nose clogged and runny, his eyes swelling like golf balls underneath his lids. He'd done nothing in his life, given his parents nothing to be proud of, no solace for their sacrifice of raising him, of loving him. He wished he were dead. At least they would have closure.

He walked through the house to his old bedroom, noting the new furniture, a new piece of sewing work that lay in jumbles of yarn and needles on the table by his mother's easy chair. Was she making a sweater for his father? A scarf? He looked at the photographs on the mantel of the fireplace—in color! They were his parents, but they were not. Their brilliant flesh tones and bright fabrics and blue skies leered at him, courtesy of the miracle of Kodak. They were people who were childless, who smiled at the camera, but their eyes belied the emptiness of those who had lost, whose eyes you could not look at for long for fear that you would fall into that deep well with them, unable to return, instead looking awkwardly into your lemonade or scotch and scratching your neck, wondering where your wife had gone. He picked one up, relieved it was not dusty, that the requirements of the household were not being neglected by his mother, that a prolonged depression had not let everything go the way of the planter. He put the picture back. These were not his parents. They were people who had simply gotten old.

Shit. His room was as he had left it. He sucked in his breath so that he would not begin to cry again. On his desk lay unopened letters. Their envelopes were yellowed, and he took them in his hands, feeling the weight of years on their delicate fabrics. His pulse quickened when he saw the return addresses, New York, NY, but then his hopes dipped when he saw the postmarks, 1947 and 1948.

Dear Calvin, the first began. *I hope you've been taking care of yourself. Fall in New York is lovely! The energy, the bustle of the taxis and subways, the awfully smart people at parties, interesting classes—it was as if New York were gift-wrapped just for me.*

I think of you often and miss you. I can't quite explain what there was between us, but I can feel its absence. Will you come to New York to visit? Yours, Kate.

He folded the letter back into the envelope and opened the second. How long had they lain like this, along with his parent's hopes for his return, on the desk?

There were three more letters from New York, before it appeared she had given up. But he had not. Twenty years, more, had been taken from him, and he deserved to get them back. He deserved another chance. Or did he? The rules that had existed in this room, this house, this earth, before he left for war—the passage of time, the guarantee of death—seemed a fallacy. He did not know what the rules were anymore. They were his to make. He would find her in New York, at least try—a day, a week, maybe longer—before trying to find Stanley. But he was down to his last few dollars from Maggie, enough to get on a bus. He would figure out how to get around in New York once he got there, eat trash if he had to.

The letters were opened now; there was no way to undo that, for his parents to know someone had been here. He put them in the back pocket of his jeans. They were his, he told himself, and he shouldn't feel guilty about coming here and taking them. He opened a drawer and pulled out a folded undershirt, where his mother had always put them, sliding it over his bare chest, then opened the closet and found a sweatshirt, one he used to chop wood in during the late falls. He put the grey fabric against his cheek and felt it wet with his tears before he pushed it to his face to muffle his cries. He was home now. He could wait for his parents to return. They wouldn't care how he looked, what had happened. They would only care it was him.

But who or what was he? He went into the bathroom and removed the bloody tissue. The bleeding from his stump had stopped, and the pain had receded to a hot, uncomfortable throb. He felt for the pinky in his pocket and took it out, pressing it to the still-open wound. Then he undid the shoelace and wrapped it around both parts, criss-crossing the thread until the pinky was loosely secured on the stump. Carefully, he washed it and wrapped it in toilet paper, flushing the bloody paper towel down the toilet. The waiting began.

He heard a car on the road. He could stand in the living room, mangled hand in his pocket, and wait. Hopefully his father's heart was still strong. He could tell them—what would he tell them? Perhaps they wouldn't ask. Perhaps his coming home precluded any explanation for his absence. He could still find Kate and Stanley.

There was time for everything. After a few minutes, he heard the turn of the Buick onto the half mile of dirt road to their home, the fat of the rubber tires on gravel.

He held his breath and slowly unraveled the toilet paper. Already he could see that the blood had congealed, that healing was taking place at some accelerated pace. The skin on the edges of his fingers was already beginning to stretch over the bone and muscle and touch the pinky, to connect the two parts.

He was not normal. He had been a Christian in the traditional American sense; reverence for a god that seemed as natural and unquestionable as Santa Claus had been when he was five. There would be nothing in his parent's Bible—theirs or anyone else's—that would explain him. And if God did not allow him to exist, then God could not exist for him, either. The chasm that was formerly God's place in his heart had been filled with cement. He thought of Kate. How could she possibly love a man who was not a man, in body or heart? How could she love a man almost thirty years—to her—gone?

And his parents, how could they understand? How could they parade him around town, their seemingly prodigal son, freak of nature? Or, they simply wouldn't believe it was him. Or maybe it was he who was scared, to see them so fragile, so aged. So human. He wadded the blood-soaked flannel shirt into a ball and ran down the stairs and, stopping before the mantel and—there was no time for aesthetic debate—took the first picture he saw. It was one he had seen before, knew very well—a black and white of his parents together before he was born. He stuffed it into the bloody hobo bundle of his shirt, hurrying through the house. He closed the back door behind him and dropped the key back onto the circle of earth.

There was nothing he could do now but wait until they'd entered the house from the front before running for his life. The cornfields, still in their spring infancy, could not hide him, nor could the dirt road that caterpillared unobstructed to town. He heard the front door close, a small locust of voices—his mother and father and probably another couple from church they'd invited to brunch and bridge—inhabit the parlor. Then he tore across the back yard, his heels kicking up the earth like a tractor hoe.

He made it to the road when he heard her voice, warbled and weaker than the bell of sound that had rung through the house many years ago.

"Calvin?!? Calvin?!? Wait!"

The toilet paper unraveled from his pinky as he ran, and he grabbed at his hand to keep his hanging digit from dropping to the earth. But, to his surprise, it was almost attached, like a maggot to a piece of meat.

He wanted to turn back and look at her, to take one last mold of her face that he could cast in his mind, and perhaps leave one for her as well, that her son was alive, healthy, and hadn't aged a day in almost thirty years.

He kept running.

The last time Johnson had been to the bus station in downtown Bowling Green, he had been coming home, from the war, to start his life. That life was now over; it had not ever actually begun. Now life would start again. Kate and Stanley were part of his past, and now perhaps they would be part of his future. But they had never felt like the present. The present was confusion, loneliness. And low on funds. He took the last few dollars of the money Maggie had

given him and bought a ticket to New York, a hot dog, a cup of coffee, two packs of cigarettes, and the daily. In the back of the Grey-
hound he opened the paper and scanned the headlines. Where to
start, to find out about the world? The Olympic summer games were
being held in Munich. Germany, now a friend to the world? Presi-
dent Richard Nixon announced that 12,000 more soldiers would be
withdrawn from Vietnam, from a peak of 543,400 in 1969. Johnson
looked at the advertisements. Watches that kept time with quartz
crystals. Televisions the size of ovens, with color screens. It was like
visiting a foreign country, except he knew the language.

As the bus vibrated to life, he sat up in his seat. His foot slipped,
and he bent over, wondering whether he had dropped a section of
the newspaper. The glossy cover of primary colors, the arching red
and yellow letters, comforted him.

A Superman comic. Some boy, twelve or maybe thirteen, must
have left it behind. Johnson opened the pages and settled into reading. He had spent many hours on his own bed as a boy, turning the
pages, reading about the man of steel and his nemesis, Lex Luther,
the love of his life, Lois Lane. He was fascinated that the forces
that pulled on Superman in different directions shared the same
initials. He was not smart enough to think further into the impli-
cations. Instead, he concentrated on Superman's strengths. A man
who could perform amazing feats, who could not die. Who had no
friends, could tell no one, as Clark Kent, of his plight. Could love
no one. Was revered as a hero. And was completely misunderstood.

It had been forty years, maybe. And every month, Superman, now
more muscular, more handsome in 1972 than ever, saved the world,
saved damsels, saved puppies. And he never lived happily ever after
with Lois, never retired to his farm or a cabin or a houseboat in Cuba,

needing time to himself. He never had a superboy or a supergirl. He kept being super. He was too young to remember his parents, Jor-El and Lara, paying homage to them in his fortress of solitude.

Johnson pulled out the picture of his parents. At the bus station bathroom he liberated it from its bulky frame and slid the black-and-white photo into the wallet he had bought at a bus station in Illinois. He looked so much like his father, the slightly wavy brown hair, the broad forehead and wide-spaced eyes, full lips. It was a face that held gravity, that was weighted with action and with heavy, laborious thoughts moving like damp sand through a straw. His mother's slightly pointed chin and dimples gave the bottom of his face more playfulness, like a rock formation whose bottom had worn smooth where it met the waterline.

Here, his parents, standing on the shores of Put-In-Bay Island, Ohio, arms linked like lace, were even younger than he. He had not even been born. And as his memory of them faded, they would remain young, their smiles, their eyes aglow with the continued sunrise of their lives.

He returned the picture and wallet to the inner pocket of his leather jacket (bought at an Army Surplus store in Montana), where they brushed against Kate's letters. How would he find Kate in New York? Would she be married, working in a museum? Would she be happy? Would she be happy to see him? Or had she moved on, like time, leaving him with his own Lex Luther, loneliness, also beginning with an L?

He held the comic tightly in his hands, like it was the Bible, or a fortune cookie. It may as well have been written in Chinese, like the rest of the world. The sun was behind them now, the bus plowing eastward, the orange horizon slipping, impossibly, into the color of typewriter ribbon. He put his hand on the window, making a fist. If his hand went through the glass, it would bleed. The blood would cover the window and the seat and his clothes, enough to kill someone. But not him. If he knew, during the war, that he could never die, would he have fought differently? If they all could not die, what would be the point of the war? What would be the point of anything? Death made so many things possible: domination, fear, gratitude.

Now, he was only scared of living. He leaned his head against the glass and tried to sleep. He was not scared of sleep, of the bus flying off the road and turning over and over, propelling him from the window like a bottle rocket, of the bus bursting into the flames and burning him to ash. He might be happy, perhaps, if those things happened, if he did not survive. He was scared that, no matter how many times he went to sleep, no matter how many times the world faded to black, he was always guaranteed of waking.

1973

She was on the television sometimes, the Grand Ole Opry and the Lawrence Welk show, and the camera panned close, framing her little heart-shaped face, fuller with age or maybe the weight of the road or the rainbow assortment of uppers, downers, and diuretics, her liver straining against the rye and vodka and wine, or maybe the weight that success, angel or demon, places on the eyelids, the corner of the mouth, the shoulders. The powder on her cheeks gave them a slightly metallic hue in the studio lights, and the heat cracked her lipstick, making little rivers, maps, in her lips that aged her like a tree.

But she was still beautiful. A shiny doll, painted and powdered and each eyelash separated, coated with mascara, her lips forming every word so carefully, so emphatically, that the deaf could hear her, the muscles of her mouth pouring the sound into one's eyes, a vessel of mouth that poured sugar water and the smell of gardenia and the flicker of twilight stars.

Stanley always watched. He sat on the edge of the couch, every muscle tense, a gazelle gauging the movements of a lion fifty yards away, far enough away, on the television, in the clearing, but close enough to leap the river, to jump from the picture tube, and sink its teeth, her grip, into his neck as he staggered across the savannah, the living room, feeling his blood, his will, drain from him.

He did not drink or smoke or talk. He merely watched, blotting time and circumstance away, her voice, the glint of her eyes, the curled and set bouffant of her hair, all for his pleasure, his pain, and no one else's. He wondered whether she knew he watched, whether she sang a special phrase for him, whether the wink between the second verse and the last chorus was for him or for someone else.

Sometimes after she sang, she would chit-chat with Lawrence Welk, Conway Twitty, whoever was the host, and she'd touch her hair absently, sprayed and unmoving, laugh a little forced, high-pitched squeal at someone's joke, talk about upcoming tour dates, an album. Then she'd be gone, some comedy sketch or standup act following her, some commercial for Coca-Cola, and he'd stand out on the porch, looking at the road, wondering how to get to her. Roads connected all of America, he figured. One could find anyone if they took the right combination of roads.

He never got into the truck. He went back into the house, sat at the kitchen table, and drank. He drank until he passed out and if he was lucky, he did not remember the evening in question until it was long past, weeks later, too far to touch or hurt him.

Heidi would be thirteen in two months. Old enough for him to tell her who her mother was. But what purpose, he wondered, did it serve? They'd received no child support, no royalties, not even a Christmas card from Cindy or her accountants, managers, lawyers. They hadn't received a goddamn cent in the thirteen years they had lived in the farmhouse. Not even a phone call. Years ago, Stanley had sent pictures of Heidi taken at the Sears Portrait Studio to Nashville Records. They probably sat in a mail bag with thousands of other letters from fans. He wondered whether the secretary who finally opened them threw them away or had passed them along, what had been discussed. He had never been offered hush money, although he had thought, from time to time, of asking for it. Not for himself, but for Heidi. He'd been laid off from the shirt factory and, except for an occasional job, relied on his pension to clothe and feed her. There was no money for anything, even as she deserved everything that thus far escaped her—beauty, biological parents, presents.

It would be cruel to tell her, insult to injury. She'd asked, once or twice, as a child, about her mother, cried at parent's day in kindergarten when Stanley had come and sat on the little kindergartner chairs with all the other mothers, his polyester church paints riding high up his shins, his clip-on tie drooping over his belt like a sad dog. She'd run to the girls room, her face red and strained like an exotic fruit, and the teacher had to bring her out to Stanley.

"Why don't I have a mommy like everyone else?" She asked in the parking lot as Stanley lifted her into the truck. She was wearing the pink and white dress she had picked out at JC Penney, one she had worn the first day of school. So proud she was of it, of herself, until she had realized that she looked different from the others, her honey skin, her angularity, her green glass eyes, Dumbo ears. She had come home asking what an Oreo was, having overheard the teacher's aide talking about her to the teacher. *It means you're as sweet as a cookie*, he'd replied.

"You have a mommy, baby." His hands gripped the steering wheel. He'd gone back and forth over the years about whether to tell her Cindy had died, had been kidnapped, was a secret agent. How to tell a child her mother hadn't wanted her, wanted them? "She'll come home. You'll see. And she'll bring with her everything you could ever want. All you need to do is wait."

Heidi looked out the window. He stole glances at her as she

looked far across the fields, the horizon, the cotton candy clouds, and he knew what she was thinking: how to get to her, where to start. He stopped at the Dairy Queen on the way home, and she'd smiled, gotten a chocolate and vanilla twist. It had satisfied her that day. But there would be many others to come, he knew, waves of days crashing harder and faster, pulling him out to sea if he was not careful, both of them unmoored.

That day before Heidi's birthday, Stanley turned on the television, hoping to catch the Orioles game. Heidi's presents were wrapped in newspaper in his bedroom: the record album *Don't Shoot Me I'm Only the Piano Player* from some nancy boy, Elton John, that she'd asked for and some Bonne Bell lip bubblegum lip gloss that a counter girl at Woolworths had found for him when he asked what fifty-five cents, the last of his money for the month, could buy a young girl. Heidi was in the kitchen, trying to bake a cake. She was taking home economics that year, all the kids were, and she'd bought some cake mix and frosting at the store with what was usually Stanley's cigarette money.

He turned the dial on the television while looking through butts in the tray, hoping for a cylindrical centimeter of tobacco to smoke, but stopped at stock footage of Cindy on the picture tube. It was not time for the Opry or the Lawrence Welk show or whatever variety show on which she may have been scheduled to appear. Rather, it was a news item, a still photo, her name and dates underneath: 1917-1973. He turned up the volume.

"What are you, deaf all of a sudden?" Heidi stood in the doorway, ghost hands spotting flour on the hips of her jeans. Her face dropped like the cake she was baking. "Dad, what is it?"

He shook his head, waving her away. A child should not have to see her father cry. He felt her move toward him, her hand dangling out in front of her as she considered whether to touch the overripe fruit of his head, red and shaking and simmering with tears. She had touched him when she was little, wrapping her thin brown arms against the pale, hairy trunks of his legs. But she had clung to him full of her fears, her disappointments, her slights. Now her face, mouth agape, confessed to him that she did not know what his fears and disappointments were, had not realized he had them.

"Dad, can you tell me, for my birthday?" She touched his shoulder, smearing the flour on him.

"Tell you what, honey?" He looked at her, his blue eyes, the bird sprout of hair and long nose.

"How you could be my father."

The words tumbled out of her mouth like change. He knew she had not meant to say them, but now they choked the air like wet-hot garbage. Her cheeks burned as she looked away from him.

"Come here." He patted the floor next to him. They sat and watched the rest of the news story. The reporter with blonde hair shellacked into a curved lampshade stood in front of Nashville Recording Studios and recounted Cindy's life in a seven-second sound byte: the struggles of being a midget in the country music world, her little girl named Heidi, who died of pneumonia after she was born, her twenty-year career that netted her five top-10 singles and two platinum albums, a tour with Patsy Cline, and her eventual death from kidney disease brought on by her condition.

"Her child, Heidi, didn't die of pneumonia." Stanley turned to Heidi. "You're that child."

He told her about everything, then, holding her hands, long and tapered and wanting mastery of the guitar or some other elegant dexterous profession. He squeezed them as they grew clammy and shook, as Heidi's eyes grew wide and then narrowed as she processed the enormity of Stanley's words.

They forgot about the cake until it burned. Heidi scraped the brindled skin off the cake and covered it in frosting, and they ate pieces that night because there was no other cake.

❀❀❀

"I wish you wouldn't make up stuff like that," Heidi said to Stanley at breakfast the next day. In the empty chair where her mother would have sat rested the newspaper-wrapped gifts. "About who my mother is. It was mean, and maybe you thought it was funny, or maybe you did it to make me feel better, but I wish you wouldn't do it again."

The trajectory of Stanley's coffee mug to his mouth stopped as he regarded her, eating the yellowest, spongiest parts of her birthday cake, shoving forkfuls into her expanding cheeks, her eyes focused on the plate, on what little goodness remained, and he wanted to cradle her back into a baby, suck the venom of this life out of her, and send her in a basket on a stream, where some fairies might find her and turn her into a princess. Instead, he picked up the Elton John record, wrapped in the comics section, and slid it over to her.

"I'm sorry, honey." He smiled. "It was awfully mean of me, and I'm so sorry. I can be a real dunderhead, huh? Now, how about some gifts?"

After he dropped her off at school, Stanley went through the rooms of the farmhouse. There wasn't much to collect. He took the record albums he'd bought of 'Lil Cindy's and the fabrics from her gaudy madam clothes she'd never made into anything else from the back of his closet, along with the quilt they'd slept under when they first arrived, a tiny perfume bottle of Shalimar. And the herb. He knew it was not connected to Cindy, but it was something he had kept alive, like hope. Hope that Cindy would come back to him. Hope that he would make peace with Johnson. Hope that he would be a better person, that Heidi would have a happy life.

He pressed the herb into the folds of the purple silk shirt he'd worn on the ferry and carried everything to the back yard with a squirt bottle of lighter fluid. He coated the pile with the clean, chemical smell of butane and felt clinical as he struck a match bulb on the side of its box. It was a surgical incision, a painless recovery, a fresh start, he hoped. He watched as the flames waved over the fabrics and turned the cardboard LP covers as black as the melted vinyl inside. He smoked a cigarette, as he watched, to suffocate and blacken any spore that might still be floating in him, threaten to multiply when it felt safe to do so.

When the pile of memories turned to ash, he took a nearby stick and sifted through them. A lump the size of coal remained. He blew the ashes away, and the fuzzy brown carcass of the herb stared back at him. He felt a sharp knock at the back of his head, as if his mother Safine had reached all the way from heaven to slap him. He squirted more lighter fluid onto it and struck a second match, watching it fall and explode on the herb. It burned like a sun, and Stanley shielded his eyes and looked back toward the house for the garden hose. But then, the brightness dimmed, the fire consumed itself, and the herb still remained, glowing orange like an ember. He leaned forward and touched it with his finger. It was not hot, as he expected, but a current of energy vibrated faintly in its core. Thoughts came to him that were not his, a house of bone and mud, a musket, suffocating dirt. A pain in his hip. He saw himself above himself, stuffing part of the herb into his own mouth, a winter forest alight with shrapnel behind his helmetless head. He looked down and, where his left leg had once rested, red meat and white chipped bone stretched on the ground like streamer paper.

He dropped the herb and waited until it glowed no longer, then he picked it up with grilling tongs and put it in a plastic bag on the kitchen table. He wrote everything that happened in the diary he'd been keeping, an old spiral-bound day planner he'd gotten free from the dentist's office that listed one day on each page along with several lines for notes and errands. Then he got in the truck and went to the library.

"Dad, what's with all the books on herbs?" Heidi sat at the kitchen table after school, reduced now to the burned pieces of cake. She flipped one book with her fork and gazed at the herb encased in plastic.

"Nothing." He swept everything into his arms and hurried upstairs to his bedroom. After telling her about Cindy, relating his experience with Johnson and the herb would probably convince Heidi he was out of his mind, a state he had not entirely disproven himself. A few minutes later, he listened to Heidi come upstairs. He held his breath like a boy as he waited for her to knock, but instead she continued onto her room, where a minute later, the sounds of her new record filled the upstairs. Something about croc rocking being something shocking. He looked through the pages of the illustrated book until he came upon the phrase his mother had uttered to him decades ago, before he went off to war: *burnette saxifrage*. And then, he began to read.

1974

He stood by the lamp post a few cars down the street, away from the doorman, his fists pushed deep into his jeans pockets, a white t-shirt and some Army boots completing him, like Dylan ten years before down in the village. At least that's what some woman, long-haired and dreamy, had told him at the mid-town library as he poured over telephone books and maps of Manhattan. It had been luck, seeing Kate's picture in the arts section of the *New York Times*. He'd been living in Coney Island, on Mermaid Avenue, not far from Woody Guthrie's childhood home, selling hot dogs to fat bored ladies and their children, when he'd happened upon the article about the forthcoming Kiyoshi Awazu retrospective in '75. The curator, her name was now Kate Strauss, talked about the importance of Awazu's contributions to urban design. He studied the picture of her in front of MOMA, the black-and-white jacquard print of her wrap dress, the softness around her waist where it did not sink inward as sharply as it had once, the fullness of her checks, the crosshatching at the top of them near her eyes, like pie crust, the wisps of silver that nested like spiderwebs in her dark, straight hair.

The same woman who appeared at the entrance to the apartment building, an attaché in one hand, purse in the other, and stepped toward the idling car.

"Kate," he said, and the doorman, who could have been a 240-pound fullback for the New York Jets, stepped in front of him.

"Do you have an appointment to see Mrs. Strauss?" He lifted the two trunks of his arms like a crossing guard, and the seams in the armpits of his doorman's coat grew wide-eyed under the strain.

"Kate Crane, I need to talk to you." He bobbed his head over the doorman's shoulder. "Don't you remember me? It's Calvin Johnson."

He did not remember what happened exactly next—her attaché falling on the ground, followed by her purse, the doorman's weight atop him, his boots scraping against the pavement.

"Eddie, it's okay."

From where he lay on his back, he could see her arm, her bangles cutting against her wrist, as she tugged at the doorman's shoulder. Her hand suddenly dove over the doorman and grabbed at Johnson's neck, pulling at the silver chain and medal from where it lay hidden in the cotton of his shirt. She gazed at the medal of Saint Christopher for a second, her brother's, before she started crying. The hand disappeared, and he heard the scrape of her heels against the pavement as she stood up.

"Ma'am, is this man bothering you?" The doorman sat on his haunches as Johnson squirmed, even at six feet, so small under him.

"No, Eddie—it's okay." She dug in her purse for some tissue for her eyes until Eddie offered his handkerchief. "I know him."

Now Johnson was standing, just as quickly as he had been pinned to the sidewalk, the doorman dusting him off like an item in a menagerie.

"Why are you...so...?" Her lips parted, but no words emerged. Her eyebrows furrowed, as if that knit them into being. "You look...like a bum."

She nodded toward the car, at the opened door and the driver standing by it. "Get in."

On the way to the museum, she ran her hands along his face, touched his lips, fingered the bent ear lobes that angled back toward his head. It had been almost thirty years since he'd seen her eyes, heard her voice, now slightly worn.

"You sure you're not Calvin's son?" She lit a cigarette. "Is this some sort of joke?"

"I swear on my soul—you left me in Ohio, but I never forgot you. I saw you in the newspaper. I've been in New York for years looking for you, after promising myself I'd only stay a week or two. Before that, I was in Montana."

"Did you tap some sort of fountain of youth out there?" She tried to knock her ashes in the ashtray but the little cakes of gray tumbled over onto the carpeted floor. "I think I need to call my therapist. Jesus. He needs to adjust my dosage."

"No—look, I didn't tell you everything that happened to me in the war, and I probably should have. But even I didn't know, when I saw you, what the truth of it was. But I want to tell you now. That is, if you even want to see me, I didn't mean to frighten you. Hey, they got the right guy for that job at the door there."

"Sure, sure," she repeated, her words not for him. A battle somewhere deep in her thoughts occurred as he watched her eyes flit back and forth. He took her hand, small and clammy, and squeezed it. He could feel her heartbeat leap from her skin into the dried callous of his palm. No other words filled the space between them until the car pulled up to 53rd Street. She began to climb from the seat, but turned to him.

"Stay here." She grabbed his wrist. "I'll be right back."

❁❁❁

They walked through the upper west side of Central Park, near her apartment. A chill crawling off the Hudson wove through the paths and danced with the litter on the sidewalk. The sky swirled uneasily with clouds, a deep sea of blue behind them. The city was a soft parade of sound that seemed to accentuate their silence rather than hide it.

"So what paper did we work on together at school?" She played with the strap on her purse.

"Beowulf," he answered. "Do you remember my grade?"

"I'm sorry." She shook her head.

"C-plus."

"Why did you go to Montana?"

"To find Stanley Polensky." He took a cigarette from the pack she extended. "A soldier I served with. It's a long story, though. I got the letters you sent from New York. Not until after I came back, though."

He had imagined the small walk-up off Times Square that they would have rented back then, had he followed her to New York, a place where they brewed coffee and fried eggs for breakfast and had a rye after work before heading over to the galleries at night for parties, more cocktails with her friends. Something he'd probably never feel comfortable with, and yet she would challenge him to do it, to prove his love for her, and he would.

"It was just yesterday I saw you," he explained, clasping and unclasping his hands. "It's as if it's only been a few years...you went to New York for school. For me, it is. It really is."

"But it's been a whole lifetime, almost," she answered, glancing at him as they walked. "At least for me."

"What did you think, when I didn't write you back?"

"I don't know," she sighed, adjusted her sunglasses with her thumb and forefinger. "That you thought I was incredibly difficult and silly and that you found yourself a nice, agreeable woman to marry. My parents always said I was too independent for my own good. But life goes on."

"For some people," he answered. "So what happened? When your life went on?"

The shadows grew long over the park as he digested, with revulsion and satiation, each morsel of her life apart from him, the stories of art world superstars and trips to Europe, her husband Harry, a surgeon, the private schools in Connecticut for her boys and the "little shack" in the Hamptons. It was a book in which he played no part, and however compelling, he could not own it, nor could he be sure a sequel would be written.

It was getting late. They'd walked over the bridge over the 79th Street transverse up to the 85th transverse and around the reservoir and back down to the Met. He stopped walking, and she trailed ahead a few steps before noticing, before he curled his hand around her arm and pulled her gently to him.

"I never got over you," he said, his hands reaching for his neck. He held the unclasped medal of St. Christopher, her brother's, before her. "I think you should take Stephen's medal back. I've finally found my way safely."

"I don't... I don't understand." She gripped the medal in her palm. He watched the chain undulate between her fingers like a pendulum, a dousing rod. "It's just not possible that you're here, and you're the same. And, even in the smallest realm of possibility that somehow this is real, you are real, why would you just show up here, all these years later, and expect to claim me?"

She opened her mouth, sucking in the air between them, perhaps so that she could scream, to exert the force of her being, to sonically disperse him, the hallucination, the doppelganger hustler before her. But before she could make a sound, he pressed his lips on hers.

❀❀❀

In the main gallery, he waited for her, studying the paintings, the drips and streaks, and it was a lot different than when he was in high school, when they studied Michelangelo and Rembrandt. Even art had moved on without him.

"Do you see anything you like?" Her voice behind him, velvet with age, and he turned with such an urge to kiss her but stared into her eyes, the brown pools of them, acknowledged the laugh lines by her lids. She took him in as well, his worn clothes, the fruity cologne he had borrowed from another boarder at the house in Coney Island. She clasped his arm above his left elbow. "I'm going to show you what I like."

They came to a painting with lots of dark boxes shaped into a grid. Gray-ghost hieroglyphic swirls and numbers were painted in the grids. A letterbox or graveyard of them.

"Lee Krasner," Kate said simply. "This woman will get her due. I will see to it. First female retrospective at MOMA. She was not just Pollack's wife—not by a long shot."

"What do you like about this painting?"

"They are the secrets of life." She moved her finger in the air over-top the symbols. "Whose meanings are private and unique to each of us and yet entirely unknown. And our greatest rewards come in brief episodes of coherence, sometimes only just one. The rest of the time, one is flailing, drowning, eyes burning with saltwater."

He closed his eyes and concentrated on the weight and warmth of her hands on his arm, the sound of her voice swimming through the air to his ears as she explained the rise of early 20th-century cubism and abstract expressionism to modern and pop art and fluxus. She had spent her life in these quiet halls, in equally quiet places in her head loving the majesty of ideals. This was her life, her voice said, the discovery of Lee Krasner, of Frida Kahlo, Willem de Kooning. He would remember all of it because he could not forget the rush of her voice, her breaths, as she spoke about color wheels and brush strokes and canons and the American identity in modern art. The excited lilt of her voice made it sound a little higher, and she was Kate again, the girl in his class at Bowling Green, laughing over a milkshake at the drug store.

"I don't love many things—my sons, my parents, my brother Stephen. I loved my husband, at some point in time. I love art," she said as they stood in front of a Robert Motherwell painting. He put his arms around her from behind and cradled his head into her neck.

"I want you to love me," he murmured into her neck. He felt her back stiffen and arch, her eyes scanning the gallery, before falling against him. "Just a brief episode of coherence...will be okay."

Kate hailed a cab and ordered the cab driver to drive them to a hotel on 31st not far from Chinatown. The smell of garlic and peanuts wafted over the sour burps of manholes as he guided her up the drab red carpet and into the lobby. In the room, they touched things—him the lightswitch plate, her the cheap wood of the dresser. Then, slowly, they came together in the middle, their bodies pressed against each other like praying hands. And then their lips connected them in a space that neither of them could see, but they swam in its calm darkness together.

❀❀❀

"I can't get pregnant anymore," she explained to him after he'd pulled out and come into a tissue. "Unless you've got some souvenir from the sixties, it's okay."

"I don't understand." He watched her across the room as she fumbled in her purse for her cigarettes. He studied where gravity had begun to tug at her, the faintest varicose vein in her right leg, and he felt alarmed for a second that he had wasted so much time dead in Montana.

"Sexual diseases," she answered, crawling back under the sheet. "Or, we can buy condoms if it makes you feel better."

"I don't have any of those...diseases, I think. I'm more worried about passing on my...defect."

"You call it a defect, my little Dorian Gray?" She lit a cigarette. "Some of us would love to look so good."

"Well, you watch your missing legs and fingers grow back like a lizard, burn to death and drown, and let me know how you feel, then."

"I don't want to think about it." She put her cigarette in the ashtray and rolled over to him. "I can't think about who you are...or aren't. I just want to think about you right now."

"What about your husband? Your sons?"

"You didn't think I'd have them—you didn't entertain those possibilities on your way here to see me after all this time?"

"No...I did."

"But you'd thought I'd leave them for you."

"I wasn't thinking clearly, exactly. I just knew I wanted to see you again. I was meant to see you again. I know they were so long ago, but the letters, your letters said to come…but I'm prepared to leave. I love you, but I know you have your own life here. I wouldn't ask you to give up anything for me. I've got people I need to see, anyway. It might not be too late for them yet."

"I don't want to think about it." She rested her head on top of his chest as he stroked her hair. "You're here now; that's all I want to think about."

The room rented for fifty dollars a week, which Kate paid. It was closer to downtown than Coney Island, so he stayed there on the days he wasn't working. She came by Monday and Thursday evenings and Wednesday during lunch.

For weeks, they studied and kissed and traced flesh with their fingers. He listened to her breathe while she sat in bed reading media releases, correspondences from international museums to procure loans of certain pieces, the quickening of the air through her nostrils demonstrating her surprise or excitement, a long sigh signaling impatience. He pretended that thousands of hours had passed before just like this one, a thousand more ahead, that their time right now really was that inconsequential.

"Chinese?" She glanced at him as she closed a folder of procurements. "I'm starving. Something else, then? On your mind, maybe?"

"I didn't come here to have an affair with you." He sat up and looked for his briefs. "I need something else. Not necessarily a promise, but…"

"Calvin, you're talking about the future again." She stood up and picked up his boxers from the floor. "I thought we agreed not to."

He pulled on his boxers and socks and sat on the bed.

"I think I should go to Maryland, see whether I can find Stanley," he said finally. He had called the operator and found all the Stanley or S. Polenskys in Maryland. There were four. Two in Baltimore, one in Annapolis. One in Fruitland.

"Why?"

"Because I need to know why this happened, first off. And what I can do to stop it. He did this to me—he needs to undo it. And maybe I just want a home. You have a home—you don't know what it feels like."

"I think you're too worked up about this idea of home." She sat on the bed beside him, let her hands rest on his shoulders. "No one has a home in the world. It's in their hearts, in the people they care about. And everyone is alone, despite what you think."

"If I was a normal person, would you consider it? A home with me?"

"You're no less normal than anyone else." She stood up and clasped her bra and pulled on her slip, her back to him. "I don't see why you can't just be happy there's this much."

"I think it's time for me to leave, then."

"I know a doctor." She turned her head slightly. "Henry Palmer. He's on our board of directors. Anyway, he's doing some very specialized, privately funded research, on genetic disorders. He has this adopted daughter who . . . anyway, I think he would be interested in meeting you."

"Why didn't you tell me before?" He stood up so quickly that she cowered, and he bent toward her, collapsing her in his arms like an umbrella. "I'm sorry. I didn't mean to scare you."

"I don't know why," she sobbed. "I'm having a hard time understanding any of this. But it's just nice to be with you. It's like . . . living in my memories. I thought things would be different back then. In a way, it's as if I still have a choice."

"This wasn't a choice for me," he whispered into her skin, tasting the salt of her tears on his lips. "I didn't choose to live. I don't choose to live this way."

"Speaking of choices, I have chosen to keep information from you." She pulled away from him and gathered her papers. "About me."

"What do you mean?"

"I didn't choose to die." She pushed the papers into her attaché. Some of them bent in defiance, tore, before she forced them in, zipping up its black mouth. She straightened up to look at him. "But I am."

1976

Heidi

Heidi Polensky was ugly, and not ugly in any way she would ever outgrow. Her father had a few pictures from when she was a baby, a young girl, tacked to the refrigerator—holding the hand of the Jolly Green Giant at the county fair, a free portrait from the Sears Portrait Studio, where a few growing incisors gleamed white as headlights, obscuring the rest of her face. It had only gotten worse from there. Things that should have grown out grew in, and things that should have stayed in grew out. Her chin and nose, sharp and long, were influenced by a gravity from which others were impervious. Her face was flat except for her eyes, which bulged like grapes. She was convinced her parents were actually a troll and an elf. In class pictures, where her country classmates, round with health, skin the color of wheat, placid eyes and smiles, stood stacked like bowling pins, her dark, ferocious features could not be hidden in the back row, half-tucked between plump Shelley Partridge and the only Asian child, Yin Soo.

"It's a shit world," her father agreed at the stove when she complained during the fifth grade of being called a witch, a booger face, a troll, a shrimp, a goblin, a chinky (not even Yin Soo was called a chinky), a fart, smelly, a dog, a Martian, stupid, and ugly—the simplest and yet most hurtful. "It's better to find it out sooner than later."

But at least, it would not last much longer. Senior year at Mount Zion high had started, and like some scene from Shirley Jackson's "The Lottery," the ritual had begun. In the first two months, Shauna Beck, head cheerleader and varsity field hockey star, with her gaggle of witches had already jimmied open Heidi's gym locker during gym class and thrown her clothes in the showers, forcing her to wear her gym shorts and t-shirt the rest of the day. They slapped tags on her back with the word LESBIAN or sometimes CUNT. They had poured soda into the vents of her locker, ruining her papers and making the pages of her textbooks stick together. They tripped and sometimes punched her in the hallways. And when a teacher, any teacher, had pledged to get to the bottom of the bullying, Shauna and her friends were the first to raise their hands, smile sweetly at Heidi, and offer to help expose the culprits.

Things were different around Ms. Webster, the junior and senior English teacher. She was, as the boys all said, a "stone cold fox." She graduated from Bennington College and chose to teach in their small-hick town instead of a private school in Georgetown because she had grown up on a farm in the Midwest, she had been known to tell her students, and she missed its wholesomeness. That didn't stop her from wearing cashmere sweaters and richly printed scarves, tan leather boots, and snug corduroys, tastes that she had developed presumably at Georgetown and Bennington and not a Fashion Bug in Kansas. Boys wanted her, and girls wanted to be her. No one risked falling out of her good graces, not even Shauna Beck.

"I really liked your essay about Beowulf." Ms. Webster grabbed Heidi's arm as she walked down the hall after school. On the days she didn't stay after for French club and the math league, her father always waited out front, 2:45 pm, like clockwork. She was the last person to leave her seventh-period classroom and then stood with her back to her locker, eyes on her backpack. When the halls were empty except for candy and gum wrappers and a lost looseleaf paper, she hurried toward the front doors of the school, expecting but not looking forward to her father's complaints.

"Thanks," Heidi answered, although she'd already been aware of Ms. Webster's opinion. The papers were passed back thirty minutes before, and Heidi's had bore an A-plus. It had been hard-earned. For the first two papers of the fall quarter, she'd gotten only As. She'd given herself an extra week to write this one, treated it as if it were her college entrance essay. "I'm glad you liked it. Have a good day, Ms. Webster."

"Oh, am I keeping you from something?" Ms. Webster let go of her arm, and the absence of her fingers on Heidi's skin made Heidi dizzy, as if she were a diver who'd ascended too quickly to the surface. She pressed her palm, flat, on the wall and concentrated on the coolness of the cinder blocks.

"No... well, I have a ride." She leaned against the wall and stole a glance at Ms. Webster, her moss-colored cashmere cardigan from one of the stylish department stores that made her hair glow. Her features were fine and milky, albeit with a heavy smattering of freckles, like cinnamon on top of toast. Heidi wondered how someone so delicate had come from the heartland, where she imagined its inhabitants to be as fleshy and firm boned as her classmates.

"Wait here." Ms. Webster disappeared into her classroom and returned with some catalogs. "You've already applied, I know, but if you're still unsure, I really think you'd be a good fit for these schools."

Heidi fanned the catalogs outward in her hands. Bennington. Bryn Mawr. Swarthmore. St. John's College. All had tuitions beyond their means—she had looked up the costs of in the *College Guide* last winter. They were more than her father earned in a year with his pensions and odd jobs.

"Thanks—I'll take a look." Heidi slid off her backpack and fiddled with the zipper.

"Let me know if you need any help with anything, okay?" Ms. Webster locked her classroom door, and Heidi peeked in her Indian print purse. Marlboro Lights. A beaded wallet, an elongated calendar with a plastic cover.

"Thank you, Ms. Webster." They walked down the hall to the front door. "I applied to some out-of-state schools, but I don't know... if I can be that far from home."

"Oh, nonsense. You remind me of me when I was your age. Shy, but dying for adventure, for something, someone to validate her. There's no one here you feel validates you, is there, Heidi?"

And she couldn't answer her because she was crying. In the vestibule, she saw her father's truck through the front doors, its monstrous orange chassis shuddering, smoke pouring out of the damaged muffler like some ancient, grouchy dragon. She leaned against the wall, not sure what would upset her father more: getting into the truck cab now, in tears, or composing herself and wasting precious minutes, perhaps not getting in the cab until 2:55. She dropped her backpack on the ground.

"Heidi, what's wrong?" Ms. Webster put her hand on her cheek, her hazel eyes blinking, her small lips frowning. "Was it something I said?"

Heidi shook her head, crying harder. She had worked so hard that fall quarter to immunize herself to the cruelty, to stare blankly through Shauna and her friends as they taunted her. She hadn't thought it necessary to make herself immune to kindness. She felt Ms. Webster's arms around her, and her shoulders relaxed, the weight and warmth of Ms. Webster's body steadying her, the smell of her shampoo and perfume making her relaxed and sleepy.

"Oh, Heidi, I am so sorry." Ms. Webster pressed her like she was a ragdoll, and her will drained from her, and her father could go to hell. "I know what they do to you."

The front door opened, and her warm nothingness dissipated into the air, replaced by the emphysemic breaths and stale-tobacco smell of her father.

"What have you done to my daughter?" Stanley Polensky eyed Ms. Webster like she was a three-dollar bill. He stood pitched slightly forward, the grizzly wrinkles of his cheeks pushed up into his blue eyes. "Who are you?"

"I'm Ms. Webster, one of Heidi's teachers." She extended her hand which, after a tortured few seconds of deliberation, he shook. "You're Heidi's father? What an honor—I always wanted to know who was responsible for molding such a fine student."

It may not have been bullshit, in Ms. Webster's mind, but her father's expression, a cocked eyebrow, clenched jaw, made it clear he took it as such. He mumbled something in return that wasn't quite words but wasn't quite a growl, either. He clapped Heidi's shoulder, the way one might herd cattle, and pushed her toward the door.

"I've been waiting," he explained, although he offered no further clarification. "Nice to meet you, Miss Teacher."

"Heidi, we'll finish this later, okay?" Her eyes met Heidi's, and Heidi nodded, although she was not sure if she wanted to. There was nothing to say, really. But there were other things she wanted to talk with Ms. Webster about; she wanted to pour out all her dreams, all her questions about life, how one shed one's life, like an ill-fitting coat, and found another. And how much it cost.

"She's going to help me with my college stuff," Heidi explained vaguely, in the truck. She had already been accepted to the local university, Salisbury State, and figured she would be eligible for some Pell Grants, a few local scholarships. She hadn't dared to dream much bigger.

"You'll get into a college," he answered. "There's no need to cry about that." The voice, sweet, like a child's but rich, honeyed, filled the car, and her father snapped off the radio. Heidi wondered whether her father waited to hear 'Lil Cindy on the radio, only to be overwhelmed when he finally did. He had told her many years ago who her real mother was, and she had allowed it to be true, in small increments, like ipecac. That way, it had not hurt. It had not even mattered that she had come from the womb of that tiny dead singer, that the tiny dead singer who rejected her own child, her father, to be loved by strangers. At least, Heidi told herself that. In small doses, she had looked at articles about her mother on microfiche at the public library, mostly record reviews and concert listings. She had listened to her records with headphones in the media section, pouring over the pictures on the albums, trying to find something that she shared with the tiny dead singer. She felt she saw something in the eyes, the nose, not of Cindy, but Dwayne Johnson, the guitar player. It had occurred to her then, the summer of her fifteenth year, who her real father was.

"I wish I'd had the chance to go to college, but there was the war." Her father coughed and spat phlegm out the window. "And I got a real education, then."

She felt the burn of the salt in the corner of her eyes as her father began to talk about the war. He talked about it so much, she actually knew scant little; her worst grade in history, ever, was her score on the tenth-grade unit test for World War II. And yet, if he suddenly were to die, she would know nothing about him, the definitive experience of his being. She promised herself she would listen one day, although, she decided, this was not the one.

There were other things to worry about. Like the racing green Volkswagen that had been following them from school. Ms. Webster's 1966 Squareback, the coolest car, according to the boys, at school. It wasn't for its engine, which was loud and slow, or its chassis, which was essentially a VW Beetle, but because it was in almost factory condition, the result of Ms. Webster's father storing it in the garage and presenting it to her as a college graduation present. She knew these things because she remembered everything Oliver Truitt, her crush since seventh grade and Shauna Beck's boyfriend, had ever said, in reverse proportion to everything her father had ever said.

She wondered whether Ms. Webster wanted to find out where she lived, whether she would park the car at night up the road from their house and watch in the darkness, wondering whether Heidi was okay. Whether she would let herself be rescued by Ms. Webster. To what length Ms. Webster would go to show her concern, her devotion. Whether she would plead with Heidi's father to surrender her to her care so that Heidi's life would reach its correct trajectory, radiate correctly, and explode like a perfect snowball in a 4th of July sky.

Heidi's stomach knotted as they lumbered in the gravel driveway, spinning stones that she hoped would miss the Squareback's pristine paint job. She watched the Squareback park on the side of the road, away from the gravel, and Ms. Webster emerge.

"My backpack." She said to her father as Ms. Webster held up the dark blue Jansport backpack. "I left it at school."

She hurried stupidly over to Ms. Webster, hoping her eyes would not telegraph all of her fantasies.

"Thanks," she said as Ms. Webster held it out to her. "This is...where I live."

"What a beautiful old farmhouse." Ms. Webster looked up and apparently did not see the broken shingles, the chipped paint and soggy wood window frames, the sagging of one side of the porch. The weeds, the junk her father had dragged for the past twenty years from the dump to the front yard. "It reminds me of my family's old place."

"Did you...want to come in? For tea?" Heidi was stunned that her lips moved and sound came out. A few packets of Lipton, probably moldly, awaited in the cupboard.

"Oh, I can't today. I've got to run. But I'm taking a raincheck." Ms. Webster backed toward the Volkswagen, her arms wrapped around herself, gave Heidi's father a little wave with the flick upward of her right palm. "See you tomorrow, Heidi."

"Bye, Ms. Webster." She was not leaving forever—Heidi would see her the next day. And yet, as the Squareback spun around tightly on the road and zoomed away, that's exactly what it felt like.

Johnson

"She'll be home at 4:30." They sat in the study. Palmer had the handsome carriage of a doctor—clean shaven, a tanned, lined face and wavy hair layered with silver and dark locks. "But shall we get started?"

That afternoon, Johnson had taken off work. Kate had brought some clothes she'd picked up for him at Pierre Cardin, which he changed into at the apartment. He absently petted the soft corduroy of his fitted camel-colored blazer. She had also bought him two pairs of smoky gray wool slacks, slightly flared as was the fashion, and a mulberry-colored V-neck sweater, which he wore along with a crisp white oxford shirt. He slid the buttery soles of his new leather loafers on the Persian rug, feeling like a child at church as Kate lit a cigarette in the leather-backed chair opposite him.

Papillary serous cystadenocarcinoma. A form of ovarian cancer, she had explained to him over dinner that night. A late-stage diagnosis from a routine checkup. She was dying as soon as she knew. It seemed so strange that she could be so composed, a black-stocking leg dangling over a knee, her hair tucked neatly into a bun, as she inhaled and exhaled through her nostrils, a half smile, reassuring, for him. The faintest frailty had begun to show, like ivy in a crack—

strands of grey hair, a fold of fabric by her waist that had been filled with flesh previously. She worked four days a week at the museum, the other reserved for doctor's appointments, treatment. How many months would the vacuum inside her continue to grow, suck in her cheeks, the fat from the bone, the moisture from her eyes?

"Do you think there is more of this herb, in your friend's family?" Dr. Palmer sat at his desk, palms spread on the blotter, the placid expression of a poker player.

"It's possible—I don't know. I'm going to visit him." Johnson looked at Kate. "If that's all right."

"Of course." She touched the top of his hand, withdrew. He thought he felt the tremor of her fingers, but perhaps it was the medication, the barbiturates he'd seen in the plastic amber tumbler in her purse. "I'll do whatever I can to help."

There was a knock at the study door. The cook brought tea on a silver service. She was followed by a young, dark-haired girl in plaid schoolgirl jumper, white knee socks, and patent leather Mary Janes. She did not carry herself with the slinking shyness of a grade-schooler; she strode to the left side of Palmer's desk, piercing him with her dark eyes before gazing at them like they were curiosities in a shop window.

"My new parents?" She clasped her hands at her waist as the cook set out the tea. Johnson concentrated on the steaming liquid filling the china rather than look back at her, eyes dull blades.

"No." Dr. Palmer stood up. "This is Kate Strauss and her friend, Calvin Johnson. Calvin Johnson has a lot in common with you, I think you'll find."

"How old are you?" She walked to him, grabbed his palm and ran her fingers over its smoothness.

"I'm 53." He leaned forward as she looked in his eyes, touched his chin with clinical dispassion.

"You are baby. According to Palmer, I am 169 years." She stepped back, hands on her hips, rocking with pride. "I come here in 1964. I am in the last grade of your schooling here, and then what do I do? I am nine-year old girl in body, not mind."

"Ela's been asked to stay on full-time at my institute after high school, for observation, but she'd like to go home." Palmer leaned back in his chair, playing with a pen. "My wife, frankly, thinks this is a good idea. Of course, I'm reluctant to let Ela return to Poland unless..."

"You have another subject," Kate answered. She looked at Johnson. "Of course, it's preposterous. Calvin can't be a lab rat."

"I'll do it." He took her hand. If Polensky could not cure him, perhaps he could cure Kate.

"He'll think about it," Kate said, blowing on her tea.

"The herb you get from Poland, Dr. Palmer say," Ela spoke to Calvin. "Where from Poland?"

"I don't know. A fellow gave it to me during the war. I don't know where he got it from. Named Polensky. From Baltimore."

Her eyes widened. She nodded to Palmer. She plopped on an overstuffed chair by the fireplace with a Chips Ahoy! and her tea and attacked them hungrily.

The room was not quite what he imagined for a girl—green walls onto which were painted murals of trees and forest creatures, glowing eyes and sharp claws grasping tree limbs. A thick brown shag carpet covered the floor. There were no toys, no dolls, but of course, she was not a girl. It was easy to forget until she looked at you, until she spoke. Ela sat on the canopy bed munching on her final Chips Ahoy! Her shoes, no bigger than his hands, rested against each other on the floor. She had explained to him about the lightning, the herb—burnette saxifrage—Stanley's mother Safine, they understood now, taking it to America. Johnson filled in the rest. Stanley to Johnson. It all seemed so random, so unremarkable in the cosmic scheme of things. They had not saved lives, heralded a new age. They couldn't even hurt themselves. The origin of the herb's magic didn't bring them closer to God, any god, but it did not push them closer to hell. They remained suspended, the frame in which the gyroscope spun wildly before them.

"What's wrong with us?" He sat on a desk chair made for a grade-school girl, his knees almost grazing his ears. "Is Palmer helping you?"

"He knows nothing." Ela shook her head derisively. "If he cannot put numbers on a sheet and make sense, it is not real. And if he cannot make money from it, it is not important. The herb with your Stanley—it is what is left of the only herb. The bewitched herb, the one my mother gave me so long ago. If you could get it to me, perhaps I can figure it out yet."

"You don't want Palmer involved?" He scratched his ankle. He thought of Kate, the years he was robbed of her, the years he would be robbed of yet. "Can we test it on others?"

"Too dangerous." She shook her head. "It is not clear how we upset the order of the world, but we do, and more people will upset the world more."

"I can't watch her die." He pleaded with her, as if she held the key to Kate's fate. But she didn't; Stanley did.

"This is only the beginning for you." Ela stared at him. Her eyes softened, a glimmer of moisture on her rims, before they returned to that vacant place. "You wait until your first hundred years."

"What are you going to do with the herb?"

"Take it back to Poland." She pointed at him. "You get the herb. You take me to Poland. We will go back to Reszel, and I will have what my mother had to make tinctures. No one will bother us."

He did not mention to her that the little village she had remembered from her youth did not even exist, possibly, especially after the Nazis decimated most of Poland. But he had no other plan. If they found the herb, it should go to the person who knew the most about it, he thought.

"How will we get to Poland?"

"The Palmers do not want me here anymore. Mrs. Palmer is scared, think I will put spell on her. They do not understand what I want. I don't want to make miracle drug for Americans. I want to die. I miss my mother. I miss Ferki."

"All right, then." He slapped his hands together, stood up gingerly from his semi-squat. The chair had not broken, and he smiled. A chair made for him. "I'll see if I can find old Stanley and the herb. You get us some plane tickets to Poland. Get us three now, okay? I think there might be one more."

"There is one more of us?" Ela looked at him incredulously. "How do you know?"

"Stanley might have taken it, you know," he said. But that was not what he was thinking. He was thinking of Kate, immortal, warmfleshed, her hand in his as they ordered sirloin tips from the stewardess. "Just try to get three in case."

❀ ❀ ❀

"I can't, in good conscience, let you do something like this." The car lurched along in Sunday evening traffic to Penn Station. He had not told Kate about Ela's plan. It was best to spring that on her last. That when he saved her, made her immortal, he hoped she took to Eastern Europe. Kate drew a line on her upper and bottom lips before filling it in dark red. "Who knows what Palmer will want to do to you at the Institute? Blood tests, then experimental surgery? It's a slippery slope."

"If there's anything I can do to...help you." He stared at the buildings, the New Yorkers on the sidewalk. They walked through him, their orbits collapsing into his, and he would always know their pains and joys. The solace of humanity is that pain is temporary. There is always death. But that pain had to go somewhere. He wondered if it went to people like him, like Ela.

"Calvin, I'm scared." She clenched his hand. He could feel the bones in her fingers, her wrist. He tried to remember if he had always felt them so starkly. "My legacy here...I'm not nearly finished at the museum. My boys...one is still in college. I want to see them get married, have their own children."

"I've got nothing to lose." He placed his hand on her thigh. Even in her fear, he desired her. He would rip open his throat so that she could crawl inside, live in him, a pupae, until his or her transformation was complete. "I'll find Stanley Polensky. I'll get the herb, and this will fix itself."

"Your optimism is always endearing." She laid her head on his shoulder. "But do you expect him to believe you, just give you his knowledge, or the herb, if he even has it?"

"I don't know." He smelled her hair. She always smelled of young, fresh flowers, but also of propriety. "You did."

"I'm not the best sample from which to draw." The cab pulled up to Penn Station. She had given him money for a ticket, for expenses. More than he thought he needed.

"Why don't you have dinner with me?" He kissed the top of her head. "Or we could get a hotel…"

"I'm having dinner with my husband. I really need to get going. It'll take an hour to get uptown." She sat up straight, dabbed the corner of her lips with her pinky finger. He dimly expected, in some way, that she would be here for him, in New York, even in dying, when he got back. And, to come back, he still needed to believe it.

"I love you, Kate." He took her face in his heads. Her lips seemed fuller as he pressed them to his. Disappointment? Resignation? Possibly medication. "I won't be long, I promise."

"Hurry back, darling. Be safe." She smiled, ran her hand the length of his face. Then, he watched the back of her head, exposed in the window of the cab, disappear uptown.

Heidi

"This is my favorite time of the year." Ms. Webster explained to her twelfth-grade honors English class. Heidi wondered why; it was the end of January. "Because we get to do group projects."

Heidi stared at her notebook until she thought she would burn a hole through it. Group projects were the equivalent, she thought, of choosing teams for gym, and she was always chosen last. She couldn't believe Ms. Webster would have such a tin ear for classroom politics. Whoever she wound up with, at any rate, she would be assured of doing more than her fair share—one, because anything less than an A was unacceptable to her, and two, because taking on more than her share had been the only way to present her as an appealing member of any group that didn't consist only of the school's downtrodden.

"Before you get all excited, I should introduce a caveat—I will be doing the pairing. I have taken the liberty of already pairing everyone with someone on the basis of your strengths and weaknesses so everyone will participate in the strongest groups possible. And, I have also chosen your topics." Ms. Webster paced the front of the room, hands in her khakis. "I've given this a great deal of thought, and I don't think you'll be disappointed. First group—Oliver Truitt and Heidi Polensky will do T.S. Elliot's *The Love Song of J. Alfred Prufrock*."

There was a chortle from the left edge of class, where Oliver Truitt and Shauna Beck sat with the jocks and cheerleaders, and Ms. Webster frowned and continued reading the lists of groups and authors. But Heidi could no longer hear them. She snuck a glance at the back of Oliver's curly head and considered whether she could ask Ms. Webster to change the assignments. Not that there was any way now, not without it looking suspicious or bad or crazy.

She didn't know whether Ms. Webster simply paired the overachieving Heidi with the clearly underachieving Oliver or whether she had some other sort of matchmaking designs in mind. Not that Heidi had a chance. Oliver Truitt, for a small-town hick, had a distinctly suburban style that everyone envied. His father, who was in upper management at the chemical plant in nearby Delaware, outfitted his family and his home handsomely. The Truitts often went on shopping excursions in Annapolis, Baltimore—even Philadelphia—to find the latest in designer fashions.

Yet Oliver could not be pinned down by a store receipt. He was a forerunner of "shabby chic" before people in town even knew how to pronounce "chic." His curly hair grew over his eyes and ears like a shaggy mutt, although Stacey Benkin's mom often referred to his coif as a "JFK Jr." He wore ratty t-shirts under expensive Ralph Lauren oxford shirts that were left untucked underneath Merino wool sweaters. His jeans were ripped strategically at the knee, and his Adidas were always untying themselves. He was an effortless god of a boy, and Heidi had no more business having a crush on him than she did Robert Redford.

However, even if it was more out of cluelessness than chivalry (for a jock, Oliver was a real space cadet), he did not tease her like the others. In fact, he always acted as if she was a perfectly normal human being, deserving of polite and sometimes extended conversation. After class, Oliver walked over to her desk and punched her lightly on the shoulder.

"Hey partner." He smiled. "I guess I lucked out, huh? You want to go to the library later today and get some source materials?"

"I could." She nodded. She knew where everything was; it would certainly be the fastest and most efficient use of their time.

"So you want to me to pick you up, or do you want to meet there?"

"Oh—you meant together." She felt a lump the size of an egg in her throat that she hoped wasn't lasagna from lunch.

"Yeah. How about we go grab a bite to eat beforehand? I've got basketball practice, but I can meet you at six-thirty. How about Taco Olé?"

"I'll meet you there," she answered. Other than from Ms. Webster, Heidi had kept her house a well-guarded secret, fearing that Shauna and her friends would egg it, or worse. She insisted that her father take a long, winding route home from school every day, one in which she could tell, on the open country roads, whether someone followed. She never put her address on her backpack or in her books. And she would never let Oliver come to the house to pick her up, no matter how much she wanted to ride alone with him in his Mustang, show her father she was popular—maybe—or at least had friends, other than "the donut boy at the library," as her father called Darren—"softer than an éclair."

Oliver chucked her on the chin, almost knocking her to the ground in her weak-kneed surprise, and then jogged out of the room, leaving only a whiff of cologne behind. She stood up and didn't bother to wait for the class to empty. She strode to her locker in a daze, the buzz of the hallways' white noise around her, and when she climbed into the truck cab at 2:45, Stanley sat up straight in his seat.

"Well." He lit a cigarette and muscled the stick shift into submission. "You're late."

"Dad, I need you to drive me to the Taco Olé tonight at six-thirty," she said, ignoring him, asserting herself in such a way that her father snorted but, for once, kept his mouth shut. "I have work to do."

Oliver was late, and she was very early. Early enough to study the menu and see what she could get for dinner with a dollar ten, the amount her father had scraped from the pockets of his two pairs of pants. She could get one large taco and a cup of potato olés, but no drink. She spread her notebook and papers on the table and went through the basic outline of a presentation she had scribbled down at home. She'd read Prufrock many times, had jotted various plans of attack they could pursue. She could do all the work in a few days, complete construction visuals and Oliver's own neatly written index cards, which he would merely have to read to the class.

But Ms. Webster had not assigned them together to do that—she had wanted Oliver to care about something other than baseball and cars and Shauna—to see the love of the world, of learning, through another student's eyes. Or at least prepare him for the workload of college. And maybe, Ms. Webster figured, Heidi would taste a glimpse of the leisurely life of the senior class's royalty, the non-shit world.

"You look prepared." Oliver appeared, smelling like the soap in the high school locker room showers, clad in a t-shirt, running shorts, and flip flops, even though it was still a little chilly—January, to be exact. "You eat yet?"

She shook her head, suddenly not very hungry, and followed him to the counter, where he ordered three tacos, two potato olés, a large Pepsi, and one cinnamon chalupa.

"What do you want?" He nodded to her as she fumbled for the change her father had thrust into her hand, although with lint and a bent nail. "Don't worry; I'm buying."

She ordered a taco and a diet Pepsi, and Oliver added to her order a cup of potato olés and a cinnamon chalupa.

"God, I hate when girls don't eat," he explained as he guided the overloaded plastic tray to their table. "And then Shauna pukes it right out in the women's room. You seem too smart to do that kind of shit, though."

"Thanks for dinner," she replied, not sure how to respond. It did not surprise her about Shauna, but if she was supposed to feel sympathy, she had a hard time mustering any.

"No problem. Ms. Webster is the one who deserves all the thanks. I mean, what did I do to get paired up with the smartest girl in the class?" Oliver opened his mouth and inserted half of a taco in it. He chewed thoughtfully and swallowed. "Not that I mean you'll do all the work."

"I have some ideas." She moved her hand to her notebook.

"Let's eat first." He smiled. "We can work when we get to the library."

She tried to eat her taco neatly, even though across from her, chunks of meat and lettuce and tomatoes frequently fell out of Oliver's taco, remnants that he shoved in his mouth with his fingers, licking them between slurps of his Pepsi.

"So, your father still have that orange truck?" He asked, unwrapping his cinnamon chalupa. "I've seen him pick you up sometimes in it."

"Yes." She blushed at the thought of him observing her unnoticed.

"You know, I let the guys in shop work on my car. They put some really great struts in and added the racing stripe. You should have your father take his truck in. I bet they'd do some work on it ... maybe free, for the experience."

"Thanks. I'll bring it up to him."

"They had a really sweet Pontiac they rebuilt—a 1966. They only want a couple hundred for it, if you're looking for a set of wheels."

"I can't really afford a car." She carefully folded the waxy paper of her taco. "I don't know if you've noticed."

"Can you get a job or something? I know Buildaburger is hiring."

"Shauna works there."

"Yeah, she likes it okay." He took a large, broken piece of taco shell and swept the remaining rubble of ground beef and shredded iceberg lettuce into a final bite. "I know the manager gives her a hard time about not working hard, talking to the customers too much. She can't help she's popular."

"I don't think Shauna likes me," Heidi said carefully, taking a sip of her Diet Pepsi.

"Really?" He crushed the wax paper and arched his arms like a basketball player, aiming for the hole of the boxy trash can a few feet away. "I never noticed. I mean, Shauna is kinda bitchy, like most girls. I try not to get involved in that kind of stuff."

The paper bounced off the rim of the trash can and settled on the floor. Oliver jumped up and retrieved it. Heidi blotted her lips with her napkin. She felt deep behind enemy lines, talking to a squirrel she had mistaken for the cavalry, while the enemy waited in the bushes, training its sights on her.

"You know, if Shauna is mean to you…" Oliver began when he returned.

"Don't worry about it. I never said anything, okay?"

"Then I'll talk to her about it. There's no reason for her to treat you bad. All right?"

"Please…"

"Don't worry; she'll never know." He winked. "I've got your back, Polensky. You ready to go to the library?"

Later that night in bed, she carefully unwrapped the chalupa she'd saved and ate it quickly, licking her fingers and the wrapper. She wondered if she would develop an eating disorder, like bulimia. Anorexia seemed to fit more with their budget. All she knew was that she had been a complete fool with Oliver at the library, and a next step down the slippery psychological disorder slope seemed imminent.

It had started with such promise. He had sat next to her at the study table, not across, and gentlemanly, he turned his head away from her to burp softly, excusing himself. He asked what schools she had applied to (Bryn Mawr, Swarthmore, NYU), what she wanted to do when she graduated. She told him she was considering pre-med or art history, and he surprised her by wanting to major in history and asking if her father was a veteran. He was interested in military history and sometimes talked to the old men at the nursing home where his grandfather lived. Oliver invited her and her father to the nursing home next Saturday to meet his own grandfather—it would be cool, he figured, if both men had a buddy from the older days.

She even confessed, swearing him to secrecy, that 'Lil Cindy was her mother.

"But country music stars are rich, aren't they?" He tried to reconcile the facts of her situation with what he knew about life.

"Yeah, but we've never seen any money," she answered, picking at the spine of one of the books. "My parents were never married. I don't even know if she knew anything about me. My father said he sent school pictures, but I never met her...my father didn't even tell me about her until the night she died."

"Don't cry." He put his arm on her shoulder as she sobbed. "They'll make us leave the library."

"You don't understand." She shook her head. "Your mother *wanted* you."

She had stayed in the library bathroom, bawling, until her father came, drunk as usual. He dented the mailbox at the corner of the library with the front bumper of the truck as it shuddered to a stop and then left rubber on the road in front as he gunned it for home. She wondered whether she would be allowed back, her lending privileges suspended.

She had retired to her room with her leftovers, content to eat herself half-satiated to sleep. But her father's step was heavy, unsure, on the stairs. She stuffed the chalupa wrapper under her pillow and pulled the sheets high. Her father tied one on frequently, and his favorite—his only—audience for his boasts, laments, and insecurities was Heidi.

Sometimes, if she pretended to sleep, he'd leave her alone. His face would dip uncomfortably close to hers, the sweet-sour aroma of whiskey penetrating her nostrils as she tried to keep her face from an involuntary twitch or sneeze, and he'd whisper "Heidi" at a decibel that most would not consider a whisper. Sometimes, a sprinkle of spit would coat one of her cheeks, the bridge of her nose. She would lay still, and the mattress would rock violently as he stood up and clomped out of the room to his own.

"Heidi." His hands grabbed the edge of the sheets near her face and shook. "Heidi."

"Dad, I've got school tomorrow." She launched herself to her side, where his emphysemic breath just went into her ear.

"Heidi, this is important." The bed rocked as he settled himself and his books. "I've been doing some research into the family's... history."

"Can't you tell me after school?"

"No." Apparently her father thought that his powers of elocution existed only when he was shit-faced drunk. "Listen. My mother, she emigrated from Poland, you know. She brought a lot of knowledge about herbs and stuff, always rubbing something on our chests for colds, awful-smelling pastes on our cuts, powders in our tea. Anyway, before I enlisted, she gave me an herb—burnette saxifrage. She told me to eat it, and that it would save me during the war. It would make me immortal."

"Did you?"

"No." His weight shifted on the bed a little. "I gave it to my buddy Johnson. He got his leg blown off by a mine. I put it in his mouth and made him chew, and then the medic came. Here's his picture."

"Did he live?" She looked at the black-and-white, so old it was grey-and-white, photo of a slight, blond man with a wrinkled forehead and kind eyes next to a well-built, taller man with dark hair and a square face. They were leaning on the rail of a warship, cigarettes dangling from their smiling, crooked mouths. They could have been the seniors at Mount Zion who graduated the previous year.

"No—he was dead when I ran off. The shelling was something fierce. Not only were there mines everywhere, but they were shelling the trees... it all came down on you. A lot of men died that way. Spent four months in the dead of winter hugging trees, trying to keep away from that shit."

"So the herb didn't work."

"I didn't think so. But I took some with me. Don't know why—pulled some out of Johnson's mouth before I left."

Her father stood and flipped on her desk lamp. The orange inverted triangle of light that filled the corner of her bedroom set her father's face in sharp relief. He almost looked like a prisoner in a concentration camp, she thought. The years, the alcohol, the war, her mother, had consumed him. He sat back on the bed and pushed a shriveled brown mass in a sandwich bag toward her.

"I tried to burn this not too long ago... with all of your mother's stuff. All this... past, it isn't doing us any good. But I couldn't burn it. It refused to be burned."

"What do you mean?" She wiggled up to a sitting position and looked at the bent, dried stalks and fragile white flowers molded into a shape resembling a dog turd.

"I mean I squirted it full of lighter fluid and it didn't burn. Maybe there's something to it after all. I tried to do some research at the library, but there's not much about burnette saxifrage. It's also called *Pimpinella saxifrage*, and it grew in the area where she said she and her mother lived in Reszel. She also told me and the other children that she grew up playing with a witch. We always thought she told the stories to scare us—of course, Cass and Thomas never believed any of it, but I used to sleep with Julia or Kathryn at night after your grandmother got done talking about the baba yagas. Heh—I still get a shiver now."

"How come I've never met any of my aunts and uncles?"

"Would you like to? I'm sure you must have cousins or something."

"I don't know." She drew her knees up to her chin. They would probably be blonde, blue-eyed starlets. "So, did you ever figure out what happened to Johnson?"

"Over the years, I've wanted to. After I stole you from your mother, I really couldn't do much traveling. But when you graduate high school and go to college, I'm thinking about traveling to Ohio, where he's from, and DC, to look into the Veterans Administration records."

"Wait—you stole me from my mother?"

"She didn't want you, baby." He reached over to grab her shoulder but missed, his palm landing on her pillow. "I babysat you on the road—she never wanted to go home. Always one more gig, one more radio performance, one more thing that would make her famous. And I guess she did all right for herself. But one day, I decided I didn't want to be her nanny anymore, especially since you weren't even... well, anyway, I couldn't leave you there. You needed stability, not formula in a hotel room at four o'clock in the morning."

"Is my father... still alive?"

"I imagine." He sighed, looking at his hands. "I imagine you could find him."

"I don't want to find him... I mean, you're my father."

"Well, it makes me feel funny to hear you say that." He smiled. "I mean, you were pretty free with your words when you was little, but as an adult, I'm sure you wonder how you got to be so unlucky."

"I feel lucky fine," she said, although she certainly did not feel lucky all of the time.

"Listen, I got this diary." He pressed an old datebook from the drugstore into her hands. "It ain't much, but I been scribbling down my memoirs and what I remember of my family. I've been wanting for you to know your roots."

"What about the herb?"

"I'm giving it to you. Don't ever feed it to me in the event of my demise—I don't want to find out if it works. I want to die as soon as I am eligible for its benefits. But maybe you can use it somehow—a science experiment or something."

"You're giving me an immortal herb for a science experiment?"

"This is all I've got." He put the baggie and datebook on her night table. "I know it ain't no Corvette. I got to take a piss."

He ambled out of the bedroom like some wounded animal, hanging on her doorframe until she thought he might pull the house apart from the inside. When he was gone, she turned off the light and tried to sleep. Her father's drunk stories were always crazy, and this one was no different. She picked up the baggie, wondering if the dropout who lived in a van by the zoo had sold her father a dime bag of pot outside the liquor store. She opened the baggie and smelled it. It smelled burnt and stale, not what marijuana was supposed to smell like. Maybe it was oregano. She put the baggie in her school backpack, wondering whether she could sell it to Melanie Huber, the girl who listened to the Happy Dead or whoever that druggie band was, for a little spending money, and held the datebook in her hands. Did she really want to know the true extent of her father's instability? She heard that train barreling down and opened the datebook, resigned to her position on the tracks.

When she got to school the next day, she noticed Shauna looking at her from across the room in Calculus class, her face placid and not twisted in its usual contortions when she met Heidi's eyes. She wondered whether Oliver had laid down the law already, if he took her aside before school, where they hung out on the bleachers with all the jocks and cheerleaders, sneaking cigarettes and sometimes pot, and told her to knock it off, maybe all of them, in his detached, no-nonsense way, taking a swig from a bottle of chocolate Yoo-Hoo, and speaking no more of it.

Mr. Davis, the math teacher, walked in and began to write derivatives on the chalkboard, silencing the chatter in the classroom. Then it started, Shauna and her girlfriends, like frogs: "Mid-get mommy, mid-get mommy, mid-get mommy."

Stanley

For once, he rode on the damn right horse. Years of Friday afternoons betting five or ten dollars of his pension on horses to show, and never had he left Delmarva Downs with as much as a nickel. Today, an unseasonably cool Friday in May, when he saw Cindy's Girl, a squat Palomino, posted at $15.50, he put down forty to win and walked away with almost 400 dollars.

He never actually thought of what he'd do with the money, since he'd never won before, but he stopped at the bus station and bought two bus tickets to Baltimore. He was not getting younger. He needed to find the other Polenskys, his brothers and sisters, and he needed to ingratiate Heidi into their care. She needed to know she had a home if his heart stopped, and by the slow, dull weight of it, the gasps of his breath at night, he figured it might be sooner rather than later.

And a steak. He wasn't due to pick up Heidi for another couple of hours. The Golden Corral restaurant had $7.99 sirloin tips. He could count on his fingers, since he had Heidi, when he'd eaten steak. Ten dollars for lunch, thirty for the bus tickets, and the rest for Heidi to do what she wanted. To live a little, for chrissakes. She had appointed herself house accountant over the years, and it broke his heart to see her move the expenses into his column—for medications, for Ben-Gay, for orthopedic shoes, a cane—and not into hers. She put her Christmas money and birthday money into her savings account for college, and although it accorded with the stinginess of his cheap Pollock heart, he didn't understand why, when she'd brought home straight As for the past five years, she didn't think she'd be eligible for a scholarship or five.

At the Golden Corral, he loaded up on the sirloin at the salad bar, along with a baked potato, green beans, and a few breaded items that he assumed were vegetables. He slid into a booth and took his wallet, bulging with tens and twenties and the tickets, and put it beside him on the table because its newfangled shape burred into his ass. He cut the steak and guiltily wondered whether he should have waited for Heidi, taken her to dinner. She'd always given him larger portions than hers at dinner, even though she was technically the one still growing and required adequate sustenance. But he wondered whether he'd just embarrass her. He saw her face every day when he picked her up at school, even crying the one day he met her teacher, Missus Fancypants. He'd thought of letting her have the truck during the week, if it weren't so unreliable. He imagined her breaking down at school and getting a lot of crust from her schoolmates, or worse yet, she'd break down on the way home and have to huff it for six miles. She had enough crosses to haul ass with every day; being with him, in public, no less, was not another he'd hoist on her back.

His stomach gurgled. The fried mushrooms and zucchini must not be sitting well with him, or maybe it was the fried egg he'd sneaked in for breakfast after Heidi was at school, washing the plate but leaving a clean bowl in the drainer to make her think he'd eaten oatmeal. He stood up and hauled off to the men's room as fast as his stiff leg and back would work, and while he sat on the hard, cold, slightly moist toilet seat, expelling large volumes of liquidated food, he remembered his wallet, sitting fat like a stuffed duck on the table.

He could not stop the waterworks, the grunting. Now his chest was getting into it, too, a little heartburn. He grabbed at his knees and remembered the days back in Germany, when he had the shits so bad and Johnson made fun of him, shitting in his helmet like that. He cleaned it out in the river, in the frozen water, but for the rest of the war, he could still smell it, the faint whiff of shit, and it got to the point where the next pile of dead they came upon, mostly newbies, he took a shining, clean helmet off a dead boy's head, not even dead a few hours, and left his on the boy's chest. No sense making the boy's hair smell like shit, too. Not that he wouldn't smell worse than that by the time he got to the Graves Registration Department.

Kind of the way he smelled now. Christ. He grunted and shuddered and forced what seemed like every spare drop out of his ass and then hurried back to his table. He felt light and achy, like he had a fever, but he broke out in sweat when he saw the table empty of his plate and his wallet. How long had he been in the bathroom?

"My stuff." He grabbed a short Mexican man who was wiping down the table next to his. "Where's my plate, my wallet?"

"I dunno." The man shrugged. He pointed to the plastic dish bin, which sat on the table. At the top was the plate with the remains of Stanley's sirloin.

"You stole my wallet, you dumb spic." Stanley grabbed at his t-shirt, but he knew, even being a head taller, that the little wetback could have him on the ground faster than a rodeo cowboy than rope a steer. "Where's your manager?"

"Can I help you, sir?" A woman, a black lady with a cross hanging on her neck larger than the ones displayed outdoors at some churches, appeared. One of her breasts, large and pendulous like a sock filled with change, brushed against his arm as she forced her girth between them.

"He stole my wallet." Stanley's hand went to his chest, not so much to get away from the oblong breast—he took what he could get—but to scratch at the sudden burning there.

"Ernesto, did you take this man's wallet? Empty your pockets, please." She peered into the dish bin and began shifting the plates.

"There is man, he leave before I bus table. I thought he eating there. Maybe he took wallet." Ernesto pulled out the white cotton pockets of his jeans and displayed a marble, and lighter, a coin purse, and a gas station receipt. Not even his own wallet. What kind of man didn't carry a wallet? He stared at them, three-quarters-size Ernesto and the Baptist who needed to pray to God about her droopage, and decided he didn't like the world. Not when some sleezeball stole his wallet and these two were left as his booby prize.

Someone needed to take control of the situation. Stanley moved to the front of the restaurant, scanning the parking lot. It was sparse, the lunch hour long over, too early for dinner. No cars pulled away. He wondered what was on the security cameras. He imagined himself as Colombo, salivated at the sudden promise of importance. Then he remembered his heartburn, that he was old. That he couldn't even be trusted with his own wallet.

"Sir, if you'd like to sit, I can call the police." The manager touched his arm. "Maybe Ernesto can give them a good description. Maybe there's something on the tapes we can go on."

"Don't matter. It's gone." He shrugged her off. The pain moved into his stomach and crept toward his left leg. He wasn't sure what he was saying anymore. "It's all gone."

He got in the truck, but he couldn't pull away. His chest felt water-logged and he began to sob, his head on the steering wheel. He could never do anything right for Heidi. But the worst part of it was, she had accepted that, and accepted it long ago. The water-works from his eyes did not dispel the drowning sensation he felt inside his body, so he flung the truck into gear and gunned it home. He'd take an aspirin and lie down for an hour. When he got to school, Heidi would know what to do. She always did.

At home, he limped toward the house, his leg heavy now, and he took the stairs carefully, one at a time, was pleased that he made it. By then, he felt completely underwater. When he closed his eyes, he heard the whooshing of it, like the ocean, and he felt himself sinking deeper and deeper into its tide, sweeping him from shore.

On the porch stood a young man, tall and square, his jaw set like concrete. Stanley couldn't place him, even though the chill of recognition settled in beads on his forehead, the back of his neck. He wore a leather jacket, jeans, strange boots with caulks on them. Probably the young tuff who stole his wallet at the Golden Corral. Stanley figured he'd noted the fat wad of cash in his wallet and probably thought there was more at home. But the tuff had no car. He would have had to have flown to get there before Stanley.

"Who the hell are you?" Stanley puffed out his wheezing, concave chest and strode up the steps.

"Don't you remember me, pole?" The man smiled. "It's me, Calvin Johnson."

Johnson

Stanley was old, older than he should have been. His hair was white, parted to the side but long, growing over her ears, and his blue eyes seemed watered down, buried under tissue-paper wrinkles. Johnson felt his heart, slippery, in this throat, as he digested what the years had sanded off, sucked from him. The soft, blond boy with the crinkling blue eyes, the toothy smile, had become a caricature. Stanley lifted an arm, spotted with age, toward him.

"You stole my wallet, you punk." His grip was firm on Johnson's wrist. "Over at the Golden Corral."

"Stanley Polensky, it's me, Calvin." He shook him off and took a step back. "Don't try to intimidate me. Did you ever win any of our wrestling matches during the war?"

"You aren't Calvin Johnson." Stanley moved closer and frisked him. "If you've got a gun, boy, I suggest you drop it. I'm retired Army—I'll break you in half."

"Stanley, I was state wrestling champion of Ohio once—you know that." Calvin pulled out a pack of Lucky Strikes. "Why don't you invite me inside? I got some business with you. About the herb."

"How'd you know about that?" Stanley peered at him. "You one of Heidi's friends?"

"Heidi?"

"My daughter. Look, you got your money. As you can see from the house, we ain't got nothing else. Now get the hell out of here before I put a beat down on you that'll make you cry for your momma."

"Stanley, look at me." Johnson grabbed his arms. "Do I look familiar to you at all?"

Stanley squinted, so close to Johnson's face, he could lick him.

"Shit, if you don't look a little like him." Stanley softened. "Christ. Are you a ghost or something? Come back to haunt me for what I done?"

"What did you do to me, Stanley?" Johnson's stomach filled with butterflies. "I need to know."

But Stanley was already opening the door. "I need a drink. Every time I try and stop, I start seeing shit."

Johnson followed Stanley into the house uninvited. Stanley moved heavily through the living room, occasionally massaging his chest. He seemed unaware he'd just talked to Johnson a few moments before, or perhaps he had convinced himself that Johnson was some alcohol-induced hallucination and decided not to acknowledge it. He fumbled in the kitchen cabinets for a bottle of aspirin and a drinking glass that he filled half with Wild Turkey, half with water.

"Are you all right, Stanley?" Johnson sat across from him at the kitchen table.

"I knew it would come to this," Stanley said, bringing the aspirin to his mouth with shaking fingers. "They all visit before you die. Is my mother coming next?"

"I'm not a ghost, you asshole." Johnson grabbed the bottle of

Wild Turkey and took a swig. "Now listen, you stuffed that god-damn herb in my mouth back in the Hürtgen Forest and I lived. Look at me—you need to undo this."

"Undo what?" Stanley held the glass to his lips and stared at him. "Are you telling me I can't get into heaven?"

"Look, you're not going to die. At least, I don't think so. But that's the point. Whatever you did to me, I can't die. I've been looking for you for years—you need to give me the antidote."

"Antidote?" Stanley finished his whiskey and began to pour another.

"Is there another herb that undoes the effects of the one you gave me?"

"I don't know, boy." Stanley lit a cigarette. "I tried to burn that herb, you know. It wouldn't even burn. I gave it to my daughter. I don't want nothing to do with it."

"Where is it?" Johnson stood up.

"Why?"

"Because I think you should eat it, too, so we'll be even." He began to rummage through the kitchen drawers, pushing aside utensils, matchbooks, losing lottery tickets, lint.

"You're not real." Stanley set his glass down. "I'm going to lie down and take a nap, and when I wake up, you'll be gone, okay?"

"Stanley, why did you save me?" Johnson turned from the cup-boards. "Why didn't you just save yourself?"

"Because you were my friend." Stanley shrugged. He fell against the doorway of the kitchen, and Johnson cupped him under his armpits, helping him to stand straight. "I never had one of those before. Haven't had one since."

"Where is the herb, Stanley?" Johnson helped him to the couch.

"I'll find it, you'll take it, and we'll both have friends for life. What do you say?"

"I'm taking a nap." Stanley closed his eyes. Within minutes, he snored, a wet, sonic clatter that Johnson could hear from any location in the house. He wondered how Stanley's daughter slept. He looked at the framed school picture on top of the television. She was an unusual bird, feral and dark with her honey hair feathered back the way he'd seen some of the young girls, the Charlie girls on television or whoever they were, style it. He went upstairs and started in her bedroom, going through drawers of what he thought were rather immodest undergarments for a teenager, gaudy blouses and slacks. With the exception of Kate, beautiful Kate, he wondered whether women even wore dresses anymore. The women he'd watched on the television at the hotel in New York were angry at men or they were overly painted, sparkly silver and blue eye shadow that made them look like space aliens. And the men weren't much better—long sideburns and strange fabric one-piece suits that zipped. But he was in a better position to roll with the changes, to absorb them in his eternal chameleon skin, than Stanley, who did not have to advertise to the world that he was hopelessly out of touch.

Johnson sat on Heidi's bed, ran his hand over the plain green bedspread. There weren't many feminine appointments to the décor: a poster of a black music singer, a rainbow. A bookshelf made of cinder blocks and cut plywood held titles by the Brönte sisters but also Norman Mailer. He stood and pulled up the mattress then looked under the bed. In the drawer of the nightstand, he found the datebook filled with Stanley's wavering, blocky text. He put it into his back pocket and finished searching Heidi's room. Then, he moved onto Stanley's.

He was saddened by the bareness of their personal spaces. In Palmer's brownstone, achievement was framed, importance shown through meticulously dusted furniture, the number and symmetry of objects. Stanley had a bed and a pile of clothes on the floor where he must have pretended there was a hamper. He walked over to Stanley's closet, noted the revolver on the top shelf, his musette bag hanging on a peg. He unhooked it and touched the canvas to his face, smelled the fabric. He wondered whether his own still rested at the bottom of a mountain in Montana, whether his things had been recovered, himself reported dead again.

But it was home, this creaking box of boards. At least they had that much, each other. He went back downstairs and sat on the rocking chair, smoking cigarettes while Stanley slept, reading the datebook. He fingered the picture of them taken on the warship, a few days before they were dumped on the shores of Omaha Beach and their lives changed forever. That day, while it rained monsoons, the gray sky and gray sea undulating, crashing into the horizon line, he and Stanley built houses made of matchsticks as the boat rocked like a carnival ride. They had been through battles, through Troina in Italy, in Algeria. They had no thoughts about their survival. One got up and hoped to go to sleep that night, or a few nights from then. Enough days and nights strewn together, like enough matchsticks, were all one could think about. And somehow, forty years had passed, and here they were.

"Shit, you're still here?" Stanley eased himself up to a sitting position. "Why are you haunting me like this, Johnson? Dreams weren't enough for you? You want my mind now, too?"

"I want the herb." Johnson put the datebook on the coffee table. "Seems like you've been doing a lot of thinking about it. And me."

"I don't have it."

"Then we'll wait for your daughter, then." Johnson leaned back in the rocker. "So you and 'Lil Cindy, huh? I can't tell you how many songs I heard of hers on the radio and never once thought of you."

"I wish I could say the same about myself. Cindy's the only woman I ever loved, besides my mother. The only woman I ever hated, too."

"You had a child together?"

"She ain't my child." Stanley shook his head, swinging his feet to the floor. "Can't you tell? She's Cindy's, but she's not mine. Not that I don't love Heidi. Smart as a whip—at least she does the Polensky name proud."

"Well, they say family isn't always blood," Johnson answered. "Tell me what you've been doing since Hürtgen, Stanley. You get all the way through, or did you get wounded?"

"I made it through." Stanley rubbed his forehead in his hands. "I always thought that was going to be you. You were braver than the rest of us, that's for sure."

"I was scared shitless. I acted like a big-shot asshole, but I was a little liver belly."

"And you would have lived, too, if I hadn't voted to go back. I never forgave myself."

"I did live, Stanley. You saved my life with the herb."

Stanley could still move. Like a cat, he leapt at Johnson, knocking him and the rocking chair over backwards. He felt the splinters of wood dig into his back as Stanley grabbed at his face, pulling on his lips and cheeks.

"You're a real person, but who the hell are you?" Stanley leaned back on his knees, his face a tomato, panting. He turned halfway and took the datebook from the coffee table. "Where'd you get this? You been reading this and pretending to be Calvin Johnson, haven't you?"

"I wish I had something to show you, a picture, my old dog tags." Johnson pushed himself from the floor. "There was a fire, back in '47. I haven't had much since. Oh, wait—*the metalanthium lamp!* The rays of immortality."

"That's not in here," Stanley said, looking up from his datebook diary. "So how…"

He stood up, dropping the book on the floor. He took a step backward toward the stairs. Johnson wondered if he thought of the revolver in his closet.

"I never told anyone the code." Johnson took a step toward him. "Did you?"

"Johnson." Stanley held out his arms. "I believe you."

Johnson opened his own arms as Stanley pitched forward into them.

"I'm sorry, Johnson," Stanley cried, burying his head in Johnson's shoulder. "I never forgave myself for getting you killed. It ate me up for so long."

"I forgive you, Stanley. I'm not mad. Just happy to see you," Johnson laughed as Stanley hung on him. He squeezed his eyes closed so that Stanley would not see him cry. His life became real again, everything between their separation a fever dream. He felt his back relax, his shoulders. "All right, Stanley, let's not get too emotional about it. I forgive you."

But Stanley became heavier, his grip on Johnson's back looser. Johnson wrapped Stanley up in his arms as he began to slide down his shoulder and set him on the landing of the stairs.

Stanley was dead. And Johnson had no idea where the herb was.

Heidi

It had been twenty-five minutes, and her father had yet to show up. She had always expected this, that one day the truck would finally die. Every day that her father waited for her, on time, the dragon filling the air in front of the school with its special blend of toxic fumes, was an anomaly, and today was expected. But if it were expected, she did not know why she had never drawn up a contingency plan.

She walked back to her locker and opened it, feigning a search for a forgotten book. She waited for Mrs. Webster to lock her door and begin her way down the hall.

"Whatcha doin', Polensky?" Oliver smacked the open door of her locker with his palm. His signature scent of Wrigley's chewing gum and aftershave worked its way into the space between her and the dark hollow of her locker.

"Nothing," she answered, fingering a copy of *Les Miserables* in French. What could she be doing here? She played no sports; math club was on Tuesdays, science on Wednesday. "What are you doing?"

"Getting the hell out of here. Want a ride?"

It was not a divine intervention, and it didn't feel like one, but Heidi was strangely at peace with whatever serendipity was in the works, with her father's absence today, Oliver's seeming chivalry. She'd let him drive her home, see where she lived. Maybe he would stay and actually meet her father this time, since the aforementioned nursing home visit to meet his grandfather had never materialized. Or maybe he'd break up with Shauna. Her torture of Heidi had not stopped, contrary to Oliver's belief; instead, she'd just grown more clever, more careful about it—saying hi to her in his presence, complementing her on a shirt she must have worn for three years—while Heidi still found used tampons in her locker, her clothes still stolen from the locker room during gym; once, underwear doused in vinegar, and crushed potato chips in her shoes.

Maybe, in his guilt, Oliver thought of her at night, some innocent fantasy of seeing the Jasper Johns exhibit together at the university in town and ramming his tongue into her throat in the back of his Mustang, flowers, long, fluent letters on looseleaf detailing his long-kindled devotion, and a date to the prom secured. Maybe he had staked her movements out for the last week, two, seeing an opportunity as she idled by her locker and seizing it.

Or maybe she was just delusional. They walked silently through the hall, filled with amateurish posters advertising this year's theme—Enchantment Under the Sea—out to the student parking lot, a square of concrete where plans were made, alliances between cliques forged, and impromptu trips to Buildaburger taken. It was a hub at which Heidi had never bartered, only heard about in the aftermath of newsworthy events. Oliver whistled. His aluminum varsity baseball bat lay across his shoulder. At the end of it, dangling, rested his backpack, and with a flick, he catapulted it across the parking lot, where it landed at the back of his Mustang like an obedient dog.

"Nice aim," she said.

"You want me to do yours?"

"No." Although she was flattered that he would show off for her. "I've got breakables."

"Yeah—I broke my trig calculator once," he conceded. "Um, so do you have a date for prom yet?"

"I don't have any plans," she answered. She could not believe he was actually asking her. Her father would have to splurge for this—a dress. Perhaps she could even ask Ms. Webster for a loan.

"Yeah? Maybe I'll see if one of the boys wants to take you. Richard Young doesn't have a date."

She felt her backpack slide off her shoulder and onto the tarred pavement. Richard Young would probably be as unpopular as she was if he was not batting .478 as the Tigers' left fielder. He was an orangutan with pimples and braces and always smelled like mayonnaise and salami. Oliver scooped the bag up with his bat and flicked over on top of his, figuring, perhaps, that whatever fragile piece rested inside was already broken.

"So, yeah, I'll ask Richard." They reached the car. It couldn't get any worse at that point, she figured, how could it? Except that when she grabbed her backpack and went to open the passenger door of Oliver's Mustang, Shauna was already sitting in it. Her eyes widened as she cracked her gum.

"Jesus—yuck, you scared me." Shauna pulled the door closed on her. "Go away, troll."

"I'm giving Heidi a ride home." Oliver said, opening the driver's side door. He threw his own backpack roughly into Shauna's lap. "So shut the fuck up."

Shauna's jaw dropped at perhaps the same velocity and speed as

Heidi's. They stared at each other as some weighed balance rolled, like a roulette ball, between them. For a moment, there was a pinhole of vulnerability in the irises of Shauna's eyes, the beginning of a tear on one of her eyelids, before their gentle, pulpy black hardened irreversibly, and Heidi knew that her remaining days at Mt. Zion would be as cursed and unforgettable as a nightmare.

"Get in." Oliver said to Heidi, nodding toward the front seat. "Shauna was just leaving."

"I just remembered—my father is going to pick me up soon." She backed away, unable to unlock her gaze from Shauna, a medusa busy turning Heidi's limbs and stomach to stone the longer she stayed put. "Thanks, though."

At an alarming and embarrassing speed, Heidi ran back toward the school, hoping to catch Ms. Webster before she left. She could get a ride and perhaps some advice on how to avoid the freight train of Shauna's wrath that would be barreling through the school at her as early as Monday morning. But the halls were dark, smelling of dust and adolescence—an eau de gym sock, bubble gum, and hormones. She stood outside in front, willing the orange monster to make its slow turn from State Avenue and lumber before her.

After forty minutes, she traced the route her father would take to the school to get her, if he was indeed coming. Six miles. It was breezy, and she scurried along the side of the road like an opossum for two hours, ready to duck into the high grass or ditch at any vehicle that wasn't the truck. She had been stupid not to take Oliver's offer, and for some reason, this made her angry at her father, rather than Shauna or Oliver. Her father was at fault, along with her stupid mother, for her existence in this shit world. And Ms. Webster, too, for giving her a chance. She became angrier every step she took, and by six o'clock, reaching the driveway of their farmhouse and seeing the truck parked in the driveway, she was furious.

Right away, she knew something was wrong. All the lights were out, and her father was a notorious waster of electricity on account of his glaucoma. Even during the day, at least the kitchen light burned. She stepped inside the hallway and there he was, like a pile of laundry that had settled at the bottom of the steps.

"Shit." She lifted his face between her hands, his head the weight of a bowling ball. Some of his drool smeared across her right palm, but he was cold, unmoving. She pinched his nose and blew in his mouth and pushed his chest, trying to approximate the CPR she'd learned during swimming classes years ago. Finally, she rested on top of him, feeling her short, beleaguered breaths press against the rigidness of his chest.

She got a glass of water from the kitchen, gulping it greedily by the sink, pressing her lips tightly so that she would not immediately throw it up. When she turned, he was still there, where she'd left him. She sat down and took one of his hands. It was strange to think that the only person she'd ever known on earth, really, her only home, had gone to some other place, some other home. And left her here to fend for herself, with thirteen sixty-eight in his checking account until his next pension check.

She picked up the phone and called Ms. Webster. She waited, strangely composed, as the rings went unanswered and she hung up. If she spoke of it, it therefore would be true, and the thing, strong and green inside her, would rot and snap and never grow again. She could not speak of what had happened just yet. She willed the tears from her eyes and went back to the stairs. She grabbed her father's shoulders and pressed her foot aside the side of the step for leverage, pulling him up to a sitting position. He looked like he did when he slept, except he was cold and everything about him was weighted down with gravity, enclosed in a faint smell of urine.

"Why'd you have to go and pull this? Jesus," she asked, smoothing the collar of his shirt. Her thoughts began to gather speed, when his pension would come in, how much she could cash at a time, when she could pay the bills and get gas. She'd already done so much of it with and without him present, that it didn't seem so hard. So hard to what? To pretend nothing was wrong? It was her senior year, and in a few months, she'd graduate. She didn't want to go into foster care, for the state to sell the house, to evict her from the only memories she had. She didn't want any extra attention at school, or even pity. And, mostly, she didn't want to believe it. He'd left her. She sat on the stair above him and dropped her head in her hands.

She heard it then, creak in the kitchen, not the creak of mice or settling foundations, but the creak of an intruder, a slow moan on the soft spot of the kitchen floor near the stove.

A young man appeared at the entrance to the living room, wearing a white V-neck undershirt and jeans, a leather jacket, some undetermined type of mountain boot, a timeless nondefinitive style, certainly no one she'd ever seen before.

"Wait…" He held out his hand, but she was already up the stairs, the charge of survival electrifying her limbs like a cattle prodder. She locked her father's bedroom door and made for the shoebox at the top of her the closet where he kept his .22 pistol. It felt heavy and foreign, like an alien transponder, and she wished she'd taken him up on his numerous attempts to train her in firearms. Unfortunately, he was usually drunk when the offers had occurred, and she spent more time trying to talk him out of shooting the empty

Wild Turkey bottles he'd lined on the fence for his own safety than wondering when her own marksmanship would come in handy.

She crouched by the door and listened to his boots squeak on the wooden planks of the steps. Each board pressed against her heart, pinning it against her throat. She moved the safety with her finger, thank goodness she knew that much, and pointed the gun at the door.

"Heidi?"

The knock, his voice, startled her. She held the gun as steadily as she could with two hands and waited, her breaths quick through her nose. He knocked again, and she felt the sweat build in her armpits and begin in run down her sides. There was no third knock, and as the boots moaned again on the planks down the stairs and outside the house, she moved to the bedroom window, peering out. He turned, and she caught a glimpse of his face—placid, square— and she leapt back, wondering if he saw her. She thought of a Joyce Carol Oates story Ms. Webster assigned them last semester—about a convict with a motorcycle jacket and too-big boots who talks a girl out of her house and into his car while her parents are gone.

He walked toward the truck. She took a deep breath and flew down the stairs, hurdling over her father's body to the front door to lock it. She let the gun fall to her side and glanced through the curtains. At the truck, he had turned, staring at the door, realizing what had happened, and he trotted back up and tried the doorknob before disappearing around the side of the house. Her heart flittered in her ears as she moved back through the house to the kitchen. Sure enough, he was coming around the back of the house.

She locked the back door and ducked as his form filled its six glass panes. The handle jiggled, and then he knocked again. She tried to imagine herself part of the wallpaper, a chameleon.

"Heidi, I don't mean you any harm. Please—answer or something."

But he didn't knock again, and after a few seconds, she could see smoke lazily spiraling up to the sky. She stood up to find him sitting on the back porch steps, smoking. She wondered how long he would wait.

A long time, apparently. Fifteen, twenty minutes passed, and she crept from room to room, peering through different windows. She could not turn on the lights as the sun began to disappear in the sky, could not turn on the television, not even take a shower. She thought about slipping out the front and running to the Harris's house a mile up the road, asking Mr. Harris to come back with her. But she was a terrible runner; surely he would catch up with her. It would be better to be bold. It was not, she realized, as if she had anything to lose. Her life was no longer anything she knew and she would have to walk through the storm's eye and get to the other side, wherever that would be. She sighed loudly, walked with the gun at shoulder level, and opened the door.

"What do you want?" She growled. The man stood up quickly in surprise.

"I'm sorry," he answered calmly, backing down the steps and into the yard. He seemed unbothered by having a gun leveled at him. "I came to see your father, Stanley Polensky."

"And you killed him?"

"No—he had a heart attack." He twisted the cherry out of his cigarette and crushed the filter in his hand. "I'm sorry."

"You're trying to rob us? Does it look like we have anything? I called the police, just so you know."

"Oh." He looked at his boots, his lips tight. One of his shoelaces was stained with ketchup or blood. She squeezed the handle of the gun, hoping the former. "I wish you hadn't."

"I bet." She felt tears on her face, but there was nothing she could do. Her arm began to warm and ping and numb from pointing the gun at him.

"No, it's just that I wanted to explain." He held his hands up over his head. "I'll stand here like this and we'll just talk and then I'm going to beat it out of here when the police come."

"Hurry, then."

"Heidi, I'm so sorry about your father." He blinked his eyes, and for a moment, she felt as if his eyelashes had wiped her face dry, had held her chin, caressed her cheeks. She noticed how stunning he was, like Robert Redford in The Great Gatsby. "I surprised the hell out of him, that's for sure. We haven't seen each other... for years."

"Are you... my *brother*?" It was entirely possible that, if her mother had hidden one child from the public eye, she had hidden another.

"Oh, no." He laughed. He shook his head and chuckled again, as if sharing in some inside joke to which she was not privy. "I'm a little older than that. I'm an old friend."

He poked around in his leather jacket for his cigarettes and pulled out a pack of Pall Malls. "Want one?"

"I don't smoke. My father doesn't—didn't—have any friends."

"So you're his daughter, huh?" He looked up at her and cocked an eyebrow. "You really don't look anything like him."

"Doesn't matter."

"Hey, come on—you gonna level a gun at me all day?"

"Until you get out of here and don't come back. I told you, the police will be here any minute."

"Listen." He inhaled his cigarette and squatted on the ground. "Did Stanley Polensky—your father—ever mention a Calvin Johnson to you?"

"Why?"

"Well, Stanley and Calvin were in the war together, which I guess you'd know if you know Calvin Johnson. I just wanted to get some information from Stanley about the war. I've come a long way. I'm not here to rob you or anything, I swear."

"What kind of information?"

"Yeah." He scratched the back of his head. "Probably a strange request. But I'm interested in a—corsage—that Stanley carried around. A dried flower that he kept in his helmet. I always figured it was probably a corsage from a girl at a dance or something, right, although Stanley never talked about any sweetheart, from what I can recall. Anyway, it's really important that I see the herb. I've wanted to get in touch with Stanley for a long time, but I lost track of him after he moved from Baltimore. I finally find him, God, it was so good to see him, but he got all worked up seeing *me* and had a heart attack. I tried to resuscitate him, but...anyway, the herb isn't important right now, is it? Your father is dead. We should help him, not leave him there like that."

"He's staying where he is." She waved the gun as if to remind him it was still there. "How do I know you didn't hit him or choke him or kill him some other way?"

"You don't." He flicked his cigarette onto the ground and stepped on it.

"So maybe you'll explain that to the police."

"Heidi, *I'm* Calvin Johnson." He looked up at her. "*I* served with your father during the war."

"Stop it." She shook her head. "Do you expect me to believe that? I don't know what's going on here, but we're going to wait here until the police come. And if you try and run, I'll shoot you."

"It wouldn't matter if you shot me or not, but I won't run." He sat on the ground cross-legged. "I'll wait."

"I'll be right back." She backed into the house toward the phone to call the police. In the kitchen, she poured herself a glass of water and watched him through the window. He remained on the ground, smoking another cigarette, as if resigned to his fate. Something about him seemed so harmless, so familiar. And he knew about the crazy herb in her backpack, the one her father had told her about, the one Melanie Huber told her was definitely not pot, but if her father was growing any shrooms, to please let her know. Suddenly, a stranger was her only familiar face in the world. She sighed and poured another glass of water and took them outside.

"Here—if you're thirsty." She put the glass down between them, then backed away, pointing the gun at him. He took the glass and gulped it empty.

"Thanks," he answered. "I'm glad Stanley had a family. He was so shy with the ladies while we were in the army. I bet he was good to you, huh?"

"Don't." She wiped the sweat from her brow and sat on the porch steps. "Don't try to play my sympathies."

"I'm not. I'm just really sorry you had to come home . . . to this. Were you in school or something?"

"Why are you curious about this—corsage?" She interrupted him. He studied her, but she could not tell what he was thinking.

"Well, it may have some medicinal qualities. Do you know anything about that?"

She looked at her water glass and then past his shoulder.

"Do you know what I'm talking about?" He stared at her. "The flower? You are aware of its existence, right?"

"Yeah—I've heard about it," she answered finally, and his face lit up. His hands dug into each other as if he were trying to keep himself from her.

"Is it in your possession? Stanley said he gave it to you."

"What's it to you?"

"Listen, I don't have any money. I can't pay you anything, but I'd do whatever it takes to get to see it. You see, a friend of mine, a scientist, he wants to examine it."

"Can't he get his own somewhere?"

"That's the thing." He stood up and lit another cigarette, running his hand through his hair and pacing back and forth. She felt her body stiffen. Her hand with the gun followed him back and forth. She grabbed the railing with her other hand to steady herself. "It's very rare, this herb, he thinks. Maybe a few patches existed in Europe a few centuries ago, or maybe this particular piece that Stanley owns was tampered with in some way. But we'll never know until we test it."

"Why do you think there's something medicinal about it?"

"Because." He stopped pacing and looked at her. "Because Stanley Polensky fed it to me in Germany in 1944 and then left me for dead...but I lived. And I've been like this...young, undead...ever since."

"What are you saying? That Calvin Johnson is still alive?" Heidi thoughts raced, constructing a man as old as her father withering away in some nursing home in Ohio. Her heart swelled for her own father, that he did not live to have the incident that weighed him down reclaimed, like lost baggage, years later.

"Yes." he smiled. "I survived. And we—the scientist and I—think it might have to do with the herb Stanley gave me."

"You are so full of it," she said, even though she felt herself shaking. "What's my grandmother's name?"

"Safine."

"My aunts and uncles?"

"Henry, Thomas, Cass, Julia...and Kathryn. Linus was your grandfather."

"What about my mother?"

"Don't know." He dug his hands in his pockets. "I only knew him until 1944. Listen, did your father ever eat the herb, to your knowledge?"

"No, he didn't."

"Did you?"

"Of course not." She picked at her tennis shoe. "But you expect me to believe you did."

"I don't know how much I ate. I remember your father stuffing it into my mouth, my wound. It was pretty bad, the wound. I was missing most of my leg from taking a shell."

"I know this. I also know the paramedic pronounced Calvin Johnson dead at the scene. And, theoretically, you're just a guy who knows it, too, since I saw my father's diary on the floor of the living room."

"Police sure take a long time in these parts." He cocked an eyebrow toward her.

"Well, I guess you have more time to make shit up," she answered.

❀❀❀

Over the next hour, he told her everything as if he expected her to believe it. She wondered whether he had stolen anyone else's identities aside from Calvin Johnson's, whose Social Security checks he had stuffed in the backpack she'd noticed lying in the living room. Whoever he was, it puzzled her why he cared so much about Calvin Johnson's past enough to come here and involve her father. Did he have some serious cash tucked away that she did not know about, perhaps recording royalties from her mother? Had he lied to her all this time, forcing them into some austere existence for the sake of making some point about his own frugality?

"I can prove this to you," the man said. "The herb. I'm telling you, that herb is magic."

"Either that or you're a nut." She sighed. He seemed smaller, shallower, to her, a con man off his meds. She figured that, like most con men, he thought he had his in with her and now he wouldn't leave unless she got the police involved.

"We should do it now." He stood up. "Come on."

"What?"

"I want you to shoot me." He stood in the backyard, arms and legs spread out. "I'm proving to you that everything I've said is true."

"I'm not going to shoot you, you moron." She felt sick to her stomach. It was turning out to be some crazy Joyce Carol Oates story after all. Maybe she had wanted to shoot him a few times in the past few hours, but this was not the same. "I don't want to go to jail."

"Nobody will hear. I'm sure gunfire isn't that foreign a sound in these parts," he said. "Now, come on. You think I'm a con artist, that I'm trying to milk you dry or something, right? All I'm saying is shoot me in, here, the hand, and you'll see."

He held his palm open toward her, far away from his body.

"And then what?"

"Well, it'll hurt like hell, and it'll bleed for a bit, but a few hours from now, you are going to see the wound start to heal. In no time at all, it'll be completely gone."

"Either you're a fool or I'm dreaming." She scrunched her eyebrows. "And I'm supposed to take care of you during your convalescence?"

"Not if you don't want to. If you'll kindly lend me a towel, I'll sit out there in the cornfield by myself."

"Couldn't you just rob us like a normal person?" She laughed at the unreality of her evening. Perhaps she had fallen asleep during seventh period. Everything, from Oliver to her father to this faux Johnson had morphed stranger and stranger as if she'd eaten chocolate before bed. "Why did you have to bring my father into this, and poor Calvin Johnson, too?"

"Do you think I want to be twenty-two years old forever?" He narrowed his eyes as he felt for his cigarettes in his jacket. "You think it's fun watching the people you care for age and get sick, knowing that every person you meet, you're going to watch die? Believe me, I'm secretly hoping that this is the bullet that *will* kill me."

"Well, since you're not going to back into the truth anytime soon, how about I start? We have nothing. There isn't any money for you to take. We live on $230 dollars a month. You know what that buys, besides gas, when the truck is working, electricity, water, and food? Yeah, nothing. Sometimes, it doesn't even buy water and food."

He turned from her and walked away, toward the cornfields, kneeling down on his hands and knees, eyes closed. She saw the bands of muscles in his arm, his legs, and his jaw tense before he started to cry, big bawling sulks, his head shaking, a cry even worse than any she'd ever had. He pounded the ground with his fists, his eyebrows slanted in fury toward his nose. Then he sat up, the residue of his anger rolling off him.

"We can still give him the herb." He nodded his head as he stood up, as if it had never happened. "He might wake up. Where's the herb? Let's give it to your father."

"He's been dead for hours." She fell back on the step, relieved that he was no longer angry, perhaps a little less dangerous.

"It doesn't matter how dead—it can't matter. My whole leg was gone. I must have been dead for a month."

"But you already had the herb in you when you were alive," she pressed, and then grabbed at her hair. "What am I talking about? This is all a bunch of bullshit."

"Look." He sat back on his haunches. "I know this is all very, very difficult to swallow. I wouldn't believe it myself, if you came up to me with the same story. But there are others like me, even. I can show them to you, if you want. There's all sorts of classified research going on to isolate what's going on in me, the others, and the flower, to see whether the secret to immortality is finally known. Even if you don't believe me, at least let's go inside. I know you didn't call the police. I know you must believe in something, Heidi."

"I don't know what I believe." It was dark. She wanted to talk to Ms. Webster.

"Believe me when I say I want to help you." He walked toward her slowly, his palms facing outward. "I want to help your father, help you, and then maybe you'll help me."

❀❀❀

She let him come inside. They sat on the couch and looked at Stanley across the room. In the deepening twilight, he looked asleep. Everything in her father that Heidi had always assumed to be available to her, her father himself, had been washed away as if it were written in sand.

"I feel so selfish for never having asked him anything about himself," she said, to the man or to herself. "I've spent all my life worrying about myself."

"You're young. I didn't think about my parents, really think about them, until we shipped out from Fort Benning and I thought I might never see them again." He pulled out his wallet and showed her a folded black and white photograph of a man and woman. The woman wore a shin-length polka-dot dress with white lapels folding out over a square collar. "Here they are, in front of our home. I wasn't born yet, so it's probably the 1920s."

"That's very nice." Heidi studied the man, who had thick Brylcreemed hair, a straight nose, and a square jaw. "You look a lot like that man. Even the slicked hair. And you definitely look like the guy on the ship."

"Heidi, get the herb. I want to save your father."

"He didn't want to eat it. Look, I will give you the herb—I don't really care about it. But you're not giving it to my father, okay? I have to respect his wishes."

"But I need to know if he can undo this." The man pressed her arm. "I can't be like this the rest of my life. Don't you want your father to live?"

"No...yes...I don't know." She shook her head. "He never asked anything of me, except for that."

She rummaged through her backpack and put the sandwich bag on the table. His hand hovered over it, but he did not touch it.

"Do you think it'll work?" She stood up, her legs like paper, unsure whether she was scared or hopeful.

"It has to," he answered. "I'm living proof."

"But if you give it to my father, there might not be any more. Maybe the scientist should try and replicate it first...if it's that important to you."

"Heidi, your father is dead over there." Calvin picked up the bag. "Don't you want him to live?"

"Of course...but not if he's going to be some Frankenstein."

"Is that what I am to you?"

"I don't know." She wrapped her arms around herself. "I didn't ask for any of this. I just wanted to get through high school. Yes, please save him."

The man bent over her father and pinched open his mouth, manipulating the herb out of the plastic sandwich bag with the other.

"I'm sorry, Dad." Heidi held her hands in prayer. She did not know any prayers, so she made one up about her appreciation of her father, his hard life, his small enjoyments of losing money at the track and at the liquor store, his faith in the orange dragon, who might miss his erratic and drunken driving, even if the rest of the world wouldn't.

"I can't do this." The man sat back on his heels. "Why would I take from your father the only thing I've wanted all these years for myself?"

He stood up and placed the herb on the table before her.

"Here, I can't. Can you?"

She looked at the herb, the one she almost sold to Melanie, in her gym class, who sat on the bleachers singing "Sugar Magnolia, blossoms blooming" with a doctor's note about her asthma even though her lungs were stronger than an elephant's. She looked at her father. He would be pissed. He would be so pissed. But he was her only father, her only... anything.

"Will he stay fifty-five forever?" She asked the man, who absently took her father's pulse. "How long has he been dead now?"

"Over two hours. Almost three." He stood up. "Look, I don't mean to take the decision out of your hands, but if it works, he'll never die. There's another one, this girl Ela—the scientist adopted her—she's been nine for nearly two hundred years. She's watched so many people die, and she'll never become a woman. I thought I wanted your father to take it, but I don't know. He'll have to watch *you* die, which will kill him, even though he can't die. Because he loves you so much, Heidi. I've never seen someone love a child so much. He told me how smart you are, how you're going to do the Polenskys proud, that 'Lil Cindy didn't know what she missed."

"At least he gets to see her again. I don't know if she'll want to see him," she laughed. But the tears that started growing in her eyes were not funny. "He's probably giving her an earful right now."

"Well, she deserves it." The man walked over to her and put his arms around her, squeezing her, warm and soft. He smelled like his jacket, clean but wild. He kissed the top of her head and held her in his arms and she let him.

It took over an hour to dig the grave. She could barely see Johnson in the darkness, the dirt flying over his shoulder. Her father lay wrapped in the spare plastic shower liner by the widening hole. She sat on the porch drinking a glass of water. Perhaps, when her father went in the hole and she didn't see him again, it would begin to hit her. It was easier to accept that it was Calvin Johnson digging the hole than her father dead beside it. She wondered what would happen when he left with the herb. She would go back to school on Monday and try to pretend that nothing happened. Maybe she could ask Ms. Webster to lend her a little food money until the beginning of the next month, when the pension check arrived, ready to be stretched every which way.

Over the mound, Johnson crossed himself, and so did Heidi.

"Do you think animals will get to him?" she asked.

"I don't know." He mopped the back of his neck with a dish towel she'd brought outside. "I dug it six feet. The shower curtain is wrapped pretty tight. I'll put some two-by-fours I found in the basement as a layer. That might help."

"I'm sorry you had to do all that," she said in the kitchen as he soaped up to his elbows at the sink.

"Don't worry about it. You just worry about yourself." He smiled at her from the sink. "So where's the gun?"

"Oh, Christ, you're not going to ask me to shoot you again, are you?" Sweat pooled in the small of her back as she tried to comprehend the pendulum on which his personality swung. He could have been waiting all along to gain her trust, then kill her. She gripped it where it rested into the waistband of her corduroys.

"It's the only way I've got to get you to believe me. Please don't make me do it with my hunting knife. It'll take longer and hurt so much more."

"I'm done with you, really, I am." She shot from the kitchen and out the front door. If she could escape, she could drive to the police station, somehow find Ms. Webster. His boots kicked up the gravel behind her as she ran. She reached the truck and flung the driver's door open before realizing she did not have the keys. She could feel him on the other side of the door. Her heart beat in her ears, blood filling her head, as she tugged at the gun in her waistband.

"Heidi." She felt his hand on her back, and she screamed, but no sound came out as she spun, pistol in her hands, and fired. Calvin fell back on the gravel, and the rocks underneath his boots spit at her legs.

"Oh my God." She dropped the gun on the seat and kneeled next to him as he grabbed at his abdomen. Blood seeped over his fingers. It was dark, almost purple, and she felt sick. She took off her sweater and tried to press it under his hands, trying not to think too much about how it was her favorite, an old cable knit sweater she had gotten at the thrift store in town, such a rare find, because she knew it was selfish, and it didn't matter because it was soaked in few seconds.

"Can you walk?" she asked, standing up a little. "We need to get you to the house."

"I might," he grunted. "Thanks. I would have preferred the hand, but the stomach will do okay, too. It'll just take a little longer."

"What are you talking about?" She wrapped her arms around his waist, taut and smooth like an inner tube, and he wove his arms gently around her shoulders. "I'm calling an ambulance."

"No, you're not." He pushed gently on his heels, taking the gun off the seat, as she lifted with her knees, something she had learned after helping to carry her father's body through the house. "The bleeding will stop in a little while. Trust me. And in a week, you won't even know it happened."

"And what about the bullet?" she asked, as they walked gingerly to the house. "It's just going to stay in there?"

"I still have shrapnel in my leg from 1944. I can still feel it some-times when it rains." His weight gradually burned in her legs, her shoulders. She stooped but kept moving. "Let's rest for a minute. I don't want to hurt you."

He slumped to the ground, a few feet from the porch. Blood covered her skin and his skin, as if they were conjoined twins moments before, now separated and left to die. And Calvin really did look like he might. He began to sweat; his face was pale, brow furrowed.

"I'm going to get some sheets." She hurdled the porch steps to the front door. "We can make a tourniquet."

She flew up the stairs, flecks of blood splattering on the walls and wood, and pulled the sheets off her father's bed. When she got back, Calvin had pulled himself on the porch and sat on the steps, leaning against the porch railing.

"How do I do this?" She began to thread the sheet around his arm.

"We don't need to make a tourniquet. Just pressure." He helped guide the sheet around his body, and when it was finished, he took her hands in his and pressed them against his stomach. She was sickened by how cold they were, how cool the skin on his back felt. The blood on her breasts and stomach smeared sticky against his back.

"I need to call an ambulance." She moved to stand up, but he held onto her hands.

"I'm telling you, I'll be fine. If anything, let's just get inside the house so no one driving along the road sees us." His weight pulled her forward as he dragged himself to his feet and moved slowly to the door. Once inside, he took heavy, slow, teetering steps up the stairs as Heidi stood a few steps behind, wondering whether he'd fall back onto her at any second. In the bathroom, he shrugged off the sheet before sitting on the toilet and easing himself out of his jeans, the waist of which was rimmed in blood. He grabbed her arm for support as he lowered himself in the tub.

"What now?" She sat on the toilet and held the jeans in her hands, kicking the sheet to the corner.

"Nothing. Maybe if you could get me a pillow, I'll just take a nap in here after I bathe." He pulled the curtain tight between them, and she could hear the water running from the faucet. She went into the hallway closet and got a spare pillow and some washcloths, a towel.

"Are you still alive?" she said to the shower curtain.

"Yep. Just hurts."

"I'm leaving the pillow by the tub here, along with some towels, okay?"

"Thanks. Do you mind bringing me some water, too? And my cigarettes. I hate to be a pest."

"You're not a pest—you're dying. How am I going to get you out of that tub after you've died?"

"I'm not going to die—why is that so hard to believe?" She heard him laugh, then suck shallowly for air.

"I'm going to call 911."

"You do, and we'll have to explain why we buried your father outside in the woods. Just give me some time, okay? I'll tell you some things about him when you come back."

She went downstairs and filled a glass of water from the kitchen, along with Calvin's packs of boxers and tube socks from his backpack. When she returned to the bathroom, the pillow was missing from the floor, replaced by a wet pair of bloody boxers. She could hear the water draining in the tub.

"You okay?" She put the glass of water on the tub's edge. "Are you alive?"

"Yep. Just waiting for you, doll-face."

"The minute you stop talking is the minute I start dialing."

"Stop worrying, Heidi. I've already died twice." She watched his hand, big and pale, grab the water, heard it disappear in sharp gulps behind the shower curtain. "I think the bleeding's stopped. You mind giving me one of those clean towels?"

She leaned over, dangling the towel in the crack between the wall and shower curtain for him to grab.

"Oww, that hurts," he said. "You know, we always had the runs in the Army. It was easy to understand why. But your father, he had the stomach of rice paper. One night outside of Germany, we were in the foxholes, freezing cold, and he had the shits bad. From the chocolate bars we got, at that—Christ, that was practically all we ate. I'm thankful I still have teeth. All night—we couldn't leave the foxholes—he's shitting into that helmet and dumping it off to the side. I said, 'Christ, Pole, you're going to drive off the Krauts with your ass alone'."

"What's a Kraut?"

"You know, a German. I guess it's not the correct word nowadays. Not the stuff you'd find in your textbooks, anyway."

The cloth shower curtain wrenched open, and Calvin stood before her, a towel high around his waist, covering the wound. She gasped, but not because he stood before her, less worse for wear. It *was* because he stood before her—a boy/man/God, talking to her, like she wasn't a freak.

"It's already looking better." He curled the towel down slightly to show her. The hair around his bellybutton was mottled red, a dark leeching scab that left little puddles of pink on the white terrycloth. "It stopped bleeding, mostly."

She watched her fingers hover near the wound, her stomach full of glass. He grabbed her hand and pressed it against the furry, gelatinous spot, and she recoiled at the fire on his skin. She imagined his metabolism churning, little mitochondria in the cells pushing them to collect and stick and close the wound, little red elves with fire heads. But it could not be true, she thought. It was not the way she learned in biology class. It could not happen so quickly. And yet, there it was. She pulled her hand away, savoring the light pressure that remained on her skin from his fingers. She looked at her skin, clean but moist.

"You'd better get dressed—you'll catch your death," she said, in a daze. She walked out of the bathroom and into her father's bedroom, falling on the scratchy wool blanket and staring at the ceiling. Tears warmed the corners of her eyes and burrowed sticky rivers down her cheeks. She heard Calvin stepping into his jeans, pulling his t-shirt over his head. He stood in the doorway, hair wet, his skin a pleasing post-bath pink and not the gallows white it had been earlier.

"You okay?" He looked at her, and she nodded her head.

"I guess…your being here has reminded me of how lonely I am." She rolled onto her stomach and studied the dust bunnies in the corners of the bedroom, trying not to cry. He sat on the bed and put his hand, massive and warm, on her back. A chill spidered through her body, and she concentrated on her breathing, slow and steady.

"Poor girl," he said, moving his hand in a circle. "I understand." She hoped he would do it for a long time, but then he stopped, and when she rolled over on her side to face him, he was looking out the window, somewhere else.

"What will you do for me, if I gave you the herb?"

"I don't know." He smelled like soap, and she imagined placing her lips on his neck. She rolled away from him, suddenly angry. "What do you want?"

She stared at her hands. She wanted to wake up the next day and have it all have been a strange dream. She wanted her father to knock on her door and chide her for oversleeping, telling her she'd be late for school. She wanted to hear him burp and fart in the kitchen while he greased the frying pan with butter and cracked his eggs. She wanted him to drive her to school in the truck, even as it had always embarrassed her. And she wanted him to be waiting when she got out, reading the newspaper and smoking a cigarette in the truck cab.

And if she couldn't have those things, she decided she wanted Calvin.

"Let me go with you—wherever you're going back to." She stood up and looked out the window.

"Heidi, you're nothing but a little girl—a whole future in front of you. You don't want to get messed up with a guy like me."

"What am I, in a movie or something?" She laughed, and he stood up slowly from the bed and came behind her. He put his hands on her shoulders.

"Imagine being in a movie that never ended," he said, his breath tickling the top of her head. "And no matter how many times you went to the candy counter, the john, it still was playing."

She didn't answer, but that movie, with her and Calvin as its stars, sounded perfectly all right to her. She turned and wrapped her arms around his waist, her head pressed against his chest, and she was prepared to not let go, no matter how hard he pushed her. But he didn't. He slowly put his arms around her and she felt sleepy, fetal, in the expanse of him. She pushed him toward the bed and he slowly gave in to her. He lay on his side, and she pressed her back against him, drawing her arms around her, and she rested her chin on his arm. She felt his breath on her neck, and she turned into him, looking into his eyes, the impenetrable earth of them, sediment deep and layered and hardened.

There was nothing familiar about him, the curve of his chin, his smell, the unwelcome stiffness of his muscles, and yet she felt safe there, yielded to his ferocity. She wanted him to want her, to bite into her heart and puncture it, thirst for its blood, its young pulse, and the stone of him would melt, for just a moment, and she could see the soft pulp of him, the organs and boy, the things that would make him cry, his mother. She felt her lips part, anxious for him to press his against hers, to offer her everything she had been starving for, starving for so long she had no longer realized until now that she was hungry.

But he told her about Kate. About Ela, the Polish girl, his asymmetrical twin, separated by hundreds of years, destined, perhaps, to be together hundreds of years still. She listened, captivated, heartbroken, drained, watching the muscles move in his throat. They lay entwined in silence for a long time as the night spilled over the corners of the room and over the bed, and they were shadows in the dark, listening to each other's breathing, their thoughts passing boats in a foggy night.

They slept. They slept like stones until the light of Saturday moved across the walls of the bedroom, and they slept some more, like people who have been through hell ice-fire, who have traversed dark valleys and need for their souls to lick their wounds.

"It's nice to be here with you like this," he said after a while, and her heart leapt a little. "It's so hard to tell this story over and over again and wonder who really believes you."

"Don't they believe you when they get older and you don't?"

"Sometimes, even something in front of your face, if it goes against your belief system, seems unreal. I was dead in a lake for twenty years. In the ground in Germany. I can hardly believe it myself."

"Are you mad? How can you believe in a God?"

"Sometimes it's a blessing, other times it's a curse. If I hadn't returned from the dead in Germany, I wouldn't have met Kate, even though now I might have to watch her die. I wouldn't have gotten to see your father and watch him die. As for God, there's something out there, I guess, and it's made this path for me. I've given up being angry about it."

"I'm sorry my father did this to you."

"Don't apologize." He drew her close, her face against his neck. "I got to meet you, too, now didn't I?"

She pressed her lips against his skin, the slight scent of soap filling her nose, and she began to kiss upward, toward his ear. She felt his body stiffen, his groin press against her. She stopped, amazed that she had such a power over any man, much less Calvin Johnson, before kissing him again.

"Heidi, I think you're great." He wriggled away from her into a sitting position. "But I could be your father. And you're Stanley's daughter. He would want me to honor and protect you."

"What about the herb?" She got up from the bed. From the window, she could see it was dusk again. She had not eaten in over a day, but she was not hungry for food.

"What, you're not going to give it to me? You want me to be a cad, lie to you, romance you, so you'll give me the herb?"

"I don't know." She wiped the tears from her eyes and went

downstairs. She could bury the herb, send Calvin Johnson on his way. Why should she give every stranger who walked in the door what they wanted? No one had ever been there for her.

The sound of a car outside paralyzed her. She caught her breath and pressed by the window, peering outside. Ms. Webster's green Squareback was parked in front. She got out of the car and made her way to the door.

"Hey." Ms. Webster smiled from the darkness of the porch. "I thought I'd see whether you were interested in a movie. They're playing 'Wild Strawberries' over at the community college at eight."

"I can't." Heidi filled the space between the door and the frame with her body.

"Oh, does your father need you?"

"Yeah."

"Are you all right?" Ms. Webster adjusted the strap of her shoulder bag. "Have you been crying?"

"No," she answered. She felt the salty sting on her cheeks as she grimaced.

"You're going to lie to me to my face?" Ms. Webster laughed. "Come on outside."

"No... it's not anything. I'm just feeling sorry for myself." Heidi shook her head. She reached behind her and turned on the porch light, hoping that if she allowed closer scrutiny of her physical condition Ms. Webster would be satisfied.

"Oh my god, Heidi." Ms. Webster took a step back on the porch and looked around her. "There's blood everywhere."

She had forgotten about that, seemingly, the shooting. And in even the dimmest halo of light bathing the porch, she could see the red splotches on the steps and the drips heading to the truck and the bloody handprint in the doorjamb.

"I cut myself trying...to change a flat," she answered. "I just haven't cleaned it up yet."

"Heidi, if you don't let me in the house to see whether everything is okay, I'm going to call the police." She moved forward, her hand on the doorknob.

Calvin would not be stupid, she knew. She hoped. She had Ms. Webster take a seat in the living room and went into the kitchen to boil some tea water, buying some time.

"You haven't opened these?" Ms. Webster held three large envelopes from Bryn Mawr, Swarthmore, and NYU in her hand. Perhaps her father had brought them in the previous day without her noticing. She carefully slit the tops of the envelopes, Ms. Webster standing beside her.

"Oh my goodness, Heidi, three for three!" Ms. Webster beamed, kissing her cheek. "I'm so proud of you. What a tough decision you have ahead of you."

She clasped Heidi's forearms and studied her body. She ran a hand on the inside of her forearms, her stomach, the nape of her neck. Heidi blushed, thought for some strange reason that Ms. Webster was going to kiss her again, but instead she stepped away and frowned.

"I thought you said you cut yourself changing the flat." She stared at Heidi.

"Not on my arms," Heidi answered. "Actually, it was my father. He's upstairs...sleeping."

"Do you mind if I poke in on him?" Ms. Webster stood up. "I just want to make sure he doesn't need any medical assistance."

"He's asleep." Heidi shot up beside her. "I can take you up. We can look in on him, but we shouldn't wake him up."

She walked up the stairs ahead of Ms. Webster, repeating the last sentence loudly. The bedroom door was open, but no shape lay on the bed. Ms. Webster moved to the right and flipped on the bathroom light. On the edge of the sink lay the revolver.

"Heidi." Ms. Webster turned to her and grabbed her by the arms. "You need to tell me the truth about what is going on here.'

Calvin's shadowy frame filled the doorway, and Ms. Webster screamed.

"It's okay," Heidi said as Ms. Webster grabbed the revolver from the sink and pointed it at Calvin. "I can explain."

"If you try anything funny, to me or to Heidi, I'll shoot." Ms. Webster, both hands on the gun, pointed it at him.

Calvin looked at Heidi, and they burst into laughter. Nothing had seemed funnier since the beginning of time. They went down into the living room, followed by Ms. Webster, a few steps behind them.

"I don't see what's so funny," Ms. Webster said as Heidi and Johnson sat on the couch. "And just so you know, my father is a member of the National Rifle Association."

"Calvin is my friend," Heidi looked at him, and he smiled. "A friend of the family. My father's been in the hospital the past few days, and he's been staying with me."

"How do I know he didn't kill your father? How do I know that your friend Calvin isn't holding you hostage?"

"You're going to have to trust me on this."

"Trust you? There's blood on the porch, a handgun on the sink, your father is missing, and there's a stranger in your house."

"I'm safe, Ms. Webster." Heidi leaned back in the couch and drew her legs up to her chest. It could end here, she supposed. Calvin could have killed her father, held her hostage for all this time. She could have tried to shoot him, to escape. She wondered whether Ms. Webster would be appointed her guardian. She imagined Ms. Webster's apartment, a sunny kitchen, with plants hanging from hooks and records lining a corner by the stereo, records of singers and bands Ms. Webster might listen to, like James Taylor or Rikki Lee Jones or maybe Joni Mitchell. She thought of the bookcase filled with Shakespeare and Yeats and Woolf and Austen. She imagined a small, impish cat, a warm afghan, a boiling teapot. Things she imagined for her own life, eventually, after receiving a head start on them with Ms. Webster, a new start.

She looked at Calvin. He sat slouched in a new undershirt and his jeans, his hands clasped between his legs, looking at the floor, and his attempt to look small and harmless belied the powerful fulcrums of his knees, which seemed to reach Heidi's shoulders. His girth sucked the couch toward him, and her by extension, his thigh touching hers, the warm of him seeping into her skin. Would Ms. Webster understand how their short time together had already made everything monstrous and unfair and off-kilter in her life seem insignificant, had blown Shauna and Oliver and Mt. Zion High away like dandelion spores? She had spent so much time fighting the tide of a sea that had only been in her imagination, and now she was free.

"I can leave, Heidi," Calvin said finally. "I don't want your friends worrying about your safety."

"Why would you leave without me?" she asked, and looked at Ms. Webster. "Calvin is my boyfriend. We're leaving this place."

"Don't be silly, Heidi." Ms. Webster paced back and forth with her arms crossed, cradling the revolver in her hand like a baby. "You're going to get scholarships. You're going to Swarthmore, Bryn

Mawr, or NYU. That's all you're going to be deciding. You're going to have a great life."

"I'm going to have a great, lonely life. I want to be with Calvin—haven't you been in love, Ms. Webster?"

"You're not in love. There's plenty of time for that. You need to take advantage of the great opportunities afforded you. You're going to bloom in college, Heidi. Trust me, I was the same as you. I had a terrible time in high school."

"I have a hard time believing that," Heidi answered. "You're beautiful. I'm hideous…a freak."

"You're not a freak, Heidi." Calvin turned and took his hand in hers. "I love you."

"I love you, too." Heidi craned her neck and kissed his cheek. He took her face in his hands and kissed her on the lips, lingering for a second before turning away. She thought she would pass out from the lightheadedness. It may not have been a real kiss, performed at gunpoint, but it was her first.

"Well, I'm glad you two lovebirds have figured this out." Ms. Webster said. "But this still doesn't answer any of my questions."

"The truth is, I shot myself, by accident." Calvin stood up, sending Ms. Webster into a ready position, gun pointed at him. He pulled up his shirt, where a raw wound the size of a fingertip poked through his hair. "It was a flesh wound, but I bled like a stuck pig. I was opening the magazine to take out the ammo, but one must have gotten stuck in the chamber. That's why I was upstairs, trying to rest a little. Heidi's been so upset about the whole thing it—all the blood makes it look worse than it really is."

"I thought he was going to die," Heidi added.

"And Heidi's father?"

Heidi looked at Calvin, who looked back at her. Like a stick in a bike tire, their easy, shared conniving grinded to a halt, planting their faces into the asphalt. It happened to the best of liars, she figured.

"My and Heidi's fathers were in the war together," Calvin began, and Heidi dug her nails into the palms of her hands. "She and I have been penpals for years. She called me and said her father died in his sleep and that she didn't know what to do. She needed the Social Security checks so she could eat and pay the bills, and she was worried they'd put her in a foster home and sell the farmhouse. She just wanted to hang on until college, you know? I told her I'd come and help her figure something out. So I got here, and we weren't thinking clearly, I guess. He was dead, so we buried him—who could afford the funeral?"

"Jesus, you expect me to believe that?" Ms. Webster's face seemingly had aged decades since she arrived. Her right eyebrow had begun a slow dive into her right eye, a skepticism that narrowed her eyelids and drew her lips tight. She sighed, taking almost all the air in the room into her lungs, it seemed to Heidi, who held her breath. "All right, let's see this body."

Calvin, Heidi, and then Ms. Webster left the house. Calvin pulled a shovel out from under the crawlspace of the porch. He stuck it into the mound, fresh and fly-infested, and threw the dirt off the side.

"Are you sure you want me to dig him up?" He paused, looking at Ms. Webster, then Heidi.

"Heidi, go inside." Mrs. Webster nodded at Heidi. "You shouldn't have to see this."

Heidi went into the house. She took the bag with the herb off the table, along with her father's diary, and shoved them between the waistband of her pants and the small of her back. She pulled on her hooded sweatshirt and left it billowy, unzipped. Then she went to the living room and got Calvin's backpack. She went out the front door and put everything under the passenger side of the truck seat and hurried back. She glanced out the window and saw that Calvin had dug a shallow hole the length of the tomb. She ran back upstairs and threw some toiletries in her backpack, underpants, an extra shirt. She put in her own journal, a few paperbacks, and went back outside, stuffing the backpack under the dashboard of the truck.

As she got back into the kitchen and sat at the table, Ms. Webster appeared. Her face was pale as she struggled against the convulsions of impending vomit. Her right hand rested on the edge of the kitchen sink as her left rose to her face. She breathed deeply twice and then looked at Heidi.

"Calvin is reburying your father." She reached into her right front pocket, where she had briefly parked the revolver. "And you're coming with me."

"Why?" Heidi ducked as Ms. Webster reached for her hand.

"Come on, hurry—before he has a chance to finish."

She thought to overpower her, but Ms. Webster grabbed her by the arm, her grip strong. Maybe she could explain everything to Ms. Webster in private. Maybe her determination would waiver as Ms. Webster calmly explained the dangers of going away with a man she had known little more than a day, and she didn't know him, really. Ms. Webster had lived longer and knew more, and she would know what exactly to do next.

"Hurry." Ms. Webster nudged her into the passenger seat of the Squareback and hurried around to the other side. She missed the slot for the key. When she tried again, pinching the key tightly between her fingers, Heidi could see her hands shaking.

"He won't hurt you," Heidi said. "He didn't hurt me."

The engine roared, and Ms. Webster yanked the clutch into gear, shooting down the road in reverse until they were out of view of the house before turning. Heidi hoped Calvin would get to the truck on time to follow them. The orange dragon was no match for the calibrated purr of the Volkswagen, which Ms. Webster eased up to 75 on the highway.

"Why didn't you say anything to me earlier, Heidi?" Ms. Webster lifted her hand off the clutch and patted Heidi's palm. "You knew you could come talk to me."

"I don't know…it happened so fast. I don't want foster parents and to go to college in some strange city and it'll be just like high school except I won't even have you or my father."

"Oh, Heidi, I know it feels like that. It feels like that to everyone—don't you think it'll feel like that to Oliver and Shauna and any other kid at school? And for them, it will be even worse. They're used to having status. Then, all of the sudden, they'll be lowly freshman, and no sophomore or junior or senior will care about their social status at their old school. But, for you, that will be a blessing. You can make a new home, a new history."

Ms. Webster pulled into a two-story apartment complex. The brick and siding structure looked grimy and old. The siding was weathered gray, and the bricks, crumbling. Tricycles and toys and garbage paraded in the grass. Ms. Webster guided Heidi to an apartment on the second floor. Inside, it was small, a layer of exotic oils and perfume almost covering the sourness of tenants past. Heidi sat on the couch, and Ms. Webster locked the door and looked out the peephole.

"We have to figure out what we're going to do." She walked into the living room and sat at the other end of the couch. "Even if I take your story as true, the truth is you didn't alert the authorities when your father died. And you could be charged with social security fraud if you don't. I don't know whether you'd go to jail, but this could keep you from going to college for a little bit."

"I know... which is why you should let me go home and not get involved." Heidi wrapped her arms around herself.

"Oh, Heidi, no—I would never do that." Ms. Webster curled her feet up and fished a cigarette out of her purse. "We can figure this out without implicating Calvin in any of it. He can go home and no one would be any the wiser."

Heidi looked at the bookshelves at the other end of the apartment, filled with the books she had imagined. No cat. She wondered what Ms. Webster did on the weekends, aside from inviting lonely girls like herself out to the movies.

"Do you have a boyfriend, Ms. Webster?"

"No." She exhaled. "I haven't really met anyone here. But I have friends. I travel. I know that you don't want to hear this, Heidi, particularly since you struggle with it so much yourself, but people are lonely a lot. Even if there is someone. There's always a loneliness that people can't fill, that pets can't fill. And you have to make peace with it because you come into the world alone and you go out the same way."

"Have you made peace with it?"

"Sometimes." She stubbed out the cigarette. "I've been in long-term relationships, and I've been alone. I'm just saying that I don't want you to think Calvin can save you from it."

"But why be with anyone at all, then?"

"Because it's fun and we procreate and that's what we do. But it doesn't mean anything unless you're comfortable with yourself.

And you can go with Calvin or you can go to college, or you could go into the Peace Corps, but you have to find the home in yourself because everything else is so much window dressing."

"Calvin isn't attracted to me," Heidi blurted. "I'm sure it's obvious. I have something…of his father's. He came here for it. That's all. He didn't have anything to do with my father dying. We can go to the police tomorrow and tell them everything."

"I think the truth is the best way to do it. I'm so sorry about your father, honey. I'm so sorry you had to go through that all alone."

Ms. Webster reached over and touched her knee. Heidi felt rocks in her chest, in her stomach, begin to break away, a raw, soft loam beneath them. The grief would come now, she knew. Ms. Webster boiled water in the kitchen as Heidi dug her chin into her chest, trying to blink away the memory of her father's body, the dirt brushing his eyelids, mixing in his hair, his nostrils, as she heaved it from the pile into the hole.

"Ms. Webster, do you think they'll let me stay with you?" she asked when Ms. Webster returned with two steaming mugs of chamomile tea.

"I don't know, honey." Ms. Webster sat back on the couch. "I don't think it's appropriate, being your teacher. But I'm sure we can hang out. We could go the movies, dinner."

Heidi sipped the tea. This seemed the right thing to do. It would seem foolish otherwise. Even her father, she reasoned, would advise her against going with Johnson, the man with whom he shared his foxhole.

Ms. Webster folded a sheet and blanket over the couch, brought her out a pillow. Heidi took off her sneakers and slid under the sheets, thankful that they smelled like detergent and not bar soap, that they were soft and cool and that Ms. Webster's apartment, although smelling faintly of mold, the memory of residents past, felt homey. Perhaps, even if she could not stay with Ms. Webster, she would stay with a family who would make sure she was clothed and fed and loved. Even if she wound up in jail, she reasoned, she would be fed three times a day, and the shower water would be hot.

"Heidi, I'm not going to call the police now," Ms. Webster said. "But I can't stay up all night. So I trust you that you'll still be here in the morning. We'll go to the police and what happens will happen, but I will be here for you every step. It'll only be worse if you decide to go with Calvin."

"I know."

Ms. Webster bent over and hugged her. Heidi's life receded into the thick waves of Ms. Webster's apple-scented hair. If she could be Ms. Webster's conditioner, she reasoned, she would be content.

In the dark, she thought of Calvin, smelled his sharp, earthy musk, felt the pistons on his fingers pressing against her waist, her back, her shoulders. He had kissed her earlier that evening. Perhaps he hadn't been faking all of it. Their lips had fit together like skin on bone. Because of his relationship to her father, he was almost family.

And he was not human. She had seen it with her own eyes. But she was, awkward and frail and bumbling. She imagined him going to New York, perhaps saving Kate, and they would march, superhuman, divine, in the sunset ever after. And Heidi would curl up in the library of some large university on the East Coast, anonymous and destined to inherit the earth after they tired of it.

She slipped out of bed and tiptoed across the room with her shoes in her hands. As she got to the door, she listened for Ms. Webster. She wondered whether she was letting her leave, make her own decision. Maybe the secret of the farmhouse grave would die between them. She slipped out of the door and padded down the concrete stairs to the parking lot, wondering how she would find her way home, to Calvin. But she did not need to wonder long, for she saw the rusted orange truck at the end of the parking lot, the dark shape of Calvin's body behind the wheel. She pulled on her shoes and ran over.

"How long have you been out here?" She climbed into the passenger side of the truck.

"Since you've been inside." He flicked the butt of his cigarette out the open window. "Where's Teach?"

"Asleep, I think. Look, I just wanted to find you so that I could give you this." She crouched between her legs and felt along the seat of the truck, pulling out the sandwich bag with the herb in it. "You're free to go back to New York."

He took the bag from her outstretched hand and looked at it, turning the fragile skeleton around and around in its plastic casing.

He was silent, still holding the herb, and she could not tell what he was thinking.

"I'm going to stay with Ms. Webster tonight," Heidi continued. She took the straps of her backpack in one hand and placed the other on the door. "Why don't you come upstairs? Maybe I can call you a cab or we can get you to the bus station tomorrow."

"You're not coming?" He asked suddenly, looking at her.

"Um...no." She let go of the handle and looked back at him. "I need to get everything straightened out with my father. But you should have the herb. My father would have wanted you to have it. I hope you can save Kate."

"Your father also wouldn't have wanted you to be alone," he said.

"It's my responsibility as your father's friend to make sure you're taken care of."

"I'm fine," she answered, although she was not really sure. She'd already, under panic, botched her father's ascent into the afterlife in epic proportions. Who knew what else she would screw up, given the chance? "Really. You have the herb—don't worry about me."

"Heidi, I can't leave you like this." He slipped the palm of his hand underneath the straps of her backpack and tugged it gently from her.

"I was planning to go with you." She explained as he zipped open the top, exposing a crush of clothes now expanding into the open space. "I put everything in the truck while you dug up my father."

He put the backpack on the seat and thought, his eyes piercing the air that hung stale between them. She watched his eyelids blink.

"Is there anything you need from Ms. Webster, up there in the apartment?" he asked finally.

"No."

"Good." He turned the key in the ignition. "Are you ready?"

"For what?"

"To go." He threw the lever into drive. She felt her stomach tumble. Perhaps he did care for her. "I already found the herb in your things, while I was waiting here in the parking lot. I could have already left without you."

"It's all right Calvin—I'm not in trouble. At least, I hope not very much trouble. I don't think running away is going to help my case."

"I don't care about any of that, Heidi. I just want you to come. Will you please come with me?"

"I don't know, Calvin." She paused, looking through the windshield at the darkened bedroom window of Ms. Webster's apartment. "I just...everything is happening so fast."

"You're right." He pulled the key out of the ignition and handed it to her. "You're going to be okay, Heidi. You're going to have a great life."

"You too." She sighed, took the key from him and put it in her pocket. She felt it dig into her skin. "I hope you are able to get help for yourself."

He nodded, and they stood in front of the apartment complex.

"You should give me an address." He zipped up his jacket, the collar up, grazing his chin. "So I can let you know how things are."

"You can come back and visit." She shrugged, moving toward the steps. He grabbed her arm and pulled her to him. She thought of Oliver and Shauna and the other kids in her classes, saw them in varying degrees of transparency. Perhaps they were always that way, even herself, and it took someone as solid as Calvin Johnson for her to feel the weight of other things. She pulled away, and the air between them seemed to dissipate into him.

"Well, okay, kid." He nodded, shoving his hands in his pockets.

"Okay." She nodded back, feeling a weight in her throat. She watched him walk away, out of the complex, out of her life. She had been given what she wanted, and she let him walk away. She sat on the steps, cracked and bubble-gummed, in front of Ms. Webster's apartment building. Two apartments up and over, a couple's argument escalated from angry murmurs to full-throated screams. She thought of Ms. Webster in the bed upstairs and wondered whether she slept on one side or sprawled across. She did not know why it mattered. She slipped upstairs, back into the apartment and opened the bedroom door. Ms. Webster lay on the left side of the bed, close to the alarm clock, her limbs folded carefully on the sheet. For a moment, she thought to crawl in next to her, to fill the space. To wake up and know she was not alone, that someone cared for her. To be Heidi Polensky again. She shook her head. She was no longer Heidi Polensky. But who she was, she didn't know yet. She ran back to the parking lot, got in the truck, and gunned it up the street, not stopping until she saw him walking on the side of the highway. Pulling in front of him, she idled and blew the horn.

Johnson

He left Heidi at the American Museum of Natural History with twenty dollars spending money and took a cab to the east nineties. Inside, the help led him to a sunroom in the back of the brownstone. Kate lay bundled in a chaise lounge, a coffee table book of Japanese wood block prints open on the floor. He had not been gone long, but so much had changed.

"Your secretary told me you'd been home the past few days," he explained. Pictures of Kate and her husband, her sons, made a daisy chain around the room's perimeter. It was not a space for them, her private sanctuary, fortress, and he wished he had thought to leave a message with her assistant instead. "She said to visit you between 1 and 5, to miss your husband, but I can leave. I understand."

"It's okay." She waved her hand, dismissively, carelessly, he could not decipher. The help appeared behind him. "Marjorie, could you bring me some hot tea? And please bring Calvin whatever he'd like. We have a rather extensive scotch collection, courtesy of my husband."

"No, that's okay." Calvin shook his head as Marjorie stepped out.

"Why?" She laughed dryly. "Do you feel it's improper to drink another man's scotch without his permission? What about sleeping with his wife?"

"You're right—I was completely out of line."

"Calvin, I'm just joking."

"I meant I should probably have taken the scotch."

"See?" She patted the Chippendale across from her. It looked like a museum piece. Johnson sat on the edge, careful that the caulks of his boots did not catch the Persian rug. "We still have fun together."

"Did we stop?"

"Well, I started to die, and you stopped dying." She took the tea off the silver service that Marjorie brought in. "That always puts a damper on a party."

"How are you feeling?"

"A bit terrible. I had my radiation treatments on Monday."

"Can you stop them?"

"Part of the protocol." She sipped her tea. "Palmer got me into a trial a couple of months ago. An experimental drug and radiation. But now, I'm thinking of dropping out."

"Don't." He reached over and touched her foot through the afghan. "I have some news for you. I have the herb."

"Yes? Congratulations."

"I was hoping for a little more enthusiasm."

"I'm so tired, Calvin." She closed her eyes.

"Of what?"

"Of everything. Even if I could get up, I don't know if I'd want to go out, see the park, the city. I just don't know the point of it anymore."

"I was hoping…" he looked toward the window, thinking of his shoes, tissues, anything but her, and forced the tears back into his eyes. "I was hoping we could spend some time together. Now that I have the herb, that maybe, after all this time, there'd be time for us."

"That's right." She smiled at him, although it was not happiness she communicated. "You have all the time in the world. There's no urgency ever, is there?"

He sat back on the Chippendale. His chest burned, his hands shook. "The only good thing about having time is that I can wait forever for you."

"Even if I'm running out of it?" She looked toward the window. The light caught her eyes, coffee brown, and time had not mottled them.

"It doesn't have to be like that." He watched her hand sweep the floor for a pill bottle, the pills that replaced her vitality, drowned her quietly in amorphia.

"What do you propose, Mr. Johnson?" Her hand knocked over the bottle, and he squatted beside her, retrieving it, putting the large yellow capsule in her palm.

"Don't push me out." He put his face near hers, felt her breath, light and uneven, in his ear. "Don't push me away. I'm not going to listen to you anymore. I'm not going to go away."

"You're going to stay here and watch me die?" She laughed.

"I'm not leaving." He kissed her neck, felt her spine through the flesh. He lingered on her skin, cold and dry, searching for the thrill that had surged through it so many years before, in plump, pulsing veins. He felt her hands touch his back, rest there, he felt the weight of them and he fought the urge to weave his arms under her, draw her to him, lift her from the chaise lounge and take her somewhere, somewhere away from this life and these memories and fill her full of him, full of them. He felt the wet on her neck, salty roads that traveled from her cheeks to her collarbone, and he followed them with his lips up to her eyes and kissed her lids, buoyant with tears, closed.

"Don't leave," she murmured, and he kissed her cheeks, her forehead, her eyelids, her lips, but she did not kiss him back. She moved her hands up his back and through his hair.

He sat while she struggled with air, with breathing, while she coughed. He wiped the saliva that formed on the corner of her lips. She slumped, the drugs pressing down on her like a thumb. He wondered what was happening deep in her skin, what was happening in his own.

"I didn't ask for this." He clenched his fists. "You try being the last person to die, always. To know that everyone you meet, you'll watch die. To wonder what the point of it all is."

"I'm sorry." She put her hand to her face. The light dimmed, and rain drew on the windows, long blemished shapes. They symbolized nothing but seemed to mock them all the same. "I am selfish not to think of your pain. Me, I should be happy to die. At least it is possible for me."

He felt the herb in his pocket.

"You don't have to die, either," he said.

"You're going to whisk me off to the Palmer's laboratory and cytogenetically freeze me until you figure out how to die?" She smiled at him, and he felt it, a glimmer of hope, of youth. Of an intimacy they had shared once, long ago, when they were both young and at the horizon line together. Before he found out that his was an illusion.

"Take the herb." He pulled the plastic bag out of his pocket and dangled it in front of her.

"How do you know it works?" She studied the bag, but he could not determine the line of her interest.

"I got it from Stanley Polensky's daughter," he answered. "Will you eat it?"

"Is it going to turn me into a young woman? Or will it preserve me at my current age?"

"I don't know what it will do." He dropped the bag on the chair, between her hands. "I just want to be with you for the rest of my life."

"Then be with me for the rest of my life," she answered, closing her eyes. "However little is left."

"You won't take it, then?" He cupped her cheek in his hand. "Will you think about it? Kate, I've waited so long for you, and to think of all the years that will pass without us ever seeing each other again, not even in death…I will tear the world apart. I will destroy the world if you're not in it."

"I'll think about it, Calvin," she answered, then opened her eyes. "You mustn't think…that I don't love you. You mustn't think that I don't care about you. I'm in pain, and I've been in pain for so long, that I've hidden from you, looking for ways to stop the spread, and I've finally accepted that the amount of time I've been allotted is up. I'm not terribly religious or fatalistic, but the real truth of my cancer, my age, the fact that my life—our lives—didn't turn out exactly as we had hoped for doesn't mean they are invalid, that we're free to manipulate them, change them. Perhaps there was a reason things were this way and perhaps not. I'm only a person, a molecule in the sea. I don't expect to change the tides."

"But what if you could? What if I could?"

"Perhaps you never existed, Calvin Johnson," she said. "Perhaps you're a morphine-induced vision, fully formed with past and future in my mind. Someone to save me. Someone to help me cope. My own King Cnut, here to turn back the tides."

"And what if I am?"

"Cnut never turned back the tides." She looked at him steadily, her lids heavy, fluttering. He took her hands.

"I've waited all my life for you. To be told now that I've been... delusional, why not thirty years ago? Why give me any glimmer of hope? Why?"

"Don't you believe I held onto that same glimmer?" she said. "I wouldn't leave my husband. But I thought maybe there'd be a time when I'd see you again... and we did, for a little while. Now, there is no time. But what if we had more time? Would we have cared for each other more than we already do? You are beautiful, a marvel of genetics. A curse to yourself and others. I would be lying if I said I wasn't a little scared of you. Perhaps I should have stayed in Ohio with you. I was young and stupid then."

"You were never stupid." He laid his head on the edge of the chaise lounge, closed his eyes.

"But I was young, yes?" she laughed. "Not too hideous back then, I hope."

"You're beautiful." He drew the line of her lips with his finger, leaned forward to kiss her. "What would we have named our children?"

"Oh, dear—I don't know." She turned her face to his. "I always wanted a little girl named Caroline."

"I always wanted a little girl, too." He closed his eyes. "Where do you suppose we went on our honeymoon?"

"Well, I don't think we would have had much money back then. I was still in school, and you were a bit underemployed after the war. Assuming we got married at City Hall in New York, we could have taken the train to Coney Island, eaten some hot dogs at Nathan's, gone on the Parachute Jump."

"For our thirtieth wedding anniversary, we took a tour of Europe." Johnson stared at the ceiling.

"Of course—to see all the cathedrals in Italy you told me about. And I would have wanted to see where you fought, in Algeria, Cisterna, Normandy. Where you died in Germany."

"And I would have wanted to see you in all those places," he said. In different dresses, at different ages, the velvety paper of her cheeks as a young woman, the skin stretching firmer and then looser across her face, her long hair, dark chestnut, lined with strands of grey, grey strands knitting spider webs in her hair, lines drawn with a delicate hand into the corners of her lips, her eyes, the first wrinkles on her hands. These changes would be subtle at first, but he would not have missed them, would have cherished each, considered them presents, anniversaries all their own.

"Don't cry, Calvin." She took his hand. "You're supposed to comfort me."

"Tell me you'll take it," he said, wiping his eyes. "The herb. We can do everything we never got to do. We'll have all the time in the world."

"You should give it to Palmer." She played with his fingers, her words more slurred than before. "I'm sure there are a lot of people who want to live forever. As long as everyone else they love lives forever. But then, if everyone has eternal life, then the world would end, I suppose. But until that happens, you two could stand to make a lot of money."

"Would you like me to leave?" He sat up, angered. "I feel like you're making fun of me. I don't want to trouble you any more."

"No. Calvin—I could die in your arms." She moved toward him weakly, her fingers trailing along his back. "I just don't know if I can live another life."

"That's just the pain talking." He shook his head. "If the pain went away, if the sun came out, when you wake up tomorrow, you'll think differently about it."

"Maybe," she answered. She sighed, staring off to a point. "There's nothing to be afraid of, right? Why would living be more frightening than dying?"

He did not answer. She did not ask, but he did not have to explain the logistics of things. That, once she took the herb, they would disappear. That they would live among people but not with them. That, even though she was given new life, she could never see her sons, her husband, again. That she would be a ghost alive. That they would stand at the edge of the world, where souls broke the plane, births, deaths, pressing their fingers against the glass. That it would kill one dead, even though one could not die.

"Tomorrow, we'll do it," he said. "But today, let's be together here."

"I'll need to say goodbye to my sons. And then what? I suppose you are experienced in the faking of one's death?"

"Shh." He rolled over, took her in his arms. "Let's not talk about it now."

"But when?" she asked, and he kissed her, as firmly as she would allow. She opened her lips to him, her mouth dry, sour with chemicals. He understood, in some way, that Kate was part of the mutation, and that was how it would be left. That if he had survived the war without Stanley's help, they would not have met, and that the mutation, his death in Germany, set them in motion. To have her, he knew, was to be cursed, and it was this acceptance that would get him through this life long after hers had ended. Because hers would end; he loved her too much to have it any other way.

When her body slackened beneath him, when her lids were heavy and wet with pain and her lips quivered, he stood up and retrieved the herb, putting it back in his pocket.

"I love you." He touched her face, hoped that whatever memories in her circuitry would claim him, that they would fire their way into her next life, whatever feelings in her heart pulsed in the breezes, the rays of sun, the leaves, when her body had crumbled to dirt.

"Are you leaving?" she murmured. "When will you be back?"

"Soon." He kissed her head and went to the door. "I'm going to send Marjorie in, and I'm going to take a walk. I love you."

"I love you, too," she answered. "Please hurry."

She waved a little, and he wondered if she knew he would not be back. Her eyes closed; her mouth opened involuntarily. He closed the door. In the hallway, Marjorie stood with another tray, and the smell of the hot, salty canned soup cut into his stomach.

Outside, life went on as always. People brushed by him, ignored him. When he took the cab back to the museum, where Heidi weaved through the crowd out front, he swam in the tide of life like blood through veins, and he was almost invisible. When he grabbed her by the shoulders, knocking from her grip the paper tote bag from the gift shop with a t-shirt, and pulled her to him, crying into her neck, his body heaving, people stopped for a second. But then, they moved on, swallowing them up in the crowd before spitting them out.

Heidi

Heidi wanted to go to Coney Island to see his past life there. He agreed, thinking it would take his mind off things. They sat in the subway car for a long time, riding through the bowels of the city before they emerged, and late-evening Brooklyn welcomed them, the beach. She studied him from the corner of her eye as he clenched and unclenched his fists, his boots pressed against the floor of the car. He had cried like a baby in the middle of New York, almost pulling her down to the sidewalk as he clung to her. He held onto her so tightly she thought he would break her ribs. No one had ever touched her like that, needed her like that. Not even her own father, who preferred to drown in the past of his mind, mostly.

Finally, he sat up straight, rubbing his hands on his jeans, and looked at her.

"What did you get?" he asked. She pulled it out almost apologetically, a sky blue-colored shirt with a whale on it. Why she had been looking at the origins of humanity and gems and minerals and perusing the gift shop while he visited Kate, while his heart was ripped out, she didn't know. She was stupid and vile, and he if had any sense, he would leave her in Coney Island to become homeless.

Instead, he ran his hand along the fabric, held it to his face and smelled its newness. "You're going to look great in this. I can imagine you going to college wearing this shirt."

She wanted to say that she wasn't going to college, that she would follow him to the ends of the earth for the promise of his touch, his tears, his faith in her.

Instead, she said, "Thanks."

It was chilly when they got off at the end of the line, and she pulled it over her other tee-shirt as they walked down Surf Avenue. In the distance, high-rise projects stood before the sea. The sidewalks were a decoupage of cigarette butts, dirty wrappers and napkins, an occasional syringe. The smell of hot dogs and beer wove through the air and stabbed at her stomach. The lights of the Cyclone and Wonder Wheel seemed to leer at them in the salty, windy night. Everything was intoxicating, slightly lurid, like she imagined a porn film. She had never been anywhere dangerous, anywhere alone. Without her asking, Johnson slid his arm over her shoulders.

"Did she take it, then?" She looked ahead, did not turn to him when he touched her, too afraid at what she would do. What he would do.

"No," he answered.

"Is she... will she..."

"She will."

"I'm so sorry, Calvin. I can't imagine... what you are feeling."

"You want to ride the Cyclone?" He grabbed her elbow.

"Now?" She stopped and laughed incredulously. "Are you sure?"

"Looks fun." He felt in his pockets, pulling out the herb, a few dollars, a lighter. Heidi took the baggie with the herb from his hand and held it up.

"How much did my father give you of this?" She rolled the pieces through the plastic between her fingers.

"I don't remember." He flattened the bills against his jacket. "How much is a rollercoaster ride these days? Thirty dollars?"

They climbed in the car and pulled the bar down. She could smell the ocean salt, the taffy. Heidi wove her left hand into his right and squeezed.

"Are you okay?" she asked. She wanted big, important words to comfort him, important insights, but what tumbled out of her mouth was junior varsity, so high school.

"Not really." He stared off in front of him. She wondered if he was out in the cosmos somewhere, waiting to catch Kate before she rocketed away from them. "I'd better get used to it, though, huh? I mean, watching you die, too, anyone else I meet."

"I'm not going to let you." She leaned forward and caught his eyes. "I love you, Calvin."

The car jolted to a start and began climbing up the hill. There was nothing else left to do. With her other hand, Heidi tilted the plastic bag with the herb toward her lips. In disbelief, then horror, Johnson watched the dried, crumbled remains begin to tumble into her mouth.

"Jesus—no." He grabbed the bag from her and shoved it into his opposite jeans pocket. "What are you, crazy?"

But it was too late. Heidi swallowed as the car slid over the top of the hill.

Johnson

"This is not what I wanted."

They sat on the beach, Heidi hugging her backpack, Johnson plunging his fist in the damp sand.

"It's what I want," Heidi said. "Calvin, I love you. I know you don't love me, but it doesn't matter. I don't want you to be alone."

"You're too young to even know what you're saying." He was crying now, for Kate, or Heidi, he wasn't sure. Both, maybe. Each cursed, all of them cursed. All of them the luckiest people in the world to have known each other, a day or forever. "Me and Ela—you've got to know how terrible it's been for us. For her, especially. And we didn't even ask for it. And you willingly did it. I don't understand."

"I love you, Calvin." Her eyes were wet. He could not tell if it was the sting of the salt air, if she was upset. "Is it that hard to understand? Like you...and Kate."

"That is *not* the same," he spat. He grabbed her shoulder as she turned from him, to run away. "Don't go. I'm sorry. I didn't mean it like that. It's just...you're a kid. You don't know what you're feeling. When I was your age, I was going to marry this divorcée, Eva Darson. Then, I went into the Army and realized how stupid it was."

"Don't tell me my feelings are stupid." She dug her pointy chin into the top of the backpack and squeezed her eyes. "If my feelings are stupid, then all of our feelings are stupid."

"You don't even know for sure... if it worked."

"Don't worry." She pulled Stanley's revolver out of her backpack. "We'll know."

He grabbed for the gun, falling on her, as it went off. Underneath him, she moaned. He cradled her head in his hand and rolled to the side, running his hand over her shoulders, chest, down her body until he found it, the blood pooling on the top of her foot.

"If it doesn't heal, we just go to the emergency room," she said, gritting her teeth, throwing the revolver into the surf. They watched the ocean spit it back. "We'll just say we got mugged."

"You... I can't believe it." He untied her sneaker and pulled it off. He pushed his finger in the wound and enlarged it with his finger, feeling the tip of the bullet lodged in the bone. In the backpack, he fumbled for the Swiss Army knife, pulling out the tweezers.

"Here." He pulled his wallet out of his back pocket and pressed it against her lips. "Bite down. I don't care if you bite a hole through it. Just don't let go."

He sat on top of her leg so that it was between his and plunged the tweezers into the hole, holding her foot still with his other hand. The bullet slipped once, twice, through the tweezers until he was able to get a grip, freeing it from the pulp of blood and flesh and bone shards.

"Jesus Christ!" She shouted behind him. "Why the hell did I throw my life away with you? What the hell am I doing? Oh hell, hell, hell!"

"You're not biting my wallet, like you should," he answered, and she responded by beating his back with her fists. He turned and held up the bullet to her.

"It's out." He dropped into her palm. "Not everyone gets a souvenir from Coney Island like this. I'm going to get some napkins. Don't move."

"Can you get me hot dog, too?" She pulled herself to a sitting position. "The pain is making me hungry as shit."

They ate Nathan's hot dogs and French fries and watched the moon on the water. He wrapped his arm around her and imagined a white sheet lying lightly over Kate's body. He then imagined it in the morgue while her coffee mugs, her comforter, her slippers, her Krasner, lay in waiting, not knowing she had passed away. And then they would be taken from their rooms, discarded or sold, asked to hang on other people's walls, touch other people's lips, and they could not protest, not grieve that her hands, her eyes, would never caress and validate them. Quietly and efficiently, the evidence of her life would be disassembled, except for his memories, other memories that her sons and their wives and her coworkers and friends had, but to which he was not privy. He had only his version of Kate's life, and it would have to do. If she had not loved him like he loved her, she loved him somehow, the way in which she was capable. The same way he would love Heidi.

"I'm sorry, Calvin," Heidi wept into his shoulder.

"Shh—it just hurts, honey." He had put the napkins, yellow ones with "Nathan's Hot Dogs" printed in green on them, between her sock and foot and tied the shoe tightly, hoping to stem the bleeding. "Shh. Just try and get some sleep."

"We can't sleep on the beach."

"If someone comes, I'll just carry you somewhere."

"Let's go see Woody Guthrie's house. I want to see where you lived."

"Okay; that's exactly what we'll do tomorrow." He pressed his hands around the slippery sneaker, splotches of blood appearing between his fingers. He could feel his heart in his throat. If she did not clot soon, she would slip into unconsciousness, hypothermia. He took the shoe off her good foot and rubbed the foot and her hands.

"I'm so sorry about Kate, Calvin. I didn't mean to . . . to do this to upstage her."

"I know you didn't." He did not know what to say. Heidi did it for him. She doomed herself to misery because, even if she was young and stupid, she loved him. Or thought she did. He continued to rub her foot. She still shivered, and he wrapped his jacket over her. He pulled out the napkins, drenched in blood, and wrapped new ones on her foot, pulling on her sock. An hour later, he did this again. Heidi's eyelids drooped; he could not understand what she said to him.

"I'm taking you to the hospital." He got to his feet and slid his arms underneath her. "This has gone on long enough."

"No." She struggled in his grasp. "I feel better. I can feel something happening in my foot. You have to believe me."

"I don't know." He eyed the growing mound of bloody napkins beside him. "I was stupid enough to let you come along to New York and ruin your life; I might be stupid enough to let you die, too."

"You didn't ruin my life." She shook her head drunkenly. "My life was terrible before I met you."

She opened her eyes, clear and beautiful, like some alien currency, and he felt a little flush on his cheeks. He imagined Stanley loving her, loving her so much it made his chest hurt, and he felt the hurt as well, the mix of pride and bewilderment and he wasn't sure what else. Something that had grown in his body like ivy. He wanted to know her better, share things with her. He kissed her on the ear and then her lips, warming them with his.

"Stop," she giggled. "I don't want your pity. Just look—look at it one more time." She wriggled her foot slowly and grimaced as he peeled off the napkins, bright red with blood but not as bloody as the last.

"Well, I guess you don't need to be carried, princess." He held up her foot, a pale fish blanched with a red, now only weeping, wound. "Looks better."

"Holy crap." She smiled at him, and he laughed. *What could go wrong?* A lot, but right now, an ending, a beginning, was happening. A lighthouse, a buoy, a place for a night's respite, as they lay entwined, before heading back into the storm.

Heidi

The flight at JFK was delayed. Calvin stretched his legs out in a chair by the gate as other travelers, annoyed, tired, squeezed past him and filed down the promenade to the concession area, the row of payphones, the bathrooms.

"Do you have to go to the ladies' room?" Heidi leaned over and looked at Ela, who sat stiffly in her own chair, her ankles and feet draped over the edge of the seat. She could not tell whether the girl had understood or ignored her. She did not seem grateful, for someone whom they had bartered with Palmer for several weeks, with no herb to offer in exchange, after the legal department at Palmer's lab wiped clean the paper trail of files, forged them passports, bought them tickets to Kaliningrad, and issued them a credit card under Heidi's new name, Heidi Webster. She had asked for this surname, and yet when she looked at her picture on the passport, the driver's license from Portland, the birth certificate, she could not help but think she had died, that the person she was now, who moved among people but not with them, was a ghost. Her past had been replaced with a few crisp papers, laminated cards, in a travel wallet. She missed her father more than ever.

"Come." Heidi stood up and held out her hand to Ela. Dr. Palmer's wife had packed her clothes so carefully in a green hardshell suitcase, matching tops and bottoms and lacy dresses and Mary Janes. Calvin had dumped everything into a trashcan in the parking lot. *We can't lay deep stakes,* he explained, stuffing one change of clothes for Ela in the large camping backpack they shared. *We don't know what's going to happen in Reszel.*

Ela launched herself reluctantly off the lounge chair and accompanied Heidi to the bathroom.

"I'll wait here." Heidi pointed at herself and then at the entrance to ladies room. Ela disappeared inside, and Heidi stole a glance at Johnson at the gate.

Heidi's sympathy for him began with her father but ended with Ela. She hadn't run away, eaten the herb, shot herself, to babysit some 200-year-old woman who refused to even speak to her. *Put yourself in her shoes*, Calvin had murmured in the cab on the way over. She wished Calvin put himself in her shoes. She wished they all stopped caring about shoes, which made her think of her foot. It had healed, for the most part, but it still felt strange, like someone had poured cement in it. Every move she made felt numb.

Besides, there was some herb left—the littlest of crumbs, a thimbleful one could pinch between their thumb and forefinger. Something to work with in Reszel, if Ela was the witch she said she was. But Heidi had not endeared herself to Ela, that much was true. She tried not to think about it too much, that she had eaten the only thing the little woman, the little dark-haired girl who talked like Natasha from Rocky and Bullwinkle, had rested her hopes on. She could not think, because of her love for Calvin, she wound up dooming them all, lest she run away somewhere, hiding in libraries across the country, living vicariously through the classics section of Topeka Public Library, Wichita, Salt Lake City, stealing coffee and crullers from the employee break rooms.

She hoped there were books in Reszel. She thought of her classmates, just back from prom night, the flowers of their corsages still fresh, trying on their graduation robes and going to senior parties. Becoming college freshmen or perhaps getting married. And she was going to Poland via Russia.

She had always wanted to travel. She had never been outside of her town. But part of travel, she thought, was the contrast and compare, the postcards sent home. Knowing, after months of adventure, there was a place to which you could return, a place that would claim you, people who would welcome you home. Now, whenever those around them noticed Ela did not grow bigger, and that Calvin and Heidi did not age, they would have to uproot, call another place home until, a few years later, they would do it again.

"I hope it is enough time to figure the secret." Ela had stared at her little hands in Palmer's office, rubbing them together. "But Reszel is country. No one will know any better that we are there."

But Heidi knew, and so did Calvin, that the world was not like it was two hundred years ago. It was not even the same as it was ten years ago. Everything changed, as did everyone, she had been warned by Calvin. Everyone except for them.

Would his feelings for her change? Would he grow to love her? She stared at him again across the airport, his rakish dark hair that had begun to creep over his eyebrows and into his eyes, the large, well-formed knuckles on his hands, the long fingers that slid over his face and rubbed his cheeks. Since she'd met him, he'd transformed from fifties greaser to seventies malcontent, from James

Dean to Al Pacino. And what, she felt a chill fall down her back, collect in her spine, what if she fell out of love with him?

"Hold on." Heidi grabbed Ela's arm as she walked out of the ladies' room and plucked a few squares of toilet paper that had been caught in the back of Ela's waistband. Heidi laughed, imagining Ela walking through the vast concourse of JFK with toilet paper wings, and Ela frowned at her but then saw the toilet paper and blushed, smiled a little, before the frown that was set in her face like concrete resettled. *Well,* Heidi thought. It was better than nothing.

She deposited Ela with Calvin and went to the payphone.

"Ms. Webster," she said, feeling the tears drum through her, like rain on window glass.

"Heidi! Where are you, honey? Oh my goodness, I've been worried to death about you."

"I'm okay," she managed. "What a long, strange trip it's been." She imagined telling her the story, going to Poland to take a little girl woman home. To find an herb. To find a way to die. At least, to find a way to live. They would mail Palmer blood samples via partner laboratories, tissue samples, whatever he wanted, in exchange for this freedom.

"Heidi, please let me know you're safe…and let me know that I can come get you."

"How are things there? Am I in trouble?"

"Heidi, please…let me come get you, and we'll get through this step by step, okay?"

"Thank you, Ms. Webster, for everything." The only mother and father she had ever known were neither.

Heidi leaned her head against the phone booth. A woman's voice over the intercom made an announcement about boarding. Travelers hurried back to the gate. Against the tide, Calvin moved with Ela, looking for her. If they did not see her, she figured, she could walk out of the airport. She would get a cab ride to the bus station. She would go home.

"I've got to go," she whispered as Calvin and Ela spotted her.

"Heidi, please…"

"I'll send you a postcard." Heidi smiled and hung up the phone as they reached her.

"Who are you talking to?" Calvin searched her eyes.

"Nobody." She shook her head. She had nothing to return to, nothing to lose. Everything to gain.

"No contact." He touched her shoulder. "We can't mess this up."

She got in the line with them, holding their tickets, their new identities, and when the gate agent smiled and took their boarding passes, they got on the plane.

Acknowledgments

Thanks to Christine Stewart for being the ultimate book doctor! Seriously, I wrote a good book and you made it a great one. Also thanks to Rosalia Scalia, Barbara Diehl, Todd Whaley, Lalita Noronha, Patricia Schultheis, Tara Laskowski, Elise Levine, and Meghan Kenny for their suggestions and advice on earlier drafts of the novel, and for The Hambidge Center in Georgia for providing me with the beautiful vista in which to finish it. Much love to Phuong Huynh, Mom, Scott, the Phinneys, and the rest of my family for being so encouraging, supportive, and understanding. Great big hugs to Diane Goettel, Angela Leroux-Lindsey, and everyone at Black Lawrence Press for believing in my work. Finally, thanks to the vibrant and engaging writing community in Baltimore for being so encouraging and for all the drinking and laughing and listening we did together.

Photo: Phuong Huynh

Jen Michalski is the author of a collection of novellas, *Could You Be With Her Now*, and two collections of fiction, *Close Encounters* and *From Here*. She is the editor of the literary journal *jmww* and lives in Baltimore.